Chapter One

AMI

'Birthday sex.'

'Sorry, sweetie. Repeat that, would you? I think the line dropped out.'

'Birthday sex,' I repeat into my phone, a little louder this time. Maybe a little *too* loud for these thickly carpeted and stylishly wallpapered hallways.

'You've checked into a swanky hotel because you want to have . . . birthday sex? It's barely five minutes after midnight. Have you've already begun drinking?'

'Emma, it's after seven in the evening here. My birthday is almost over.'

'Oh, yeah. Right. Stupid time zones,' she mumbles through a yawn as I'm overtaken by a sudden burst of warmth that she stayed awake long enough to call. As someone who also used to spend her day wrangling five-year-olds, I appreciate she's probably beat.

'I really miss your judgmental ass.' I really do. 'Are you gonna visit me soon?'

'Just as soon as my credit card recovers from visiting you in Paris, Miss International Jetsetter.'

'I'm not sure living out of a backpack and staying in hostels falls under jet-setting, Emma.'

'Let me amend my previous statement. Just as soon as I've paid off my credit card, *and* you find somewhere else to stay. And speaking of beds, run that idea past me again, would you?'

'You mean, the idea where I'm spending the night in a fancy hotel?'

'No, the part where you said you planned to get laid.'

'Well, Mom sent me some money. She said to get something nice, so I thought I'd get myself—'

'A man.' Emma's flat tone borders disbelief. 'That does *not* sound like you.'

'It's not every day you have a special birthday.' *The big 3-0.*

'True, but—'

'And, well, I've recently realised that along with cake and candles, gifts and birthday drinks, every year since I turned twenty, I've always had sex on my birthday. So I decided a lack of boyfriend wasn't going to make a difference this year.'

'Okay . . . ' Her chuckle rumbles down the line before morphing into another yawn.

'I just decided to treat myself to a night in a nice hotel.'

'And a man,' she repeats.

DOWN UNDER

COPYRIGHT

Other Books by Donna Alam

'Because sex in a backpacker's hostel is not my idea of fun. I'll be damned if my birthday celebrations are reduced to a quick drunken fumble under a sleeping bag in a communal sleeping space.'

'Speaking from experience, are we?'

'After the past month in Thailand, I have enough experience as the audience. Let me tell you, millennials literally give no fucks who might be watching *when* they fuck.'

'So Thailand turned you into a voyeur?'

'Quite the opposite.' A shiver of distaste ripples down my spine, and I'm almost certain I heard the *ping* of elevator doors closing. *I'm heading in the right direction, then.*

'Birthday sex,' she mutters. 'Seems to me you have a bit of a wild side. All this time, you've been holding out on me.'

'Hardly. I'm like the Diet Coke of wild—wild-lite.'

'Mildly wild,' she adds with a snort.

But I get where she's coming from. If there truly is *that kind of a girl*, she's not me. And my previous accommodations aren't the only reason for my celibacy. I love sex and am a big fan of men in general, but sex is linked to intimacy for me. And intimacy equals a connection and, invariably, a relationship. And I'm far too busy for this kind of thing right now.

'You're crazy,' Emma decrees.

'Crazy horny, maybe.'

And therein lies the problem—yep, that's totally what she said. *She* being me. And *she* being sex deprived and super horny. Besides, I've been telling myself I'm all about experiences outside my comfort zone this year.

'Okay, suddenly nympho, what else have you got planned for your first visit Down Under? You know, apart from finding someone to visit *your* down under?'

'Never say that again. But I'm gonna do all the things!' I begin to animatedly tick my bucket list items off the fingers of my left hand. 'Walk across the Harbour Bridge, cuddle a koala—kiss a kangaroo!'

'I wouldn't try that one,' Emma says. 'Haven't you heard of boxing marsupials? Plus, I heard they kinda smell.'

'Visit the Opera House,' I continue undeterred, 'sun myself on Bondi Beach, and absolutely drink gallons upon gallons of fabulous Aussie wines. But first comes—'

'You?'

'*Obviously*,' I reply with a snigger. 'And hopefully, not just once. Then tomorrow, I'm going to eat my weight in macarons because ohmygod, I found this place on the web where the pastries are reported to be as good as *Pierre Hermé*.'

'Amber, don't taunt me,' she half moans.

'Emma, don't make sex noises at me,' I playfully moan back. *Pierre Hermé* is a patisserie in Paris with the best macaron ever. We'd gorged on them together when Emma had used some of her vacation time to visit me while I was living there, working as an au pair. 'Anyhoo, I'm going to visit tomorrow, and I intend to eat my body weight in macarons while drinking coffee strong enough to stand a spoon in.'

Because after that, I have to try to earn a little money. My plan is to travel around Australia for the next few months, taking in the sights while picking up a little work here and there. But for now, I'm just trying to find the elevator in this damn hotel. *Where the hell have they hidden them?*

'Ah, so that's the reason for tonight's planned calorie deficit?'

'Well, a trip to pound town is better than any gym session,' I reply through a slightly tipsy giggle. Did I mention I'd helped myself to the minibar earlier? A girl can be determined *and* nervous, it seems.

'And more fun,' she responds. 'What I find hard to believe is you didn't bang one of those cute French dudes while you were living there.'

'Yeah? Well, maybe I'm paying for it now.'

'I'm sure there were cuties in Thailand.'

My nose wrinkles immediately. 'Did you not hear me say how awful those backpacker hostels are? Nothing dampens a girl's libido like a potential lover whispering, *do you want to come back to my room. I've got the bottom bunk.*' Emma begins to snigger manically. 'Besides, most of the guys I've met over the past few months were barely shaving. And a lot of them were barely bathing.'

'*Eww.* While I'm a fan of a little stubble, not bathing would be a hard limit for me.'

'I meant they weren't shaving because they were babies, mostly doing the gap year thing. Come to think of it, they mostly smelled like teenagers, too. Honestly, I felt like an old grandma.'

'And you don't want a boy toy tonight, hence the swanky-ass hotel.'

'Yep.'

'And you think you'll find a hot guy—'

'In a suit,' I qualify from my wish list.

'For a one-night stand.' He pauses. 'That so doesn't sound like you.'

'Maybe that's the whole point.' The whole point of travelling. 'And somewhere like the Harbour Park Regency isn't likely to be full of unwashed twenty-year-olds with scraggly facial hair and dreadlocks. Not at four hundred bucks a night.' A whistle sounds down the line. 'I'm expecting a different kind of clientele. Suits, square jaws, and hundred-dollar haircuts. A Chris Hemsworth lookalike would be awesome, or even a Liam, and if he has an Aussie accent, all the better.'

'Well, I suppose it is your birthday,' she asserts, amused.

'Exactly. And I'm gonna treat myself. I'm tired of men-boys in dusty boots and grimy T-shirts.'

'So how are you going to land this Aussie stud? Just walk up to him and ask if he'd like to didgeri*doo* you?'

I groan as though I'm in physical pain from the pun. 'No, I'm just going to sit in a nice hotel bar with a nice glass of wine and wait for some nice company to sit next to me, then we'll have a very nice conversation before—'

'You leave for your room to have very nasty sex. It sounds like you've got it all planned,' she adds, still sounding amused.

'Sure have!'

Yet the truthful answer is no, not at all. Up until a year ago, I'd lived a very predictable life. I had a good job teaching third grade in my Midwestern hometown, and I was dating a nice man. A very nice man—a man I'd had birthday sex with three times! That's not to say we had sex three times on one birthday. *Because wouldn't that have been something.* No. We'd been dating for over three years. *Three birthdays, sex on each one.* And maybe it wasn't *awesome* birthday sex, but it was nice enough. I'd begun to see the path of my life mapped out before me, and those prospects were just frightening. I suppose Todd, my then boyfriend, must've been feeling the same because when I sat him down one Friday evening to talk with him about it, he was a lot less upset than I'd initially feared. *A lot less upset.* I'd worried it might come down to following my heart or breaking his, but it didn't. Truthfully, I think he might've been relieved. So the following Monday, I'd resigned from my job, effective the end of the school year, and condensed my life to the size of a backpack.

'Well, my friend, here's to you unwrapping one fine birthday gift tonight and the lightest, tastiest macarons you've ever tasted to look forward to tomorrow.'

'*La vie est faite de petit bonheurs,*' I say with a sigh that doesn't mask my terrible French accent. Oh, and would you look at that—the elevator. I must've taken a wrong turn somewhere because I feel like I've walked the whole floor looking for it.

'You do know what that means,' Emma chides.

'Come on, my French isn't *that* bad. Life is made for small pleasures,' I add in translation, though not for her benefit. Emma's French is much better than mine, even if I did spend the first four months of my adventures working in Paris.

'Your accent has improved, even if your sentiments are a little off.'

'What do you mean?' Hitching my shoulder, I trap my phone between it and my ear as I press the call button before proceeding to search through my purse for my lipstick. Peach, not harlot red, if you're interested.

'Surely the birthday girl deserves *grande bonheurs*, not *petit*.'

'Grand b—Oh. I get it,' I reply, pulling the gold tube from my purse. 'A dick joke—a French dick joke.'

'Is it?'

'*Bonheur*,' I repeat, murdering the pronunciation again, 'does sound like boner.'

It totally does. If you don't believe me, ask Google Translate

'That's not quite what I meant.'

'So you're not saying I should be looking for a *grand bonheur*—a big boner?' I taunt, my French accent ridiculously theatrical now as I push my purse under my arm again.

'Well, it might not be the worst idea you've ever had,' she replies, laughing. 'Go big or go home, right?'

'And I'm not going home anytime soon. The elevator has just arrived,' I add as the doors begin to slide almost silently open.

'In the morning. I want—'

'Yeah, yeah. You want a boner debrief—' My words come to an immediate halt as I step into the elevator, poised to use the mirrored walls to apply my lipstick when my gaze finds more than just my own reflected back.

Hemsworth who?

A man stands behind me, ticking off just about everything I'd list on my birthday sex wish list. That is, if I'd thought to make one. Tall and dirty blond— much less common than tall and dark—and strikingly good looking. A black suit jacket coats his broad shoulders, a white button-down snug against the flat planes of his stomach. I drag my eyes up from the vicinity of his belt before they're tempted to stray farther south because I *do not* need to investigate his *bonheurs* status.

I'm a little unnerved as my reflected gaze draws level with his because he's still looking at me, his amused eyes now holding mine. Amused yes, but also shrewd. And a little unnerving. *The colour, maybe.* Because his eyes are the blue of a dark sky or the deep ocean. Places you could be launched into without the prospect of a return. No, I decide. It's not the colour that's unsettling. It's not how good looking he is that's making my heart beat out of my chest. It's the way he's looking at me.

As though he'd swallow me whole.

In the few short days I've been in Sydney, I've become aware that the place is full of beautiful men. I can also say that though my elevator companion is clearly gorgeous, he's just a little too ruggedly masculine for that tag. He has the kind of stubble that only serves to highlight the angles of his jawline and the sharpness of his cheekbones, but for all his masculine features and cool eyes, he has the kind of lips that totally should be on a woman.

Preferably me.

Let me qualify this: He has a mouth that was made for wearing lipstick.

Also preferably mine.

Applied by my lips, not the tube.

I might even suggest it, test the waters with a little flirting—it is my birthday, and I have already hit the (mini) bar—but for the conversation I find myself mentally playing back. How long had he been behind me? Long enough to have heard me talk about *bonheurs*—boners? Or worse still, my plans for the evening. *My plans for birthday sex.* Could he have been behind me this whole time?

No. Surely, I would've heard him.

The doors slide closed as I turn away from the mirror, almost swinging on my heel as I drop my lipstick into my purse. There's no way I'm putting it on in front of him. With him watching. Not unless I want to look like I'd given the job to a bunch of kindergarteners.

'Are you still there?' Emma's disembodied whisper brings my attention back to the phone in my hand. I bring it quickly to my ear again.

'I-I'm in the elevator. I'll speak to you tomorrow, okay?'

'You'd better,' returns my friend. 'And to think that while I'm child wrangling later today, you'll be on your back getting—'

'Okay, good talk!' I drop my phone into my purse, hoping he didn't hear any of that or any of the other stuff. *I would've known if someone had been standing behind me, wouldn't I?*.

'Which floor?' my elevator companion asks, his voice deep and clear. And he seems mildly entertained. *Crap.*

'T-to the one with a bar?'

'Which one?' *Urgh. Of course, there's more than one.*

'Ground?' I hate how this comes out as a question, but there's bound to be a bar on the ground floor, isn't there? Jeez, this isn't going to work. How can I expect to embody the role of sexual birthday goddess if I can't even tell the pretty man what floor I want to be on? 'Ground,' I repeat, this time with a confident nod.

The stranger turns to the panel of buttons, his profile hinting at the suggestion of a deepening smile. But what the hell. Awkward interaction over. We're just two strangers in an elevator. He knows nothing about me, and I know nothing about him. Our interaction will be over quicker than you can say—

'Ground floor it is.' *Exactly. I couldn't have said it better myself.* 'I reckon that must be where the boners from pound town are found.'

Wait—what?

Chapter Two

AMBER

What the what-what?

Oh, the mortification. The abject shame. That eavesdropping fucker listened to my conversation—my *private* conversation—the whole way around the hotel!

Pound town.

Banged.

Boner.

Visits down under, not to reference the country.

My plans for birthday sex!

The sexy stranger heard it all. And look—look at how he almost bolts from the elevator as soon as the door opens. I just bet his shoulders are shaking with the effort to suppress his laughter as his long strides carry him across the shiny hotel foyer. Not that I can tell—not at the rate he's moving, obviously seeking to put as much distance as possible between himself and the crazy.

Meanwhile, I'm struck mute, watching as he strides past the doorman out into the Sydney evening as though he's escaping a disaster. *At least I don't look like a disaster*, I think as the elevator doors close.

I definitely don't look like a disaster, I repeat a little later as I take a sip of Shiraz, examining my reflection in the smoky grey mirror hanging behind the bar. That's the bar on the ground floor, though I may have taken a short detour as the elevator was called to one of the upper floors.

His loss. I push a hand through my silky smooth, flat-iron tamed hair, ignoring the niggling sensation that it was maybe my loss too because not only have I been sitting at this bar by myself for an hour now, but *that* was also a man who looked like he could take care of business, if you know what I mean.

Hell, this wine is strong . . .

Still, not to worry. Someone else will come along. In fact, I've already been hit on twice since I took a seat at the bar.

Or maybe once. And once mistaken for a prostitute.

Maybe. It was hard to tell. It's not like he got his wallet out while asking, *how much?* But he wasn't exactly trying to impress me, either. Whatever. It was still a compliment, right? Kind of. What wasn't so complimentary was when he asked me if I was a true redhead. Actually, he asked if my collars matched my muff.

I thought it was cuffs, but whatever.

Interested party #2 looked sort of preppy and seemed pretty cool until I realised he'd left the office and popped into the bar for happy hour. And then somehow forgot to go home.

Drunk. As. A. Skunk.

So the birthday sex gods aren't exactly working in my favour tonight, but the night is young and the bar is busy, so my odds are still good, even if the goods have been a little odd. I'm itching to turn on my stool and survey the goods—I'm mean the place—properly. But after *Mister Are Your Legs Open For Business* sat next to me earlier and sorta-kinda propositioned me, I don't want to look too eager.

Or desperate.

Or prostitute-y.

Channel alluring and mysterious, I intone as I slide my hand over my thigh, straightening a wrinkle in my LBD. I'm still surprised I'd been able to salvage it from the bottom of my backpack, along with a pair of strappy heels that, once slipped onto my feet, don't look so squashed. Since I'd left the States, I've basically worn a uniform of T-shirts, skinny jeans or shorts, and Converse, so this is the first time I've dressed up in months. Come to think of it, I've barely brushed my hair in months, which is hardly alluring or mysterious, except in the way the nest of my hair had hidden things. Leaves and that sort of stuff—not small animals or anything.

'How are ya?' I start suddenly as a man hefts himself into the seat on my left. He's a big guy, bigger even than the elevator hunk. *Unnaturally big, in fact.* At first glance, he looks . . . passable. Not to be too demanding or bitchy, but it is my birthday. His hair is clipped short, and he's dressed sort of smart-casual; grey pants and a button-down, muscles straining at both, though not necessarily in a good way. But at least he's not nineteen with patchy facial hair. Or dreadlocks. And what he does have going for him is that panty-melting treacle thick Aussie accent.

'Grey,' he says. *Gr-eye. Oh, Grey. What is? His eyes? His pants?*

My eyes dart back and forth between the two before I realise he's holding out his hand.

'Oh. Amber,' I respond a little breathlessly. Not that I'm channelling Marilyn Monroe or anything, but I suppose breathless can sound alluring, right? Or asthmatic. I place my hand in his . . . trying not to cringe as he turns it over, bringing my knuckles to his lips. *Yuck. And he has thin lips—unnaturally thin. Like if he were a mafioso, he'd be called Jonny Thin Lips. Or Grey Thin Lips, I suppose. Which sounds like he should be dead.*

'What's a lovely looking girl like you doin' sittin' at the bar all on her own?'

'I'm just enjoying a drink,' I say, retrieving my contaminated hand to furtively wipe it on my dress. 'Same as these here good folks.' And suddenly it appears I've turned into an extra from *Little House on the Prairie*. Great.

'Yer' a bloody septic!' he says suddenly and quite animatedly, slapping a meaty thigh.

'I beg your pardon?'

'You. You're a septic tank—a yank!'

Charmed, I'm sure . . . ly not.

'Yeah, I'm American.' And apparently, I've turned into Nelly Oleson, my back suddenly ramrod straight and my tone a little caustic. Not that he appears to notice.

'Fair dinkum,' I think he asks, his smile wide now. 'On holiday, are you, love?'

Okay, now *that* was a definite enquiry and with much nicer terms, so I won't write him off just yet. Even if I'm not feeling it and am kind of nauseated by those fishy thin lips. But Aussies have a weird sense of humour, so I've heard. It could be some kind of cultural thing. And we're just chatting at the bar, that's all. No need to get my panties in a wad. So I reply.

'I am. Vacationing, that is.' Sort of. It's easier than saying I'm backpacking, I've found.

'I've always wanted to root a yank.'

'I'm s-sorry, what?' Root me? What the hell does that mean? My eyes fall to my feet, my mind filled with the ridiculous—my bare feet stuck in a couple of terracotta pots as a shower of potting soil falls between my toes. That sounds very . . . fetish-y.

As I raise my head, his thin lips are smiling lasciviously before he says, 'I'd eat you like a dingo eats a baby.'

Eat me like. . . *Oh.* And just in case I was still in doubt, he licks his lips, his gaze falling to my lap.

I think I've just vomited a little in my mouth.

'Tell me.' His gaze rises briefly as he leans closer to wrap his thick fingers around a lock of my hair. Call me psychic because I know what he's going to ask before the words even leave his mouth. But before I can beat him to the punchline—before I can tell him my red hair isn't natural, that it's only red because I dye it in the blood of the idiots who make unwelcome advances, both our attentions are pulled by a voice from behind us.

'Mate, get your hands the fuck off my wife.'

Chapter Three

BYRON

Her mouth falls open though I don't give her time to think let alone speak as I slide my hand around her shoulder and press my lips to her temple.

'Sorry I'm late.'

'For . . . given?' she responds bewildered but so fucking cute.

My hand slides from her shoulder, a bolt of sheer electricity travelling up my arms at the sudden connection of skin against skin. I'd known her dress was mostly backless—hadn't I followed that pale smoothness half a kilometre around the passageways of the hotel?—but I wasn't prepared for this reaction, the jolt of need.

Fuck. I need to get laid more often.

I insert myself between her stool and the meathead, propping my forearm on the bar and effectively blocking her from his view. Her expression is priceless, the darkened arch of eyebrows, her mouth a soft pink *O*. Shock or recognition? It's hard to tell. Not that it matters because my view is pretty perfect. An expanse of creamy leg and full, high tits straining beneath the sheath of her dress. She inhales so deeply, the way her body moves makes me wonder if she's wearing a bra. Makes me wonder if she's silicone or as natural as her hair.

Something tells me that's not a colour created in a salon. Red, copper, and brown. And why the fuck does she smell like magnolia?

'I see you kept yourself occupied.'

Her soft expression morphs immediately, heat rising in her gaze.

I'd bet my left nut she's a firecracker between the sheets. So she wants birthday sex, according to her phone call, and I suddenly want to give it to her. That's what I call win-win. Mutually beneficial and all that.

'I'm s-sorry,' she stammers a little indignantly. While her words might be a touch irate, her expression is something else. The way she's looking at me as though she can't quite believe her own eyes.

Or maybe her luck.

'That's okay, I forgive you,' I respond evenly, adding a wink for good measure and maybe also to ruffle her feathers a little more. 'You still here?' I say, turning my head over my shoulder to the glowering lump of gristle behind me.

'Yeah, I am.' Nothing like stating the obvious. As I turn my head to him, his shoulders are hunched like a Disney beast. 'Because you know what? I reckon you're not fuckin' married 'cause she's not wearing a ring.'

'Snaps for fucking you.' Facing him, I rest an elbow on the bar, crossing one highly polished boot over the other as I give him the full attention of my glare. 'Want to guess why she's not wearing a ring?'

' 'Cause she's a slut.'

His words inexplicably ignite an angry fire in my gut.

'If she was a slut, she'd still be my fucking slut. If I were you, I'd shut my fucking mouth unless you want to risk the remaining brain cells the 'roids have left you with.'

'Fuck you,' he growls.

'You reckon you could? Find your dick, I mean?'

'You don't know what the fuck you're talking about. This,' he says, throwing out a thick arm as he pushes his stool back, 'this is all natural.'

Out of the insults I've thrown at him, that is what he takes offence to? *Fucking meathead.*

'Well,' I reply, straightening slowly. 'I'm glad to hear it, mate.' I've got four inches in height on the fucker, but he's a lot heavier than me. He'll be slower than me, and he'll hurt more than me, if it comes to it. Not that I sense it will. 'Real glad to hear it.' I take a step closer, and he doesn't step back, leaving us almost toe to toe. 'See, the reason my lovely wife isn't wearing her ring is because it tends to put men off. Doesn't it, sweetheart?'

I have to stifle a laugh as I turn. She hasn't got much of a poker face. Come to think of it, neither has the meathead. In fact, my words seem to be straining those tiny brain cells of his.

'And putting men off is the last thing I want, if you catch my drift.'

His eyes slide from mine to the redhead, and I think he's finally picking up what I'm putting down, which is mostly bullshit.

Go on, you can do it. 1 + 1 + 1 =

'A threesome?'

There you go—snaps for fucking you, meathead!

Red opens her mouth, more to splutter than actually speak, but I can't look at her. Not while I'm trying to keep a straight face.

'So long as you can cope with me being the meat in the sandwich.' I let my eyes roam over him suggestively. And you know what? I reckon if I was into men, his type would be the absolute last on my list. But his face, it's a fucking picture, before he turns, and funnily enough, I can't see him anymore in the wake of his virtual dust.

'You think that's funny?' she asks incredulously.

'Yeah, I do actually.' Taking the recently vacated stool, I catch the eye of the barman. 'Didn't you?'

'I think I'd have found it more enjoyable if he'd taken you up on it.'

'Sorry, darl. If it's a little man-on-man loving you're after, you're in the wrong bar. In fact, I might be your best bet tonight.'

'What's that supposed to mean?'

I take a sip of the scotch that appears in front of me, turning to survey the array of bar patrons.

'It's Friday night, and most of this crowd,' I say, gesturing outwards with my glass, 'are in straight from the office, making a head start on the weekend.' Men in shirtsleeves and loosened ties, women who look like librarians who've just let their hair down. 'Plenty of blokes, I'll grant you, but most of them are already three sheets to the wind. Then you've got these,' I say, nodding towards the couples sitting in front of the wall of darkened windows and those sitting in booths, most of them with attention for nothing but the phones they hold in their hands. 'I know it doesn't look like it, but most are in from the suburbs for a dirty weekend in the city.' She follows my gaze before she turns to me once more, this time frowning.

'It's true. Maybe not the kind of dirty that just frightened that fuckwit away, but maybe they've something more in mind than a quick fuck in the laundry room while the kids are watching cartoons.'

'Oh, so you mean they're not all here waiting to be offered a slot on your three-way schedule?' Her tone drips with sarcasm as she turns both her body and her full attention to me, crossing one long, smooth leg over the other and raising the stakes just a touch

'This lot?' I pull my gaze from that kissed-shaped mouth and those creamy legs. 'Faced with that proposition, half would cream themselves and the other half would fucking die.'

'You've got kind of a dirty mouth.'

I quirk a brow because that wasn't a compliment. 'Says the girl looking for a birthday fuck. What was it you said you were looking for? A large boner and a visit to pound town?'

'I'm positive I didn't say that,' she protests, the colour in her cheeks deepening, one high-heeled sandal beginning to bounce from her toes. 'And that conversation wasn't meant for your ears.'

'Then maybe you should watch what you're saying out in public.'

'A gentleman wouldn't listen.'

'No wonder they're a dying breed,' I retort, taking a sip of my whisky. Whisky, not wine like she's drinking. I wouldn't drink what they carry here, not this month, anyway.

'What?' Mirroring my own actions, she takes a sip of her drink before placing her bowl-like glass back on the bar.

'Gentlemen,' I repeat, 'there aren't many of them around.' They probably all died of boredom.

'And just how do you come to that conclusion?'

I try not to stare at her slim fingers as they toy with the stem of her glass. My guess is she's not paying attention as she slides them up, then down. Up . . . then down.

Like that's not going to make my cock hard.

'If they're not getting laid, they have to be dying out.'

Her head comes up, and I wonder if she's going to take offence to my tone. Maybe walk away. But she doesn't, and her next words are delivered with all the sweetness in a dose of arsenic.

'You know who else isn't getting laid?'

'Apart from you, you mean?'

'What are you doing here?' she asks full of exasperation. But she can't be confused, surely. I just chased away the competition. And our exchange? Foreplay.

'Here, you mean?' I point a finger at the floor. 'Or what am I doing here?' This time I use my finger to indicate the space between us.

'Both!' The word almost explodes from her mouth.

Yep, she's gonna be a firecracker in the sack, this one.

'Well, I heard there was a birthday girl at the bar.' Her features soften, her eyes both wider and darker as I reach out and push a lock of her russet hair over her shoulder. 'And I heard she was putting out.'

Chapter Four

AMBER

Dear birthday gods,

Thanks for sending me my own very own Chris Hemsworth. He's even got the panty-melting accent and everything. But bonus! This Aussie seems to have a whole lot of wickedness thrown in.

The icing on the cake would be if he has a hammer as magical as Thor's . . .

'I can't believe I'm doing this.'

'We're just walking along a hotel corridor, Red. Nothing's set in stone.'

'You mean you'd just walk me to my room? I-if that's what I wanted? If that's what I asked you to.' His brows furrow a little, though he nods. And I can see he means it. 'But then, what kind of birthday would that be?' I ask, slowing my steps, forcing him to slow, too. 'No one wants to fly solo on their birthday,' I add in a meaningfully tone as he turns to face me. God, that wine was strong, and that I can allude to a little *ménage a moi* probably means I'm still a tiny bit drunk.

Or a tiny bit lust drunk.

Drunk on the idea.

Drunk on him.

'So why are we standing here?' The soft light from a nearby table lamp—because it's that kind of hotel, the kind that doesn't feel the need to nail things down—brings out the blue in his dark eyes. And I can't help but notice the strong steady sound of his breathing. What will he sound like as his body works over me? Under me. As he breathes harder and harder as he reaches his peak.

'You okay there, Red?' Damn that smirk and those knowing eyes, and damn the way my expression barely hides my thoughts.

'I . . . I'm fine. I'm just wondering if this will be a birthday to remember.'

Or will this be the birthday I'll long remember as the one where I lost my mind. I've had friends who've viewed turning thirty with a sense of reluctance or fear, but it truly hadn't bothered me. I didn't feel like I was kissing my youth goodbye, trading in my heels for house slippers. Mainly because I turned a little crazy when I turned twenty-nine and decided my life didn't fit me anymore. That it needed shaking up. That I was going to travel. So as my thirtieth birthday approached, I'd so far viewed it with a sense of equanimity. I thought I was being Zen about the whole thing. Crazy was so last year. Turning thirty was going to be *fine*.

But what if I've been kidding myself? I mean, look at me! I've never had a one-night stand in my life, yet here I am, poised to do just that. What happens if we don't gel—if we have no chemistry? What if his kisses are sloppy and his hands like paws?

'Are you suggesting I look deficient in some way?'

'Well.' My shoulder lifts in a tiny shrug. It's an automatic movement, my lips moving of their own accord. 'We haven't even kissed.'

In less time than it takes to blink, I find myself pushed up against a door. No, not a door, a doorframe. *And not my room.* I brace my hands at the base of my spine, mainly to hide how they shake, as he raises his forearm to rest on the doorframe above my head.

Chemistry. So much chemistry. Buckets of the stuff washing through my veins. This is different from the bar, different from when he's sheltered me with his body. This time, he's crowding me and making me feel small. *Though far from insignificant.* For all the fair colour of his hair, his lashes are suspiciously thick. And dark. Wait, does he line them? As he comes closer, I decide no, not as those lashes become dark half-moons almost caressing his cheek. He reaches out, twirling a lock of my hair between his fingertips. My breath halts as he leans closer, pushing the hair from my shoulder, then pressing a fleeting kiss beneath my ear.

'You know it's gonna be good,' he whispers. 'I know you feel it.'

And I do. It's in the darkening of his gaze as the pulse thrums in his throat. It's in my body's response to his barest touch. It's in the hitch of my breath as his lips taunt mine.

His lips travel to mine, working teasing kisses across my jaw. My heart beats out of my chest, my body straining closer for his touch, for harder, for more. And finally, as our mouths meet, a sigh of sheer desperation fills the air between us. Light lips and a caressing tongue stoke a fire in me as, almost of their own volition, my hands slip from behind me, rising to wrap around his neck as I tilt my hips to feel the hard press of him. Light turns to dark, warmth to fire as his kisses deepen, his hands now in my hair, every inch of him now hard and possessive.

And I love it. Need it like I need my next breath.

'What's it to be?' The brush of his cheek is as rough as the words rasped against my neck.

'I'm good with . . . with this being good.'

So very good.

Pulling away, he takes my hand in his, and moments later, we're standing outside my room. More interestingly, he's the one who pulls us to a stop right at my door.

'How did you know which . . . ?'

'802. Mine is the room next door.'

'Oh.' *Oh.* 'You heard everything, didn't you?' My question is less accusatory and more shamed as heat floods my cheeks.

'I heard enough.'

His expression wears no smirk, just that knowing gaze which, as my mind supplies lewd snippets of that earlier conversation, I hide from, bringing both hands to my face.

'Let's just say,' he says, peeling my hands away, his gaze now level with mine, 'I heard enough and saw enough to make a working dinner last only as long as it took to inhale an entrée and down a glass of subpar wine.' I frown, not sure what he means. 'My mind was on other things. See, there was this woman in the elevator who I wanted to watch as she put her lipstick on.'

'Me?'

'Yeah.' His words are low and husky, his breath warm whisky and spice. 'Because I wanted to see what it tasted like. What *she* tasted like.' Then he kisses me, one sweet slide of his warm lips as he takes the key from my hand. 'Say the word and I'll fuck off next door.'

But I don't.

The room is cool, the drapes still open, a lamp at the far end of the room casting the space in a warm hue. I drop my bag next to a tray laden with tea things and, as I turn, find him unbuttoning his shirt.

Oh, so it's like that, then . . .

He toes off his shoes as he begins unfastening the tiny row of hinderances between my eyes and his skin, working from the bottom to the top. My breath halts, my nipples standing to attention, rubbing within the confines of my dress as he works the plackets apart without showing more than a few millimetres of skin.

'You're a tease,' I murmur. And a natural born tease at that.

'Says the girl fully clothed.' His eyes narrow almost infinitesimally. 'Incidentally, what is your name?' I shake my head, my lips rolled in on themselves. 'Are you a girl who likes a bit of mystery, Red?'

As a redhead, I've been teased plenty. Called lots of names. Carrot top. Gingersnap. Cheeto head. Orphan Annie. This list goes on and on. Curiously, though, I've never been referred to as Red.

Or mysterious.

I kind of like them both.

'Red works,' I demure as I think I'm more realistically the kind of girl who'd prefer not to spend the next six months sighing a man's name in her sleep. A girl who doesn't want to get even the tiniest bit attached to the person she's madly attracted to. If I don't know his name, or what he does for a living, or where he lives, I won't have the opportunity to obsess. Or stalk, come to think of it. Not stalk in a bad way, I'm not likely to get all Kathy Bates on his ass. Or ankles. But I might find myself stalking him on social media, or worse, derailing my Australian travel plans just to stakeout his favourite coffee shop for days on end to bump into him.

But I'm getting ahead of myself here and—

All thoughts of *ought* and *what* and *if* pop like bubbles as he slides his shirt open, pushing it from his shoulders. And, oh my God, I appreciate the dramatic reveal because he's so tanned and so taut, just as I'd imagined . . .

. . . and *covered* in ink.

Ohhhhh . . . I think I might've just orgasmed a little, a miniature burst of fireworks that consumed my ovaries. How can something that looked so perfect covered up by such proper tailoring turn out to be so sinfully sublime? My eyes devour him—the wreath at his collarbones, the sleeve of colour covering almost his entire right arm, the contrast of the almost blank canvas of his other. I suddenly want to touch the heat and the colour of him, want to trail my fingers over the vivid marks against his skin. I don't realise I'm staring, absolutely staring— or that he's still holding his shirt—until he holds out his arms as he begins to slowly turn.

His back is broad and lean, and every inch of it is covered in colour. A dragon, definitely Asian in design, swirls over the smooth surface as I suddenly find my fingers there, the body of the beast seeming to move in response to the ripple of muscles under my fingertips. It's then I realise that this isn't truly a dragon but an ouroboros, devouring its own tail. I'm not sure of the symbolism, but I can surely appreciate both the art *and* the canvas.

He's so broad and lean and, as he takes both my hands in his to press them against his chest, so incredibly warm and real.

His eyes darken, flickering my mouth. This is happening, really happening. My breath halts as I spread my fingers wide, one pinkie finger cautiously brushing his flat copper-coloured nipple. Abstractly, I recall a silly conversation Emma and I once had about the validity of the male nipple. I can't believe it's taken me until my thirtieth birthday to realise they might not just be an evolutionary leftover, but that they exist so we may hear the sound this man just made.

Sweet and agonised and rough and male.

And I made him do that.

My fingertips move over his abs, hot needy points of contact desperate to brand every inch of his skin. Who even looks like this in reality? I'm not a virgin, and I'm no stranger to a gym, but I've never been this close to a body like his.

Liam who? Chris who? Thor? Who the hell is he?

As my fingers continue to chart the ridges and valleys of him, he brings his hands to my shoulders, sliding the fabric from each. He lifts my hands once, then twice, the fabric falling to my hips. Is it the tickle of fabric or his gaze that ignites my skin? A moment later, it pools at my feet.

It's hard to discern what he's thinking as he looks at me. Just looks. My face. My neck. *Lower still.* A pulse flutters in my belly as the backs of his fingers brush away the strands of my long hair from where they reach the tips of my breasts. The flutter becomes a fire. A fire that writhes.

'Unzip me.' His voice soft yet authoritative, that accent and those two words causing a ripple of electricity to zip down my spine, the sensation exploding in my core like fireworks on the fourth of July.

I lick my lips as his darkened gaze stares down at me and my fingers fall to his belt. But it's kind of hard to concentrate enough to coordinate my movements as his lips pull and tease the soft skin of my neck, his big hands covering my hips. His pelvis flexes, my fumbling fingers plucking at his belt, barely managing to loosen it. I begin to struggle next with his button and zipper, my whole body shaking from the weight of his eyes. *The weight of my need.* His hands suddenly push mine away, and in one fluid moment, he works both obstacles free. Not to be outdone, I grasp the fabric, pushing his pants down his strong thighs, swapping our positions before pulling his eager hardness free from the confines of his boxer briefs.

'*Oh!*'

My exclamation is more breath than anything else because he's long, and thick, and I find, just what I need. *Birthday felicitations to me!* I wrap my hand around his girthy base, causing him to stagger a little, his upper back hitting the wall behind him. If you ask me why later, I'll probably say I must've been drunk on that sudden power as I place my hands on his hips, leaning over to take his fat crown between my lips.

'*Fuck . . .* ' The word is base and strained and so beautiful. 'I thought it was your birthday, not mine.' *Moy-n.*

Still bent at the waist, I look up and lick my lips. 'The birthday girl always gets what she wants.'

'Who am I to deny you?' he replies with a grin. But he isn't grinning for long, his mouth falling open and the back of his head hitting the wall with his agonised groan. '*Jesus Christ.*'

The rasp of his need pulses through me as I slide my lips along his silken hardness and bring my lips to his fat tip once more.

'I hope this is the gift that keeps on giving,' I whisper, my gaze sliding up the ripple of his abs.

'Red,' he rasps, tilting his chin as he moves my hair from obscuring his view. 'I'll give it to you all night long.'

With a wicked smile, I flick out my tongue before engulfing his length as best I can. He rasps a string of barely coherent curses, his hand tightening on my hair as I reverse the motion, my tongue working the sensitive underside.

'On second thought, I might be dead before that.' His words sound pained as I hum around him, repeating the action with a little more suction.

'Fuck, that's it. Take more.'

But as I'm pretty sure that's not how birthday gifts work, I circle his crown with my tongue, and as an encore, I flick the wet slit, causing him to gasp as his hips twitch and his fingers itch to tighten in my hair.

'Birthday and Christmas at once,' I think he mumbles as I take him into my mouth again, all wet lips and sliding tongue as I work him again and again. He should look silly, I think, half in and half out of his pants, his cock lifted free from his black boxer briefs. But as I cast my eyes up the taut, tanned length of him, I'm surprised to find he looks anything but. 'You're so fucking sexy, Red,' he rasps, staring down at me. 'Jesus Christ, I can't wait to get my mouth on you.'

I hum a pleased response, but before I can reply on any other level, his hands reach to pull me to stand. He kisses me then, long and wetly, his tongue running over the seam of my mouth as though to taste himself. Like I needed the added stimulation with as wet as I am. I find myself writhing against him, desperate to feel more of him—desperate to get this to the bed before I spontaneously combust.

He pushes me back just a little bit, his hands making a slow sweep of my body, sliding across my hips, up my belly to the tips of my breasts.

'You're sure it's not my birthday?' His expression wears a lazy half grin that should come with a warning to panties everywhere.

'Well, I don't know you.' I give a little shrug. 'So it might be.'

'I reckon it might be.' He licks his lips a little. 'It might've come early.' I refrain from making the smartass comment sitting on the end of my tongue, and he knows it, too, judging by the quirk of those shining lips. His eyes dip to my panties briefly. 'Take 'em off.'

'I will if you will.'

The words are barely out of my mouth before he's stripping out of his pants and Italian looking loafers. He's cut. *So cut.* And I know it sounds ridiculous, but he looks like Michelangelo's *David*, but for the swirls of his ink and the endowment of more than a *David*-esque tiny penis. Because *his* looks more like it belongs to a statue of a satyr I once saw in a Grecian museum.

Birthday penis for the win!

There isn't an ounce of self-consciousness in his stance—and why would there be when he looks like that?—as he glances down at my panties meaningfully. So I hook my thumbs into the elastic at my hips and wiggle them down to my knees.

'Best birthday ever.' *Ev-ah*. His tone is suddenly a little growly, his half smile a little wolfish. Put them together and I almost stumble backwards as he steps into me, his big hands on my bare butt as he lifts me, striding deeper into the room. I squeal a little and then mutter something along the lines of *I'll let him know* when he slaps my ass, then deposits me on the top of a vanity.

'Do you have something against beds?' The words hit the air a little tremulously.

'How many birthdays have you been fucked in a bed?' I shrug in the face of his expression. Not only do I not have the capacity to do the math, but I also don't quite know how to answer. 'A little birdy told me you were fucked at least once last birthday. I bet that was in a bed.'

'Is there anything you *didn't* hear?'

'Yeah, actually. I didn't quite catch how many birthdays you've been fucked on one of these,' he says, slapping the wooden surface.

'Well, that would be at least . . . ' I pretend to count on my fingers, but he's not buying it. 'At least . . . zero times.'

'Perfect. I like that you left your shoes on.' He wraps his fingers around one of my ankles, propping the pointed heel on the ledge of one of the wide drawers as he begins trailing his fingers lightly up the inside of my leg. My body jolts as he passes my knee, travelling farther until I'm gasping with the sweet shock of his fingers suddenly between my legs. His eyes darken at that catch of my breath, his knowing gaze not once leaving my face as he teases my slickness, tests my resolve, his fingers sliding the length of me, touching but not quite touching enough. *Or where I need him.* Then it all happens at once—our mouths fusing in a powerful kiss, his wrist twisting, his fingers thrusting. Curling. My hands clutch the hard wooden edge of the vanity as his sandpapery compliments whisper against my skin.

He whispers how gorgeous I am.

How hard he is for me.

How he can't wait to be inside me.

How he'll give me the birthday of a lifetime.

And I believe him.

He works me wetly, the lewd sounds of my pleasure joining my tight breaths. With a groan of appreciation, he drops to his knees. His tongue slips between my legs and with one long, flat lick, my thoughts scatter. The air is filled with my shameless moans as he spreads me wider, his wicked mouth driving me to the edge of sweet sanity. The abrasion of his stubble, his hums of appreciation against my flesh, and I'm almost immediately ready to detonate.

'Please . . . *please!*'

'You want to come,' he asserts, his gaze rising shamelessly and lustful from between my legs.

'Yes, please.' My eyes flutter closed. 'I need you.' Need to feel you. Need to be filled.

The crinkle of a condom wrapper sounds, and my heart gives an excited jump, my eyes springing open to watch him roll on a condom. The jump turns to an eager thud as he pushes my thighs a little wider. Wrapping his hand around the base of his thick erection, he lines himself up, two sets of eyes falling to where we meet.

'Just look at you.' His voice is rough, his swallow deep and, as though the action is one that requires complete concentration, his lids shuttering over coal coloured eyes. One beat, two, then he presses his lips against mine.

I can taste myself and wonder how the taste of my pleasure from his lips can be such a turn on, one extra layer to the sensation to those building and coalescing inside. I ache with the need to be filled, my insides pulsing empty and desperate. Not that he would know as he pulls away a little once more, leaving us staring down to where we almost join. To where he circles his fat crown against my clit.

'Happy Birthday, Red.'

My face in his hands and a soft curse on his lips, he pushes inside with one solid thrust. As he exhales, I inhale, the moment synchronised and shimmering and beautiful. I feel filled. Stretched, almost impossibly so.

Has it been so long?

Was the first thrust ever so good?

I don't have time to contemplate an answer as he withdraws, his hips driving forward solidly with an eager grunt that counters my cry.

'*Oh!*'

His hands slip under my ass, pulling me closer to the edge and tilting my hips. My response to the change in depth is immediate, my fingers grasping his shoulder as the pressure of his next thrust rubs my clit. My cries urge a repeat, my body meeting his undulations in the rhythm of his own as he gives me what I need, again and again, working himself deeper and deeper until we're no longer two strangers in a hotel room but one entity with a common yet greedy cause.

'Give me your mouth,' my birthday gift demands, his stubble abrading my skin as his mouth seeks mine. I roll my hips, too focussed on this moment to comply, as I throw my head back and offer him my neck instead.

'You're so fucking tight,' his dark voice rasps, the room filling with the sounds of our joint pleasure. Lifting me from the wooden surface, I slide a little deeper, the weight of my body a counterbalance to his actions. Everything moves in this position— boobs, ass, my hair—but I don't care as, with each thrust, he drives me closer to where my body tells me I need to go.

'Fuck. *Fuck*.' His eyes are glazed and his expression intense, but he's no longer looking at me. He's looking *behind* me as his tempo increases and the sensation between my legs borders on the most exquisite kind of pleasure as his rhythmic grunts sound in my ear. 'That is so fucking hot.'

I turn my head over my shoulder, belatedly realising that he's watching our reflection in the mirror, watching my body accepting his. The realisation sets off a new round of internal fireworks, the sensation seeming to affect him in the best of ways. I do the only thing I can, which is hang on, my whole being capitulating to him completely, whimpering as he pushes his tongue into my mouth at the same moment he thrusts.

'God. *Oh, God.* I'm . . . I'm . . . ' I'm a goner. Done for. Stick a fork in me and I probably wouldn't notice as pleasure crawls through me, through my thighs, my stomach and spine, the feeling building in intensity and ferocity until it bursts through my skin, white hot and intense.

With an answering shout, he undulates into me, the muscles in his neck and forearms straining, pulling my body impossibly close. Our hearts pound, pressed together, his fingers gripping my ass so tight, it's like they've burrowed right under my skin.

For a few moments, we stay like this, skin sticky and out of breath, waiting for the awkwardness to kick in. Of course, somehow, I feel the need to make sure awkward appears sooner rather than later.

'Well, that was . . . '

'Round one,' he says, carrying me across the room before dropping me unceremoniously on the bed. I land in a tangle of limbs and auburn strands.

'That was what?' I pull myself to sit, pushing the sweaty locks from my face with little success.

'Round one.' With both hands, he pushes the strands left and right to reveal my face. *Yeah, I'm sure that's super attractive, not. No wonder he looks so amused.* 'The birthday fun starts here,' he says, pulling away.

'What–where are you going?'

'Gonna run a bath,' he answers, adding far too many vowels to that word. *Baaath.*

'Why?'

' 'Cause it's the best place to drink champagne,' he says, disappearing into the bathroom.

'But there isn't any in the mini bar,' I call after him. Not even the little bottles.

I might've looked. What? It is my birthday.

'Here.'

Everything goes white. And fluffy. And towel like. I pull the robe from my head.

'What—'

'I'd put in on if I were you,' he says, appearing once more in front of me, this time, with a towel wrapped around his waist. 'Unless you want room service to know you're a natural redhead.'

Chapter Five

AMBER

'Of course, thanks for your consideration!' I reply, my smile falling as I end the call. 'I thought backpacking gigs were supposed to be easy to pick up in Australia?' Dropping my phone to the table, I pick up my paper coffee cup before slumping back in my chair. 'I suppose I'd better make the most of this.' I raise it in a weak toast. 'The way things are looking, I won't even be able to afford this soon.' I force a smile to my face for the benefit of my new friend, Rose. We met when I moved into the backpacker's hostel. Can't live five star every day. Unfortunately.

At least the air is cool and sweet after the earlier storm. It's a welcome respite from the blistering Australian heat.

'*La vie est faite de petit bonheurs,*' I say, bringing the plastic top to my lips.

'Boners? Girl, that call must've gone better than I thought.'

'What? Oh, not boners, *bonheurs.*'

'You realise you just said boner twice, right? Just once in a fancy ass French accent. What are you shaking your head at?' she asks, sending me a look that suggests she thinks I'm crazy.

'Not only was that a French accent, but it was also French.'

'Sure, French boners. But we're in Australia. There are other boners to concentrate on right now.'

'And jobs,' I add with a sigh.

'And you're just *so* sweet in the face of adversity.' Smiling, Rose shakes her head.

'Meaning?'

'You're still smiling despite *that*.' She leans over, tapping the back of my phone with her red fingernail, 'sounding like a *no* call if I ever heard one.'

She's right. It was another no. Number eight? Or was it eighteen?

'Onto the next one,' I say, now fixing that smile on my face. After all, it was my choice to travel the world. My choice to seek adventure. And what's a little adventure without adversity? 'Onward and upward!' I raise my cup even higher along with the platitude. 'It's always darkest before the ... Aw, hell, I dunno, Rose. I'm trying to stay positive here.' Rose chuckles as she shakes her head. 'I want to stay in the region—I'm not ready to head up country yet. At least, not until the weather cools a little.'

My. God. It is *hot!*

'Those cute Swedish guys?' she says, waving her own cup over her shoulder. 'They all piled in a car to travel to Queensland yesterday. They've got work on a sugar farm someplace up there.'

Urgh. More outdoor work, and in a state even hotter.

'I was hoping for something indoors, something maybe with food. Maybe a pub or a café? I think I'm currently keeping Proctor and Gamble in the sunscreen business.' I rub a hand over my pale yet lobster red freckled arm. And that's despite the liberal application of sun protection every four hours. But I love it here. Of all the places I've visited, Australia has been the most amazing. Paris had been its own kind of amazing and my ticket to an education, to experience, and a little confidence. While working as an au pair in Paris, I discovered that working with kids was still good, but that maybe I wasn't truly destined to teach forever after discovering a passion for food. I'd developed a desire to create edible masterpieces. And by masterpiece, I mean something that provided the ultimate satisfaction. It could mean the best cookies the kids had ever eaten or the most delectable three-course meal ever to grace a dinner table. I'd wanted cook for the family, and they'd encouraged me to sign up for some culinary classes, and even paid for them. And then, *mon dieu*, I'd discovered a love of baking. And a few extra pounds to my thighs.

Since then, I haven't had much opportunity to cook other than the odd stir-fry in a backpacker's communal kitchen, but Lord, I want to.

I've got a year's visa for Australia that's contingent on all kinds of things, but for now, I've been trying to snag some kind of casual work around Sydney. I just love the place—the cafés and the nightlife, the beaches and the parks, the fabulous smelling Blue

Mountains that are just a couple of hours away. There's just so much to see and do, and I can't wait to do it all.

Plus, I'm also working my way around their wines, and that might take me a while.

What's not to love about the place?

I suppose working in orchards, for one. Picking apples. Working in farms picking vegetables, or veggies as they're prone to call them here.

'Well, since you're desperate,' Rose begins, 'it's not quite Sydney, but a group of us are travelling into the Hunter Valley next week to work at a vineyard.'

'Urgh. More picking. I think I'd rather start picking my nose.'

'It's not that bad,' she says with a laugh. 'Besides, they're looking for more than just agricultural workers. The winery has a cellar door and stuff.'

'A restaurant? A café?'

'Honestly? I don't think so, but I'm sure there'll be other work. It's not Sydney but . . .'

It's not too far away. Or anywhere hotter.

'Is there space in the van?' The group Rose is travelling with have hired a Wikid Camper. That's an old camper van, vandalised to look cool or so they say.

'Sure, though you might have to blow Sven,' she says with a sly wink.

'That's Sven the dishy Swede who seems to hang on Mitch's every word?' There's a little unrequited boy-on-boy lust if I've ever seen it.

'Yeah, but I think he might be getting desperate.'

'Desperate enough to go for a girl? Or are you suggesting I try cultivating a beard?'

'Maybe you could get him drunk.'

'The size of that dude? I'm on a budget here!'

'Or maybe you could just buy him a box of those yummy macarons.'

My cheeks heat as I remember walking into the hostel last week after my amazing birthday hotel weekend. It was a weekend to remember for sure. I'd spent hours by the pool under a wide parasol, drinking cocktails and reading, or just lying on the crisp, white sheets, dining from the room service menu and hitting the minibar. And of course, there was my birthday fantasy fulfilled—sexcapades amazing enough to tide me over until I'm at least thirty-one.

Lord, it was . . . everything. Dirty and rough, sultry and sweet. My mystery man ordered champagne to celebrate my birthday, and can I say I was surprised to find he didn't charge it to my room? He looked at me as if I were a queen, then fucked me like I was a hooker. Then back to the royal treatment again as he'd run me a bubble bath, serving it with a glass of chilled champagne. Then, be still my still fluttering lady parts, he'd climbed in to join me. Who knew bathing could be such dirty fun? He got me soapy and slippery and super turned on, then carried me into the bedroom where we got sticky again, this time with sweat and champagne.

'Girl, where have you gone with that smile on your face?'

'The patisserie,' I answer immediately. 'Total macaron porn.' Rose laughs, though she throws me a sceptical look.

But I had the most amazing night, finally sleeping only as dawn began to break with my body draped over his chest. I'd next woken midmorning alone and a little disorientated, sore in places that had been long neglected. But I had plans—a date with coffee and colourful cake—and I wasn't about to dwell.

I was just about to leave to check out when a delivery was brought to my room. I could barely see the member of the hotel's guest services for a huge bouquet of the loveliest blooms; pale coloured orchids, roses, and tulips, all wrapped in the greenest tropical foliage. It was breathtakingly stylish. I'd argued they couldn't be for me until I spotted the birthday card. I might've swooned a little, even if the card turned out to be blank. But the icing on my birthday treat was the box of brightly coloured macarons from the patisserie I was planning to visit.

Better than any birthday cake.

I'd almost floated out of the hotel, maxed out on my birthday experience. There was no way I was leaving my flowers and yummies behind, though I must've looked a little odd checking into my next accommodations. But hey, the flowers brightened up the six-person room—and a six-person room is better than a mixed-sex dormitory, let me tell you.

And sharing my box of macarons made me instant friends. Like Rose, here.

'I just sent Sven a text. He says there's space in the van for you.'

'What's it gonna cost me?'

'Sven says zero sexual favours and zero pastry treats. But Rose says it'll cost you another cup of coffee.'

'I can cope with that.' Just about, especially as I'll be earning an income in a few days. 'I don't have to preregister or anything with the winery, do I?'

Rose shakes her head. 'The website said first come, first served. Apparently, we just have to turn up early enough.'

'What if there are others who get there before us?'

'That's all part of the backpacking adventure, babe.'

Chapter Six

BYRON

'You need a cold beer and a hot woman.'

I pull the key from the ignition, tipping my head back against the headrest. 'That your professional opinion?'

'As a schoolteacher, you mean?' Tom, my best friend and self-appointed therapist, asks.

'No, as a fucking idiot.'

'I'm not the one biting off people's heads because he needs to get laid. And I'm not the one skulking off out of town once a month like he has a dirty habit.'

'You've got a bloody nerve. You're the biggest root rat there is.' A manwhore by any other name is just the same.

'I'm not complaining. I'm saying if you're going to have a habit, fucking well commit! Root. Screw. Bang. Bring it on, I say!'

'You don't know what you're talking about.'

'Don't I? I guess those were mozzie bites covering you neck last month, were they? They must have been big fucking mosquitos, or maybe you were attacked by a teething puppy while you were in the big smoke on business?' When I don't answer, Tom starts up again. 'Maybe they were bird pecks? Did you get attacked by some vicious plovers, mate?'

Despite my mood, I smile. I can afford to because Tom was the first person I'd called in on my way back. Forewarned is forearmed and all that, though it was difficult to hide the bitemarks from those at home. Hunter Valley summers are hardly scarf weather.

'Man cannot live by being blown once a month alone.' This time, I do laugh as Tom taunts, 'Go on, call me an idiot again. You know I'm right.'

'Reckon I must've been wrong. I must be an idiot because I don't remember asking you what I was missing in my life.'

'B-Man, come on. Ask anyone and they'll tell you. You need to cut loose more—get laid more. Call one of your fucking tribe of brothers—they'd tell you it'd do you some good.'

I'm telling my brothers fuck all.

My gaze narrows unseeingly on the roof of my truck as I mentally run down the potential list of people who've complained about my recent attitude. I pay no mind to the setting sun, glorious as it may be, and the vines that surround my hundred-hectare plus property.

'So that's your solution. A cold beer and a woman—life's that simple, is it?'

'A cold beer and a *hot* woman. That's Uncle Tommy's prescription.'

'No need to go all creepy on me.'

'Sorry to burst your bubble, mate, but this Uncle Tommy's not interested in having your bony arse sit on his knee.' Tom's grin seeps through his words. Meanwhile, my grin is more grimace as I draw a hand down my face.

'Mate, I have beer in the fridge and two women waiting indoors for me.'

'Your mum doesn't count. And neither does the babysitter,' he replies with a snigger I probably deserve. 'Even if the sitter would like to treat you like her little toe.' He pauses for me to reply with my line, but when I don't, he pretends I've asked anyway. 'And bang you all over the house.'

'That was last week, and she was a qualified nanny.'

'Ah, shit, yeah. I remember. With a rack like hers, I can't believe you gave her the elbow.'

'Why, what would you have done?' I regret the words as soon as they're out of my mouth.

'I'd have given her my dick first. What kind of drongo turns down a hot chick dressed in a candy G-string?'

It's a good job I didn't mention that, at the time, she was also holding a bottle of beer. Apparently, she was dinner. Candy G-string, girl, and a cold beer to wash it all down. Fuck me.

'You're forgetting the bit where my children were asleep in bed so early it had to be with the aid of some kind of medicine.' *An antihistamine or something.*

'Shit, I forgot about that. You've got the Maddison's girl working for you now, right?'

'An emergency hire,' I agree.

'She's like, what? Grade ten?'

'I dunno, you're the principal of the school.' I'm sure the parents of his students would be horrified to know how irresponsible he is in his private life. Still, he's a good mate. Mostly. 'All I know is she's young enough not to joke about.'

'Like I said, you need a hot *woman*. Not your mum and not a teenager.'

My mind slips to a moment in Sydney last month. The gorgeous redhead standing before me, absently biting her lip, her anticipation almost tangible as she'd watched me unbutton my shirt. *Would she have been as keen if I wasn't suited and booted that night? If she'd known the ink I was hiding underneath?*

These are questions I've asked myself before. Moments of time I've played like a montage in my head. *Usually when I'm alone in bed with my dick in my hand.* But this time, it's different, my thoughts not on being inside or over her, or charming my way into her for the third or fourth time. This time, my thoughts snag on something else. I'd held my balled shirt in my hand as I'd glanced around the hotel room looking for somewhere to chuck it, ending up giving the girl a bit of a twirl.

Seems ink was definitely her thing.

I swallow thickly at the memory of the dusty backpack and swag roll abandoned on the suitcase stand, a pair of mud-caked boots lying underneath. At the time, I'd pushed the sight of it and the implications to the back of my mind. She didn't look like a kid, not in the elevator, and not standing in front of me, biting her full pink lip. There was no turning back. She'd caught me hook, line, and sinker. But now, weeks away from that night, I find myself wondering how old she actually was. Not all backpackers are kids. I know this now, know it after spending time scanning the seasonal pickers for her face. Australia is full of Europeans and American kids, and more, working their way around the country, spending a year in the sun. I hire enough of them to work on the vines to know they're all over the age of consent. But right now, that doesn't make me feel any easier.

She'd looked all woman, worldly and sophisticated as fuck. And she didn't sound like a kid as I'd followed her through the hotel hallways, smiling to myself at the one-sided conversation. *That isn't as bad as it sounds.* She knew exactly what she wanted. She just hadn't realised *who* could fulfil those wants was just a few steps behind her.

It was almost funny how it happened. I'd pulled open the door to my room at the exact moment she'd passed. I caught little more than a glimpse of her profile and the scent of her perfume. *Like night blooming magnolia and sin.* She was laughing, and the next thing I knew, she was telling whoever was on the other end of line that she was looking for a bloke for the explicit purpose of treating herself to a very happy fucking birthday. *Literally.* She was heading the wrong way for the elevator, but I followed her anyway. What else could I do? Stop her? Tell her I could save her time on both counts?

Excuse me, miss, the elevators are the other way, but I think what you're looking for is in my—or your—hotel room because I couldn't help overhearing you say you were looking for someone to bang tonight. As it happens, so am I.

We must be fated to fuck!

I'd followed her. Followed the trail of her perfume, her round swaying arse, and the smooth skin of her exposed back. And those fantastic legs.

But mostly I followed the sound of her throaty laugh.

But the backpack . . . she couldn't have been a kid. Could she?

'You're like a dog with a bone, you know that?' I grumble, the current discomfort tightening my gut and causing my words to sound unnecessarily gruff. 'Maybe I'm happy with the way things are. Maybe not all of us need a woman to feel fulfilled.'

Except occasionally. When the itch requires scratching.

'Bullshit. You're tellin' me you don't go out of town once a month just to get your dick sucked?'

'I go for business.' *Go for the business, stay for the dick suck.* 'And you've got a nerve.'

'I've got a fucking bunch of them, mate. I am what I am, and I don't hide it,' Tom retorts with malicious delight. 'I don't go around town pretending to be something I'm not.'

'Right. I'm sure the parents of the country high school you lead know you as Thomas Austen, upstanding school principal by day, and Tomcat by night.'

'I guess my old mum chose my name well.' Tom chuckles. 'Come on, I can't help it I'm popular with the ladies. You would be, too, if you didn't go around growling at half the town.'

'Piss off,' I reply with, in hindsight, something that sounds like a growl.

'It's true. Sometimes you even bark. But all that growling and barking seems to be doing something because, as it turns out, you've got this whole mysterious powerful man vibe going for you. The women in this town are creamin' in their undies, mate!'

'Jesus Christ,' I groan, rubbing a hand across my jaw. I need a shave. And a beer. And a bit of peace and quiet. 'What the fuck, Tom?'

'Pretty much what I said when I walked into the staff room to hear a group of 'em discussing, with relish I might add, if Byron Phillips really bites.'

'You're full of shit.'

'Fair dinkum.' Gleeful. The bastard sounds gleeful. 'The lot of them are just waiting for you to send that angry blue-eyed stare in their direction. Swoon! That was a direct quote, by the way.'

'I don't need to listen to this.'

'I kinda think you do. And I kinda think you should try socialising locally sometime. Maybe even *dine* locally from time to time.'

'Dine—what are we? Old maids now?' The reason I don't *socialise* in town is exactly this—Tom's timely reminder. Gossip and the damage it can bring. 'I'm going now,' I say, my fingers already tight on the door handle. 'I'm going to walk into my own damn house, drink my own damn beer, and I'll enjoy it so much more. You know why? Because it'll be served without the complications a woman would bring.'

'I'm only sayin'—'

'And another thing,' I say, cutting him off as I slam the door of my truck. 'Remind me next time I call that I can't expect any kind of sensible conversation from you.'

I scarcely hear my boots on the gravel or the cicadas singing from the yard. My fingers are wrapped around the door handle, and before I even realise, I'm swinging it open.

'Oh, *shiiit!*'

I stare blankly at my three-year-old son, then the puddle of orange juice and the shattered glass at the base of his stool. Before I can move a muscle, Mum appears.

'Back in your seat, back in your seat!' She scoops up Matty before his bare feet get anywhere near the shattered glass, her frustrated gaze cutting to me. 'Well, don't just stand there. Make yourself useful— get the dustpan!'

But the dustpan is the last thing on my mind.

All I wanted was a beer and a bit of peace and quiet.

My abrupt appearance might've shocked my four-year-old into dropping his juice glass, but I also have other things on my mind.

Where did Matt learn that word?

Who the hell gave him a glass?

Where is the goddamn babysitter?

And why the hell had Tom taken to yanking my chain today of all days?

Tilting my head, I crack my neck in an attempt to release the pent-up tension. *Maybe Tom's right. Maybe I need to root more often.* With that last unwelcome thought, I stride into the kitchen, pulling open the pantry door, though not before I hear my mother's impatient sigh.

There are two main entrances to the Phillips house, or *mansion*, as some of the local smart arses call it, though I know, technically, my childhood home doesn't qualify as a mansion. I'd spoken to enough realtors just dying to have a stickybeak at the place to be aware that it falls a good eight-hundred square feet short of that title. *Apparently.* But the remaining seventy-two hundred square feet are full of history and detail, plus I'd recently remodelled and redecorated, chasing away old ghosts. I can see how it might dazzle the locals.

Despite the Sydney architect and interior designer, to me the house is just my home. It always has been, even when I was living in a luxury penthouse in Sydney. This place is in my blood, seeped in soil and in wine. I couldn't give it up, even if I wanted to. I'd not only grown up here, but I'd also been born in the very bedroom I now call my own. A fact that had not dazzled, Katya, my wife, unsurprisingly.

I suppose I'd always expected to end up back home—maybe not as soon as I did—but Dad's sudden heart attack two years ago brought forward my plans quite a bit. The house itself overlooks the family business, Riposo Estates, the oldest and most prestigious vineyard in the Hunter Region. Yep, the wine and the soil of this land stains my fingers and runs in my blood, even if the name of our brand is a total misnomer. *At Rest Estates.* Rest is something I don't get a lot of, not when the grapes are grown on this land, harvested, fermented, aged, and bottled here.

Matty's butt is parked on the stool as my mother takes the dustpan from me. I notice she's refilled his juice, this time in an appropriate child-friendly cup.

'Where's Edie?'

'She went to sleep in the middle of a pile of Legos, so I put her to bed.'

Great, so no decent bedtime hour tonight. No kicking back after dinner with a glass of wine to follow my beer. Parents of young children are driven to drink, and that's a fact.

As I face the prospect of an evening playing with Lol Dolls with my daughter, an evening filled with unrelenting questions until gone ten p.m., I wonder if, just this once, I can be a deadbeat dad and plonk her in front of the Disney Channel. Tempting, but no. There's a reason it's called the idiot box, and I'm raising no idiots.

'How'd Matty get the glass?' Mum shoots me a disparaging look in answer. 'He didn't get it himself.' She still doesn't answer. 'Come on, Mum, we both know he can't reach that shelf in the fridge.'

'Byron Phillips,' Mum replies, bringing herself to her full five foot nothing height. 'If you go in there and frighten that poor girl, I'll . . . I'll . . . '

'You'll what? Tan my arse?'

'I'll starch your boxer shorts!'

Shaking my head, I leave Mum with both son and mess as I walk through the main entryway and into the sitting room. I fully expect to find the Maddison's eldest daughter sitting on the sofa with her headphones on, ears picking up whatever it is that her millennial brain denotes as music.

Fuck, I sound old. However, as I turn the corner, I see I was right about the girl.

Eyes glued to her phone, her blonde head bops like an empty bobblehead doll. So I make my way around the back of the sofa and stand in front of her, arms folded. I get no satisfaction as she starts visibly . . . when she eventually notices me. And yeah, it makes me feel like a bit of a prick. I'm pissed off, but I don't take pleasure in frightening teenagers. That's Tom's job, though he tells me that these days, teaching is mostly a velvet glove affair. *No back-handers across the head for behaving like a tool.*

But, come the fuck on, I left her in charge of a pair of four-year-olds. Yeah sure, I left Mum in charge of *her*, but this kid was supposed to do the heavy lifting.

As if I haven't got enough on my plate these days.
So she should be nervous. And she is. But it doesn't make me feel big. And I'm about to treat her like I treat any of my employees. Surely, she realised that her relationship with *my* money depended upon her relationship with *my* children, didn't she?

What was her name again? Maddie? Nah, Maddie Maddison? No one would be cruel enough to do that to their kid. Martha? *Yeah, that was it.* Martha quickly whips out her earbuds, her eyes darting around the room, presumably trying to locate her charges, therefore reassuring me, their father and her employer for the school holidays, that everything is cool and has been all day.

My arse.

'How loud is that music?'

My tone is even as I slide my hands into the front pockets of my pants. The way her eyes flick over me with a mixture of fear and interest—teenage interest—makes me glad I'm wearing a long-sleeved shirt. I can't walk through town without drawing glances. Millennials of both sexes are a fan of tattoos, it seems. The thought makes my frown all the more stern, I imagine.

'Sorry?'

'I said, how loud is the music? Is it so loud that you can't hear an emergency?'

'Oh, th-there was no emergency, Mr. Phillips,' she stammers, her voice full of uncertainty.

'What do you think would be worse? Matty getting cut on broken glass while you sit here *rockin' out*, or his sudden use of an unsavoury word?

Something like shit?' My tone is glacially cool. And once more for the record, I take no pleasure in this.

'Beg your pardon,' she asks, all big blue eyes and innocence, which is all well and good had I not just almost witnessed my own blue-eyed innocent risk a trip to the local hospital.

'It's like this, Martha. I just came home from work to witness both of these things.' Almost. 'Meanwhile, you were nowhere to be found.'

To her credit, the babysitter's first instinct isn't to defend herself. By good sense or genuine care, she asks how Matty was instead. But it's a bit too late, and along with it, a list of reasons of why a teenager isn't fit to look after my kids.

Different day, same shit, even if this girl was just supposed to be a stopgap while waiting for someone more experienced from the agency to arrive. She's not the first nanny, childminder, or whatever to get her marching orders for incompetence. Or in the case of the Candy G-string, negligence. And at this point, there's usually an outpouring of anger or tears. I'm guessing tears, given her age. And doesn't that make me feel like a total turd. But she's got to go.

But the girl makes no attempt to defend herself and successfully holds back the threatening yet welling tears.

'This isn't going to work out,' I tell her simply, slipping my wallet from my jeans. I'm not purely heartless as I pull out a few notes, paying her until the end of the week. No doubt by the weekend, she'll have told her mates what I total dick I am, and she'll have a job at the local ice cream place.

Martha leaves the room red-faced, out of shame, out of anger, I don't really give a fuck. I expect she's currently in the kitchen getting a hug from this ogre's mother before being handed a few more dollar notes.

But at least she didn't cry.

Or run from the room.

Maybe I'm getting better at this gig.

If only I could get that to translate to the hiring.

I sigh as I take her place on the couch, arms folded across my chest, my legs stretched out in front.

'You didn't have to make her cry,' Mum reproves, coming into the room.

Fuck. Not another one.

'It was probably gratitude,' I reply as she rounds the couch, holding Matty's hand. 'I paid her until the weekend.'

'That's it? That's all you've got to say for yourself?' She throws up her hands. 'Sometimes I wonder where I got you from.'

'I thought you said you found me stuck in the prickly pear bush.'

This family lore. My parents had four boys, and they told each of us a tall tale of our origins. I was the kid found abandoned in the prickly pear bush, probably on account of my sparkling wit and personality. Flynn was the son found hanging out with the koalas in a eucalyptus tree. Koalas are notoriously lazy fuckers, and Flynn is so laid back, he's horizontal half the time. *At least he was until his wife had a baby.* Rafferty came from the pumpkin patch because that's the only way they could explain the red cast to his hair. And then there's the baby, Roman, who my parents purported to have found wandering about the streets. *Just roamin'*, Dad used to say. *We found him just roamin' around, bare arsed naked, his little thumb stuck in his mouth.*

So that's the fable. The real story is a little stranger. My mother fell pregnant with me after just a month of dating my old man and following a weekend in Byron Bay 'getting to know each other'. Or as the rest of the world calls it, enjoying a dirty weekend away. Mum's parents were stinkin' rich and not at all pleased. Still, they came around once the pair had been hastily married, then farther seduced by the appearance of their first grandchild. Said first grandchild was named after the place where he was conceived—the town of the dirty deed. It could've been worse, and I'm pleased they weren't visiting somewhere like Humpty Doo or Yorkey's Knob.

Flynn was apparently conceived in a tent at Flynns Beach near Port Macquarie. Thankfully, I was probably sleeping as well as too young to remember because I was there with them, staying in their little two-man tent. The pair did love their holidays.

Rafferty was conceived at the eponymous resort of the same name, somewhere on an island in the Barrier Reef, and Roman was conceived on our very first family holiday overseas. No prizes for guessing which city they screwed in to produce him. I suppose I should be glad I don't have a brother called Riley because then I'd probably have been traumatised by tales of them shagging in some grotty Irish bar somewhere.

'Daddy, where did Marfa go?' Matty asks, pulling on the leg on my pants.

'She went home, mate.' I poke him in his soft, round little belly, causing him to giggle and squirm as he clambers up my legs, crawling onto my knee. His pudgy little arms close around my neck like a monkey.

'Little mate, how about you draw me a picture before dinner?'

'Sure!'

Kissing his head, I inhale his little boy scent deeply before he untangles his arms, squirming to the ground. He pads to the window where a pair of handsome toddler-sized wooden desks stand before opening the drawer stuffed to the gills with crumpled paper, broken crayons, and pens with missing caps. *Neat on the outside, Matty on the inside.* The thought makes me smile. I'd trade a lifetime of cold beer and hot women to keep him and his twin sister safe. But if I had to choose between living without beer or the occasional fuck, I'd become teetotal, for sure.

As I watch Matt create his masterpiece, I become aware of my mother sitting in the wingback chair to my left, just itching to speak. Leaning back once again, I let my head rest on the back of the couch as I close my eyes.

My stomach tightens as my mind leapfrogs to an evening last month. An evening where I'd made myself a beautiful woman's birthday gift. But now is neither the time nor the place to think of this.

'What was she? Number five?'

She wouldn't have been number five. More like number fifteen this year, at least. *Fuck, who's counting?* I'm a grown arsed man, and I'm hurting no one, I wear rubbers. Play safe.

'I'm right aren't I?' Mum enquires again.

My eyes spring open, realising Mum and I are talking—thinking—at cross-purposes. Red had been root number fifteen. Martha, on the other hand, had been the kid's fifth carer, at least.

I sit forward, elbows on my knees, my nod of agreement almost imperceptible. Unlike my sigh.

'What was it this time? You didn't like the way she blew her nose?'

I don't respond. What would be the point? Instead, I keep my eyes fixed on my shoes, but as she *harrumphs*, words spill rapidly from my mouth.

'She wasn't there when Matty broke a glass. She didn't even *hear* it because of that goddamn phone of hers. What if he got hurt?' I say, turning my gaze to her. 'You're not the nanny, so why were you the only one there?'

'Kids get hurt, love. They fall and get bruises. Sometimes they bleed. No amount of nannying, parenting, or cotton wool, or coddling will stop that.'

I ignore the point she's really trying to make, opting for the easier path instead.

'And what about him swearing. He didn't get that from me.'

'Oh, I agree,' she replies, folding her arms under her ample bosom. Because that's what the older generation have, according to Flynn. Women have tits. Mums have something else. Not that we have conversations about our mother's . . . although, with him, conversations can often be much weirder. 'I know Matty likely got that word from Martha because if he'd picked up something from you, it'd be ten times worse. He's likely to get expelled from kindergarten before he's even started.'

'I'm careful around him.'

'Too careful,' she repeats. 'That's the point I'm trying to make.'

'Don't start, Ma. I'm not in the mood.'

'How many times have I heard that, I wonder? Thousands probably. What?' she asks blandly in response to my glare. 'You always were a temperamental little bugger. That's not news to me.'

'Yeah, well, now I'm a big temperamental bugger.'

'No, son. You're just a man who's hurting.'

I don't answer. I can't. Even when I think things are getting better, sometimes even the most innocuous words whip the wind out of my sails.

'All I'm saying is he was fine.'

'He might've stood on the glass. That would've been a trip to the emergency room.'

'Probably. Stuff happens, love. Why, when you and your brothers were little, I thought we should've had our own entrance to the ER, we were there so often. Do you think that made me or your dad bad parents?'

'No, of course not. But things are different for me. The twins only have me, and I can't be there to watch them myself. And as you've said yourself, you've got your own life to lead, so I can't expect you to look after them, either.'

It's a low blow, but one Mum chooses to ignore. I know she needs to do her own thing—I want her to live a full life. But I also want to tie her to me and the kids, even if that makes me a self-interested arsehole.

'You'll find someone,' she asserts in that no-nonsense tone of hers. I choose to ignore that her words lend themselves to more than just childcare. 'As for his swearing, who knows where Matty picked up the word? You have so many youngsters coming through the property now that it's picking season.'

'The kids aren't hanging around itinerant workers, Ma.'

'Then there's the handymen, your market reps –'

'They're not all rough people.'

'Not rough? You should have seen what one of them did to my nighty last week!' Mum caws with laughter, ever the joker. I guess this is another of her hints to say she won't be here forever, that she's ready to move on and that I should be, too.

That I can't expect to mourn the death of my wife forever.

That I'm still young.

And she's right on both those points. As hard as it is to mourn her, I'm still not looking to get involved. I'll stick to my monthly escapes, thanks.

'Didn't you say you had something to do?' I thought that was the reason Martha was here today.

'I do have something to do. I also have places to go.'

'Where?'

'London, for starters.'

'London? To see Flynn?' My younger brother lives there.

'To see my newest grandbaby,' she replies with a nod. 'Then maybe I'll go on to Paris, then maybe Switzerland.'

'Switzerland?'

Mm-hmm, and India.'

'India? Come on, Mum.' What the fuck?

'I want to go anywhere and everywhere, Byron!' she says, the words bursting from her mouth. 'I want to travel, see the world. Your father and I were going to do all that before the old bugger went and died on us. He worked too hard, and he passed that down to you. But I've done my bit. I've been here while you've gotten back on your feet after . . . '

Her words trail off as though to spare me the pain of hearing them. But I can hear them and I can speak them, too. *Before Katya died*. It's somehow both easier and harder that no one knows the state of our marriage before Kat passed.

Katya was beautiful, full of energy and determination. She was going places, and I was going with her. We met in Sydney, and I'd fallen in love with her just as quickly as she'd fallen out of love with me. But that happened later. She knew I'd be taking over the family business one day, moving out of the bright lights of the city. The way I saw it, I had years before that. Dad was going nowhere—he was as strong as an ox. So long as I took care of the commercial side, he was happy on the land. Yeah, we had years . . . until Dad had a massive heart attack, and we didn't anymore.

'Well,' Mum continues, 'let's just say that I don't exactly see you on your feet yet. But you will be, and once the twins start kindergarten, things will be much easier. But you need to get help, Byron. And let that help stay. One nanny not working out can easily be explained. Two nannies, and well, maybe you've been unlucky. But five nannies, Byron, and the problem isn't them, and it isn't the job. It's the employer.' She reaches over, poking my knee.

Exasperated, though trying hard not to show it, I get up and move to the bureau, opening it up to the neat stacks of household bills and paperwork. *Paper clips and staples. Highlighters and pens.* I pull out a manila folder standing on its end, open it briefly before closing it again. Then I deposit it in my mother's lap.

'The running file of nanny applications.' Well, call it foresight that I'd downloaded everything from the agency's website. 'Why don't you have a go at it this time. I thought I was getting better at it, but maybe I'm not.' Mum looks up at me, unsure. Maybe she's wondering if *better* included the candy G-string episode. 'Go on, I trust you. You can't make a worse job of it than me.'

'Daddy, look.' Matty comes barrelling over, waving his masterpiece. 'That's me,' he says, pointing at a wobbly circle. A stripe of brown hovers about it, the shape itself covered in dots and scribbles. 'I'm at the window, looking at you drive to work.'

'That's great, bud. But what's this on your face?'

'That's my face, silly!' he admonishes. 'I'm crying.' I feel a pinch in my heart. I'm driving to work, and he's crying. 'Because I want to go to big boy school.'

Ah, well then. 'You will, son. Next year.'

'We'll get my nuniform?'

'We will. The stupid hat and everything.'

'Byron,' my mother chastises. 'What was it you were saying about him not repeating what you say?'

'Come on, Mum, he's four. What does he need a formal hat for? Tea with the Queen?'

'I don't wanna have tea with the Queen,' Matty asserts, screwing his little face up in concentration. 'Edie can do it. Can I jus go to her castle, instead?'

'I'll ask her next time I see her, yeah?' I ruffle his hair. 'What are the scribbles over here?'

'That's not scribbles, Daddy,' he chastises. 'That's Nana kissing Dave-o goodbye before you got home.' *Dave-o the foreman? And my mum? Nah . . .*

Mum pretends not to have heard, instead feigning complete interest in the applications on her lap. But the foreman? Well, maybe she is truly ready to move on. Or bribing Matty to help make her point.

She'd said herself that she'd never find another love like she'd found with Dad, but she's too young not to have joy in her life.

But would I begrudge her the kind of temporary joy I allow myself? The illicit coupling in darkened hotel rooms. I shut down the thought immediately, glancing at my red-faced Mum. I wouldn't begrudge her any kind of dalliance because that would make me a hypocrite.

If I bump into her at the Park Hotel in Sydney, I'll have no one to blame but myself.

'Great,' I mutter without enthusiasm, causing Matty to look up at my flat tone. 'Really. Great picture. Fridge-worthy!' I ruffle his hair again, bending to kiss him this time. 'Thanks for the picture, son.'

'You're welcome, Daddy.' I hold his warm little body for a moment longer, just long enough to think about poor motherless Matty crying at the window while, in this picture, his dad drives in the direction of the big city for the purpose of getting his rocks off ... and going through nannies quicker than most folks have hot dinners.

Mum's right. They need some stability in their lives. They *deserve* it.

'Go put your crayons away, bud. Time to clean up for supper.'

Matty makes his way back to his desk and picks up his crayon box upside down, all the colours of the rainbow scattering across the floor.

'Ah, shit,' he complains, with the intonation and finesse of, well, me.

I rub my temples and the beginnings of a headache away as my mother has the good sense to turn her chuckle into something resembling a clearing of the throat.

Chapter Seven

AMBER

The drive from Sydney to the Hunter Valley was just about how you'd expect it to be when travelling with a group of guys barely out of their teens. Raucous, testosterone-filled, and a little smelly, but it was only a couple of hours or so before we'd reached the winery. Huge brick pillars heralded the entrance to the place, black wrought iron gates open in welcome. The camper van trundles up a long and winding driveway, flanked by a sea of green vines which runs for almost as far as the eye can see. There's a house in the distance shaded by trees— two stories with what look like iron lattice worked balconies. It's very heritage kind of looking and quite imposing. Maybe a little Italianate?

This isn't just money, I catch myself thinking. *This is wealth and history, a gate between worlds.* But I only want a job in the kitchen or working a bar. I'm not moving in.

We pass a creek with a jetty and pavilion flanked by old wine barrels, set with tables and chairs, then what looks like a huge old stone barn, though I note it's signposted *The Cellar Door*. My heart beats a little faster as we follow the signs, pulling to a stop at what looks like the backend of this operation.

With laughter and aching moans, we climb out of the van, squinting into the bright sunlight as I begin to mentally rehearse my opening lines, trying to prepare for any questions that might come up. I catch a glimpse of my reflection in the window, kind of horrified to think I might be heading for an interview. I have my hair in pigtails, and I'm wearing a grey T-shirt knotted at the waist and a pair of old denim shorts. As I look around, it's clear than none of us are looking our best, including the two guys suffering severe hangovers.

I take a deep breath as we collectively head to the offices, reminding myself of how very impressive my French connections might sound. Plus, I have a teaching degree, which speaks of dedication if nothing else, and I also have a little culinary experience.

'I wonder if it'll help if I tell them I have lots of experience drinking wine.'

Beside me, Rose sniggers. 'That makes you more sophisticated than this lot.' With her thumb, she points at the rest of our motley crew.

'No, that just makes me older. Their day will come, though.'

A thought suddenly strikes me: French and Spanish backpackers probably know more about wine than me. Aren't they raised on the stuff? I swallow against this wave of irrational anxiety. I suppose it's all fun and games until you're down to your last few dollars. But things aren't that desperate. I still have a little left on my credit card, and I know I can borrow from family if I'm desperate. But I don't want to be desperate. I want to succeed. It's a little untethering not knowing exactly where the money for your next meal is coming from. It almost makes me regret spending so much on the night in the hotel. *Almost.*

Screw the European backpackers with their worldly, sophisticated palates, I decide, throwing back my shoulders. They might have been drinking wine longer, but I bet I've still downed more of the stuff. But I'll keep that to myself, I think.

'I can't see sophistication hitting me when at twenty-five,' Rose retorts. 'You can take the girl out of Kentucky, but you can't take Kentucky out of the girl. I think I'll stick to Pabst Blue and the occasional shot of bourbon.'

'Maybe you should keep that to yourself.' Because we all have our little secrets.

'Pshaw! I'm fine with picking grapes. I don't want no job in hospitality. Customer service blows.' Her gaze travels over me. 'But I guess looking as pink as a shrimp thrown on the barbie also blows.'

'Prawn.' It's an odd word, even odder spat from the side of the mouth of a gnarled-looking man. He's walking the same path as we are, only he's going in the opposite direction. 'We don't call 'em shrimps. They're prawns,' he calls over his shoulder. And not in the nicest tone.

'Excuse me?' I ask, sugar sweet, turning to face the way he's travelling.

'Bloody backpackers,' he grumbles without stopping. 'Don't know their arse from their elbow.'

'Thank you,' I call after him with a little wave. 'Thank you for that unique cultural observation, strange little man.' The last I add under my breath. 'And I thought Australia was supposed to be the friendliest place on earth.'

'Come on, Pollyanna,' Rose says, throwing an arm around my shoulder. 'Crotchety old men exist in every corner of this wonderful planet.'

We join the end of a line, the one with the kind of length that makes my heart sink. Yep, it's a long, long line.

'What's going on, do you think?'

'Looks like there are a few too many people for the jobs.'

'You mean we didn't get here first?' I ask with a twist of my expression as my heart sinks a little bit more. Looks like I'm about to start living on my emergency credit card.

'I guess that's what happens when you're travelling with guys with weak bladders.'

'Or guys who drank too much beer the night before. And to think I shared my goodies with those fools.'

A girl standing in front of us in the line snorts.

'Don't you know it's rude to listen to other people's conversations?' Rose demands, her hand on one cocked hip. The girl feigns not to have heard or to have snorted, for that matter.

'For the record, I meant I shared my pastries,' I mutter.

To underline the point that she has nothing to do with this scene, the girl begins babbling to her friend in French.

'That's what I thought,' grumbles my self-satisfied companion.

Honestly? I'm too old for this, and the midmorning sun is beginning to sear my skin.

'I'm going to have to go back to the van and get a shirt or something.'

'And a hat,' Rose replies, peering at my forehead.

'I'm burning, aren't I?' I bring a hand up immediately, almost as though I'd be able to feel the heat as you would with a hot kettle or skillet.

'Go wait under the tree,' she suggests, pointing at large eucalyptus nearby, its leaves swaying in the scant breeze. 'Oh, look, Amber,' she says quite suddenly, one hand clutching my arm as the other points to the rows of vines in the distance. 'They have miniature kangaroos!'

'Those aren't roos,' a small voice corrects from the vicinity of my knees. 'Those are wallabies.'

'Walla-what?' asks Rose as we both look down. A kid of about four years old stands before us, his solemn little face almost obscured by the bill of his ball cap.

'Wallabies. They're a different amimals, you know.'

'No, I didn't know,' I reply, hunkering down to speak with him face to face. Did I mention I love little kids? I sometimes even miss teaching the little boogers, though I definitely don't miss their boogers. 'Thank you for telling us that. Where we come from, we don't have wallabies or kangaroos.'

'I know,' he adds with a serious nod of his head. 'We only got them here in 'Straya.'

'Is that so?'

'Matty! What in the blazes are you doin' over there!' A middle-aged woman comes bustling down the path, her blond hair falling to her shoulders in pale waves, a little girl of about the same size balanced on her hip. 'I take my eyes of you for one minute and poof! You're like Houdini, I swear,' she continues gesticulating wildly with one hand, though not in anger or fear. I get the impression for a woman short in stature, hers is a personality that's on the large side.

I stand, taking a moment to dust the seat of my shorts, then shield my eyes as the woman draws near. Despite her large sunglasses, I'm guessing she's not the momma. Their auntie, maybe?

'I was jus talking to the lady, Nana.'

Oh, a young grandma. One who takes care of herself.

'He was just setting us right on the nature of wallabies,' I say with a smile. 'Can you think of anywhere else wallabies might live?' I ask, looking down at the little guy once more. It's hard not to slip into teacher mode sometimes.

'I know!' I look up at the slightly jumbled words, realising the little girl has spoken. She pulls her thumb from her mouth with a pop before replying, 'Ina zoo!' She shoves a pink wrinkled thumb back into her rosebud mouth again. Twins, they have to be. And just the cutest yet almost reflections of the other. The little boy has a mop of dark curly hair, and the little girl wisps of silver blond. Where they don't differ are in their big blue eyes and rosy cheeks.

'Come on, you two,' their nana says. 'You've been to another place with wallabies.'

'Was it . . . another country?' I ask, my words heavy with hinting as the little boy's face screws in thought.

'Amber,' Rose laughingly chastises. 'Don't give the kid a pop quiz during summer vacay. Save those for back in the classroom.'

'Professional habit,' I say with an embarrassed shrug.

'You're a teacher, are you, love?' The woman's smile is a little wider now. 'What grade do you teach, if you don't mind me asking?'

'Third grade mostly, but I have taught younger grades, too.'

'You on a career break?'

'Yes, Ma'am. I decided I wanted to see some of the world this year.'

'A girl after my own heart,' she announces. 'Where've you been so far, darl?'

By the way, I love being called darl, though maybe not so much when a creepy guy on a barstool says so. But in other situations? Definitely.

'Scuse me darl. How's your day, darl?

I love it! And as Aussies abbreviate everything, I assume darl is short for darling. Who doesn't want to be everyone's darling!

'So far I've been to Paris, Greece, and Spain. I saw a little of London but not much of the rest of the UK. Then India and Thailand. And now I'm here.'

'Lovely! What do you think of Australia, then?'

'It's such a beautiful country, and I might've fallen in love a little with Sydney, which is pretty much all I've seen so far.'

'My oldest boy used to live there,' she says, her smile slipping just a touch. 'But here I am gabbing on when you've got things to do, no doubt. You'll be here for the picking season, I suppose?' The little girl begins to wriggle, so she sets her down, both children running off to inspect a patch of nearby grass.

'We are but . . .' My expression twists as I turn back to Rose momentarily. 'I was hoping to get a job in the kitchens or something.'

'She's a bit of a whizz with pastry,' Rose says, cutting in. 'Paris trained. She even speaks French.'

'Hardly,' I put in before her nose grows Pinocchio style as she tells some even taller tales.

'What a shame. We don't have any sort of commercial kitchen. The only food we serve here is, funnily enough, fruit and cheese. Just at the cellar door,' she says, waving her hand in the vague direction of the large barn we'd passed on the way in. 'You know, for tastings.'

'Oh, that is a shame.' For both me and this place. This spot has to be the ideal setup for a little tourist attraction action. It's just so pretty. I can almost see people dining by the creek or surrounded by the peace of the silent vines. And the view is breathtaking. I'll just bet sunset out here is simply amazing.

But did she say we *don't have any kind of kitchen? Could she be one of the owners, maybe?*

'It's not exactly kitchen work, but I think I might have a bit of a proposition for you.'

'Oh.' Really? 'Well, I'm all ears,' I reply with the weirdest sort of jazz-hand wave. 'I'm not afraid of a little hard work, but I'm kinda coming to the conclusion this inherited Scottish skin of mine just wasn't meant for the outdoors.'

'Well, come on up to the house. We'll have spot of morning tea and a chat.'

This seems to catch the children's attention, two heads whipping around. 'Can I have—' one of them begins.

'Milk,' she replies mock-sternly. 'I don't know why your dad thinks it's okay to give you coffee.'

' 'Cause he doesn't like to find my biscuits floating in his cup,' the little boy answers reasonably.

In the periphery of my gaze, Rose looks like she's going to puke. *Okay, not really, but she does look a little confused.* 'He means cookies, not biscuits,' I explain.

'No, I doesn't,' he protests. 'I mean biscuits.'

'I like jam drops and TimTams,' Edie, the little girl, begins to chant.

'But not biscuits like *biscuits*,' I continue to explain. 'At least, not like back home.'

'Are you coming, darl?' the older woman asks, taking both children's hands.

'Oh, but my friend . . . It looks like the picking positions are all full.'

'Leave it to me,' she says with a wink. 'Come on and have a chat. We'll sort something.'

At Rose's insistence, along with her reassurance that she'll find the guys, I follow the family up the hill to the house, allowing myself to relax enough to take in the view. The undulating lines of vines, the odd head of a curious wallaby peeking through, and the blue-green mountain range rolling in the distance. The house itself is encased by a beautiful white porch and wrought iron lattice work as I'd thought. We avoid the double-doored entryway, slipping in through a side door and into a small entrance as the woman turns and offers me her hand.

'Sally Philips,' she says. 'And this is Matty and Edie, my grandchildren.'

'Amber Greeves.'

Sally's hand is small and warm.

'Edie and me are twins,' Matty announces, hopping around our feet. 'And Nana also has more grandchildren wif Uncle Flynn!'

'That's right, I do,' she agrees. 'Flynn, my son, lives in London.'

'Well, I'm pleased to meet you both, too,' I continue, holding out my hand to each of the kids. Matty's hand is a little sticky, and Edie keeps her thumb in her mouth, reluctant to offer me her other hand.

'My real name is Maffew,' the little boy adds as he retracts his grubby hand, 'but you can call me Matty, like my nana and Daddy does.'

'Your nana hardly looks old enough to be a nana,' I say. Instantly, I wonder how insincere my thinking aloud sounds. *Buttering up the lady of the house, eh?* Unless, of course, there's another lady of the house. Like the children's mom, though given Matty's phrasing, I'm almost certain she doesn't live here.

'That's kind of you to say, love. My Tony and me started our family young. Mainly because we couldn't keep our hands off each other, if you know what I mean.' She accompanies the statement with a ribald laugh and the light squeeze of my elbow as she leads me out of the room and into a large hallway, when I feel a little tug at my hand.

'Dana,' the little girl says around a thumb.

'Take your thumb out of your mouth, darl, and introduce yourself properly.'

The little girl does as she's told, rubbing her mouth on the back of her hand before speaking. 'My name is Edana.'

'That's a very pretty name, angel.'

'I'm not an angel,' she replies shyly. 'I'm a mermaid.'

'Let's swim our fishy butts into the kitchen then, and I'll put on a nice pot of tea. It's a bit early for wine, wouldn't you say?' she adds, throwing me an enquiring look over her shoulder.

'Absolutely,' I answer as sincerely as I can manage because it *is* midmorning, after all, and that's practically lunchtime.

'Liar,' she replies with a knowing look. 'It's always wine o'clock somewhere. Especially in a winery.'

I follow her through the grand entryway, past a very grand carved staircase and into a light-filled breakfast room. Beyond is the kitchen, the likes of which I've only seen in magazines. It's so stylish yet homey and huge! The sun streams in from the window as my gaze travels the room, delighting in the features—the heritage-style door handles, the pale marble countertops, the butler's pantry and Belfast sink, plus an oven I could easily cook multiple cakes in all at once! The floors are wooden as are the beams overhead, from which two huge glass chandeliers hang.

'Sit yourself down,' Sally instructs, gesturing to the row of plush stools on one side of the central island block before she bustles off to fill the kettle.

'You have such a beautiful kitchen,' I say as the children climb up on stools next to me. I hold out my hands to catch Matty as he wobbles, but he's very independent, judging by his frown.

'Thank you, but I don't live in the house. I have my own little place out in the back, though I do seem to spend quite a bit of time in here recently.' Her expression clouds, clearing again so quickly I'm not sure I imagined it. 'And I try to keep little mouths fed around here when I can. Though some people are getting harder and harder to keep fed, aren't they?' she adds with an arch of her brow as Matty's little hand retracts from the fruit bowl, a fat ripe peach curled in his fingers.

'I'm a growing boy,' he mumbles around a mouthful. 'My dad says so.'

'Fruit is very good for you,' I say, sliding him a napkin from the holder nearby, though he doesn't appear to mind the juice dripping down his chin.

'So is pizza,' he calls, sticking his hands and dripping peach in the air.

'I think I can guess pizza is your favourite food.'

'Yep.' He nods solemnly. 'Edie's, too. What's yours?'

'Well, I have a bit of a sweet tooth, and I do love cookies. I bake a pretty good cookie, too. Biscuits,' I correct, just for translation sakes, not that it appears needed.

'Nana bakes chocolate chip cookies from a tube,' Edie says softly, 'but she burns them most of the time.'

'Letting out all my secrets,' she grumbles good-naturedly as she brings over a grey-coloured teapot and two blue cups filled with milk, plus a small chocolate cake. Shop bought, but I'm in no place to judge. 'So,' she says, taking a stool adjacent to me. 'Let's talk about you, and if you'd like to take a job helping me and these two.'

'Oh, goodness. That would be . . .'

Better than outdoor work but not quite catering. I cast my eyes around the beautiful kitchen as Sally begins to serve the children, my mind filled with a million things.

'Drink up, love.'

So I do as we talk, or at least, I do. I tell her about my job back home, and why I'd left, though I sort of paint over the bits that might make me sound flaky or irresponsible. But it quickly becomes clear that she's only looking for someone to look after the kids until they start kindergarten next year. Maybe eight weeks tops, which is pretty much perfect. And the figures she's throwing out in terms of salary would certainly refill my travel funds. The more she speaks, the more eager I am to have this job.

'I don't have my resume on me. It's in my backpack back in the van.'

'There's plenty time to get to that.'

'Oh, but I do have some photos on my phone. I'm sure my host family in Paris wouldn't mind me showing you them.'

Sally seems delighted as I flick through the images of my classroom back home, photographs of the little kids and their cuddles on my last day. I show her a few from Paris—my host family and their kids, all happy faces. And I show her the school I helped build in Thailand. Yeah, I did that, and it makes me feel so proud, even if I mostly spent my time there putting together classroom resources.

'You know, I think this could work,' Sally says, her cup chinking against the dainty saucer. 'Subject to your references and things.'

'Oh, sure. Absolutely. Just email the Montrose family. They said they'd be more than happy to give me a reference. Same with the school, though it might take a little longer. Bureaucracy.' I shrug. 'But I have copies of my qualifications and teaching certificates, plus I also have a copy of my State background check. No criminal record for me,' I add, maybe a little too effusively for it to sound true, even if it is.

'I'm sure it's all in order, love,' Sally answers, amused. 'We'll get to it soon enough, but for now, I think I'd like to offer you the job.'

'Really? That's so wonderful. What about Rose?' I ask because, sure, I'm excited for myself, but I'm not the type of person who thinks only of herself.

'I'll make sure Rose has a job here, too. And if we can't get work for the rest of your crew, the Allanson's place is just a few clicks, a few kilometres, away. I know they're looking for help.'

'Th-that's awesome, Sally. I really appreciate it.'

'We haven't confirmed exactly what the wage is yet.' She'd said earlier she'd have to okay it with her son.

'Honestly, right now, anything would do.' Because this kitchen, these sweet kids, this lovely lady, plus not picking grapes in the sun. What's not to love!

'Don't sell yourself short,' she says, laughing. 'Like I said, I can't make promises on his behalf, but I do know he's a shrewd business man, my boy. It's a good job he didn't hear you, or he might hold you to exactly that.'

'Might hold her to what?'

At the gruff interjection, I turn so fast on my stool, I almost fall off the damn thing. I've been drugged— there must've been something in the tea. Some kind of hallucinogenic? Or maybe I have sun stroke because no way. No way what I'm seeing is real.

Those broad shoulders, the same ones he'd balanced my ankles on.

That thick, dirty blond hair that I'd held tight in my hands.

That dark expression.

'Daddy!' yells Matt, not that I can be trusted to hear correctly through this fog of abject shock.

'Byron. This is Amber.'

Oh, God. There's nothing wrong with my hearing, which means there's nothing wrong with my eyes.

I'm so plucked.

Chapter Eight

BYRON

Of course, she is. Everything about her is fucking Amber. A warning. A red-coloured flag. Watch out, Amber ahead. Situation hazardous.

She's Amber from those ridiculous red pigtails to the smattering of freckles now decorating her nose. *Too much sun.* Or not enough, maybe, judging by the rest of her milky skin.

Get a hold of yourself. It's not like you've never seen a girl in shorts before.

Except I haven't seen this girl in shorts. I have seen her in a slinky backless dress. And I've seen her in her underwear. *What little she wore of it.* And I've seen her wearing heels. *And nothing else.*

I've seen her naked.

I've tasted her warm, musky wetness.

Licked her honey-like skin.

Yeah, she's Amber all right.

From outside in.

And now I've got a hard-on *and* I'm fucking pissed.

'What's going on, Mum?' I drop the large and well-used backpack at my feet, its presence adding to my annoyance. The thud as it meets the floor causes her to physically start—Amber, that is. Mum just rolls her eyes.

'Amber, here, is going to help us with the kids over these next few months.'

'No.' No. And fuck no. I ruffle Matty's hair and give Edie a quick peck on the head all without looking at the girl. Or touching her. Or inhaling her floral perfume. I move around to the other side of the island so I'm not looking at her in those shorts. Looking at those legs. Remembering the red outline of my fingerprints on them. Recalling their silky softness as they'd wrapped around my head.

'No what?' Mum asks, though by her unimpressed tone, I know she gets exactly *no what*. I grab a glass from the cupboard and fill it with water from the dispenser on the fridge, keeping my back to her.

'No, a-a *backpacker* isn't going to look after Matt and Edie.' I've nothing against backpackers, but they're just kids. Cheap labour. Itinerant workers who I've found to be mostly reliable, so why is my tone derisive? Because it's my kids we're talking about here, not my business. Speaking of which; 'Kids, go put your togs on, and I'll take you for a quick swim.'

'Now?' Matty asks, his surprise evident to the whole room. It feels like a deadbeat dad moment, but fuck it, I'm doing my best here.

'In the middle of the workday?' adds Mum.

'Yeah, a quick swim.' See, I'm not behaving like an arsehole because I don't want a backpacker looking after my kids but because I don't want a nameless woman I've fucked looking after my kids.

So I'm doing my best to escape the situation. Sure, I've a million things to do today—time, seasons, and viniculture wait for no man—but I'm also mindful of not involving my children in this, especially when they already seem to have had time to build a rapport with this girl. *Woman*, I remind myself. She was all woman that night, even if she does look like it was only a few short years ago she was watching cartoons.

Like that thought was fucking helpful . . .

Matty whoops at the unexpected treat, scrambling down from his stool as I turn my gaze to the kitchen window and the pool beyond. I can feel her eyes on me, the prickling sensation making the hair on my arms stand on end. And yeah, the touch of her gaze has me reacting in parts elsewhere. So I'll keep my eyes glued to the pool and my back to her, and though the water is so still it's a perfect mirror to the sky, it still doesn't stop me from wondering what the universe is playing at by sending her here.

'Sir, for your information, I'm a teacher as well as a backpacker.' Her response rings clear and a touch haughty, and fuck if that doesn't work for me. *I'd like her to* call me Sir . . .

Concentrate, man. She'd be a ticking timebomb working here. It'd just be a matter of time before she'd blow you—I mean blow. Like a bomb, not like a blow job.

'I just happen to have taken a little time off from my profession to see more of the world,' she adds, making it quite clear that she doesn't appreciate my reaction or my words.

But why the fuck would she want this job? She'd almost fallen off her stool when she'd copped a look at me as I'd entered the kitchen. I'm surprised she didn't bolt then. Why the fuck would she want to work in the house of the man who'd bent her in shapes her body had probably never been? The man she'd covered in bites—hickeys—that had somehow left me both impressed and annoyed for days. There is one sliver of a silver lining, though. As a teacher, she can't be as indecently young as I'd begun to fear. *Despite the pigtails.*

'Amber is the perfect solution,' Mum begins. 'She's agreed to stay here until kindy starts, which will give us time to make more permanent arrangements.'

'I said no,' I growl . . . even though I promised myself I'd growl less this week.

'And I said pull your head out of your *a-r-s-e.*' As I whip around, water spills from the glass to the floor. 'That doesn't count.' She quirks a brow. 'The twins can't spell yet. Byron Phillips,' she adds in that tone, the mum tone, adding the weight of one pointed finger gunning for me. 'Don't you pull that face. It doesn't work. And it didn't work when your father pulled it, funnily enough, either.'

'Mum . . . ' I can't look at *her*—I won't—choosing instead to face my mother's resolute expression.

'You said I could choose, and I have. What happened to "I trust you? You can't make a worse job of it than me?" Well, I've chosen. And guess what? It's Amber here.' This is my cue to answer, and when I don't, she adds, 'You won't get better than this girl here.'

She's not wrong, but not for the reasons she thinks. My interest lies in the qualifications my mother hasn't mentioned. It's in the way she worked my cock, of how she'd looked up at me, her mouth full of me, her gaze dark and guileless. It's in her muffled moans and how those sounds had tightened my balls. My interest lies in her sweet sighs and her even sweeter pussy, and the snapshots of the evening I've viewed on autorepeat since I'd forced myself to leave her wrapped in a tangle of hotel linens.

I can't have her here. Not here in my own home.

The temptation would be too great because *Amber* is fucking right. This is dangerous territory.

My gaze drifts to her then, and I wish it hadn't. Why does it have to be her? Why now?

'We don't have anywhere for her to stay,' I continue in the same surly vein with the same arrogantly uninterested façade.

'Yes, we do,' Mum counters. 'She can stay in one of the cottages out back.'

'In one of the half-fitted cottages, you mean? I wouldn't let the dog stay out there.'

'Or she could stay here. It's not like there isn't room. It's not like you haven't already—' I cut her off with a severe look. Yes, a couple of the previous nannies had stayed in one of the guest rooms, but that was before "Candy" and her edible tiny G-string. She was a nutjob. She had to have been. And I'm going to ignore the fact that Mum looks about to burst out laughing. Next, she'll be making some crack about locking my bedroom door if I'm worried for my virtue.

I breathe out, slow and even, fighting the feeling that I'm losing this fight. But no, whatever kind of fuckery brought Amber here, isn't going to keep her here. I'll make sure of that.

'Right.' I put down my glass. 'Okay. I'll interview you.'

'You will?' Amber asks, visibly stunned.

I nod just once, a terse movement of my head, my teeth clamped so tight I'm liable to crack a fucking molar.

'That wasn't the deal,' Mum interjects. 'You said—'

'I know what I said, Mum, but I meant from the file I gave you.' I turn my attention to the woman in question, though my words are more for my mother's benefit than hers. 'You'll appreciate this is a little unorthodox.'

'Of course.' She wears a slash of colour high across her cheekbones. It reminds me of— 'An interview is fine.'

Business. Remember, this is business. I nod stiffly and turn to Mum.

'When the kids come downstairs, tell them I won't be long.' Well, only as long as it'll take me to piss her off badly enough to make her run out of here. *This is business. Only business.*

I stride from the room, leaving her scurrying after me as I make my way to the formal dining room. We never use this place because who dines formally these days? Plantation shutters keep out the sun, protecting the heirloom furniture in here. Dust motes dance in the sun dappled through the slats, the air still and a little stale. In my great grandparents' day, this room would be opened on both sides for parties, allowing the space to be used as a ballroom of sorts. But not only do we not dine formally these days, but we also don't party.

Discounting the kind of partying done in distant hotel rooms, obviously.

I hold the door open, allowing Amber to pass through, then close it solidly behind her once again. Mum isn't beyond being a bit of a stickybeak, but I doubt she could listen through the solidness of this door. Which is just as well as I could do without her overhearing what I've got to say.

'Take a seat.' I do the same, seating myself at the head of the table, watching her hesitate where to sit before eventually taking the chair to the left of me.

'Amber Hardy,' she says, holding out her hand as she sits. I look down at her pale and slender fingers, devoid of any kind of polish, not fighting the amused curl tugging at my lips.

'So we're gonna play it like that.' My tone drips with derision, causing her to frown as I take her pale hand lightly in my darker, larger one. The touch is like a memory, one I swallow down.

'No, sir. I just thought that we hadn't been properly introduced,' she says, bringing her hand back to the table in front, clasping both as though in prayer.

'If you say so.' I lean back in my chair. *Fucking sir.* 'Though I wouldn't myself. The way I see it, we've had a *thorough* introduction.' My gaze very deliberately roams across her T-shirt. Okay, her tits. Either way, she doesn't bite.

'This is a beautiful house,' she remarks instead, her eyes drifting through the room, seeking to look anywhere but at me.

'Yes, it is.' Yes, it's dark but sumptuous, I suppose. But I'm not a man prone to flattery. The sooner she realises, the better. 'We're not here to talk about my home, but rather what you think you're doing inside of it.'

'What do you mean?' Immediately, she sits straighter. 'Wait,' she adds, her expression morphing through a range of emotions. Confused, bemused, then thoroughly amused. 'You don't think I've tracked you down here, do you?'

I don't see how she could have, but there's always the chance, especially when I consider the G-string incident.

'Oh, honey,' she adds, treacle thick. 'You were good but not good enough to chase.'

'Did a bit of acting during your teaching degree, did you?' I respond evenly. 'A bit of drama?'

'I . . . no?'

'Not that I thought you were acting that night. That kind of pleasure can't be faked. You're a pretty good little actress right now, though.'

'And you're a colossal douche.'

Amusement to anger, and now we're getting somewhere.

'No, darl. I'm just a bloke who doesn't want some chick he picked up in a hotel being around his kids.'

'You picked *me* up?' She scoffs a little. 'The way I remember, you've got it the wrong way around.'

'Yeah?'

'Yeah.' She slides a lock of hair behind her ears then fold her arms.

'Regardless who picked up who, we still fucked.' The colour is still high in her cheeks as her fiery gaze finds mine.

'Don't worry,' she begins, her words biting and clean. 'A good teacher can separate the children from their parental shortcomings.'

'Shortcomings?' I bark out a laugh. My dick is neither short nor short in coming. We fucked multiple times—both came multiple times. But . . . that's not where this conversation should be going. 'Well, that's good to hear, but as you won't be looking after my children, it's of no consequence.'

Her chair scrapes against the parquet floor as she stands. 'Then what the hell are we doing in here?'

'Letting you down gently without the assistance of an audience.'

'Gently?' she spits. 'Thanks, you're a real *gentleman*.'

'I feel like we've had this conversation before, darl.'

'Shove it up your ass.' And with one last death glare in my direction, she storms out of the room.

'It was lovely to meet you, Sally.'

As I enter the kitchen, Amber's back is to me, and my mum is pulling her in for a hug.

'What on earth has he said to you?' Mum's gaze shoots me a questioning glare over Amber's shoulder. A glare with an edge of *I'm so gonna bend your ear about this.*

And she can. So long as the woman she's hugging is no longer here.

'Have you got a tummy ache?' Matty asks, tugging on her hand. Both kids have got their swimming togs on, Edie trailing her aqua mermaid one behind her like that kids from Snoopy. A more sanitary version, maybe. 'My daddy always gives my tummy a rub when I'm feeling sad. Maybe he should give you a magic rub, too.'

Ah, out of the mouths of babes.

'I'm not sad,' she says, dropping to her haunches to speak with him. 'Well, maybe just a little bit.'

'Then maybe you should make some choccie chip cookies. I reckon that'll make you happy.' He nods eagerly. 'It'd make me happy, anyways.'

'Sorry, honey. I'll have to take a rain check. I'd better be getting back out to my friends before they leave.'

'*Ah, fuck.*' Today, the universe can just fuck right off. I'm sick of it riding my arse.

'Daddy said fuck,' Edie announces, her tone one of awe as four pairs of eyes turn my way.

'Were you with the lot in the graffitied camper?' Amber nods stiffly at my growled question. 'They've gone. I saw them dump your shi—your backpack at the front door and drive away. That's why I brought it in.'

'No. No,' she repeats, her eyes turning to my mum. 'Rose wouldn't do that. Besides, you said there'd be work for her,' she adds almost beseechingly.

'I hadn't spoken to the foreman yet, darl. I wanted to be sure this job was the job for you first.'

'So your mates have shot through—they've left you?' Her gaze drops to the floor as though she can't quite comprehend. 'Did they call at all?' She blinks heavily, her hand sliding into her pocket and slowly pulling out her phone. She looks so forlorn as she shakes her head. 'What a bunch of . . .'

'Meanies,' she suggests, her gaze darting to the kids. I was thinking *bastards* was probably a more suitable word because I suddenly feel pissed off on her behalf.

'What kind of mates ditch you in the middle of nowhere?'

'Not very good ones, apparently,' she answers, giving into a small smile. 'And after I shared my birthday macarons with them too.'

Chapter Nine

AMBER

'So you met Matty and Edie. They've just turned four, and I suppose they'll be your primary concerns.'

Byron's tone is resigned, which is a whole lot better than how he sounded in the dining room, which was just plain assholery. He didn't behave like a douche but a mega douche. And though he looks like Michelangelo's *David* come to life, for all I know, mega douche might be his default mode. And speaking of flesh, it's kind of hard to concentrate on what he's saying given the amount of it available to my gaze. Tanned and wet, his colourful art glistens in the sun. He rubs a towel through his hair as I try to keep focussed on the blue fluffiness of his towel rather than the rest of him. Those strong arms and golden shoulders. The ripple of tan abs, sans ink, and the trail of hair dipping under the waist of his board shorts, to where I know his resemblance with David ends.

No Ancient Greek under-endowment here.

'Daddy! Watch me divebomb!' calls Matty from the side of the pool.

'I'm watchin', bud.'

From the stylish wicker patio chair adjacent to mine, Byron pulls the thick towel from his head, his eyes glued to his son at the far side of the pool. I try and fail to suppress a heavy sigh. My memory of him hasn't done him justice at all. I remembered him as handsome but not like this. Maybe it's the sunlight or maybe it's how he delights in his son. Maybe it's those darked spiked lashes and the bead of water rolling down his defined cheekbone.

No amount of contouring could deliver that effect.

Stop. Staring.

I turn my gaze to study the rest of the pool area instead. At the far end of a lap pool is a pool house open to three sides with just as many zones. One houses a built-in outdoor kitchen, all gleaming stainless-steel, a built-in bar, and an outdoor dining setting—you know, just in case the one we're sitting on at *this* side of the pool isn't enough. The central zone is home to a matching L-shaped sectional and an outdoor hearth. Zone three houses a pool table and what looks like a dartboard. The whole area is an entertainer's dream and makes me wonder if he's the kind of man who has parties. Friends, even. I can imagine carefree, sexy *Hotel Byron* having friends but uptight, autocratic *Byron the Dad*, not so much.

Matty cannonballs into the blue water as Edie squeals in delight before climbing out of the pool for her turn in their father's blue-orbed limelight.

'Watch *me*, Daddy!' his daughter calls.

'I see you, love. Good job!' His smile for his child is . . . wow . . . just dazzling. I shake my head a little as though shaking off its spell. Is this the real Byron? Where's Mr Surly-Growly? Or Mr Birthday Sex? I shut the last thought down *tout de suite*.

'Listen, Mr Phillips.' God, that not only sounds weird but feels weird, too. Why do I feel like I'm in some alternate babysitter porn universe?

'Just call me Daddy.'

'W-what?' I don't know which is worse—the way I know my cheeks are burning suddenly red or the secret flutter between my legs. Stupid body.

'I said, just call me Byron.' He sort of glowers in my direction. Clearly, I'm not the only one feeling weird. But it's this job or a bus ticket back to Sydney booked on my credit card.

Breathe in, breathe out. I can do this.

'Byron.' My voice drops a touch as I say his name. This also feels weird, saying it for the first time. Saying it *to* him. It's like the world has shifted somehow. Fantasies aren't supposed to become reality, are they?

From my periphery, I see he's still watching the kids. I wonder what the deal with their mother is? Not that I'm asking him. Nope. Not today.

'I just wanted to say thank you for the opportunity.' He turns his head slowly, those perceptive eyes now on mine, one brow raised rather sardonically. 'For the opportunity to work, I mean.'

'Don't read too much into it.'

'What's that supposed to mean?' He can't mean I think I want to screw him again because—

'It means you've got me over a barrel. This isn't a good idea.'

'You think I can't separate what happened in Sydney?'

'Well, can you?'

'You've a mighty high opinion of yourself, mister.' And I'm back to being Nelly Olsen again. 'If you can't stand the idea of me being here, then why did you tell me to stay?'

'What else was I supposed to do? Tell you to walk back to Sydney? I'm a bastard but—'

'Well, you got that right,' I grate out, folding my arms across my chest.

'I'm a bastard, but I'm not unreasonable.'

'I'd say that's a matter of opinion.'

'Miss Amber! Watch me dive!'

'I'm watching, Matty!' See, I can separate my feelings for you from your son.

'Mum says you're thirty?'

His expression suggests my age is something he also can't believe, so I slide him a scathing look.

'I did just turn thirty. I can show you my passport, if you want. Though I seem to recall you were there at my party.'

A party for two. The best birthday of my twenties, including that one time an ex booked a weekend in Vegas. Sadly, the reminder doesn't seem to elicit the same kind of memories, judging by his expression.

'And you cook.' Talk about changing the subject. 'That's like, your hobby, right?'

'I love to cook,' I answer begrudgingly. 'I was an au pair in Paris for a few months, and while I loved living with the family and Paris was just wonderful, the food really opened my heart and my mind to other things.'

'So more than a hobby? You don't think you'll go back to teaching?'

'Who knows?' I smile, not because I feel he deserves it, but because I'm tired of fake positivity. 'I'm kind of taking one step at time, looking down both paths, but those paths are in the future. For now, I'm happy to see more of the world.'

'When do you think you'll go back to the States?'

'I'm in no hurry.'

'Nothing to go back for?'

'I have family, if that's what you're asking.'

'And in the meantime?'

'In the meantime, I'll be the best damned nanny your children have ever seen.'

'Won't be hard,' he answers gruffly. 'We've had some disasters.'

'Yeah, and I'm sure you're just peachy to work for.'

At this, he smiles a real smile with dazzling white teeth and everything. My girly bits flutter a little, but I'm not panicking. It's just muscle memory, I think. Nothing to worry about.

'Tell me about your long-term goals.' He leans back, folding his arms across his flat stomach. *Cue the onset of more muscle memory twinges.*

'Why? I'm not going to be here more than a few weeks.'

'You don't have to tell me. I just thought we could get acquainted a bit better.'

'Better acquainted than seeing me in my underwear?' My tone is severe, and no more than he deserves.

'Our acquaintance goes beyond seeing each other in the semi-buff, though doesn't it?'

My cheeks begin to burn with remembrance rather than embarrassment. This is going to be a long few weeks if he keeps reminding me in that bedroom voice of his how good that night was. *Of how good we were together.* It's bad enough that he's sitting there in all his wet glory, heightening my senses and taunting me with more than just his words.

'Okay, that was a cheap shot,' he adds when I don't answer. But I don't answer because I'm lost in my own memories, not because he's annoyed me. But annoyed I can go with and quirk one brow as a little reinforcement of the look, because annoyed is preferable to him being able to read my actual thoughts.

Hell, this *is* going to be a long few weeks.

'I wasn't trying to get you to leave.'

'Really? You mean *this time* you weren't trying to make me leave.'

'Not this time,' he agrees evenly. I suppose this is as close to an apology as I'll get.

'Just so you know, my being here is a complete fluke of fate. Also, I wouldn't be here if my so-called friends hadn't decided to leave.'

'The friends you shared your birthday cake with?' His mouth curls, but it's more taunt than smile.

'It looks like that's a second strike against my ability to judge folks.'

'I suppose I'd be your first?'

I shrug, a sort of *if-the-shoe-fits* kind of motion.

'You think I'm an arsehole.'

His is a statement, not a question. I shrug again, and he smiles, like we're playing a game.

'A bit of a bastard?'

Once, twice, *thrice* I shrug.

'Then I'd say your judgment is spot-on.'

Way to take the fun out of the game.

'What happened in Sydney?' he says, completely serious now. 'It stays there.'

'Hey,' I reply airily, 'you're the one who keeps bringing it up.'

Byron's nostrils flare, the muscles of his jaw drawing tight. 'Maybe I'm the one who needs reminding,' I think he mutters, his gaze returning to Matty who appears to be wrestling a large inflatable pink flamingo in the middle of the pool. 'We're stuck with each other, and while that night was . . .'

'That night was in the past.'

'Yeah,' he adds softly, his gaze sliding momentarily to mine, his expression almost thankful. 'So movin' forward, why don't you tell me a little about you.'

'I want to cook.' My decisive words are in the air before I've even realised.

'What, you mean like a chef?'

'Baked goods. I want to eventually open my own bakery. After all the travelling I've done, and the years I've worked in the education system, I've just found the most happiness in a kitchen.' As I say the words, I realise they're true. I've always loved to bake. Rare was the day I showed up at a friend's house without a tray of cookies or a dessert of some sort.

'A bakery? Like with bread and pies?'

'Maybe more like a patisserie, I think. I learned to bake at my grandmother's side, standing on a step stool, helping her measure out the ingredients. Gosh.' I bring my hands to my face. 'I can't believe I just remembered that. Anyway.' My hands fall away as I add a self-conscious shrug. 'I've since spent some time studying the intricacies of patisseries in Paris, and well, that was it. I suppose you could say I fell in love.'

He looks surprised . . . but not even a little bit impressed.

'You'd need a fair chunk of start-up capital.'

I speak of love, and he speaks of money.

'I'm aware.'

'So why go squandering cash on travelling when you could be saving and putting away money to achieve your goal?'

'I didn't know I had a goal until I left teaching, so that would've been a little difficult, don't you think?' My tone this time is a little *a-screw-a-you!*

'Those kinds of businesses are notorious for having margins that stink.'

'I'm sure you are well-versed in the business life, but wealth doesn't interest me as much as happiness does. I follow the joy, not dollars.'

'Yeah, right.' *Roi-t. Gah, that accent!* He stretches out those long legs, his whole presence seeming to take up so much space.

'It's true,' I protest.

'Yet you find yourself seated on the largest property in the region, asking for work.'

Why, the egotistical . . .

'I wonder how hard it is to have claimed that big title of yours in this small part of the world?' I smile sweetly, not caring if there's sufficient sugar in my tone to take the bite out of my words.

'Australia small? And Riposo Estates produce can be found in stores all over the world.'

Right about now, I wished I had a foot-long dick so I could slap in on the table next to him. That's what this is, isn't it? A game of who's got the bigger dick?

'Congratulations,' I reply sweetly. 'Can't say I've ever tasted your stuff—your wine,' I qualify, lest he think I'm talking about tasting other things: 'I mean, I haven't seen it around.' Probably because I mostly buy my wine by the box. That and Walmart probably isn't his market.

'What I'm trying to say is, I work hard and I don't screw around.'

Except on nights away. Nights with random girls in Sydney hotels. But I don't correct him because it looks like Byron and I are just gonna have to agree to disagree on a lot of stuff.

A little while later, I'm returning from a trip to the powder room when I overhear Byron and his mom talking in the kitchen. People who listen at keyholes might not hear what they want, but it doesn't stop this girl from slowing down to catch what's being spoken about.

'Well?' Sally prods.

'Yeah, she good, but . . . '

'But what?'

'I dunno. I just don't think she's right for us.'

'Have you been out in the sun too long? The girl is perfect! She's sweet and personable and, don't forget, a qualified teacher.'

'She is . . . sweet, I'll grant you. Nice.' Be still my pitter-pattering heart, not. I've been anything but sweet or nice to him, and I intend to keep it that way. One, I need the money, and two, children are involved. We're keeping it purely professional, mister.

'She's as cheery as one of those kids' presenters on ABC,' his mom begins. 'She has a teaching degree, she's looking for work, and she can cook. What more do you want, Byron? A rack like a porn star?'

I hold my hand over my mouth as I giggle quietly, then pull the neck of my T-shirt to check on my solid

Cs. *Yep, still there, and I wouldn't want them to look any other way.*

'She's travellin', Mum. Like an itinerant. And I'm nearly ten years older.'

'What's that supposed to mean?' Yeah, tell us, Byron. What's *that* supposed to mean? 'You're not dating her. You're employing the girl.'

'What kind of thirty-year-old gives up a career to travel the world?'

'An adventurous one. One looking for another kind of existence.'

'Or an irresponsible one.'

Annoyed, I creep closer to the kitchen door. Sally sits on a stool, her elbow bent and resting on the island countertop. Byron leans against the open French door as he watches the kids still playing poolside. His profile is as dark as the outdoors is light, and I'm beginning to wonder if his parents naming him was prophetic or if he's somehow grown into his name. Though he's not mad, or really bad, as far as I can tell. But he may be dangerous to know—at least, for me—as he stands there in all his brooding, frowning glory, those damp board shorts glued to his strong thighs.

And I thought blonds were supposed to be more fun.

'She's not here for a handout, son. She seems as genuine as they come. She was here for the picking season, for goodness' sakes. She's got to be hardworking, and I'm sure her references will be fine.'

'I dunno, Mum. I know it's only for a few weeks, but I think she'll be a pushover. I don't want my children raised to be flaky.'

'Sure, you'd rather they grow up to be crabby like you.' He looks about to argue with Sally when she holds up a hand.

'I love you, son, but you're aged beyond your years. They're only little. Let them know fun and happiness. It won't make them soft—for God's sake, allow Matty to be a child before you expect him to be a man.'

A moment of silence passes between them before Edie begins to yell for her father. As Byron steps out onto the patio, his parting words are delivered over his shoulder, full of bitterness and hurt.

'It's the lot of the oldest son, though, isn't it, Mum? Freedom is a fairy tale. The sooner he gets used to it, the better.'

Chapter Ten

BYRON

Kicking my feet up on the chair in front, I take a sip of my whisky, relishing the peaty burn. At times like these, I wish I still smoked. Not because I feel like the evening air needs polluting but more for something to do. Something to take my mind off what's going on inside—inside upstairs, more specifically. And more specifically still, what's going on inside the guest room where Amber is currently. Where she's probably getting ready for bed. Washing her face, brushing her red mane of hair. Maybe showering. Sliding soapy bubbles across her creamy skin . . .

What the fuck am I doing?

My feet hit the tile with a thud, my glass skittering across the darkened table. I came out here for some peace following a dinner where, in the kitchen, she'd sat opposite yet barely looked at me. My own fault. I'd been curt at best. At worst, a total dickhead. On the surface, it looked like I'd ignored her, speaking to her only when absolutely necessary. On the surface, it looked like I'd spent the meal listening to the kids chatter while encouraging them to eat their greens, my gaze and attention as far from her as it could be. But beneath the surface, hidden from all, I'd been aware of little but her. The cadence of her soft accent as she'd chatted quietly to my mother. Her delicate fingers as she'd reached for the bread, and those kiss-shaped lips as she'd brought her glass of wine to them. My wine. Is it odd that I got a kick out of watching her enjoy it?

Jesus, this isn't happening.

'It'll only be a few weeks,' I grumble, pushing a hand through my hair as I imitate my mother. 'You're not dating her, you're employing her,' I parrot.

The thing is, I don't want to date her, and I sure as shit don't want to be her employer. I want her out of this house, away from temptation. Only, that's not really true, is it? Because what I really want is to be upstairs in whichever guest room she is, spreading her silky thighs wide and torturing her with my tongue, because just looking at her fills my head with dirty ideas. And that right there is a fucking problem.

'Fuck.' I throw myself back in my chair, blowing out a breath, long and low. Coming outside was to be respite, not an opportunity to torture myself. I need to crush these images and get a fucking grip on my thoughts.

A curlew wails like a newborn babe in the distance, a familiar sound I hang onto as I try to concentrate on the sounds of the evening instead. Though we live some way from the nearest town, the evenings are never quiet. Cicadas sing, insects buzz, a chorus of frogs somewhere out of sight striking up a song. Batwing and birdsong. Possum feet scurrying across a branch. These are familiar sounds . . . and do fuck all for my concentration because all I can think about is her.

In the hotel room.

Upstairs in bed.

How the fuck did she end up here? Was it not torture enough that she'd been my go-to girl since that evening, my wank-bank material consisting solely of her? Evidently not. Someone upstairs wanted to make me bloody suffer.

How long had it been since I'd been stirred like this? Probably not since those early days with Katya, my wife. Not the pretend one I'd picked up in a hotel bar that had somehow followed me home. *Christ knows she'd looked tempting enough that evening in that backless dress, but in pigtails and shorts, she's fucking edible.* I swore I'd never get involved with another woman after Katya because she left me a shell of a man.

A widower. Christ, how I loathe that label.

Katya was never really happy in the country, and I've often wondered if it was the Sydney lifestyle she fell in love with and not me. The trips overseas taken in the course of running the corporate side of the business. The endless gatherings and parties all over the world. Selling wine is a very sociable affair, and we'd had our fun or so I thought. But having kids was supposed to make you want to settle down.

When she fell pregnant, I couldn't have been happier—I was fit to burst—and she seemed to feel the same. Naturally, our social lives slowed. Katya had a difficult pregnancy, and I put the changes in our relationship down to those difficulties. To hormones. But then the babies came, and the love we had seemed to blossom and multiply because there was more of us to love. At least, that's how I'd viewed things. I didn't realise she wasn't happy. Not until it was too late.

She spent hours at the gym, insisted on a tummy-tuck and liposuction, determined to get back to her pre-pregnancy shape. I couldn't see the problem. She was always a beautiful woman. *Maybe too beautiful.* Not that it stopped her from Botox at barely thirty years old. She hated what pregnancy had done to her body. Or so I thought.

Those were rough days. But there were worse days to come.

Katya's terminal cancer diagnosis. *The kids were only babies.* Then Dad's heart attack. All within a few weeks of each other.

Dad's death devastated us all, and we gathered around Mum, desperate for comfort, desperate to offer comfort. When my brothers returned to their lives, I found I couldn't. Things with Katya weren't . . . great. And Mum needed me. Besides, I couldn't leave the running of the estate to the managers. It was his life's work and hadn't he always expected me to take over? As it turned out, we moved back to Riposo as a family, even if weren't really a family anymore.

That's what it felt like. We were just going through the motions, waiting on the inevitable. Katya passed, leaving me with two small children, anger, and grief. And I just did what I could, putting one foot in front of the other. I made sure the kids were fed. Well. Looked after. Loved. But it was a good job Mum was about, too. The dead stay dead and the living move forward, if not on. With kids, you really don't have any say in the matter. They say anger is a natural part of the grieving process. What they don't tell you is what you're supposed to be angry about.

And I'd be lying if I said there hadn't been other women since Katya, but only one besides Amber had made it into my home. *Rebecca Keogh*. The experience fucked me over so badly that *since* Becci, I'd made it a point not to fuck anywhere near home. There's only one thing worse than a woman who throws herself at you, and that's one who lives near enough to *keep* throwing herself at you.

We'd gone to school together, and she was there at Katya's funeral to pay her respects. I didn't pay much attention to anything that day, let alone her. If I had, I might've realised she wasn't the only girl from town scoping me out.

We kept bumping into each other—on purpose, I reckon now—and I remember thinking adulthood suited her. She became good to have around. A mate, same as Tom. And we began to hang out, though purely platonically. *Except that one time.*

I knew it was an accident even as our lips touched, but I needed the kind of comfort a man could only find in a woman. And then, afterwards, I was too tired, too much not myself—Dad then Katya, the kids, Mum, and the business to look after—that I wasn't seeing things straight. I didn't realise the town thought we were in a relationship, not until one of her mates told me what exquisite taste I had in diamonds. Apparently, she was flashing the thing around town, wearing it on her left hand.

If Katya's death left me hollow, Becci's games left me done.

I intentionally turn my mind back to Amber. She obviously takes from life what she wants and gives zero fucks about opinions. *Particularly mine.* She seems genuinely happy. Genuinely good. But she isn't for me.

None of them are.

I have my kids and my business, and that's enough for me. I don't need a woman. *Period.*

I was right to ditch Becci, and I was right about not having Amber in my home, too. I know it. It's just a question of time before the rest of the world agrees. I can feel it. The sense of things stirring, rearranging themselves around me, the tiny unseen cogs around me seeming to shift. It's almost imperceptible, but it's happening. Or maybe it's the whisky talking, bringing out the maudlin, superstitious Irish blood in me. *Courtesy of my mother's bloodline.*

In the meantime, I just have to live with the remembrance of that night. Her soft sighs and even softer skin. With that last, unwelcome realisation, I throw back the last of my whisky, then drag myself off to bed.

Chapter Eleven

AMBER

One more deep breath in front of the mirror before I head downstairs for my first day of work, where I need to impress parent, grandparent, and toddler. It's a good thing I'm not freaking out.

Nope, I'm cool as ice.

Cool as a cucumber.

And I'm absolutely *not* intimidated.

Especially not by a certain man whose heavy footsteps I'd fooled myself into thinking had paused by my bedroom door last night. A man whose apparent attitude is as bad as he is good in bed.

Don't think about it, I silently chastise myself. Nothing good can come of remembering the way his stubble had deliciously abraded the soft skin of my thigh. Of how his heavy, hooded eyes watched my responses as his bronzed body had worked over me.

Gah!

I slide an errant piece of hair behind my ear, tugging on the front of my T-shirt. I'm showered, my teeth are brushed, and my hair is . . . well, my hair is doing its own thing—I'm not flat-ironing every day even if I am staying in the house of a man whose mere glance makes my skin tingle. A man whose accent makes my throat dry and my panties wet.

Not helpful, brain!

I wonder if he wanders around in the morning in his pyjamas, or if he's the type for grey track pants and white T-shirts. *Lord have mercy!* But I suppose I better stop wondering and go find out.

The house is quiet as I walk down the impressive staircase, butterflies like velociraptors swooping through the pit of my stomach. I'm not nervous about the job—I'm sure I can do the job standing on my head. Looking after twins isn't going to be difficult. Difficult is trying to keep a glass of thirty in line while also educating them. Difficult is running field trips and making sure you return with the same number you had when you left. Difficult is paying supreme attention to answering an eight-year-old's question while the eyes in the back of your head watch over the other twenty-nine of them.

So if I'm not nervous about the job, I guess that means I'm nervous about seeing him. Not surprising, I suppose, given his arrogance yesterday. And despite telling myself I shouldn't be thinking about him, I seem to be doing anything *but*.

It's like . . . birthday cake, I tell myself. The best tasting kind that you can't help but imagine tasting again and again, even if there's no evidence left of that cake.

Not even crumbs.

Oh, well. You can't make a cake of out crumbs, anyway. Even if the crumbs are a little dark and delicious, like the best kind of ganache, not to mention a lot intriguing. What did he mean about freedom being a fairy tale, I wonder?

Stop. Thinking. About. Him!

Whatever. If he continues being a colossal douche, I'm out of here. Especially as it turns out that Rose and the guys didn't abandon me at all. The stupid signal on my phone had dropped out, so I'd just missed the text she'd sent which read:

There isn't work here for all of us so we're heading to the next place about five miles away. If it doesn't work out for you, holla. Sven says he'll come pick you up. Either way, call me, girl!

So, last night, I did. Rose told me they found work on the other side of town, in another vineyard, the same one that Sally had mentioned because they couldn't wait around in case they missed out there, too. I feel a bit of a wuss admitting to myself that they're my security blanket right now. So I won't. At least, not out loud.

As I reach the bottom of the staircase, I realise Byron probably isn't even at home. I imagine he's been up since the crack of dawn to do . . . whatever vineyard owners do. Milk the wallabies? Feed the grapes? Maybe I can ask Matty or Edie. Kids love to tell grown-ups what they know, and this grown-up is ready to listen. What I won't ask the kids about is their mom. It's best I hear that from one of the adults.

I'm at the kitchen door at five minutes to eight, and while I'd love to say my motto is *if I'm five minutes early, I'm ten minutes late*, I'd be lying. I'd dearly love to be the kind of person who shows up early for appointments, dates, and meetings, but it's not in my blood. However, I have never been late for work a day in my life.

True story.

It's a boring story but nevertheless true.

Poking my head inside the kitchen door, I smell a hearty breakfast. Or maybe that should be a heart attack breakfast. Bacon, sausage, coffee, all while my stomach sings out for a croissant.

'Hi!' I call out, pushing the door a little wider. 'It's Amber! I'm here for work!'

'Morning, darl'.' Sally and Matt, and Edie are seated on stools at the kitchen island with empty plates and juice glasses before them. Sally is polishing off a cup of coffee but slides off her stool to take my hand in both of hers. She still wears her wedding band, I notice, though her husband has passed, along with a diamond encrusted band on her other hand.

'How did you sleep?'

'Amazing,' I lie because the sounds of the countryside are going to take some getting used to. The nightlife here is almost as loud as the city nightlife. Okay, so maybe it isn't as loud as drunken revellers and police sirens, but it's chirpy and screechy and all other kinds of noisy.

'I'm glad.' Sally pats my hand, still smiling before pulling away.

From his stool, Matty sends me a shy wave, though Edie shrinks back a little, like a turtle trying to retreat into its shell. After yesterday's friendliness, it looks like today we're starting from scratch again. Their father had mentioned they'd had a lot of nannies, so maybe that's it. Maybe I'm just another strange face in their home. And I wonder, and not for the first time, where their mother is. Is she dead? Or is this a custody thing?

As Sally clears the dishes, I make my way over to the little ones.

'Good morning, Matty. Morning, Edie.' I hold out my hand to Matty, the more open of the two, but he gives his little head a shake. 'That's okay. I'm still glad to see you. I think we're going to have a good time today.'

'There's a plate of breakfast on the counter for you,' Sally says. 'And some coffee left in the pot. You can eat while the kids get their chores started. Byron has gone out already, but he left you a note, and a list of things he'd like you to take a look at today.'

'Chores?' I question, hoping I don't look too surprised as my gaze slides to the note on the kitchen island held down by a silver paperweight shaped like a bunch of grapes.

'Byron has . . . very particular ideas on parenting.' The way she looks at me, her eyes full of sympathy, makes my heart sink just a little bit. 'But I'm sure you'll find your feet. There's a list of contact numbers on the fridge,' she continues. 'I'm at the top of the list. If you've got any questions, give me a yell.' She gives me an appraising look than a warm smile. 'I got a lovely email back from your family in France.' Ah, so that's probably the reason I'm being left alone with the little cherubs today. 'If there's an emergency, call Byron first. He's working over at the winery this morning, then he's got a meeting over in the office this afternoon.'

'The big man is on the premises,' I repeat, the velociraptors giving another swoop through my intestines.

'Well, he's certainly got a big enough opinion of himself, I'll give him that much. But then again, none of my boys are wallflowers. I blame their father.'

'It's always the father's fault,' I add in a mockingly stern tone.

'Clever girl.'

Giving Matty a kiss on the head and Edie one on the cheek, Sally makes her way to the door.

'Sally, are the twins expecting visitors this morning at all?' Her expression clouds with confusion. 'I'm sorry, I don't want to appear nosy or anything but . . . ' With a quick glance at the kids, I confirm they aren't listening, I say quickly, 'What I'm trying to say is, I get Mr Phillips is a single dad, but should I expect a visit from their mom?'

I know what the answer is before she even speaks. Divorce doesn't cause loved ones to look pained. 'No, darl. Byron's on his own.'

A few moments later, the door closes. I stand in the same place feeling inexplicably sad. Widowed. And at such a young age. This poor, poor family.

A few moments later, the sound of nails on a chalkboard causes me to wince and turn to where Matty has pulled out a step stool and is rinsing his plate in the sink.

'Getting started on your chores already?' I look down, realising I still have the chore list in my hand. 'You have to do all this?' I ask Matty. Turning off the water, he looks over his shoulder at me.

'We have 'sponsibilities before we can play.'

'I'm surprised you get to play,' I mutter. I mean, I know about learning through play, but come on, there are eight things on this list! 'And you do these things every day?'

He nods, rinsing his blue cup before handing it to his little sister who props it on the upper shelf of the dishwasher.

'Chores are boring,' Edie offers up. 'And the chooks bite.'

'The what bite?'

'The chooks,' Matty repeats, handing Edie her pink princess cup, which she pops next to the blue.

'What's a chook?'

Matty pauses, turning his head over his shoulder, his brows pulled together in a perfect imitation of his father. But before he can answer, Edie chimes in.

'Chooks are chickens.' She closes her lips around her thumb again.

'They're hens,' Matty replies in a superior tone. 'Not chickens, silly.'

'You're silly,' Edie says, stamping her foot on the tile. 'Just like the chooks. And you're a chook because your hair is sticking up like a chook's bum!'

'Is not,' her brother counters, stepping down from the stool while smoothing his wet hands against the crown of his head.

'Your hair is perfect,' I interject, stepping between the two. Sliding my hands under Matty's arms, I pop him back on the stool, sliding my hands into the sink full of water, reaching for a sponge. 'Maybe I can help you, and then we can play sooner.'

'Like Nana does?' Matty tips his head, and while his smile is slow to grow, it's there.

The dishes take but a minute to rinse, and by the contents of the dishwasher, it looks like Byron ate earlier. I clean my plate, both by eating the food, and then actually rinsing it, and try some coffee.

Act in haste, repent at leisure.

The coffee is . . . well, put it this way; I think I'd be better served drinking the dirty dishwater. As I clean the coffee pot, the kids wander out of the room, and I wonder if they've gone off to play. I'm eager to know what puts a smile on their faces.

'Kids?' I call, walking into the entrance hall. Above, two little faces poking against the railings of the mezzanine floor. I follow them upstairs, noting the area open to a sitting room as Matty appears from a doorway, a calico laundry bag with a pirate cartoon in his hand.

'Is this your laundry?' I ask, looking down at the little sack and the pirate's squashed face. If that wasn't a clue enough, I'd also previously noted *laundry* was somewhere on *the list.* It's a pity I don't respond well to instructions . . . 'Shall we gather the laundry later?' I suggest brightly.

'We've got to put it in the washing machine,' he says glumly. *Geeze!*

'Well, maybe you could show me around first?' Matty sends me a reluctant glance, probably because the prospect doesn't seem much of a step up from picking up his clothes, but he eventually nods as I take the sack from his hand and drop it on the floor.

His hand in mine, he leads me down the hall.

'Dad's room,' he says. Though the door is ajar, it doesn't reveal very much. Shame. I suppose I'll have to continue my investigation later. 'The barfroom.' Matt pauses briefly by the sleekly stylish *bath*room. An oval tub big enough to house the family sits under a plate glass window framing views to the mountains. A double vanity painted chinoiserie style chests, fluffy towels stacked beneath. The black and white tiled floor looks original as does the imposing chandelier. This is a bathroom that looks ready for a home magazine photo shoot, but for the toy-filled net festooning the bathtub.

'Bedroom, bedroom, bedroom,' Matty chants, sounding bored as he points at the doors along the wide hall. 'And this is our bedroom,' he says, pushing open the adjacent door.

'The one with your names on the door?' He nods rapidly, pulling on my hand and guiding me into the room. 'Who'd have guessed?'

I laugh when I see his bed, which is quite a grand affair fashioned to look like a pirate ship.

'These are so cool!' On the opposite side of the large room, Edie lies across a bed fit for a mermaid, complete with a headboard fashioned to look like pearly clamshell draped with a gauzy teal canopy. Both beds have been made. Well, in a fashion.

'You make your own beds every morning?'

'Yep,' Edie replies. ' 'Cept when we camp out in the garden.'

'Do you camp with Nana or Dad?'

'Dad!' Matty answers for her, his tone clearly noting how ridiculous he thinks the question is.

They show me their favourite stuffed animals, then Matty shows me his favourite books as Edie empties a large box of mixed Legos on the floor.

There's a playroom next door filled with every toy known to man, or at least it seems that way, plus a game console that Edie tells me they're allowed to use but only *when Daddy says*. Every figure of farm animal is paraded from its box, and board games are pulled from closets before we lose ourselves in dress-up until the sound of a dog barking drifts up through the open window.

'Dave!' Matty cries, his wide blue gaze meeting mine. 'We're 'posed to feed him after laundry! And the pesky chooks!'

'Chooks?' The word is just so ridiculous.

'The chickens,' he says with an air of long suffering before the pair dart out of the room.

So we feed Dave the dog before moving on to the chickens, who live in a fancy coop a little ways from the house. Matty isn't comfortable with them, and it doesn't help that we're late with their food.

'We have to get the eggs,' he says mournfully. 'And the white one bites my toes when I wear thongs.' He stares down, wiggling his flip-flop clad toes. 'I shoulda worn my gum boots.'

'Helga,' Edie says, tugging on the leg of my shorts. 'The mean white chook's called Helga.'

'S'not what Dad calls her,' Matty replies from under his brows.

'Oh, I'll bet it's not,' I sort of singsong in response. 'How about I get the eggs?' My suggestion is a hit, judging by the swift nods of their joint little heads.

Unhooking the lock, I step into the coop and am immediately assaulted by pecking beaks.

'Ow! Those are my toes, not food!'

'Told ya they bite,' Matty calls, throwing a handful of grain in through the wire mesh. 'Quick, grab the eggs, I'll distract 'em!'

'There are chick—chooks in here,' I call out once inside the little chicken house, eyeing the chickens occupying three of the six boxes.

'You gotta pick them up,' Matty calls.

' 'Cause they're sittin' on eggs,' his sister adds helpfully.

'Oh. Pick them up.' Easier said than done, I find, as I'm forced to lift three of the squawking, pecking feather-balls, one by one.

'It bit me!'

'Told ya.' Matty's tone is self-satisfied. 'Bet it was Helga.'

With my little basket and half a dozen eggs, I escape from the enclosure, and at my suggestion, we throw the food—vegetable peelings and the like—over the fence before getting the heck out of the place. Next, we go back to Dave, who is, Matty tells me, a cattle dog. And Dave, as it turns out, has his own set of chores. He walks alongside Matty to be delivered to the foreman who is heading out somewhere to do something I don't care enough to ask.

On the way back to the house, I notice a large playset under a cream sail shade. It's quite a fancy affair and includes a large cubby house with two slides shooting out of it, a couple of swings, and a climbing frame for aspiring, pint-sized gymnasts.

'Do you play often here?'

'With Daddy and Nana sometimes,' Matty replies. 'The other nannies liked to be in the house.'

'In that house?' I ask, pointing at the wooden piece of architecture, making him laugh.

'No, *that* house!' He points a finger in the direction of their home. 'They liked phones better.'

'Talking on the telephone?' I ask even though I know hardly anyone uses their phone for calls these days.

'For games.'

'Marfa let me play on her phone,' Edie adds, sliding her hand shyly into mine. 'Can we play on the slippery dip, Miss Amber.'

'You might. If I knew what the slippery dip was.'

'This,' calls Matty, running over to tap the base of the slide.

Honestly? That's what a slippery dip is? Australian is like a whole other language.

We play until we're good and sweaty, and despite the shade sail, the growing morning heat has us beat. So we head inside, gulping down cool glasses of water and a little lunch.

It is cosy sitting at the island together, eating cold sandwiches and fruit, and when we're done, the pair tell me they're usually allowed a treat and ask for something called a *slice,* which turns out to be a little like a brownie. Shop bought again, not that there's anything wrong with that. I should know, I was practically raised by packet Betty Crocker. Unlike my grandmother, my mom didn't care to bake.

As we chat, the kids tell me about all the things they would do if they never had to complete another chore in their lives, and while I realise we didn't bring the laundry downstairs, I'm really too comfortable to do it now. Besides, the twins and I are just getting acquainted, and I'm not in any hurry to break that spell, especially not as Edie leans her head against my shoulder, her pudgy fingers stroking my hair.

'You have hair the same as Ariel,' she murmurs. 'Did you used to be a mermaid?' Her little head peers down at my legs as though to check for fins.

'Sorry, honey, but no. I do have a pretty cool mermaid swimsuit, though.'

'I have mermaid swimming togs, too,' she replies enthusiastically. 'I can show you, and we can go for a swim!'

Beyond the French doors, the pool does look pretty tempting. Barely a ripple mars the surface as a kookaburra sings from a tree somewhere, almost as though encouraging our company outdoors.

'Maybe we can swim later,' I tell her. 'The sun is pretty fierce right now. I don't want us to burn.'

'We have rashies,' Matty offers.

'That's like a sun shirt, right?'

He nods. 'And we have swim hats, too.'

'But I don't. And I look like a lobster when the sun burns my butt.' I make a clawing motion with my hands, pinching his ribs and causing him to giggle. 'Who told me yesterday their favourite thing to eat was cookies?' Tapping my bottom lip with my index finger, I pretend to contemplate the answer as I'm met with a chorus of,

'*Me! Me!*' along with raised hands.

'Maybe after lunch we can make some together?'

I end up laughing as I have to remind the pair to slow down as they precede to shove the remainder of their lunches into their mouths.

So we bake. Matty shows me where the aprons are hanging, passing out the one he says his Uncle Flynn gave his father for Christmas. It has a very suggestive looking cob of corn poking provocatively out of its leaves, leaves that sort of resemble underwear. Under the cock of corn—because that's kind of what it looks like—are the words *Corn Star*. The kids ready themselves with their own aprons, completely oblivious to how I stare at mine.

But cookies. It turns out not only is the Phillips's kitchen a true luxury, providing space and every high-end kitchen gadget imaginable, it's also stocked to the gills. We make chocolate chip cookies along with a healthier (barely) oatmeal, and the kids help me measure, pour, and stir.

The kitchen smells like bakery heaven as we sit down to warm cookies and cold milk an hour later, and when Matty promises not to tell they ate slice as well as cookies, I laugh, despite realising that I've maybe made my first mistake. But as my gaze slides to my note and the kid's to-do list, I decide that's probably not true.

I've made a tonne of 'em!

Maybe I'll be making my way to Rose and the other vineyard today after all.

As the afternoon sun begins to dip, we decide it's time to hit the pool. I follow the kids upstairs, and though they insist they need no help with their swimsuits, I keep my door ajar as I wrestle myself into my own, struggling a little with the halter top before slipping on a short beach kaftan.

'Oops. We nearly forgot the sunscream,' Edie tells me just as we're about to step out onto the tiled deck.

'Here,' Matty says, handing me a bottle of sun*screen* with a pump dispenser he'd grabbed from a nearby cabinet.

After covering the pair in the thick goo, I pull the kaftan over my head and begin creaming myself with the stuff, too.

'*Ohhh,*' Edie coos. 'Miss Amber, you do have mermaid togs!' She looks down at her one piece and the glittering image of a mermaid. My own swimsuit is a bikini, the material shining almost iridescent in the sunlight. And it might be a little over the top for playtime with little ones, I decide as I mimic Edie's examination. Edie's swimsuit is as cute as a button, meanwhile I'm shimmering like a drag queen in the spotlight. Speaking of over the top, the cut of the garment, or what there is of it, is a little revealing. Strange how I'd felt glamourous at the poolside in Sydney, yet here, in the privacy of secluded home, with only two children as witnesses, I feel a bit conspicuous. A little slutty, even.

Come on, they're just little kids. Matty doesn't appear to care, and Edie is just a little mermaid-struck.

The pool feels like bathwater as I wade in, confident that both children can swim after watching them yesterday with their father. And boy did I watch. It was hard not to, not just because he's easy on the eyes, but also because it was like seeing another side to him. He wasn't the suave sophisticated man who screwed me seven ways from Sunday, the man who worshipped me with his body in a Sydney hotel. And he certainly wasn't the total ass who tried to drive me running and screaming from his home. Nope, he was just a man who delighted in his children. A man who let them climb his strong body like he was a tree and they were little wet monkeys. A man who allowed them the appearance of being strong enough to dunk his head, only for him to rise from the water, flipping back his wet hair with the confidence of David Gandy filming a cologne commercial.

Gah! Enough of that.

Matty and Edie follow me in like little ducklings. Confident and playful, they swim to opposite sides as they each grab a hand-sized torpedo, taking turns to throw them into the deep end for the other before counting, sort of, how long it takes their sibling to reach the surface again. Watching them gives me time to think. Their father and grandmother clearly dote on the pair, and while I'm perplexed by the need for a chore list, I wonder if this might be their father's attempt at some kind of control. The death of a loved one can leave a person feeling out of control, so I suppose it might make sense. Whatever. What I need to do is separate the man from the hotel. I work for him now, and no matter how gorgeous he is, there won't be a repeat.

The twins tire of their game, moving quite happily on to playing with an assortment of pool floats, dragging in one after another until there's almost no space to swim. And it's on one such mission to retrieve the pink flamingo when Edie slides poolside, falling and bumping her chin. I'm out of the water in a flash, the sodden and tearful little girl wrapped in my arms almost immediately.

'It's okay, baby. It's okay. Let me see your chin.'

'*Nooo*!' she wails, 'It hurts! I want my daddy.' Her fingers wind tighter around my neck, her cries so close to my ear that I'm almost certain I can feel my eardrum rattling.

'Stop crying, Edie!' From the side of the pool, Matty claps his hands over his ears with a scowl as his sister's cries reach a crescendo. 'You're such a sook.'

The little girl's tears halt almost at once.

'Am not,' she counters, her expression matching his. *Thunderous.*

Tears and ick streams down her face as I shift her onto my hip when it becomes clear she's trying to wriggle down. That's probably not the best idea. Unless I want to explain to their father and grandmother how they tragically drowned while fighting.

'*You* are a sook,' Edie retorts, her squirming now a little more frantic. 'Matty cries like a baby—waa, waa, waa!'

'Do not!'

'That's enough, both of you.' I use my calm but authoritative teacher's voice. And it turns out I may as well be speaking Dutch as they continue to argue and snipe from opposite sides of the pool. 'I think it's time we went inside,' I say, continuing with my teacher tone, my tolerance tweaked as Matty instantly drops into the water with a look of supreme disdain. Then he proceeds to swim into the middle of the damn thing before climbing onto the pool float.

'Get out of the pool, Matty.'

He doesn't answer but for glaring at me.

'Matty, you get your butt out of this pool this very minute.' With an imperious look, he turns his back to me. Well, as imperious as a child can be while clinging onto a blue inflatable whale.

'That's it. No more cookies for you.' This time, I get the little prince's profile as he pokes out his tongue. 'Would you stop wiggling.' I tighten my arms under Edie's butt.

'I want to get down,' she demands.

'Why? So you can float in the middle of the pool, too?'

'No, 'cause I'm gonna smack him,' she grumbles, still wriggling, one thin hand pushed against my breastbone, her arm out straight.

'Lord alive. This is why I moved to teach older grades,' I grouse. 'This is disappointing.' And now I'm apparently channelling Mary Poppins. I wish I had her magic carpet bag because then I'd at least be able to stash Edie in it while I get into the water to grab her brother. Scooping him out with the pool cleaner is probably against some kind of child protection code. 'Yes, this is quite disappointing after all the fun we've had.' *Bibbidi bobbidi bullshit.* 'Stop squirming, Edie. Matty, you get out of the pool right now. I don't know what's gotten into you, but I think that's quite enough from both of you.'

'I'd agree,' comes a dark voice from the other side of the pool.

Ah, fuck a chook . . .

Chapter Twelve

BYRON

It was fun for a while watching her squirm. She probably thought looking after twins would be easy—a piece of piss. But the thing with these two is, they're best of mates a good ninety percent of the time. They even share a bedroom at their own request, like best buds. But that ten percent that they're not? They fight. Fight each other. Fight for attention. Fight for shits and giggles sometimes, I'm sure.

It's normal, I'm told. I paid good money for the information because there's no one who needs more reassurance than a single parent, no one more frightened. What my dollars bought was the information that the relationship between twins is complicated one. Multifaceted.

Apparently, this is completely normal. Of course, Mum also got to say "I told you so," laughing that I'd wasted nine hundred dollars on a psychology report. I should've listened more closely to her telling me how me and my three brothers spent many an hours punching lumps out of each other as a way to just pass the time.

So their fighting is normal but fucking hard to take sometimes.

The fact that we were boys and the twins are one of each sex doesn't seem to have any bearing. And if I'm honest, Edie has the worse temper out of the pair. She's also the one who usually starts the blue. Though not always . . .

'Matthew.' My son physically starts at the sound of his name, pool water arcing around him as he turns to the sound of my voice. 'Get out of the pool. Edana.' I flick my gaze to my daughter, though only briefly. 'Stop pulling at Miss Amber and get over here.' She slides down Amber's body as Matt paddles his way over to the side of the pool. Two damp and very contrite children make their way over to where I stand. I'm not an ogre, but they know they are in trouble so move slowly. Matthew's lip trembles while Edie's feet slap against the wet tiles, her expression one of sheer petulance.

'What have you got to say for yourselves?' I ask, lowering myself to their level. I usually meet them eye to eye when I'm telling them off, but today, the lowering of my gaze is necessary more than normal. As if looking at her ordinarily doesn't fill my head with smut, today the prospect of keeping my thoughts clean is almost impossible.

'Sorry,' Matty mumbles at the same time as Edie's brows pull down as she exclaims,

'Was Matty's fault!'

'The two of you will apologise to Miss Amber, then you'll get your towels and get your butts inside. Go wait for me in the living room.'

The children murmur halfhearted apologies before trudging inside, Matty even going so far as throwing his arms around Amber's legs as she makes her way to where she'd abandoned her own beach towel.

'I had it under control,' she says quietly, skirting the edge of the pool.

'Looked like it,' I retort, immediately wishing I could swallow back the words. 'They caught you by surprise, didn't they?' I offer up a little softer, studiously keeping my eyes above her neck. Let me tell you, that is *not* an easy task.

'Yeah.' Her word hits the air as a tremulous laugh, like the realisation and the admission take her by surprise. 'They really did.' Her eyes shine with a mixture of disbelief and embarrassment. 'I can't believe it, but they did.'

'Matt's a stubborn little bugger, and Edie has the devil's own temper.'

'Might've been nice if you'd warned me.' Her soft tone matches my own, though holds a touch of reprimand. 'Forewarned is forearmed, Mr Phillips.' A teasing, playful reprimand.

For the first time, I get a flash of the girl from the hotel. The confidence and attitude. Sure, we'd sparred verbally since she'd arrived, but this is different. This is a reminder of that woman, the one who'd been the tempting push to my shove. The one who'd fought me for control in the bedroom, the way she'd gone down on me once the hotel door had barely closed. The way she'd smiled wickedly as though I couldn't read her intentions the moment she'd wrapped her legs around me, rolling herself on top, her expression turning to triumph.

'I thought you liked surprises.' I hadn't meant to sound so familiar, not this time. I'm not trying to push her away. My words are a soft enquiry, not a reprimand as I'm suddenly not so keen on keeping a professional distance between us.

Maybe it's the way she's dressed. *Barely.*

Or maybe, just maybe, it's because I've thought of little else but her all day. Done little else but watched her and the kids eat breakfast and make cookies.

And suddenly the installation of a nanny-cam last month doesn't seem so clever anymore.

'Who doesn't love surprises?' she answers, turning away as though to grab her towel.

Her skin is sun-warmed as I wrap my fingers around her forearm, words spilling from my mouth without thought.

'You can swim, though, right?' She might've spent her birthday a little recklessly, and sure, she'd recently given up a good job to go play Romany traveller, but that doesn't make her irresponsible. Not with kids. *Not with my kids.* The thing is, I don't want her to turn away. I don't want this small moment to be over. Also, I might be a bit of a pervert.

'Of course, I can swim.' Towel forgotten, she turns to face me, her eyes glittering with annoyance now. 'What do you take me for?'

Jesus Christ, I'd like to take you. Right here in the sunshine. Loosen the ties on that tiny bikini, lie you across one of the loungers, and stuff you full of my cock.

'I brought the children to the pool safe and fully prepared.'

'Speaking of being prepared.'

I chance a look at her eyes. They're not brown but gold and amber. They're also wide and a little bit wild.

But she doesn't stop me.

Not as, hand still wrapped around her arm, I catch her bikini tie at the juncture between her neck and her shoulder, sliding my index finger underneath.

Not as I pull the fabric away from her body.

Not as I slide that lucky finger down her chest.

Her breath hitches, her back arching almost infinitesimally as my knuckle glides across the bud of her nipple—her hard and exposed nipple—covering it with the shiny fabric once more.

'There.' My dick throbs as I loosen my grip on her arm and step back, swallowing thickly against the instinct to kiss her. I want to kiss her. Why can't I kiss her?

Fuck. I remember. Because this isn't right for so many reasons, least of all sexual harassment in the workplace. All of a sudden, the weight of my actions press on my shoulders as I realise what I've done.

Of how she might interpret this, because how can she not after all I've had to say?

But she laughs, a small, tremulous sound. Then another. And another a little louder before she claps a hand to her mouth.

'I've been walking around the pool with my . . . with my . . .' Her eyes are still wide as she begins to giggle manically, her hands starfishing across her chest.

'Yeah, Edie must've—' I don't need to fill in the blanks, mainly because I don't need the added stimulation of uttering nipple, tit, bare, or breast. It wouldn't help the situation in my jeans right now. *Maybe I should take a leaf out of Flynn's book and go with bosom. Or maybe I should just stop thinking about her tits altogether.*

'And here I thought you wouldn't look at me because you were angry.' She snorts. 'A close second was that it had to be my swimsuit.'

'Your swimsuit?' My incredulous words are out in the air before I can temper them, and my eyes? Utterly un-fucking-controllable as they roam over said swimsuit. I think I've got socks that run to more fabric, which is fucking fine by me. In fact, she can wear that thing around the clock, as far as I'm concerned because it's fucking fantastic.

'It's a little hard on the eyes.' Hard on the cock, she must mean. 'Gaudy. Sort of like a disco ball.'

This time, my gaze follows hers down the path of her body, which isn't helpful. But it's not just the suit that's dazzling. She's utterly unconscious of how gorgeous she is. Completely unaware of the effect she has on me. She's just quietly breathtaking. Beads of water cling to the weave of her braids, the ends curling in response to being damp. Her lashes are darker on the ends, I realise, and her eyes are—

'Your eyes are almost the same colour as your hair.' She blinks heavily, once, twice, and I swear they darken a touch more. 'I thought they were brown.'

'Makeup,' she whispers, immediately discerning my mind had slipped to that night. I wonder if she thinks about it? 'It was my makeup. My mom says my mood is reflected in the colour of my eyes, that they change according to my mood, but I don't think so.'

'I reckon the darker the colour, the more turned on you are.'

Fuck. Flirty was not what I'd aimed for there. It wasn't supposed to sound like a dirty invitation. I don't think, anyway. To her credit, and my disappointment, she doesn't bite.

'I think they're more likely they appear to change in response to the clothes I'm wearing.'

'Or not wearing.' My eyes make a slow perusal of her body again, lingering over the tight buds of her nipples. I want to put my mouth on them. Cover them in cold wine. Come on them. So many avenues and I want to take them all.

'I mean colours. The colours I'm wearing. And if we're talking about that night . . . ' Colour suffuses her cheeks as her gaze falls to the ground, seeming to find some fascination with the tiles. 'The darker my eye makeup, the darker the colour.'

'What about now?' My tone is lower, husky, and my body works on intuition rather than thought as I slip my finger under her chin, raising her eyes to mine. 'You're not wearing makeup or much of anything right now. The way I see it, my theory stands.'

Her gaze is still dark but entirely guileless, unlike the night in the hotel. It should be a warning. A warning of how wrong this is—of how wrong she is because she's not that woman anymore, and here, in my home, I'm not that man—but as a tiny slice of wet, pink tongue darts out to moisten her bottom link, I levitate closer. A pulse trips in her neck, and I suddenly want—no, *need*—to feel that pulse thrumming against me. Pulsing around me, tempting and taunting me to fuck her harder, deeper. Sensory memories tug at my brain and surge through my body as, without thought to anything but having her, I slip my hands around her waist, pressing them low on her spine. She gasps, her whole body yielding as our bodies collide and my rock-hard cock presses into her softness.

'Your eyes are so dark right now. Must be because you're wearing me, eh, Red?'

Without giving her time to answer, I press my lips against hers, possessing them, pulling on her tongue. I slide my hands down, cupping her firm, full arse, grabbing it, pressing her harder against me, causing us both to groan.

'Byron . . .' She wants to speak, and I want her to scream, despite the knowledge dancing on my periphery that this isn't right currently.

'Let me taste you.' Her head rolls back as I bite her jaw, lick her neck. 'Let me touch you.' She whimpers as I dip my knees, drawing my hands from her thighs to the backs of her knees to hook them around my waist. 'I need to fuck you.' I sound like I've been running, my jaw tight, compressing the words, and though Amber doesn't verbalise her agreement to my sentiments, I still hear it. And feel it. It's in the movement for her lips against mine, the flex of her warm centre against me, and in the fingers tight in my hair.

With a growl, I stumble towards the patio furniture, my hands continuing to maul her arse cheeks, my fingers desperate in their quest to feel her wetness. She shudders as I manage to do so, my dick fit to burst as the very tips of my fingers are coated in her.

'You're—'

'Before you tell me I'm wet,' she murmurs, her mouth at my ear, 'you should remember I've been swimming.'

'*Ungh*.' Her grazing teeth tighten on my earlobe as I pulse into her. 'Fuck that. You're wet because you want this again.' I rub her against me, then shift her higher up my body, wanting to reach her centre with more than just my fingertips. 'Admit it. You want to fuck me. You want—'

'Ow! I'm tellin' Dad! Dad, Edie hit me.'

'Did not—Matty hit me first!'

Blood turns to ice water in my veins as the thunder of small feet sound on the kitchen tiles. And as if that wasn't reminder enough of what a selfish bastard I am as I slide Amber's legs from my waist and her feet to the ground, the outer kitchen door opens, too.

'Hello, my little possum—'

'Nana, Edie hit me!'

'Matty hit me first!'

'Did not!'

'Did, too!'

'Is it too late to pretend I'm not here?' my mother mumbles as the door clicks closed behind her. I step away from Amber, not sure whether the knot in my stomach is from letting her go or having her in my arms in the first place. Whatever the reason, I'm just grateful we're out of view. 'Where's your father?'

'Here,' I call, throwing Amber her towel as I pass the chair it's draped over. I can't look back at her— I won't. 'Here. I'm here,' I repeat, stepping into the kitchen, pretty much treating my mum the same way. I can't look at her, and I won't. I'm a long time out of short pants, but I'm not sure my poker face is up to adulting standards right now.

'Where's Amber?'

'She's, er, out.' I sniff. Rub my nose. Stare at the kids. Hair no longer damp, their dark waves are gnarled and knotted, towels no doubt abandoned farther into the house on the floor somewhere. Fighting again. And it's my fault. I should've followed them in like I promised. *Okay, threatened.*

I feel like a total shit. Despite this situation being my own fault, I turn my stare into a glare as though rejecting the responsibility.

Avoidance, anyone?

'What do you mean, she's *out*? I swear to God,' Mum says, puffing up like Helga, the most irate of our chooks. 'If you've kicked her out, I'll—'

'Easy on. She's outside. At the pool.' As though the statement requires farther clarification, or as though she might be unsure where the pool is, despite the house being in the family for generations, I hook my thumb in that general direction. My gaze follows, though I'm almost fucking sure my brain wasn't supposed to allow it to travel Amber's way. Thankfully, she's not in view. Maybe she found the outdoor shower?

Fuck, that is not *helpful.*

Why didn't I think of hiding us there?

Because you're a responsible adult and a decent father.

But still, that would've been a hell of a good time.

Stop. This. Shit!

'So you haven't . . .?'

Sadly, no. Though I did feel the heat of her pussy through my jeans. The touch of her wetness against my fingertips.

'I said no, didn't I?' I snipe. 'What? I haven't fired her!' But I should have. I should've nipped this in the bud when she first walked in.

'All right. Keep your hair on,' she snipes right back. 'Oh, there she is,' she adds mildly, glancing out the window now. 'She's gone for a swim'

The equivalent to a cold shower, or a reason not to partake in this clusterfuck? Either way, Amber has the right idea.

'That's right. She's having a bit of time to herself after spending the day with these savages.' I bring my gaze to my offspring. 'What have you got to say for yourselves?'

'She hit me first,' Matty begins.

'I don't give a flying f—flip who hit who.'

'Whom,' my daughter corrects. 'Nana says it's whom.'

'I'll get to you in a minute,' I warn, my gaze sliding back to Matty. 'I'm talking about what happened at the water, son.' His face scrunches a little as though the effort of recall is currently beyond him. But I give him points for playing dumb, especially given his sister's bold expression. 'When you were in the pool,' I remind him. 'When you wouldn't get out when Miss Amber asked.'

'Oh,' he answers simply. 'Sorry.'

'It's not me you need to apologise to. And you,' I say, turning to Edie. 'What have you got to say for yourself?'

Unlike Matt, this little madam is rarely contrite, her little fists balling by her side as she stomps her foot and suddenly yells, 'What I've got to say is . . . is . . . Matty has been 'noying me in the front room.'

'Have not.'

'You're a lying bloody bastard!'

'Where on earth did you learn language like that?' my mother says, though likely her horrified sounding gasp might've been an attempt to swallow her laughter.

'I learned it from Dave,' she decrees, her attention swinging to Mum.

'Dave didn't teach you that,' Matty retorts, defending our cattle dog's honour. 'He can't speak!'

'Not the dog,' she responds, her tone far too snide for a four-year-old. 'I meant Dave-o.' The foreman, who—whom, ah, fuck it!—she no doubt overheard.

The pair begin to squabble in earnest now. 'That's enough,' I growl, bringing my hand to my face. *I can smell her on my fingers. How is that helpful here? And how is it that half the town is purported to be affected by my growl, but it barely registers with these two?*

'Edana Elizabeth Phillips,' I say, filling my tone with censure, 'I suggest you take yourself off to your bedroom to cool down.' She doesn't move. At least, not immediately. 'Now!' Raising my voice gets her moving. I dislike shouting, but sometimes it seems to be the only thing that works.

As Edana stamps from the room, I concede she doesn't look overly upset by the noise. *More like severely pissed off.* Christ knows what strategies I'll be left with as she gets older when yelling no longer works.

'Dad.' I look down as Matt tugs on my pants. 'She's just grump because it's nearly dinnertime. Don't be too cross.'

'I'm not, little mate.' I run my hand over his hair—
my other hand, the hand I've touched her with I
save for myself. Matty winces as my fingers snag on
a knot. 'Why don't you go upstairs and get ready for
the bath? Give your room a wide berth though, eh?'
He shoots me the kind of grin that doesn't leave
much face, wrapping his arms around my thigh.

'Love you, Dad.'

'Love you, too, son.' So much. Too much to be
putting my dick in front of their well-being. Mum
bustles about the kitchen as my eyes slide out to the
darkening pool. I can hear the quiet movements of
Amber in the water, but I can't see her as I realise
I'm thankful the pool lights haven't yet switched on.

'What's for dinner?' Matt questions from the door
to the hall.

'Steak,' Mum answers. 'And leftover potato bake.'

'Nana,' my son responds chidingly. 'You know
there's no such thing as leftover potato bake!'

'Ah, you're right. Suppose I better make some
more then, hadn't I?'

'Yum!' And with that declaration, he darts from
the room.

I'm quick to follow, keen to avoid the pull of the
siren swimming in the pool.

Chapter Thirteen

AMBER

Sweet. Mother. Of. God.

What has gotten into me?

As my head breaks the water at the far end of the pool, I give the little devil on my shoulder the opportunity to speak.

I'll tell you what hasn't gotten into you: Byron Phillips.

That would be who, not what.

Who cares!

And I'd be out of a job.

Totally worth it.

More like a total clusterfuck.

You're sure you don't mean the hottest fuck of your life? The way he carried you across the patio like a motherfucking caveman. The way he'd growled and bucked when you sucked on his ear. The way he'd lifted you up his body to feel the heat between your legs. You know what was coming next, don't you?

Me?

Your back against the wall. Your thighs around. His. Head.

That only happens in porn.

And with growly Aussies, apparently.

He wore that expression—the one that seems to see right through my skin. And that damned watch drawing attention to the knuckle of his wrist and those great big hands.

Even his wrists turn me on. Oh, God. I'm in so much trouble.

God can save you, sure. But only the Devil knows how to work that tongue.

Unhelpful, but thanks anyway. Uncurling my fingers from the sandstone, I pinch my nose and submerge once more. Feet flat against the pool wall, I use the motion to propel me in the direction of the far end, managing to do so without once coming up for air. And still I stay beneath the water line, under until inky stars explode in my head and my lungs feel like they're about to burst. But the effort not to push above the surface robs me of all thought and all feeling but this. I'm no longer pulsing and heated, my insides clawing with need. I'm no longer listening to the warring voices in my head, and I'm no longer tainted by guilt.

They're not your kids. You're not responsible for what they see.

'*Gah!*' I breach the surface, allowing my thoughts to roll off me with the water streaming from my shoulders and hair.

The sky has turned the colour of watermelon, the mountains in the distance as dark as night. With my arms resting on the pool coping, I listen as the birds sing their dusk chorus, watching as they jostle for perch and position in the trees. A trail of ants moves across the tiles, attracted by some stickiness on the surface, moths swirling around the outdoor lights. I watch it all, not because I'm particularity observant but because I'm avoiding the inevitable climb from the cooling pool. The kitchen lights are still on, the French doors open though screened. The door on the far side of the kitchen opens before slamming shut, so I take that as my opportunity to avoid Sally first. Scrambling from the pool, I grab my towel, giving my body a hasty wipe down before wrapping it across my chest, then, sliding my feet into my flip-flops, I slip in through the screen door. The oven hums quietly, the scent of cheese and cream drifting from it, salad fixings spread across the island countertop. I hear the shuffling of shoes from beyond the kitchen door—Sally is in the place she calls the boot room, the laundry lying just beyond. Before she can return, before she reads what I've been up to from my face, I hurry out into the hallway and up the stairs with only one more person in mind to avoid.

The man standing at the top of the stairs. And he's no longer wearing that expression. I'm not sure if that's a good or a bad thing.

'What's the laundry still doing here?' In his hand, he holds the pirate emblazoned sack that I'd taken from Matty this morning.

'What's that? In your hand?'

'I know what it is. What I want to know is why it isn't in the laundry room. In the washing machine.'

'Oh, that's totally my fault. I told Matty to leave it,' I reply airily, refusing to make eye contact as I take the last three steps to the top of the stairs. I skirt around him. *Don't look at the handsomely angry man, Amber. It's not good for you. Or your libido.* 'We, er, got caught up doing other things.'

'Laundry was on the list.'

'List?' I repeat casually.

'I left you a list.' He looks anything but casual, a tiny tic flexing in his jaw, his eyes more granite than blue right now. Yet out of all the things I should be thinking, what my mind snags on is the fact that those cheekbones are wasted on a man.

'Ah, yes, the list. I did see it. In fact, I put it in my pocket . . . ' *of the pants I'm no longer wearing, yet reaching for.*

'Fat lot of good it'll do in your pocket.' His eyes don't flicker from my face, not to glance at where I'm feeling for my pockets like a dog scratching an itch, or even just to look at me. *Like he did at the pool.* I get that he's angry, but is it about that or that the kids have played hooky from their chores? I'm having problems processing anything while he's standing so close to me. Strange that his proximity doesn't stop me from noticing a myriad of other things. Like how his shirt is a little dishevelled but no longer damp from the press of my swimsuit, but wrinkled instead. I notice the tic in his jaw and that his hair seems to have been the recent recipient of more than just the attentions of my fingers. And I notice how his eyes positively burn. How can such a cool colour burn with such heat, I wonder. His pure, unadulterated lust at the pool I recognised. But now?

Who is he angry with? Me or himself?

And does he know when he's a little mad, he's a lot sexy?

And is he really counting off the chores—reciting from the list—on his fingers right now?

I wonder if he washed them. His fingers, I mean.

And I wonder if he'd use them on my properly if I asked him nicely.

Gah!

'The list.' My decisive tone halts him in his tracks. 'Personally, I feel it was a little . . . unreasonable.'

'Unreasonable?' Judging by his expression, I'd say this is something we don't agree on.

'Especially for my first day.'

'The list wasn't for your benefit, but I'm beginning to think I shoulda left more explicit instructions.'

'Explicit, like clear? Or explicit, like what just happened at the pool? What exactly are you angry about? For what it's worth,' I continue in the lull and in view of his angry stare, 'I was just as responsible for what happened.'

'I fucking mauled you.' And there we have it. The answer. Well, at least one of them.

'Yeah,' I agree with a small shrug. 'You're kinda good at that.'

'That's not helpful.' His frown falters—it's still there, but not from anger now.

'Maybe not, but it's true. And I didn't say no. I should have.'

'And I shouldn't have touched you.'

'And Edie shouldn't have aided in my flash-fest, and Matty shouldn't have decided to play deaf, and Dave the dog probably shouldn't have licked my leg, but hey! We all make mistakes. And all of them today.'

'I'm sorry.'

God, I'm not. Actually, I'm only sorry we were interrupted even if that's wrong.

'Me, too.' Like a child, I cross my fingers behind my back. 'Maybe we should rewind.' I close my eyes and take a deep breath. 'I think—I think my birthday was amazing. And I think you thought that, too. It's only natural we should be drawn together.' I say the words in a rush, not giving him time to deny them or contradict me in any way. As I open my eyes again, my heart beats once—*ba-dum*—in the face of his expression. Crossed fingers, closed eyes, and rushed words may have been childish reactions, but they were also reactions fearing his scorn. In the place of scorn, I see want. I see need. I see a man on the edge of reaching for me.

'But we can't. It wouldn't be sensible.'

'No.' He swallows deeply, his gaze lowering and shuttering his thoughts. 'I see that.'

Before he can say anything else, I point at the calico laundry bag. 'So, that laundry bag . . . I get that the kids have responsibilities, applaud you for it, even, but today was my first day. I didn't want to come in all guns blazing.' As he looks up at this and I realise that he's looking down at my hands. My hands that have made index finger guns. *Pow-pow!*

Way to go, Amber. Oh, so attractive. I doubt he'll ever look at you with desire in his eyes again! 'I wanted to take time to play with them, to learn a little about them and get to know their personalities.'

'Okay,' he answers carefully, his blue eyes no longer stormy. Or bemused.

'But also, I don't agree.'

'Agree with what?' *Uh-oh.* Looks like the storm is rolling back in.

'The list was just too much. They're too little.'

'So you're a psychiatrist now?' He folds his arms across his broad chest, the little calico laundry sack hanging forlornly against his belted waist.

'No, sir.' Is it just me, or did his gaze just flare a little? Does that mean something else to him? 'I just want to make sure I'm relating to them on their level. The more I understand about them, the better I can care for them.'

'This isn't Paris. We're not sitting around sipping tea and eating croissants all day.'

I roll my lips inwards from correcting the sacrilege of his pronunciation. I may never speak like a Parisian native, but *cross-ents* will never do. Annnd . . . he's still complaining.

'We have shit to do—a business to run, vines to keep healthy, employees to pay, and wine to produce. The expectations I have for my children are reasonable enough that they've never complained or skirted their duties until today.' *Oooh, burn.* 'They understand they're a part of this land, part of this machine, and parts are what keep us moving. Their chores provide them with a sense of purpose and responsibility.' I realise he's gotten closer during his monologue. Hell, we've gotten closer to each other. Our feet may be glued to the same spot, but our upper bodies lean in.

'A sense of responsibility is one thing, but don't discount play,' I reply firmly, unwilling to give an inch. 'Play allows a child to learn, too. I feel as though you understand this, based on the playset outside and the bins of toys in their room. Play brings joy and creativity to the forefront, exercising parts of the brain that aren't in use while they're forced into the monotony of feeding violent poultry and doing laundry.'

The corner of his mouth quirks, his blue eyes seeing what, I don't know. 'Come 'ere.' Without giving me a chance to respond, Byron's paw of a hand lands on my upper arm as he begins to steer me in the direction of the bathroom. My heart begins to thump, that thump resonating someplace a little lower, whether from the contact or his expression, or both, I'm not sure.

We stop just by the door, his gaze amused, though almost a little reluctantly so.

'I'm sure I don't need to tell you that children need consistency.' As he uncurls his fingers, I feel the loss of their heat. 'I aim to be that consistency, and as their father, I mean what I say and say what I mean. And when I say they need to be responsible for their own laundry, I mean exactly that.'

'But—'

'Watch,' he decrees quietly, pulling open a small hatch built into the wall. Pulling open the rope on the laundry sack, he reaches in, pulling out what appears to be a pair of Matty's pyjamas, along with presumably, yesterday's clothes. Then, with more than a little self-satisfaction, he pops the clothes down the . . . laundry chute. 'There,' he says, closing the hatch once more. 'Matty's laundry chores done.'

'But—'

'Course, he'll have to go out into the yard later. Heat the water over a fire. Drag out the washboard and the mangle, taking care he doesn't squash his tiny fingers.' As he waggles his not-so-tiny fingers under my nose, I can't even muster a little appreciation for sight of them or those strong wrists. Not as my cheeks begin to burn and not as he folds his arms across his chest again, leaning his shoulder against the wall. 'And God forbid he forgets to starch my shirts,' he adds with comically widened gaze. 'That'd earn him a birching.'

'Very funny, I'm sure,' I mutter acidly, playing back this morning. Had I jumped to conclusions too quickly, fed too eagerly on his children's tales of woe? Or had I subconsciously wanted to create tension? Draw his attention to me?

Urgh. What is wrong with me?

'Funny? Well, I think so.' His subsequent chuckle is a dark, velvety sound. 'I'm not some hard-arse father or Fagin character.'

'And what about the chickens? You must know they're frightened of them.'

'Do you know why we have chooks?'

I sort of shrug, though I'd guess for fresh eggs. That is, if I could bring myself to speak. I think I'd rather choke on my tongue right now.

'We have chooks because about eight months ago, the twins went visiting with Mum. Mum's friends had chickens, so when they came back, that's all I heard night and day, chooks, chooks, bloody chooks. So I gave in, but not before discussing—at length—their responsibilities.'

'You can't expect four-year-olds to be responsible for raising chickens!'

'Why not?'

'The . . . the cleaning, for one thing. They couldn't possibly.'

He shrugs, a careless motion. 'I'm sure there are lots of country New South Wales nippers with bigger responsibilities. It's not beyond my two. That said, they don't clean the coop. I do.' I might not know him very well, but I still find this very hard to believe. 'Or I get one of the labourers to do it.' Now, *that* I can believe. 'All they need to do is collect the eggs and chuck them a bit of food, usually the scraps from last night's dinner. Automatic feeders do the rest.'

'Yes, well, they don't like feeding them,' I retort a touch acidly.

'Tough shit.'

'And what about the dog? Did they ask for a dog, too?'

His chest moves with a deep sigh. 'Every. Bloody. Week. But Dave was my dad's dog. He's a working dog but semi-retired these days. And before you get your undies in a bunch, they only feed him a treat in the morning, and they only walk him to the foreman because Dave loves their company.'

'Oh.'

Byron slides me a look that says *idiot*. Or *I win*. It's hard to tell.

'About earlier.' Gone is his teasing tone and half smile. 'I truly am sorry.'

'I've forgotten about it already,' I reply with a dismissive wave of my hand, hiding how his continued apologies feel like a sudden slap to the face. As his eyebrows retract, I find myself blundering on. 'I did happen to be flashing you,' I sort of stutter through a fake laugh. 'Let's . . . let's call it a momentary madness.'

'That seems fair because God only knows I feel a little crazy around you.' That smirking half smile is back again, as if his accent alone wasn't hard enough to ignore. 'I'm only glad I'm not going daft alone.'

I'm saved from a retort—oh, who am I kidding? I'm saved from my guppy expression by Edie's appearance. She stumbles from her bedroom, a dark curtain of wet hair covering her eyes, and a tiny pink brush sticking from her head like a crown.

'Daddy, I can't see, and I gots it *stuuuck!*'

'How many times, Edie?' he asks, getting to his knees. 'You know you can't brush your hair with a dolly's brush.'

Slightly dazed, I take the opportunity provided by Edie to slip along the hallway to my room. What the hell just happened?

I really don't know.

~*~

'What can I do to help?' I ask, coming into the kitchen a half hour later. Sally stands in front of the window, a magazine open in front on the countertop.

'How are you, darl?' She turns with a smile. 'How were the kids for you today?'

'Good. Both good,' I reply. 'We had a bit of a moment out at the pool.' Lord, didn't we? And I'm not just talking about the twins. But as Sally's expression falters a little, I suddenly feel like kicking myself. 'It was no big deal.'

'They were fighting, I'll bet.'

'Yeah, a little.' My words come out high and reedy.

'Little heathens,' she says, pulling out a large pair of salad forks from a drawer. 'They're as nice as ninepence most of the day, then bang! Out of nowhere, all hell breaks loose. Still, that's siblings for you. I bet you fought with yours, too.'

'Actually, I'm an only child.'

'Oh?' Sally's slim eyebrows retract in an echo of Byron's.

'Born late to older parents, so I didn't even have cousins to speak of. I think that's why I went into teaching, in a way.'

'Well. I'm sure you're a comfort to them both.'

'Not as much as the retirement village in Florida they moved to a year ago,' I reply, not without a touch of chagrin.

'Oh?' she repeats, this time with a little chuckle.

'I think they're reliving their early twenties.' My overshare comes courtesy of my scrambled brain as my eyes flick out to the pool, a flash of sensory memory grabbing me between my legs. 'When they said they were selling and moving to the Sunshine State, I imagined they were moving to a quaint little retirement place, but it sounds more like little Vegas. And you know what they say about Vegas.'

'You mean what happens in Vegas stays in Vegas?'

'If only,' I mumble, swiping a dish towel from the countertop. 'I've told them, *don't tell me any more of your stories. You're making my ears bleed!*' Sally sets off laughing, an honest to goodness belly laugh. I'm pleased she's entertained by a daughter of parents who may or may not have become swingers, but I can only force a small smile. 'Seriously, Sally, the things my mom tries to tell me . . . I'm surprised I haven't gone grey.' Why didn't I think about my parents earlier?

Thoughts of my parents doing the dirty deed = Amber libido turning off.

I must remember that.

'But that's fabulous! Getting older shouldn't mean giving up.'

'Yeah, but I don't want to hear about them . . .' I fail to resist a shudder. 'Never mind.'

'Getting it on?' Sally's words are wavery with laughter, making me bury my face in the tea towel as I nod. 'Maybe that's what I should do. Threaten to move to Florida, too.'

'Why?'

I look up from the towel. Sally seems to be weighing her words. When they eventually come, they hold a note of wistfulness. 'I didn't expect to be a widow at this time of my life. I loved Tony. He could be a grumpy old bugger and always liked to think he was right. Of course, like most men, he was usually on the opposite end of the scale.' She smiles sadly, opening another drawer, pulling out placemats this time. 'But I didn't hold it against him. We loved to travel—always had. And I miss it. Like I miss him. I still have my boys, of course, even if they're all grown. And I'll be here as long as Byron needs me, but quite frankly, love, I've already raised my kids.' I nod. I get it. She has her own life to lead. 'Speaking of his nibs, how'd it go with him today?'

'Well, I had a great time with Matty and Edie,' I answer brightly . . . before lowering my voice. 'I kinda messed up, though.' Boy, did I.

'The ogre's not here,' Sally assures me. 'You can spill the beans.'

I take a deep breath, ready to tell her anything but the truth about what happened between us. 'It's just that I didn't follow the itinerary precisely. I mean, the list.'

'Oh, *the list*.'

'Chores are chores, and I get it. But I blew them off in favour of hanging out with the twins. Getting to know them. Letting them get to know me. And well . . .

'Byron seemed a bit tense when I saw him.' She slides me a dry look.

Suddenly, I have a hard time keeping my mouth shut, words spilling from my mouth like water from a burst dam.

'He was so hard-headed and frustrating and arrogant, and I–'

I clamp my lips closed, abruptly remembering who I'm talking to. I can feel my cheeks redden and not just because I've railed at her boy but also because I almost said the unthinkable. I almost told her he's hard-headed, and frustrating, and arrogant, his temper as changeable as the weather, and that I find it—find *him*—so incredibly hot. That I want to climb him like a tree. That I want to make him use his satanic tongue on me. Yep, I was about to horny word vomit over her own little boy. Who, incidentally, isn't small in one place. Except maybe in his professional regard for me right now.

What's with that, Amber? Where's your self-respect?

Probably still in my backpack.

'I apologise, Mrs Phillips.'

'It's Sally, and save your apologies, darl. They're not necessary.'

'Still, that was unprofessional. I'm just trying to balance things in a new setting. And it's such a lovely setting that I'd be devastated to find myself fired.'

Sally chuckles. 'If being fired is what you're worried about, you'd know it by now. When Byron fires someone, they leave with their butt smokin'.'

'Maybe so,' I add with a sigh, sliding my hands into the pockets of my sundress. 'But it's safe to say that he wasn't very impressed.'

'*Pssht!* Byron never looks impressed. Since he's been old enough to talk, he's expressed his disdain for all things not Byron. But don't worry too much, love. And don't take him too seriously. Lord knows, I don't. You've just got to understand that he's a man with a lot of weight on his shoulders, and he operates under a short fuse. The weight comes with the territory. He inherited it when he inherited this place, but don't go thinking he didn't have a choice about it because he did. He went off to college, then went off to Sydney to run the corporate side of the business. His dad and I never expected him to move back here. In fact, before Tony passed, we were putting plans in place so we could travel.'

Sally smiles as though catching a glimpse of herself and her late husband on a distant beach somewhere as she absently picks up a dishtowel.

'The short fuse, that comes from his grandfather. His dad and me? As laid back as you can get. At least, running an operation this size. His grandad, though, he was a tough nut. A tough nut usually has a hard shell, and inside is something a little more tender. For his grandad, the tender spot was his son. Byron's tender spot?'

'The twins, of course. Like any father.'

'Exactly. But more than that, he's the only one responsible. Sure, he has me right now, but he knows I won't be here forever. Since Katya, his wife, passed, he's been pretty much solely responsible for the pair. I worry about him sometimes because he feels that duty so deeply, I'm not even sure he sees himself.'

Her words hit me in the solar-plexus. Here I am, wondering if he's angry that we almost did or didn't do the dance with no pants poolside, or if it was because I'd had the temerity to deviate from his chore list. No, I hadn't seriously thought him as petty. Frustrated? Maybe. Sexually frustrated? Also possible, though looking like that, he can't be short of offers.

But maybe the man hates himself for reacting to me, to need. But then a second, much less pleasant thought hits; maybe he's angry with himself because he still loves his wife?

'Oh, Sally, that's so sad. He must miss her terribly.'

Yep, I hate myself just a little right now. *Also, dig, dig, dig.*

Her hands tighten on the dishtowel, her gaze gliding to the window for a beat. 'I don't know that he was happily married. There was some... tension. I can't say for sure, but something was going on. I saw it at Flynn's wedding, but Byron wouldn't have thanked me for prying. Still rivers run deep with that one, I'll tell you. He's been the same since he was a little tacker. I never knew what he was thinking, not unless he was angry. But the rest of the time? It's like he wears the weight of the world on his shoulders. He feels deeply, not that he shows it.' She sighs, seeming to rouse herself from the past, her attention coming back to me. 'Byron needs to surround himself with patient people. If you have the good grace to offer him that, these next few weeks will go fine. Just remember, two short fuses don't make a long one, darl. They just make things blow up quicker.'

I swallow thickly, the advice a little hard to ingest. A few weeks. I'll only be here a few weeks. Surely, I can keep my thoughts, comments, and hands to myself. Because if I don't, I'm likely to find myself fired and picking grapes someplace else. Or maybe pushed up against a wall with my thighs wrapped around his head. While the second scenario has its merits, something tells me I'd still wind up picking grapes elsewhere. And what's worse, maybe Byron would end up hating himself.

It's time to move on and put Byron back in the fantasy pile.

'Is there anything I can help with?' I ask. I peer into the huge salad bowl filled with an array of leaves and vegetables of every colour. 'That looks delicious.'

'I'm not much of a cook as my darling grandson might have suggested already,' she deadpans, 'but I do make a mean salad. The salad is done, potato bake is in the oven, and the steaks are seasoned. All we need to do now is wait for the man himself to cook them.'

'I can handle a barbecue,' I offer up.

'That's good to know but—'

'No one touches my barbie.'

The sudden deep rumble of his voice makes the hairs on the back of my neck stand. He's changed out of his almost-sex-wrinkled shirt and is wearing grey shorts and a pale sleeveless T-shirt.

'I see how it is. Never come between and man and his meat, huh?' The minute the words are out of my mouth, I'm trying to reel them back in. 'Barbecue. Never come between a man and his barbecue—his barbie, that is.'

'Oh, no, love,' Sally offers, chuckling. 'I think you got it right the first time. Men are a little precious about that end of their anatomy.'

From the other side of the kitchen island, Byron groans. 'Come on, Mum. Not now.'

'What?' she answers innocently. 'I'm just acknowledging a universal fact. Men are very attached to their penises, and not just literally.'

Byron groans again, turning to pull a bottle of red from the concealed, purpose-built storage. Apparently, according to Sally, wine needs a consistent temperature, among other things. Byron had the cooler thing installed because the house doesn't have a cellar, and the wine of Riposo Estates deserves to be served the right way. But I digress.

'Prepare yourself,' he mutters as he passes behind me, retrieving three glasses. 'Mum's about to tell you about one Christmas when we were all kids.'

'Really?' My attention swings to Sally. 'I'm all ears!'

She proceeds to tell me about how when Byron was fourteen, she stuffed all four boys' Christmas stockings with the usual fare; smellies, which I gather is cologne and deodorant sets, chocolates, and this particular year, condoms.

'Tony wasn't happy,' she tells me, laughing as she does so. 'What kind of mother gives her sons condoms? *This one*, I said.' She points her thumb at her chest. *'I don't want to be a granny before I'm forty,'* I told him. *'And I will if they take after you.* That shut him up, I'll tell you. Well, until Rafferty took one out and shoved it over his head. Then the silly bugger started to blow it up.'

'That answers a lot of questions,' Byron says, pushing a glass across the countertop my way.

'Are you saying he's into that auto-erotic-whatsitsface?' Sally asks, a little horrified. 'You know, where they—'

'Jesus, Mum, I know what it is. And no—just no!' With a look that's pained but that would wither flowers on their stems, Byron splashes wine into three glasses. 'And if he was getting his rocks off from auto-erotic asphyxiation, do you think he would tell me?'

She seems to consider this for a moment before answering, staring into the bowl of the glass of red he hands her. 'Probably. Rafferty can't keep a secret to save his life.'

'Well, he can keep *that* one.'

Our eyes meet as he hands me my glass before moving to the other side of the kitchen, leaning his large frame against the sink. This man does not look like someone's dad, let alone two someone's dad. Try as I might, I can't help but stare at the ink covering the bulge of his bicep and the way it peeks from the top of his T-shirt.

'What I meant was.' He brings the glass to his lips, his tongue clearing a drop from his lip. 'Rafferty's brain must've been starved of oxygen that Christmas.'

Sally chuckles as she agrees that Rafferty is the family clown. I don't speak, lost in the memory of his tongue. *Wife. Dead. Tragic. Widower.* I run the words through my brain as Sally carries on.

'He and Flynn keep sending each other T-shirts with ridiculous slogans. They've got some competition going on. Who can wear the rudest T-shirt in the strangest part of the world.'

'Pair of drop kicks,' her son mutters. By his tone, I guess that's not a compliment, even if he's still sort of smiling.

'What did Byron do with his pack of condoms?' I ask before hiding behind the bowl of my glass.

'Used them,' he answers immediately. His lips curl in a smile of half invitation, half provocation.

'See, he's a dark horse. What did I tell you, love?'

'Can I have a cookie, Dad?' Matty asks, padding into the room in his bare feet and batman pyjamas, complete with a cape.

'Biscuit,' his father corrects. 'And please may I.'

'Do you want one, too?' the little boy asks evenly as he makes his way over to counter where the container of chocolate chip cookies is.

'No, bud.' I'll note that Byron makes a good show of hiding his exasperation as he makes his way over to the refrigerator, pulling out a tray of dinosaur-sized steaks. 'And no one's eating treats before dinner.'

'Did you bake treats with Miss Amber today?' Sally interjects as Matty nods, his grin stretching from ear to ear.

'I did, too,' says Edie, bouncing into the room in a manner very unlike the one she'd left the space.

'I think you have something to say to everyone.' At her father's voice, her little shoulder slump.

'What?' she asks, perplexed.

'Come on,' her father cajoles. 'Your ears, they aren't painted on.'

'Oh. Yep.' The little girl bounces towards me, not at all contrite. 'I'm sorry for using bad words. Can I have a cookie now?'

'Biscuit,' Byron and Matt answer in unison.

'Later,' Sally answers. 'Dinner first. It's such a lovely night, I thought we'd eat outside.'

'But the mozzies nibble my toes,' Edie complains, looking down to her bare feet. As I follow her gaze, I notice her tiny toenails are painted pink. But mozzies, I've learned, is Aussie speak for mosquitos. I'm pretty sure dislike for these bite-y bugs is universal.

'You'll be right,' Sally answers in another display of laconic Aussie speak. *You'll be right. She'll be right. She'll be apples.* Basically, everything will be fine. You could be living in a cardboard box under the freeway, but the words *you'll be right* should be the reassuring balm to your soul. No, I don't understand it much either. 'I've lit the torches and the candles,' Sally continues. 'And there's ice cream out in the freezer.'

'Yum!' cry the twins in unison, making for the door out to the patio. As Byron passes, I furtively inhale a lungful of his scent. He smells so clean and delicious. Not that he smells bad at any time, as far as I can tell.

Cologne, soap, a little man-musky, sweaty from exertion . . . it's all good.

Oh, Lord. This is going to be a long evening, one where I may need to consume a vat of wine just to get through it.

Chapter Fourteen

BYRON

No worries, Byron, Mr Phillips, Sir.

Don't give what happened out by the pool a second thought!

Me? I've forgotten it already!

I blow out a breath as I stare up at the darkened ceiling. *I bloody wish I had.*

Dinner was . . . an ordeal, and as a consequence, I've drank more wine than I would have normally on a weekday evening. I live and breathe wine. Grow, produce, sell it. Wine is pretty much my life. In fact, Dad used to say it ran through my veins. Just mine. Not through Flynn's or Rafferty's or Roman's. Just me out of the four of us. The others had never shown any interest, so maybe that's why I always felt, as the oldest, I had no choice but to be in the business. But tonight I think it runs through my veins a little more literally than he meant.

Rolling onto my side, I punch my pillow a couple of times before rolling back. There's always wine at the dinner table, though I usually just stick to a glass or two, sometimes opting to drink a beer or two instead. But not tonight. Tonight, we'd finished three bottles between us, and I even had a whisky nightcap to aid me to bed. But then again, I've never had dinner with Amber in touching distance.

Huh. Look at that. I just ate dinner with a woman I've *ate out*.

I can't remember the last time that happened. Maybe with Becci, though I can't be sure. Probably on purpose because just the thought of that woman is enough to make my dick shrink. But it's not really her I'm thinking about. She's not the reason a small family could currently camp out under my sheets, and she's not the woman I just ate dinner with.

Sadly, eating alfresco is the only eating out that's happening tonight.

Whoever said only women can multitask should be shot because not one of my tablemates tonight were aware of the directions of my thoughts. *Just as well, considering the table was occupied by my mother and my offspring.* But I'd grilled, talked with the kids, involved myself in conversation, ate my food, and I did so while taking in all the details. Amber likes wine, preferring white over red. One glass makes her less fidgety. Two and her eyes glow. I'd topped up her second glass, making it a less than even third, and even though she'd protested, that extra half glass made her movements a little more languid, her laughter a little more throaty.

Yeah, she likes wine. Maybe almost as much as she likes me. Or maybe almost as much as she wants me, I should say because despite her protests, I saw the signs. The looks. The way she'd moistened her kissable lips as I'd brought my own glass to my mouth. And all the other little tells. When Mum had insisted on clearing the plates before helping the kids to ice cream, she talked to fill the void created. But she barely looked at me. Almost like she couldn't trust herself.

I sigh again, folding my arm beneath my head. I can fucking empathise. I can think the right words— say them, even.

'The last thing I need in my life is to get involved with the woman I'm paying to look after my children.'

Maybe I should've thought about that before I mauled her like a horny teenager by the pool. What happened to self-control? To not messing with the nanny? I'll tell you what happened—my plans all went to shit. Because of her damn nip slip.

And now I'm kidding myself because I've been thinking of her since I left the hotel room. I only need to close my eyes to play back the memory of the way she walked in front of me. The dip in her spine and the sway of her arse. At night, I've dreamed of her cat-like tongue.

'Jesus, I'm so fucked.'

You have nothing in common, my mind supplies. *She's travelling the world, living from moment to moment, and meanwhile, your next twenty years are mapped out.*

Wine. We've got wine in common.

I'd opened a light, oaky Semillon, bottled here just a year ago. I got a kick out of watching her drink the stuff. My wine, my glass, in her hand, at her lips. It made me think about the hotel when I'd doused her in champagne. I'd like to do it again, maybe one of the Estate's full-bodied Cab Savs to stain her skin and the sheets. I'd pour it over her and chase the rivulets with my tongue. Drink it from her natural dips and curves, lap it from her pussy, and tease her with the neck of the bottle this time. My hand grips the head of my cock as I imagine the scene. Hair spilling over her shoulders, the only thing besides wine and my body covering her.

'Fuck . . . '

I slide my hand down my length, my grip a little tighter than normal, my eagerness overtaking need, pushing me a little faster than normal to where I need to be.

Her body bows as I fill her with my fingers, torturing her clit with my lips and tongue before spreading her thighs impossibly wide, all for my view.

I bring my hand from behind my head, cupping my balls as I kick the sheet from my body, fighting to untangle it from my feet. The room is stifling, the evening breeze almost non-existent tonight despite the fan whirring overhead. I chuck my pillow next, every outward sensation unwelcome but for where my hand meets flesh.

Moonlight shines through the window, highlighting the drop of moisture on my slit, turning it the colour of pearl. I hiss as I drag my hand up my hard length, squeezing my cock head and rubbing my fingers through the pearly bead at the tip.

With a bite to her thigh, I rise to my knees, jacking myself slowly.

See what you've done to me? I should make you lick this clean.

And just like that, the images change.

Bent at the waist, her small hand wrapped around my hard dick as I stagger, my back hitting the hotel wall.

Her hands on my hips, the crown of my dick disappearing between her lips.

'Fucking Christ!'

Eyes screwed tight now, I work myself harder, faster, my hand sliding from root to tip, my knees falling open as I recall her wicked tongue and sinful mouth.

The way she'd hummed as I'd wrapped her hair in my fist, the way I'd felt the vibration right to the core of me, making it so fucking hard not to ram myself down her throat.

A hot pulse shoots down my spine, drawing my balls tight.

Her hot body encased in that tiny little swimsuit, her hard nipples begging for my tongue. The desperation deep in my belly to feel her heat around me.

Her body under me.

Her kissable lips just begging for mine.

Begging to be defiled.

I call out as liquid heat lances through me, my climax like a fucking missile. Undulating into my hand, the stream of cum seems to be never-ending, and fuck knows if I'll ever gain use of my legs again.

With one final squeeze, I run my fingers through the sticky remnants. I'm usually smiling like a fucking loon at this point, high on the euphoria of release with my mind as empty as my nut sack.

But not tonight.

If anything, I've just made my need for her greater.

I'm fucked.

~*~

The alarm clock goes off a little before five thirty, as it does most days. I turn it off, stretch my body out along the bed, and yawn, all while ignoring my morning hard-on. Rolling to sit at the edge of the mattress, I run a hand through my hair as I recall the pleasant dream I seemed to have been having. I'd dreamed I hadn't woken alone, my body wrapped around a softer one, one with the smell of magnolia in her hair. The dream dissipates, as dreams do, leaving me with the sense of having empty, lonely spaces and robbing me of contentment. I close my eyes, turning my face to the sunrise as I imagine this dream woman again. Her hair a halo against the white pillows, her naked skin glowing, painted in the soft hues of sunrise. I ignore the fact that I seem to know who this dream woman is. The red hair and her sweet scent all point to one place I'm not willing to go in the daylight.

I make my way into my bathroom, shower, contemplate and decide against a shave, then pull open my closet. Today calls for something more than last night's shorts and singlet. Bringing out my black Armani, I consider it before sliding it back. I wore this last time I was in Sydney. *The weekend I fucked the nanny.* The thought makes me flinch as I pull out the grey-blue instead. Savile Row, I had this suit made at Flynn's tailor last time I was in London. The joint thoughts of *Flynn* and *tailor* make me smile. Up until recently, Flynn was more likely to be found dressed as a mermaid or wearing a helmet and a morph suit than something tailored. *Just for shits and gigs.* My smile widens as I step into my pants, recalling Flynn's freak-out moments as a new dad while watching my pair careen around the Natural History Museum. It was a good holiday. Good to see my kid brother and his new family, and a fucking excellent opportunity to wind him up about his wife's company.

Fast Girl Media.

My sister-in-law speaks like the queen and looks like she should be holding a wand and sitting on top of a Christmas tree, yet in her professional life, she produces porn. Ethical, women-centric erotica. They're still dirty movies.

I've had fucking heaps out of this, and I reckon I'll get at least another decade of winding Flynn up about it. He can take it, even if I call bullshit on the taunt that he's responsible for half of Chastity's ideas. But I'm glad he's found someone and settled down. The pair are solid, and my brother is in love with his little family.

Buttoning my shirt, I glance out the window. The lorikeets are beginning their squawking morning chorus as they feed from the equally brightly coloured eucalyptus flowers hanging in the front yard. I'm amazed anyone can sleep through their noise.

When I open my door and step into the hall, I can already smell coffee. A distant part of my brain reminds me that yesterday afternoon, I'd asked Mum to ask Amber to set up the coffee pot for this morning—we have a built-in espresso machine, but the thing is as temperamental as all hell. If I wanted to fart around with coffee, I'd have become a barista, so I never use the thing. So I'd asked her to ask Amber to set the old coffee pot up. That way, I saved her a mauling along with my request. She must've put it on a timer because I can't imagine she'd be up yet. She's probably still out for the count, wrapped in cotton, her head full of dreams.

Wish I was there, watching her.

Pervert, my mind then whispers.

I guess Amber made this heavenly brew because Mum's coffee is as weak as piss. It's so bad, I usually fire up the Moka pot for a morning ristretto.

Downstairs, I flip on the kitchen lights through habit rather than necessity, chucking my suit jacket over one of the stools. I pull out the coffee pot before bothering to take down a mug. The liquid is full and velvety and moves like dark treacle. If this stuff doesn't wake you up, nothing will.

I wonder if her desire for kick-arse coffee came from living in Paris because this isn't like any coffee I've tasted in the US. This stuff is like liquid crack. So I drink my mug of liquid crack as I shove some toast in the toaster and whack open an avocado, drinking a second cup while I eat. When I leave the house an hour later, I'm pretty fucking caffeinated.

These days, I work from an office within the grounds, just a short walk from the main house. I'm suited up because I have meetings later today, and I'm in the office early because I've a mountain of emails to go through. Today, as most days, I have time to pop home to have a second brekkie with the kids and Mum. I reckon I'll just have another coffee this time.

As I make my way into the kitchen, Mum is adding hot water to her coffee as she looks up.

'This stuff will blow your head off!'

'Yeah, but you'll die with a smile on your face.'

'If I drink it like it is, I'll end up having a heart attack.' Chuckling, I kiss both kids on the head, then deliver a smacker to her cheek. 'Morning, darl,' she says, puckering her lips to the air.

'I remember a dream last night,' Matty pipes up.

'Me, too,' chimes in Edie, though it's hard to tell if she has or if this a little sibling rivalry. 'What was your dream about?'

'Miss Amber and me were going down the twisty slide on my playground. We fell off the end, and she bumped her butt, but I didn't because I was in her lap.' He doesn't look at me while he talks, just keeps on eating his food.

Looks like Miss Amber has been on a lot of our nocturnal minds.

'What did you dream about?' Matty asks his sister.

'Lol Dolls and sharks.'

Or maybe not.

'Good morning, Phillips's!' the woman herself calls from the doorway, her head poking around the door before she steps into the room. Her hair is back in pigtails, and she's wearing another pair of denim shorts along with a white T-shirt I can see the outline of her lacey bra through. Tearing my eyes away, I end up dragging them down the smooth expanse of her legs.

Why don't you just make your way over there and feel her up? You're being obvious enough.

I keep my eyes glued to her feet—her battered pink Converse—but it doesn't settle long before my gaze does another sweep of her hips. As an encore to my idiocy, I swallow hard enough I nearly bloody choke.

'Mornin', darl,' Mum returns.

I glance at the clock, then Ma, then Amber once again, who hasn't spoken since her greeting. Unlike last night, she's looking at me. Really looking.

'You're early,' I offer blandly.

She doesn't answer, not immediately, though she seems to come to abruptly, singsonging her answer.

'Ten minutes early is half an hour late!'

I bite my tongue from asking her if she'd turned into a lorikeet since last night. It seems she really does like the suit.

'No, it isn't.' It comes to something when you're grateful for your four-year-old daughter, who has no concept of time, saving you from filling the space. Because I'd like to make her sing. Or scream maybe.

'Well, pumpkin, that's something my dad likes to say.'

'I'm not a pumpkin,' my daughter responds with a giggle. And a giggle is better than a glower, and believe me, it could have gone either way. 'You're the one with the orange hair.'

'Edie . . .' I slide her a *don't start* look.

'What? It is orange,' she complains.

'I like pumpkin,' Matt says. 'And the colour of Miss Amber's hair.'

Yeah, me, too.

'Thank you, Matty, and Edie is right. It's really just a silly saying.'

'One of your dad's saying, eh? Your swinging dad?' Mum's eyes glint with devilment as they turn my way. 'It sounds like retirement in Florida is quite the thing.'

'Don't get any ideas,' I drawl before chancing a look at Amber, her expression now a picture of discomfort. She so doesn't want to discuss this in front of me. 'Swingers, eh?' *Oops. It slipped out. Okay, I'm lying.*

I steal a piece of bacon from Edie's plate, popping it in my mouth. Chewing doesn't stop me from smiling, though. Neither does the way my daughter points her fork at me menacingly.

'They're not, that is to say—'

'Don't knock it until you try it, love.' Mum chuckles. She pats Amber's shoulder as she leaves the room. 'I'm gonna see if the postie came yesterday. I forgot to check. You,' she adds, pointing a finger my way, 'stop teasing the girl.'

'I think I'd like to hear more about this topic,' I say, my smile now a mile wide.

'I'm not discussing my parents' s—s-e-x life with you.' The more I laugh, the pinker her cheeks become.

'Do you like to swing?' my son asks her, keen to be involved in the thing that's amusing the hell out of his dad. *You don't know the half of it, little mate.*

'I'm afraid I'm not that adventurous, Matty,' Amber answers a touch primly.

'There's no need to be afraid—not if you swing with my dad. He'll take real good care of you, won't you?'

I can't answer because I suddenly recall involving my children in flirty morning banter was not on the horizon this morning.

Chapter Fifteen

AMBER

Day nine of working for Byron Philips, and I'm still alive!

Horny, but alive!

I unbuckle the twins from their car seats, taking care to make sure I'm holding each child's hand as we make our way to their weekly swimming lessons. Despite the pair being absolutely fearless water babies, their gorgeous father insists they need to learn technique. So, to swimming lessons we must go! This must be their third lesson under my watch.

Matty and Edie are already wearing their swimsuits, or togs, under shorts and T-shirts, and having already been slicked with sun*scream* the prerequisite twenty minutes prior to exposure, they abandon their thongs, or flip-flops, and toddle off in the direction of the instructor, swim goggles in hand.

'Don't forget to wait for Miss Maddison to invite you into the water,' I call after the pair. I'm not sure the instruction is warranted seeing as they've been coming to lessons for months, according to Sally.

But as Edie slaps Matty with her goggles, I stand in the bleachers, preparing to intervene.

'Leave them. Maddy will sort them out.'

The class is small. In fact, Matt and Edie are half the number of the pupils, though quite a few classes are going on under the blue and white striped awning. And quite a few moms are waiting in the same set of *burn-your-butt* bleachers, but this is the first time in almost two weeks of lessons that one of them has spoken to me. They usually just chat with each other, though I have seen a few questioning glances thrown my way in the midst of their conversations.

'Jacinta,' the woman says, introducing herself as she pulls her Mulberry purse onto her lap, her hand dipping inside, her arm consequently disappearing as far as her elbow.

'Amber,' I reply, still hovering between following the twins and being polite. As the instructor gestures them into the pool, I fall into my seat.

'Keeping you on your toes, are they?'

'Just a little.'

'You should try managing three,' she replies with a laugh, pointing at the car seat at her feet complete with sleeping baby. 'It's enough to drive you to drink. At least, at the weekend. When I'm off breastfeeding duty.' She laughs again, delighting in my expression. 'Sorry, that was probably too much information.'

'No, it's fine. Totally fine.'

She pulls out a ring of keys, pushing the hair from her face that's escaped from her blond ponytail.

'Thank Christ my hour in purgatory is up,' she says, standing and somehow simultaneously swinging her purse onto her shoulder and the car seat into the crook of her arm. 'It's too hot to be sitting this side of the pool. See ya, Amber. And sorry for opening you up to the gossip vultures.'

'I'm sorry, what?'

'You know this lot,' she says with a jerk of her head, 'are just dying to know what the go is.'

'The go?' I repeat.

'Yeah. What the deal is—who is the cute redhead looking after gorgeous Byron Phillips's kids? And under what capacity is she looking after them? And what happened to Candy, the girl who brought the twins to swimming before? The girl who'd taunted this lot with tales of his holy hotness.' Her eyes dance with mirth, and as I open my mouth to answer, she holds up her key holding hand. 'I didn't ask, but it was pretty hard not to hear, the size of the mouth on her. She ruffled some feathers, I can tell you. None of my business, but if I were you, I'd look too busy to speak with them.'

With a wave, she leaves, and I'm not sure if it's her words or if the women sitting nearby *are* actually watching me. As stealthily as possible, I look around at the other occupants of the bleachers. An indiscreet girl named Candy? Or a lying one? Whatever the story of *Candy and the Hot Widower*, I decide I'm not going to be pumped for information. Information I don't have, I realise more than a little bitterly, as I pull my battered notebook from my battered canvas satchel. I stash my bag under the seat and pull the kids backpacks onto Jacinta's vacated seat, just in case anyone thinks about sitting there. I flip through some of the recipes I've picked up on my travels, the pencil chicken scratch smudged in places, realising I'm annoyed about this mystery girl. I suppose I could text Sally and ask, but that might give her the wrong impression. I suppose I could also go straight to the horse's mouth. After all, hasn't he been nothing but polite since our poolside moment?

Ha! Like I even would.

No, instead, I concentrate on my notebook, raising my head only to wave at Matty as he calls out, 'Watch me!'

Madeleines. A Greek semolina cake, the name of which I haven't noted. The recipe for *torrijas* from Spain. And then there are also recipes of my favourites from home. One for cake that brings back memories of eating on Grandma's back porch, counting fireflies at dusk. One for cherry scones, perfect for strong coffee and lazy mornings, those days when the sun turns everything white and brilliant. I smile, wondering what memories my baked goods might conjure in the future. Will Matty and Edie think of me at the scent of chocolate chip cookies? *Will he?*

I flip the page a little bitterly, determined not to go there. If I can't go there literally, I'm not going to go there in my daydreams.

Candy. The nanny with the stripper name.

Urgh!

The rest of the hour passes uneventfully, discounting the tantrum Edie threatens to throw when we learn the concession stand is out of chocolate Paddle Pops.

'Just have a banana one,' Matty says with a long-suffering sigh. 'Stop being a sook.'

Recognising this as uncomplimentary—though in what capacity, I've yet to find out—I step in.

'How about a different kind of ice cream, Edie? What about this one?' I ask, lifting the yellow packaged treat from the freezer.

'It's not an ice cream, it's an ice block,' she responds petulantly.

'Then pick another.' Any other.

And wouldn't you know it, she picks the largest, most chocolaty ice cream there is. The kind that is going to melt down her hands before the air conditioning in the car has had a chance to kick in.

'Oh, no. Edie seems to have disappeared,' I say, opening the rear passenger door when we reach the house. 'And there's a mud monster in her place.'

'No, there isn't.' Her tiny white teeth glitter in the sunshine, her face from nose to chin covered in ice cream and chocolate. 'Look, it's me!'

'It sounds like Edie, but maybe I need to wash the mud monster's face, just to be sure.'

The car doors close with twin *thunks*, Matty having loosened himself from his seat and climbed out. The pair chatter as they trot towards the door, but all I can think about is *stupid Candy*. I make a mental note to take off the cover from Edie's car seat and wash it before we use it next, before he bans me from using the cute little Jeep I've been allowed to use as a *runaround*.

I chuckle as I unlock the door at the side of the house. *As if I'd take any notice of him. Or stupid Candy.*

After lunch—which makes me realise I probably shouldn't have allowed Edie to choose an ice cream as big as her head—the children's piano teacher arrives.

I know. Precocious or what?

I keep one child busy while the other plays their variation of nursery rhymes along with what I assume are scales. Joy, the tutor, has to be in her seventies. But she keeps the little ones on course, their attention focussed, and they each end their half an hour lesson smiling. While one child plays the piano, the other plays an educational game on their electronic tablet.

It's all part of the routine. *Le sigh.*

After Joy leaves, I pull out my notebook once again, sketching a few ideas for the layout of my mythical patisserie. I sketch images of a storefront, a small patio at the front with two or three tables, *tres Parisienne.* A chalkboard menu set out on the sidewalk for the table specials and maybe messages to catch the attention of passing foot traffic. Those who aren't lured inside by the sinfully sweet smell.

As I doodle, I try a few out.

Skinny people are easy to kidnap. Stay safe—eat cake.

Meet you for Pilates? I thought you said pie and lattes.

I sketch another layout. This one has a window with a counter, no need to even walk inside. Sit at the counter or order and go.

'You aren't like our other babysitters.'

At Edie's voice, I look up. Matty is still playing on his tablet, oblivious to the fact that he's doing math. Meanwhile, Edie has pulled the ever-present thumb from her mouth.

'Aren't I? In what way?'

I expect to be told it's my pumpkin hair or my funny accent—honesty may come from the mouths of babes, but I can't help but think little Edie is more honest than most.

'You're more funner,' she offers up. 'And you don't look at your phone all the time.' High praise indeed! 'Even if you do make Daddy angry.'

My heart sinks to my dirty pink Converse. 'Why do you say that, honey?'

' 'Cause you're always drawing and you let us play outside.'

'And you think that makes By—your daddy angry?' *Did Candy make him angry? Maybe she was too sweet—ack!*

She seems to think about it, for at least two seconds, then shrugs. 'He just looks at you all angry. Dunno why.'

Really? The man who *means what he says and says what he means*?

So what isn't he saying here?

~*~

I'd known in advance that today neither Byron nor Sally would be home for dinner. Consequently, it was a quiet affair, the twins tuckered out by their busy day, rounded off by a late afternoon walk and a trip to play on the gym equipment. After a bowl of mac and cheese, the comfort I found I craved myself, both children were bathed and asleep by seven. I watched them slumber a while, wondering why sleep made them look like cherubs from a Rubens painting. I stroked Edie's silvery hair, smiling as her rosebud mouth trembled around her thumb, marvelling at Matty's long silky eyelashes. Matty also has a hint of freckles appearing along the bridge of his tiny nose, spilling onto his chubby, baby-like cheeks. At the bedroom door, I turn once more, hoping that their dreams are sweet. I hoped they were dreaming of playing mermaids and friendly in the pool or dreaming of playing in the grass and dirt. I hoped they dreamed of their mother as I sometimes dreamed of my grandmother. With a twinge of hurt on their part, I recall they'll have no memory of her. Just photographs, like the ones on their dresser.

Their mother was strikingly beautiful. I see where Matty got his hair colour from. If he's extremely lucky, he'll have inherited his mother's high cheekbones. Warm eyes smile out from the picture frames, the images obviously taken so recently it seems so strange that the woman staring out at me is no longer here.

In one frame, she's standing in the snow, wrapped in a woollen hat and scarf, clutching the fur of her fluffy hood under her chin. In another, she's dressed for a wedding, a tiny hat of feathers worn stylishly to one side. And in a large silver frame is an image that's particularly poignant. One from the delivery room. Her smile is so wide in this one, her dark locks piled on the top of her head. In her arms, she holds two precious, wrinkled bundles, one with a wisp of silver hair, one with thatch of dark. Perfect babies, and one of each in more than one sense.

Whatever happened between the pair, they certainly made beautiful looking babies.

It's good that they have pictures. At least they'll know their mother's face. Know that she once held them in her arms, that she stared at them with wonder and joy. But they wouldn't remember. They wouldn't know what it felt like to be held close to her heart, or remember the shape of her face in their little hands. So much they won't know. I close the bedroom door, hoping they're dreaming of love.

As I make my way downstairs, I take a mental trip through the house, realising I can't remember seeing any photographs of their mother anywhere else.

How strange.

I halt halfway down, my hand on the thick balustrade, my mind not on the downstairs, but the upstairs. I wonder if Byron has a photograph in his bedroom? I've been here three weeks, but I haven't yet ventured into that hallowed space, either with or without an invite. I don't want to do so while the kids are home because you never know what's likely to come out of their mouths.

Dad, Miss Amber was sniffing your pillows in your bedroom today. Do you have a smelly head?

Not that I would . . . I don't think. I'm more likely to smell his cologne.

My heart bangs against my rib cage as I push on the door. I mean, it's not like he keeps it locked. Or even closed. I might've just been passing and tripped and fallen in. I snort at my ridiculousness, the snort turning to a giggle as I remember a night out with Emma and one of her friends who happened to be an ER nurse. She told us about her shift earlier that day, a sunny afternoon in June, when a guy walked into the department, very carefully I would've assumed. His problem? He had a cucumber stuck up his butt. How did it get there? Naturally, it was an accident—he tripped and fell onto a foot-long specimen while he was gardening.

Still sniggering, I step into the room. A large wooden framed bed dominates one midnight blue wall, flanked by matching nightstands. As I step closer, I run my hands over the cover. *A blue waffle weave.* Then I pull open the nearest nightstand's drawer. I'm not naturally nosy and don't exactly feel comfortable as I snoop, but it doesn't stop me taking a cursory look through all three drawers. *On both sides.*

But I'm not just being nosy for the sake of it.

I'm looking for evidence. Evidence of a sex life.

Condoms. Toys. That kind of thing.

As I imagine they'd say in a TV detective show, my search comes up clean. There are also no pictures of his wife. Not in or on the nightstands. Not sitting in frames on the tall set of drawers. A large TV hangs on the wall, a wing backed chair next to the French doors with shorts thrown carelessly over it. A dark rug on the wooden floor, the colour matching that of the comforter and walls. All are complementary tones of blue. It's a calming space, sure. Stylish, too. But very impersonal.

I freeze suddenly, worried I heard something downstairs. Maybe a door? But as I strain to listen again, I realise it's just my guilty conscience bothering me. Not that it stops me making my way into Byron's walk-in closet. Surprisingly, it isn't as organised as the bedroom. T-shirts spill from open drawers, shoes left in piles on the floor rather than put back in their places. I pull one open drawer a little wider to see beyond the spill of socks, finding a large open box of condoms. Is it wrong that I find myself a little pleased to know he doesn't store them in his bedside drawer? If they're hidden in *here*, he's not likely to be having sex in *there*. I close the drawer again, only to open it again approximately in the position I found it.

I wonder why a man would have such a large closet, one with racks and display cases, and other bits of storage deliciousness? And then it hits me. This wasn't just Byron's closet. *And the bedroom wasn't just his.*

A quick peek in the bathroom where I sniff his cologne and shampoo before I retrace my steps, leaving the door to his bedroom in the position I found it. I feel like such a shit as I make my way downstairs. I knew I'd feel like this, yet the knowledge didn't stop me.

Act in haste, repent at leisure! My grandmother's words echo in my head. *Few people care, the rest are just busybodies, Amber!*

Oh, man.

I hurry down the remainder of the staircase as I hear my phone ringing from the kitchen and manage to grab it before it rings out.

'Girl, I've been ringin' and ringin'.'

'Rose. Hi. Sorry, I was upstairs.'

'You are the only person I know who doesn't carry their phone *with* them. You know, it being a wireless and all?'

I refrain from answering that I'm probably *not* the only thirty-year-old who isn't permanently attached to their phone. I suppose I should be flattered that she sees me as someone closer to her age.

'The only thing I'm attached to is my teeth and my hair.'

'What?'

'Nothing. It was . . . nothing. How's the picking going?'

'Oh my God, it's so tough! But better than looking after kids.'

'You think?'

'My sister has four of 'em. I *know* so. How's things going over there?'

'Fine. Good, actually.' When I'm not feeling bad for snooping.

'Tomorrow night, you're not tied to the kitchen or babysitting or nothin'?'

'Nothing planned as far as I know. Why?'

'Sven's gonna pick you up in the van. We're going into town for a few beers and a dance.'

'Okay.' My one-word answer is filled with amusement. 'Thanks for asking. Or telling. Whatever.'

'Cool. Pick you up at seven? I have it on good authority that the waitstaff at the joints in town start clearing your table if you're not done by nine.'

'Ha-ha. Very funny.'

'I'm serious! And bring your own wine or whatever. I'm told they're also B-Y-O-B.'

'They're what?'

'Bring your own beer. Or wine. Or whatever. Something to do with the licensing laws or something.'

'Okay,' I answer doubtfully.

'Okay. Saturday night, lady!'

Chapter Sixteen

AMBER

I open a bottle of wine from the magic cabinet before picking my way through a half block of Margaret River cheese. *A cheese and wine party pour moi.* I spend the next hour flicking half-heartedly through TV channels I don't really see before forcing myself to go to bed. Sally texted earlier to ask if all was good on the home front. She also mentioned that Byron wouldn't be in until late. She's back on the property, though, at her little cottage out back, but she offered to stop in if I had plans.

Plans. Ha. Plans with my pyjamas maybe.

My mouth tastes metallic as I climb into bed, despite having brushed the taste of wine and cheese from my mouth thoroughly. I sigh then turn over. Then turn over again, extending a little violence to my pillows I do so.

Byron is out, probably painting the town red.

I'm not sure what I expected, but somehow, it wasn't this. And why? The man clearly isn't celibate. *See exhibit A in his sock drawer.* And it's not as if I can complain. Even if it is the magnificent Candy he's seeing tonight.

The room is dark, the blinds are open, but the moon is hiding behind the clouds, and there isn't a breath of air in the room.

That's what I get for leaving off the air conditioning.

But I've begun to prefer to leave the French doors open to the balcony and the evening, allowing the night breezes to blow in from the mountains, both cooling the room and bringing the scent of eucalyptus with them.

If he's out with another woman, you've only yourself to blame. You could've jumped him rather than pushed him away.

I could've. True. But it's not professional. And it's also wrong. Even if sometimes I catch Byron looking at me hotly. Or maybe with anger.

But, Lord, it's so hot. I don't think I'll ever get to sleep . . .

I stir sometime later, the sheet sticking to me. I push it off, turning in the effort to find a cooler patch of mattress when I roll into an even hotter body than my own. Hot, large, and naked, our skins fuse immediately in the heat of the room. Which would mean we're both . . . *naked?* And how? I went to bed in pyjamas—small pyjamas, but pyjamas all the same. But didn't I also go to bed alone?

'Byron?' My whisper breaks the silence of the room. I'm going to ask him what he's doing here— why we're naked, but all thoughts disappear—poof, gone!—out of my head as his large paw of a hand finds my shoulder in the darkness, rolling me once more onto my back. The sheet beneath us rustles as his body moves with mine, bringing with him the faint scent of soap and the strong musk of man.

And sex.

Did we already . . . ?

Between my legs seems to pulse with the memory. I guess that means . . . I need to stop drinking wine by myself in the evening.

'What are you doing here?' A bird screeches in the distance, cicadas humming like anticipation across my skin.

'I was sleeping.' His hushed tone is smooth like velvet and as dark as chocolate and sin. 'But you can wake me up anytime.' *Any-toy-m.* That accent—it hits me right where it shouldn't. 'Anytime you want to fuck.'

Harsh words and soft intentions, I feel myself melt across the bed as his shadow looms above me, blocking out the little light there is. His flat stomach next to my hip. Byron trails two fingers between the valley of my breasts, my breath becoming a staccato, stuttering thing as they travel over the soft swell of my belly before dipping between my legs. Like we've done this a million times before, my legs open, and he presses two fingers so deep inside me, I cry out.

'Shush, sweet girl.' His thumb bushes my clit, and I arch from the bed, this time my pleasure smothered by his mouth. I'm all gasping breaths and heaving chest as his fingers work me, and all grasping hands as I seek to hold this feeling, to hold him.

'Please. . . I want . . . ' I can't articulate my need, particularly as Byron adds a third finger, bringing with it such a swell of relief.

'That's it . . . you take my fingers. Make them good and wet.' His thumb pets my clit as his fingers fill me, and God, I want this. Want it all—am greedy for more, greedy for the feel of him inside—over me— and whether the shroud of the evening brings with it secrecy or whether it's plain selfishness, I place my hand on his shoulder, urging his body over mine. The press of him against my centre—the coarse hair on his thighs, and the sound of his rough sigh—I relish it all. Sliding my hand between us, I take him into my fist. He's long and so impossibly hard—satin over steel as I slide my hand over the length of him. Byron's forehead touches mine, his tight breaths, one, two, three, blowing over me as I work him in my hand.

'Put me inside, Amber.'

My pulse pounds everywhere as I widen my legs. We both shiver as I slide his head through my wetness, placing the fat crown were we both need it. I'm so ready from his fingers that my body offers no resistance as, with one thrust, he drives inside.

'That's so . . . *fuck*.' He doesn't need to tell me how illicitly perfect this is—the darkness, the sound of his strained breath, how my muscles tremble around him, taut and tense.

One second thrust, a solid third. A fourth with an accompanying growl before his movements become wild. The sound of skin against sweat-streaked skin, the sharp gusts of his breath and his rough groans in my ear drive me to climax almost instantly. His hands on my breasts—his mouth—my legs stretched impossibly wide across the bed. I feel him everywhere, consumed by him.

'I'm so fucking close,' he pants in my ear. 'Tell me I can come inside.'

The answer?

'Yes!' A thousand times yes—I want this, need it, primally. And I'm coming—so fucking hard—and so is he. Undulating, hips grinding, cursing, his palms planted firmly by the side of my head. I feel his pulse everywhere.

'Jesus, Amber, you're so fucking wet . . . ' I hear the pride in his words, or is it amusement. 'Are you sure you haven't peed yourself?'

'What?'

'Do you need to go?' His tone—it wasn't like that before. And what the fuck kind of question is that? And why does he sounds like a dad?

With a sharp breath, I sit straight in the bed, sweat-streaked, panting, and alone. I'm not naked. Well, not technically, even if much of my body is exposed. Yes, I'm wet, but I haven't peed the bed. *Thankfully.* My hands shake in the moonlight as I lift my breasts back into my tank top when a chink of light under my door catches my attention. There's a rustle and the sound of creaking floorboards. And whispers, one childlike and one deep.

Good God, did I wake the whole house getting myself off? In my sleep?

I don't move, I don't dare, not even to throw my head into my hands. Or my mortified self from the balcony.

A door opens. More rustling. More murmurs. Please say I haven't actually woken the whole house. *Of course, I haven't. I'm not that loud when I, you know. If my nocturnal activities were loud, surely someone would've pointed it out before now.*

Of course. You're being ridiculous.

A little more settled and a little less shivery, I grab my phone from the nightstand; it's a little after three. I don't feel the usual surge of excitement on realising I've woken but there are still hours of sleep ahead, strangely. In fact, I feel like I might never sleep again.

As voices travel past my room once more, I slip out of bed and pull the door into the hall ajar. Byron is pushing what look like Matty's sheets into the laundry chute as his son stands beside him, rubbing his eyes.

He's home. That shouldn't make my heart lift; just because he's home doesn't mean he hasn't had sex. *It also doesn't mean he has*, my mind whispers right back.

Gah. Pathetic!

'It's okay, little mate,' he murmurs.

'Go on, hop into my bed.' His broad back is bare, athletic shorts hanging low on his hips. Which means only one thing; Byron Phillips sleeps naked. Like my mind needed the extra detail.

'I dreamed I was on the toilet.' Matty sounds so forlorn, the poor kid.

'Everyone has bad dreams,' Byron replies, turning to reassure his son.

'Even Miss Amber,' a sleepy Matty replies with a nod. 'I hope monsters weren't chasing her in her sleep.'

'She'll be right,' he reassures him quietly. *She'll be roi-ght.* I inhale a sharp breath as, over the little one's head, Byron's darkened gaze finds my own. 'I reckon she was the one chasing something.'

His eyes never leave mine as I silently close the door. I might not have woken the household, but Byron heard.

I bring a shaking hand to my tight chest. So much for giving up wine with dinner. Tomorrow morning may find me pouring it on my cereal as well.

~*~

I wake at six. Who wakes at six on a Saturday? I'm not ready to face the day or Byron, but there's only so much a girl can do at this hour. I could sit on the balcony and listen to the birds. Take a long shower. Go for a swim. Pack my bags and run away. Crawl into a corner and die from mortification.

With a quick calculation, I decide to call Emma. She'll still be awake.

'Hey, it's the intrepid traveller!' Her exuberance and the beat of the music playing in the background suddenly makes me feel a little alone. Sun streams in through the window, and the lorikeets are doing their morning squawking. It's so weird, not only are our days reversed, but also the pace of our lives right now.

'Hey, buzzed Emma!'

'Guys, say hello to our own littlest hobo!' She calls, 'Amber's on the phone.'

There follows hoots and hollers, and one or two yells of *hi* from our mutual friends.

'I was just calling to catch up, but I'll let you go. We can do this later.'

'Oh no, you don't!' she decrees. 'I wanna know how things are down under. Did you get any didgeridoo yet?' She sniggers at her own joke. 'You know they're made from wood?'

'We all need a little wood in our lives,' offers one of our friends in the background. Aimee, maybe? 'Hey, scooch up,' Em demands. 'Imma take this call outside.'

Suddenly, the noise disappears and the call becomes clearer.

'How're you? Are you good? Did you meet Thor yet? Screw any prime Aussie man meat?'

Her eagerness makes me giggle a little. 'Not since my birthday.'

'Welp,' she says short sigh, 'that night was more fucking than most of us get in months.'

'It was more sex than *I'd* had in months, for sure. And about that. You know the job I emailed you about?'

'The one in the country in the café? Did you get it?' We haven't spoken since just after my birthday, and I'm not great at email. Mostly, I forget.

'I did, and I didn't. It turns out there wasn't a catering gig here, but they were looking for a nanny.'

'I thought you were done working with kids?'

'I'd have preferred a café, sure,' I agree. 'It would've been easier.'

Emma snorts. 'Says the girl who didn't experience the hospitality industry while at college. Waitressing blows, I told you that. Oh God, it's so cold out,' she says, her teeth beginning to chatter. 'But how many kids?'

'Two. Twins actually, super cute four-year-olds. But they aren't the issue.'

'So what *is* the issue?' She giggles a little drunkenly.

'The dad. It's him—the guy from the hotel.'

'Your birthday fuck?'

'Wait. I'm just going to hang up—I'm pretty sure I can hear you shouting from the other side of the world.'

'Oh my God!' she continues, her laughter stuttering down the line. 'Only this would happen to you, I swear!'

'Yeah, well, I swear I'm screwed.'

'You've screwed? Woo-hoo!'

'No, *I'm* screwed.' This phone call might not have been the best of ideas.

'He's married? I knew it—I knew a man like that had to be married.'

'No, he's not married,' I protest, but Emma isn't listening.

'Do I have to come over there and deliver a beat down? Don't tell me you're calling to say you're considering a sister-wife deal. No *D* is worth that, no matter how magical.'

'Em, calm down,' I say, laughing now. 'There's no dick sharing going on. He's not married. His wife died.'

'Did he kill her with the D? That would be some way to go.'

'Em, be serious. How much have you had to drink?'

'Raz is paying.'

'So . . . I'm guessing a lot?'

'Hush. Tomorrow's Saturday. I can stay in bed all day. Now, how old did you say he was?'

'I don't know. Mid-thirties, maybe?' I swallow back last night's confession, the words balancing on the tip of my tongue. I'm not telling tipsy Emma that I came so hard in my sleep last night that the whole district heard. She's likely to go back and regale the table with that tale.

'Oh, so not old. So? I don't see the problem?'

'There is no problem. It's just—'

'That he's handsome and has a magical unicorn dick? What're you lookin' at?' she adds a little aggressively. 'You got some advice for my girl here?'

'Em, who are you talking to?'

'I've got all the advice she needs here, baby.' Oh, God, she's engaging the local drunks by the sound of things.

'Em, what are you doing?'

'Now, why would she need your pencil dick when she has unicorn dick,' she protests sharply.

'Em,' I repeat louder. 'Go back into the bar. We can talk about this some other time.'

'Hey, babe, I'm going to go back inside before my nipples fall off.'

'Yeah, that sounds good idea.'

'Just one thing; you're on a big ole adventure right now. I say you make the most of all the things. You get what I'm saying?'

'Yeah, I do.' I do totally get what she's saying, even if drunk Emma is saying the opposite of what regular Emma would.

'You don't want a digeri that don't. You want a digeri that *do*. Love ya!' With one cackling bout of laughter, the line goes dead.

If it only it were that easy.

Chapter Seventeen

BYRON

'Where's your brother?' Hunched over her colouring book, Edie mumbles something unintelligible. 'What?'

'It's not what, it's pardon,' my daughter corrects.

'A thousand apologies, princess smarty pants.' I tug on one of her tiny pigtails. 'Since when have you been wearing your hair like this?'

'Since this morning,' she responds with the attitude of someone at least ten years older than she currently is. 'Miss Amber dided it for me.'

'Did,' I correct as I make my way over to the coffee pot. *Damn.* Not only is it empty but it looks like it also hasn't been on at all.

'Did what?' Edie looks up at me from her stool, crayon poised like a judge about to sign my death warrant.

'Miss Amber did your hair.'

'That's what I just said to you. Sometimes I fink you don't listen to me.'

'Oi, watch the attitude.'

Edie mumbles something again, returning to her colouring.

'Feeling a bit dusty this morning, are we?'

Mum's sharp tone causes me to turn to where she's standing in the doorway to the kitchen. 'That's supposed to be the kid's job,' I reply, gesturing to the egg basket in her hand.

'And that wasn't what I asked.'

'No, I wasn't dusty. I only had two glasses of wine over dinner. Why?'

'Your car wasn't in the driveway.'

'Am I on a curfew now?'

'Don't come the raw prawn with me, young man. You know fine well Amber was left looking after the kids last night.'

'I was back before midnight. Was there an issue?'

'Only that you hadn't the *n-u-t-s* to ask her if she had plans. You just assumed she'd be there at your beck and call. Typical *b-l-o-o-d-y* man.'

'Woah, woah, woah. What's rattled you this morning?'

'You have.' She puts the eggs basket on the kitchen bench, folding her arms across her chest. Evidently, she's less than pleased. 'I didn't know you had plans last night until I was already out at dinner with Marj. If I'd known you'd be *otherwise engaged*,'— Jesus, Edie isn't the only one full of attitude this morning—'I would've made sure Amber didn't have any plans before I went out myself.'

'I was in Sydney yesterday. I told you I had meetings.'

'Yes, well you usually stay over.'

But why would I want to stay away when the only woman I want sleeps under my roof these days?

'So your knickers are in a knot because . . . I didn't stay at a hotel?'

'Don't you talk about my knickers. You might be too big to put over my knee, but there are plenty other ways to skin a cat.'

'Skinny cat?' Edie pipes up.

'Next time you want to go galivanting,' she says, bustling from the room, 'remember, life isn't all about you.'

'I was at work,' I protest.

'Yeah, yeah,' comes her distant reply.

'Someone hasn't had her coffee this morning,' I find myself muttering.

'Tell me about it,' my daughter replies. 'I haven't had my coffee and biscuits this morning either.'

I pretend I haven't heard her complaint as I make my way upstairs.

Matty isn't in his room. I tell myself that's why I knock on the door to Amber's room.

'Come in.'

The door is ajar, so I push it a little wider. 'Have you seen Matty?' I ask, sliding my hands into the pockets of my shorts. But I don't need her to answer as I spot him curled under her arm. They're snuggled on her bed, a nest of pillows the only thing keeping Amber upright. *Sort of.* In her free hand, she holds Mat's favourite Winnie the Pooh book.

'I've been looking for you, bud.'

'Miss Amber was reading me a story.' My son nuzzles his face into her T-shirt, a lock of her fiery hair trapped between two of his pudgy fingers.

I lean my shoulder against the doorframe, thick emotion swirling through my insides. He looks at home there. Content. And I feel like an intruder to their time. Is that a ridiculous notion? Is it jealousy? Because I'm pretty sure she wouldn't welcome me crawling onto her bed to curl up on her other side.

No, I'm certain it's not jealousy, but it still feels odd, especially as she uses her thumb as a temporary bookmark as she turns her attention to me.

I wonder what she sees when she looks at me.

'I'm sorry about last night.' Her warm eyes blink innocently, though her cheeks take on an immediate pink hue. 'About being late home,' I qualify. I don't want her to think that I'm sorry about hearing her cry out. Hearing the unmistakable sound of her joy. Was she dreaming about me, I want to ask. But I won't.

'That's . . . okay,' she answers softly.

And if she was thinking about me, will she let me watch the next time? Let me taste?

Now who's fucking dreaming?

'You're sure? Mum's just chewed me out for not being home earlier. I was in Sydney. Meetings ran over, an early dinner. The usual sh—stuff.' I leave out the bit where I sat in manic traffic for hours rather than stay overnight in a hotel, because—

'You're a big boy, Byron.'

Excuse me for not being able to tamp back my smile. Actually, you know what? I don't want to, not if I get to see her blush like that.

'A big boy?' I shrug a little as though embarrassed, as though the title is a little too telling. *It's not.*

'You know exactly what I mean,' she answers quietly.

'I'm starting to feel like a pariah in my own home.'

'What?'

'Don't look so delighted,' I say, casting my gaze to the ground. 'Mum's got the shi—got the *s-h-i-t-s* with me, Edie's turned to a teenager overnight and decided her dad's a total dag.'

'A what?'

'It's the poo-ey, yucky fur hanging from a sheep's butt,' Matt whispers, holding his hand up against the wrong side of his mouth as he tells his secret. 'Pooey Dad!' he adds giggling.

'That must be why no one wants to hang out with me. Do I smell?' I make a show of sniffing my pits.

I think I might be winning as Amber's gaze narrows, and she collapses the book against her chest.

'What is it you want, Byron?'

To be part of bed and story time?

'Some company. Wanna go to the park, little fella?' When in doubt, use bribery.

'Yes!' Matty begins to bounce. 'Yes, yes, yes! You'll come, too, won't you, Miss Amber?'

'You go on with your dad, Matty. We can finish this story anytime.' Without looking at Matt or me, she places the book down.

When in doubt, use bribery. And not just against your kids.

'You want Amber to come?' He nods vigorously, his expression lightening. Yep, me too, little mate. 'Look at his little face. You can't say no to that. I'll bet Edie would love you to come, too. Come on, I'll even shout you ice cream.'

'You'll shout for ice cream?'

'I'll *shout* you one—ice creams are on me.'

'Yes!' cries Matty with a little fist pump as Amber rolls her eyes . . . and concedes.

And what a shame—Mum says she's too busy to come along.

The park is a child jackpot, and though the twins are always keen to go, we don't go often. Usually because I tell myself they have enough stuff to play on at home. Not to mention acres and acres of land. But we don't have a splash pad, which is the first thing the kids head for, despite—dad fail—not being dressed for it. And the kids are playing there alone as I follow Matt under an arc of water over to a water cannon made from colourful piping. Amber squeals as the cold water hits her. Turns out I've a pretty good aim.

Or course, she doesn't take the soaking lying down. Her and the kids gang up to make sure she's not the only one dripping wet.

Tired from laughing and still soaking wet, we lay out in the grass to let the sun warm and dry us as I try not to stare at Amber's nipples threatening to poke an eye out.

The kids chatter happily about wallabies and cakes and swim lessons and bloody cookies while I stare at Amber lying against the grass, eyes closed, a small smile on her face. She really is beautiful. In fancy dresses. In shorts and Converse. In nothing at all.

Then it is on to the playground; a large spider web climber, a slippery dip painted to look like a snake, swings, every possible thing to exhaust a small family. For all intents and purposes, I think that must be what we look like from the outside. A thought confirmed by an old dear who sits herself on the bench next to us.

'Children are such a blessing,' she says, watching her grandson play with Matt. 'You made some beautiful bubs, darl,' she says, patting Amber's knee affectionately. I reach for Amber's hand, squeezing it against her burgeoning protestation. I'm not sure why. Maybe because, for the moment, I want the illusion of our family being real. Whatever the reason, I don't get to dwell as the woman carries on with a saucy wink. 'I bet number three's a bluey, eh? I'll just bet you're doing plenty of practising.'

'I . . . ' Amber's gaze moves between us, confused and maybe a little shocked. Thankfully, the question she asks is, 'What's a bluey?'

'A redhead.' God love her sweet, confused face. 'Another piece of madness for your Aussie dictionary.'

'You haven't heard that one before?' the oldie asks, but before she can add anything else, her gaze snags on the playground. 'Tyrone, you put that little girl down. Not on her head!' With a tut and an eyeroll and a muttered complaint of *why an earth couldn't they have called him Peter or something*, she dashes off in the direction of the playground.

'You've never called me Bluey.' I can feel the touch of her curious gaze, but I don't turn to her. Instead, I tighten my fingers over hers. *I'm holding the nanny's hand because I want to. And I don't give a fuck who might see.*

'It's sort of generic Aussie speak.' My shoulder rises in a careless shrug. There's nothing generic about her. 'You've always been Red to me.'

The moniker rolls from my tongue like the most decadent of treats. Sweet, almost sinful, instantly melting away. Fleeting, like the idea we could be anything but what we are.

Employer. Employee.

She's leaving soon, my mind supplies. *Don't get attached.* So I do what I've done since she arrived. *Swallow the words back.*

'Always Red?' she questions, her knowing tone causing me to turn to her now.

'Just because I haven't said it since'—*since the pool*—'doesn't mean I'm not thinking it.'

'What else are you thinking?' Colour suffuses her cheeks, like she hadn't meant to say anything.

'Stuff that would turn your hair from red to blue. Or grey, at least. You're not the only one plagued by dreams.'

Her gaze is melted, liquid copper, and her lips soft. I want to pull her onto my knee and make her mouth mine. My body's reaction is purely visceral—I'm hard immediately, my heart softened by her clear and honest gaze. But as a father, acting on these impulses here, by the children's playground, would be all kinds of fucked up.

'*Daddeee!*' Edie comes barrelling towards us, unheeding of the fact that Amber's hand is in mine. She lands between us, her arms spread out across our knees. 'Is it time for ice cream?'

The sun is setting by the time I park the truck at the side of the house. The twins, though half asleep and after munching practically the whole afternoon, rouse themselves enough for food.

'You can't be hungry, surely. Have you got hollow legs or something?' The pair nod solemnly before climbing onto a kitchen stool each. 'Seriously?'

'We haven't had lunch,' Edie complains, even as she yawns.

'We did have lunch,' Matty says, turning to his sister. Atta boy, Matt. 'It's dinner we haven't had.'

'Do you two count meals or something?'

I offer the pair cheese and vegemite on toast, and they counter with cheesey-mite scrolls *that Miss Amber made*, along with a glass of milk and as they tuck in, I realise Amber isn't in the kitchen. It's not that I expected her to make them dinner, but I thought . . . whatever. I'm acting like a teenage girl. Maybe she's just gone to change.

There's a note on the fridge from Mum which says she's out for dinner, so I pull open the fridge to survey the contents. The kids might've spent the day grazing, but I'm hungry. I pull out a couple of steaks—my culinary repertoire isn't great—and open a bottle of wine to let it breathe.

'Right, upstairs you two. Shower time.' As the pair leave the kitchen under a wave of complaints, Amber is coming back in. 'You've changed,' I say with a smile I couldn't contain even if I wanted to. Dark, tight jeans and a white button-down, her hair curling around one shoulder like a—'

'Miss Amber, your hair looks like a mermaid!' Edie exclaims.

And her lips are suspiciously pink.

'You didn't need to dress for dinner.'

'Oh.' Her expression clouds, her expression quickly replaced by a grimace. Then I realise she's holding a pair of shoes in her hand.

Fuck me, I'm slow on the uptake.

'You've got plans,' I say, clapping my hands together like a total prick. 'Course you have. It's Saturday night.' Rather than avuncular, which I think was what my fucked-up brain seemed to think was a good idea, my words come off as bitter.

'Is . . . is that okay? I mean, you don't need me tonight or anything, do you?'

'No, no. Of course not.'

'Okay, well, I'm going into town with Rose and the guys I travelled here with.'

'That'll be the lot that dumped your pack on the doorstep before fucking off.'

'I told you about that,' she answers softly. Soft but not subdued. In fact, her gaze is fiery and not a little pissed off. 'They didn't leave me exactly.'

'Ah, okay. My misunderstanding. I didn't realise that them driving off wasn't them leaving you.'

'Okay!' she answers brightly. 'I'll leave you to your evening.'

She turns a little violently, making her way down the hall.

'Wait, Amber.' As quick as a flash, I'm behind her, my hand on her shoulder as she turns.

'What?'

'I-I had a good time today.'

Her eyes soften, her chest moving with some semblance of a smile. 'Me, too.'

'I know I might not always seem so, but I'm really happy you're here.'

As she opens her mouth to answer, a car horn sounds obnoxiously outside. 'That'll be my ride.'

'Is that them?' My tone is incredulous as she steps out into the warm night, leaving me on the threshold. And why the fuck have I followed her? *Because I want to see what the competition looks like.* The competition for her company, I mean, not for anything else. And the competition looks like . . . 'Are they even old enough to drink? Look at the bum fluff baby beard on him. And that one with the dreadlocks looks like a fucking drug dealer.'

'Shush, they'll hear you.' Her words quiver with laughter.

'Fuck me. You're really blowing me off for a night with that lot?' I gesture to the battered camper, something that looks like a throwback to the nineties.

'I didn't know a night with you was on the table.'

For a moment, my heart stops, the blood in my body heading south at her tone. Is she . . . giving me the come on?'

'What if that's what I'm offering you now?' A night with me. On the table. The bed. The fucking floor!

'Raincheck?' she asks, in the same flirtatious tone. 'I already have plans.'

As the camper door creaks closed, one of the fucking twelve-year-olds hangs out the passenger window.

'Cool tats, man!'

The thing backfires, exhaust fumes polluting the air as it pulls away, and I'm left at the door wishing I'd warned her to watch for strange men slipping gear in her drink, while looking like a total knob-job.

Chapter Eighteen

AMBER

It's morning, the sun is shining, the birds are chirping. I need coffee, sunglasses, and a gun.

'Urgh.' Why did I say yes to that final drink? Dragging myself upright, I rub the heels of my hands against my eye sockets. Rookie. Error. Always refuse the last round, Amber! Did college teach you nothing?

But this is what happens when you have a boring, boring night.

After spending time with grownups, with Sally and dare I even say it, Byron, I'd forgotten how hard it sometimes is to relate to millennials.

Memes are always a good talking point. And funny cat videos. But the rest? It's kind of difficult. Even the places we've visited mean different things.

For instance, visiting Thailand. I got to help build a new school, which was super rewarding and made me feel good about myself. Meanwhile, Lars enjoyed drinking so much in Kho Tao he blacked out.

Just give me good conversation and a nice glass of wine.

And don't ask me to go to the pub with you again. *Ugh!*

Post Shower Update:

Upon reflection, my travelling friends are nice.

They just happen to be a little young.

I need to think nicer thoughts about them and remember they were good enough to invite me out last night. And good enough to drive me here all the way from Sydney.

The least I can do is hang out with them.

I think my opinion was coloured by how different Byron was yesterday.

I didn't want to leave him in the evening. I wanted to stay and drink his amazing wine. I wanted to spend time with him, possibly spend time with him inside me . . .

And I'm really happy I don't keep a diary right now.

Chapter Nineteen

BYRON

Being distracted while I'm working is not typically an issue I have. I've done time in just about every position there is in the company, from picking grapes as a kid to dabbling in the science of winemaking, to selling our product into multinational markets. Family always come first in my life, but Riposo Estates is a close second. And as I raise my family, my business is honed to the finest detail. There has never been an occasion when I couldn't keep my eye on the ball. Even when Katya was sick, and when she passed, I was back to work the same week. Maybe not full days but I had the kids to think of, even if they were too little to fully comprehend they'd just become motherless.

So I'm busy—always busy—whether I'm in the office or not, and I'm as focussed as any man running a multimillion-dollar business would be. An average day for me is one where I work fifteen hours and still get to spend time with the kids. I work before they're awake, and I work after they go to bed, dealing with stock projections and emails, and communicating with other time zones. There's always some fire to put out or some deal to be made or someone who needs a piece of my time. And I thrive on the chaos of the week—it's where I'm at my best.

Or at least it was.

Slipping my fingers from the bridge of my nose, I try to refocus on the email in front of me. I've read it three times so far without absorbing a word. My focus shot—it has been all day—so I give in. Give up for the day. And as the screen in front of me blackens, I lean back in my chair with a groan.

Over these past two weeks or so, I've found myself being much less productive. I'm still working like a fucking Trojan, but my mind is often someplace else than it should be.

Meaning my mind is often on Amber.

Especially after watching her walk out the door Saturday night.

It's not like she was dressed provocatively or that she came home late. Or drunk or smelling of sex. And if she had, would it have been any of my business?

Fuck, yeah, it would have been my business.

Despite what I've been trying to tell myself, I feel like she's mine. And the thought of anyone putting their grubby mitts on that pristine skin? It makes me feel fucking ropeable.

Why her? Why now?

She makes that big house feel like a home again, which is strange to say as I've always thought of it as my home, whether I lived there or not. Truthfully, I think the last time it truly felt like home was when I was a kid. Ma was a lot like Amber back in those days. Always around, filling the place with love . . . along with her threats of a wooden spoon to the back of the legs. She helped Dad run the business, sure, and when the place passed onto them fully upon the death of my grandfather, she injected a good deal of her inheritance into it. She's as much a part of this place as anyone. She was feisty—still is—but she made that big old house a place of comfort for her family. Mum has never been any great shakes in the kitchen, but what she could do was make an outstanding breakfast and usually made enough to feed the five thousand. Unless she burnt it first, though that was usually Dad's fault.

How the fuck did I only just remember that?

He was the source of many a ruined breakfast, dragging Mum off into the laundry under the pretext of "needing her help with something". I was about twelve before I realised the thing Dad needed help with was likely his dick. I think it was also around this time that Flynn discovered Dad's code, too, only he wasn't quite so lucky. He went looking for a clean school shirt or something one day, only to find Mum sitting on the washing machine with Dad between her legs. At the age he was, he didn't know exactly what they were up to, but he knew he never wanted to see it again. He still brings it up to this day just to see Mum blush, I'm sure. Meanwhile, Rafferty likes to tease that the event has somehow repressed Flynn's sexuality, which is clearly not true given he married a pornographer.

Piklets. God, I loved it when the house smelled of piklets from breakfast. More recently, Mum makes pancakes for the kids, which is essentially the same thing, I think. Some days, when I got home from school, the smell of chocolate cake or Anzac biscuits would greet me at the door, ready for afternoon tea. There's something about coming home to the smell of baking. Something welcoming. Something that fills holes you didn't know were there, and I'm not talking about filling the holes in your stomach but maybe the battle-worn patches of your soul.

Jesus, since when have I been such an introspective bastard? And if I grew up with this, why do I find myself resenting Amber for making my house feel like a home? Because I do. Not every day, but some days. I worry about how well she's fitted into the place and how it'll make the kids feel when she's gone?

You keep tellin' yourself you're only worried about the kids, fuckup.

Maybe I should've just hung out for a professional nanny and not been so short-sighted. It would've benefitted the kids better in the longer term. Because if she hadn't stayed, I wouldn't be sitting here wondering what deliciousness will be in the kitchen tonight. And I wouldn't be wondering if she's wearing shorts or one of those fucking sundresses. Or if her hair is in braids or a bun, or if my daughter will have insisted on wearing her hair the same. Or if my son had adopted another of her mannerisms. Yesterday, when I asked him if he wanted avocado on his toast at breakfast, he answered *yes, sir*. He's four years old, for Christ sakes. He's not in the fucking military.

And if I'd hired a professional nanny, I wouldn't keep finding myself staring at her. Thinking about that tiny catch in her breath as I'd slid into her. Wondering what it'd be like to greet her daily with a kiss, dreaming of being the man leading her into the laundry room on a whim.

I push the thoughts and the questions away along with the ache deep in my stomach. I'll go home. Take myself off upstairs and into the shower. I'll wash my need for her from my body, watching it swirl away with the strain of the day.

She's not for me. None of them are. Besides, she's leaving soon.

I close my eyes tightly and reopen them, trying once again to refocus but with little effect. Leaving my office, I walk down to where Dave-o is smoking with one of the maintenance crew. I wave to him as I pass, not in the mood for talking. I feel a bit untethered right now, unsure of my intentions as I head to the house. *Maybe I'll cook an early dinner.* We haven't cooked a meal together in a while. It'd be a good distraction. Keep my mind busy, plus it's good for the kids. Matty always likes it when I fire up the barbie, and Edie enjoys choosing what to add to the salad, even if she can be a bit experimental at times. *The cherries weren't so bad. Pity I can't say that for the anchovies.*

I enter through the side door, sure the twins will be finishing their allotted tech time, when I'm hit with the scent of gingerbread. And the kitchen? It's a wreck. Flour, sugar, dishes, and pans seem to cover every surface. What a fucking tip.

Amber and the kids appear from the patio, our eyes meeting over the expanse of kitchen. I register her surprise, the hitch in her breath before the light in her eyes quickly dulls as she come to the realisation, quite correctly, that I'm in a foul mood. I'm absolutely pissed off—I was before I even took a step in through the place, not that she'd know, but it's like my mood has intensified. Maybe it's the mess or maybe it's the way the kids are hanging off her every word. Maybe it's the smiles on their faces, or maybe it's because I just need to get fucking laid, but not even my offspring's delight at my arrival take a bite out of it.

'Daddy looks cranky,' Matty whispers, sotto voce.

Daddy's spewin', more like.

'Why is it, whenever I come home these days, I feel like I'm walking into a bloody Hansel and Gretel story?'

'Does that make me the witch?' she asks blandly.

'Dad, we made cookies! 'Cause when we came back from yesterday, you'd eaten 'em all.'

Yeah, so? That's what happens when the whole family abandons me, leaving me to my own devices. Fuck, I have turned into a teenage girl—one who eats her feelings.

Instead of saying any of that, I mutter, 'Biscuits,' under my breath. Cookies, my arse. They're called biscuits. 'Looks more like the site of an explosion than a kitchen,' I add, surveying the mess with a critical eye. Anything other than look at Amber.

'Sorry about that,' Amber-Poppins says with her indifferent air. 'We were just getting some fresh air. I wasn't expecting you until later.'

'So this is how the kitchen always looks?'

'Not always,' she replies lightly. 'Sometimes it looks even worse.'

'Is that supposed to be funny?'

'I thought so.' Now it's her turn to mutter under her breath as she begins to move the edible creations into containers.

'Did the kids get their chores done today?' If I was expecting this to take the smile from her face, I'm mistaken.

'Mostly,' she replies with an untroubled shrug.

Scraping my hand across my jaw, I turn to the kids. 'Why don't you go draw a picture for Nana, you two.'

'What should we draw?' asks Matty. I'm guessing *I don't fucking know* is not the answer. 'Daddy, why are you such a cranky pants today?'

From the other side of the kitchen, Edie sniggers, neither of my offspring paying any attention to my suggestion.

'Go on, off you go. Daddy needs Amber's help with something, and that's not code, by the way.' Who am I kidding, and who the fuck am I disputing this with? I could think of a million things she could help me with. Right now, the feel of her arms around my waist would probably make me feel a little more sane.

'Code?' Matty's expression is perplexed. Meanwhile, my temper is hanging on by a fucking thread.

'I have an idea,' Amber interjects. She stands by the sink as soapy water rapidly fills it. 'Why don't you both go and draw a picture of what you think Nana's hair will look like when she gets back from the salon?'

'I think she'll be getting pink stripes.' Edie cackles.

'Or dinosaur blue,' suggests Matt as the pair make their way into the other room.

'The kid's schedule,' I begin once they've gone. 'You either did or you didn't get everything done.'

'We moved a few things around,' she non-answers, beginning to pile the dishes into the hot water. 'And the kids really wanted to bake.'

'The kids did, or you did?' I demand.

'Oh, I always want to bake. Baking is like therapy.'

'I've told you they need structure. Not therapy.'

'And I've told you, baking *is* structured. Actually, it's an exact science, even if they're a little young to understand that right now. It teaches literacy and math as well as motor skills.' She sounds like she's reciting information at a parent-teacher meeting. I don't want to hear rote words—I want her to agree with me. Or maybe I want her to get on her knees for me.

'I'm sure I don't need to tell you that the first five years of their lives are the most critical in terms of development.' My tone is snide on purpose. If anger won't sway her attention, maybe nastiness will. 'And you're just filling them up on chocolate and sugar. They're never going to use this stuff.' As she turns, I gesture to the mess with my hand. 'Not in real life!'

'I do, all the time.'

'And see how far that has gotten you!' It was a low blow, and one she certainly felt. Or maybe that's just my own wishful thinking, because yes, I meant to lash out.

With her back to me now, Amber places on final mixing bowl in the full sink before beginning to load silverware into the dishwasher. I can see her reflection in the window. She looks so calm. So unconcerned. So fucking uninterested.

And me? I'm spewin'. In the face of her indifference and industry, the pressure in my jaw is matched only by that building between my ears. Whatever plans I had about coming home early are gone, quickly replaced by irrational anger, and it's got fuck all to do with the flour on the countertops, or the sugar under my shoes, and it's got even less to do with the state of the kitchen, and everything to do with the fact that I want her to look at me. Just look—right now, I'd forgo everything else I want for a tiny morsel of interest.

'Byron, what is it you want from me?' she asks quite suddenly.

The sink is full of dishes, her arms submerged to the elbow almost. It makes me think of that night. Of the hotel. Of how her arm had draped over the bathtub as she'd held her champagne glass by the rim. Of how beads of water glistened against her skin, at least, what I could see of it, the tub filled almost to the rim with soapy bubbles. She'd looked blissfully happy, her head resting back against the porcelain, the humidity creating little curls in her hairline.

Then her toes rose through the mound of bubbles, a surprising glimpse of bare wet skin. Toes. Then an ankle. Then a knee. It was the most erotic thing I've ever seen.

And that, as they say, seems to be the straw that broke the camel's fucking back.

Enough.

I close my eyes and pinch my nose once again. 'I need you to look after the kids till Mum comes home because I'm going out.'

~*~

'What are you doin' here?' Tom asks from behind his desk. I still find it weird to see him sitting on that side of the desk, given all the years we found ourselves on this side wearing contrite looks on our faces.

'Did the school buy a job lot of this paint?' I ask, closing the door behind me. 'It's been this green for fucking years.'

'It's got nothing to do with me, mate. Bureaucracy picks the colour. I just have to stare at it. Did we have something planned today 'cause if so, I've completely spaced it.'

'Nah, nothing, I'm just off to the pub.' I lean my arm on the ancient filing cabinet as Tom makes a show of looking at his watch.

'On a Monday?'

'Stop fucking around.' We both know he's going to say yes. I'm grateful I'd noticed his car still in the school carpark as I passed, or I'd be going to the pub on my own. If you call on Tom at home unannounced, you never know who you're gonna find or in what state of dress.

'Go on then, you've twisted my arm.'

Without bothering to pack anything up, he picks up his phone. We drive separately the two blocks over to O'Grady's, a small pub on the corner of the main drag through town.

'What's on your mind?' Tom asks, once two cold ones are set before us. 'I haven't seen you in weeks.'

'Why does there have to be something on my mind?' I bring the glass to my mouth, refusing to look at him.

'Because I'm usually the one having to drag you out, not the other way around. It's not Becci again, is it?'

My head whips around. 'What makes you ask that? Have you heard anything?'

'Is there something to hear?' Tom's expression is uncharacteristically guarded. I can't be sure if he means business or something else.

'That's what I'm asking you. I haven't seen her since I was in Sydney last month.'

'Did the pair of you root?'

'What makes you think I'd tell you if we'd fucked?'

' 'Cause I'm the bloke who hears your confessions. And, mate, there haven't been many of them lately. What have you been up to?'

'You mean, who have I been up? Not Becci, that's for sure.'

'Good call,' he replies, taking the first mouthful of his beer. 'Especially after the last time.' I lean my forearms on the bar—it's early and it's clean, thank fuck—and my right boot on the brass rail.

'How's the family?'

'Kids are good. Mum is in rare form, as usual. Flynn and Chas are coming out for a holiday soon.'

'The lady pornographer? Reckon she'll give me a mate's rate subscription?' he asks with a comical leer.

'I reckon Flynn will knock you the fuck out if you go anywhere near her. Besides, her films are probably a little art house for your tastes.'

'What's that supposed to mean?' Tom's tone drips with fake aggrievement. He's like the little boy who never grew up, though without the tights and little green hat. I have no fucking idea how he came to be principal at the local high school.

'I should imagine your tastes run more to forced deep-throating and anal.'

'Get a room,' Charlie, the ancient barman grumbles as he passes on the other side of the wooden bar top.

'I would, Charlie, mate,' Tom retorts, 'but he can't take dick like you do.'

'Watch it,' Charlie answers as he fills another customer's schooner from the tap. 'Or you'll be ingesting your next beer like an enema.'

'You say the sweetest things,' Tom coos as Charlie passes once again. This time, Charlie doesn't bite, but he glowers.

'Getting back to it,' Tom begins, turning to me. 'I suppose you'd know all about it because you've watched.' I don't reply or even smile, though maybe I should, just to annoy him. Instead, I just take another mouthful of beer. 'Women centric, you said. If you ask me, that sounds like pussy licking. What's not to like about that?'

'Keep your voice down. Seriously, how do you keep your job?'

'I've got a magic touch,' he replies with a wink.

'If that means you're screwing someone in the Department of Education, I don't want to know.'

'Probably for the best. And how's the nanny going?' Something in his tone sets me on edge.

'I didn't tell you we had a new nanny,' I say, straightening from the bar.

'No, Sally did. Of a fashion.' He shrugs, then scratches his nose but doesn't offer further details. *Bastard.*

'Meaning?'

'Just what I told you. That you'd hired a new nanny. A lovely American redhead, she said.' Each of his words provokes a reaction. The hairs on my neck begin to stand. My jaw getting tighter. The knot of tension coils in my stomach as my foot comes off the railing and I stand.

'You stay the fuck away from her.'

'That's pretty much what she said.' His words hit the air with a dark chuckle. 'Only she was a bit more frightening.'

'I'm warnin' you. If you want to keep your teeth, you keep your fuckin' hands to yourself.'

'Course, mate.' He pulls his phone from his pocket, beginning to mess about with it. 'Might not have to, though. Not if you haven't been able to seal the deal yourself.'

'What's that supposed to mean?'

'Just this.' Tom sets the phone down in front of me, the darkened screen flickering to life. And there. Is a picture. Of Amber.

It's just a picture of Amber. Dancing. Having fun. On Saturday night. There's nothing too untoward or salacious about the photograph, so why does my heart feel like it's beating out of my chest? And why do I feel like ripping Tom's dick off and shoving it down his throat.

'You're a fuckin' creep,' I retort, sliding the phone back across the bar.

'And you're not fucking that.'

I turn to face him. 'Fuck you.'

'Thanks for the offer, but I like pussy, By, not dick. You know that. Just look at the young bucks hanging around her.' In the photograph, Amber's sitting at a table with at least eight other blokes. Young ones, sure. But they're old enough to fuck.

'What the fuck am I doing sitting here with you?'

'I take it that one was rhetorical.' Tom doesn't look up from his glass. 'Or did you mean, what are you doing here with me when you could be at home doing the nanny?'

'This one's on me.' I throw a twenty on the bar, clapping my hand on his shoulder on my way out.

Thanks, Tom, I don't say, even though he's hit the nail on the head.

Chapter Twenty

AMBER

'Nighty-night, Miss Amber.'

'Night, kids,' I answer for the seventh time. I've made it as far as the doorway, having read them two stories already. Byron never seems to have any problem putting them to bed, but they've pretty much run rings around me.

My hand is on the light switch as the next question hits.

'When will Daddy be home?' Matty asks in a voice that sounds a little sad.

In the weeks that I've been here, Byron has been home to put them to bed every night. Well, except Friday. I'm a little worried that his not being here right now might be the result of me poking a growling daddy bear.

It took every ounce of my self-restraint not to give in Saturday night, not to turn on my heel and slam the door on Rose and the guys. Because those looks he was dishing out at the park? Pure dynamite. And then tonight, he goes and spoils it all by coming home and acting like a total dick!

Right now, I feel like I'm in a Katie Perry song.

'Miss Amber?'

'Yes, honey? Oh, your dad. I'm sure he won't be long now.' Switching off the light, I pull the door closed. 'Sweet dreams.'

Downstairs, I run into Sally, who hasn't been around this evening up until now.

'Amber. Just the person I was looking for. Have you got five minutes to help me?'

'Sure.'

'Thanks, darl.' As I reach the bottom of the stairs, she thrusts an aerosol can in my direction. *Wasp and Hornet Spray*, the can reads. *Kills the entire nest! Kills Wasps and Hornets on Contact*

I groan internally. First, I had to deal with a mean Byron and now stinging insects. This is turning out to be a shitty day.

'Is that okay?'

'Great. No problem,' I manage, though without an ounce of enthusiasm.

We spend thirty minutes outside drenching the nests that are tucked under the eaves of both the house and the outdoor entertainment area. Sally assures me that we'll stay clear of being stung, but what do you know? I don't, despite the majority of the inhabitants dropping to the ground like the helicopter seeds off a sycamore tree. One black and yellow ninja bursts through the poisonous spray, exacting its revenge on the back of my shoulder.

'Ow. Shit!' I drop the can, the sudden stinging pain taking me by surprise. I don't think I've ever been stung by a wasp before—especially not an

Aussie steroidal enhanced one. Okay, so I might be exaggerating a touch, but redheads have more pain receptors than most folks. It really does hurt!

Slapping the beast away, Sally exacts revenge, spraying it to the ground. Tears prick behind my lids, my whole mood plummeting down a few notches farther. I don't cry, but I want to. In fact, I want to storm away like a temperamental teenager because this evening blows. Instead, I silently grab a broom and take my frustration out on the dead bugs and nest debris, pursing my lips to keep my grumbling thoughts from tumbling out because dammit, pest control was not in my remit, lady!

'We're all good,' Sally decrees once the great wasp massacre of November is deposited in the trash. 'Thanks for your help, love.'

'S'okay.' So long as I can leave now.

'There's some *Sting Goes* in the cupboard above the fridge,' she tells me as she turns away. 'It'll take the bite out of that sting. Night, love.'

'Sure, thanks. Night, then. Oh, Sally!' She turns. 'Your hair looks good.'

'You are a sweetheart,' she returns, patting her new ash-blond do.

I make my way across the patio as Sally's footsteps draw away. At one end of the pool, I decide on another remedy for the pain in my shoulder and, hopefully, my mood. Opening the glass pool fence, I loosen the button of my shorts, slide them down my legs, and pull my tank top off. Within seconds, I'm diving into the deep end of the crystal pool. I won't stay long—not when I'm still in charge of the little ones—just long enough to cool the sting and cheer myself up, maybe loosen the toxic cloud from my head. *And I don't mean just the wasp spray.*

I swim a couple of lengths staying mostly under the water, relishing the feeling of air building in my chest, and the subsequent gulps of oxygen I take as I reach the surface. On my fourth or fifth length, I break the surface once again and reach for the pool edge with a suitable mix of tiredness and exhilaration. My fingers grasp the still warm coping tiles as I use my free hand to wipe water from my eyes. Vision cleared, it falls on a pair of bare feet. Attached to jeans. Jeans attached to a dark T-shirt, colour swirling from one arm.

'It's not quite a midnight swim.'

'It's not even an eight o'clock swim,' I reply, twisting water from my hair one handed. Silence settles between us as I suddenly remember I'm not wearing appropriate swimwear. I glance down at my cotton bra, immediately seeing the problem— immediately and literally.

Cool water, nipples, and cotton are not a modest threesome.

I swear I didn't think this would be a problem. Swimming in my underwear wasn't meant to provoke him. For one, he wasn't home. And for two, the way he left showed he wanted to be anywhere I wasn't.

'You're a real water baby, aren't you?'

'I used to swim a lot at school as a kid. Play water polo, that kind of thing. Byron?' I add, 'I kinda can't get out of the pool.'

'Course you can,' he replies, thrusting a hand in my direction. 'Here, let me help you.'

'No,' I answer, swatting his hand away with a smile. 'I can get out of the pool, just not while you're standing there.'

'Because?'

'If you *must* know, I'm swimming in my underwear.'

I'll credit him as attempting to restrain his smile. 'And I say again because . . . ?'

'Because I was helping your mother get rid of the wasp's nests—'

'And she got you stung?'

'I'm pretty sure the wasp stung me,' I mumble, crossing my arm over my chest because he can probably see a little too much from where he's standing. 'Are you gonna stop staring?'

'No.'

'That's not very gentlemanly.'

'I think we already established I'm no gentleman. In fact, I think we've established that fact a couple of times, if my memory serves.'

'You're so . . . exasperating!' The words burst from my throat, his resulting smile languid and seductive.

'I'm exasperating?' he grumbles. 'Well, you're driving me crazy.'

'Oh, because you're pure sweetness and light, right?'

'Too bloody right!'

'Oh . . . go away!'

'Nah, I think I'll wait for you to get out of the pool.' He folds his arms across his broad chest, his expression resolute and, unless I'm mistaken, amused.

He's getting a kick out of annoying me, and that just makes me—urgh!

'For goodness sa—why?'

'Because we can't keep on like this, dancing around this.'

Wait, what? Is he for real?

A small part of me wonders if this is it—is he going to fire me while I'm wet and bedraggled? Or even in the pool? Because it'll be hard to be dignified from either of those positions—but a larger part tells me that's not where this is at. My heart beats a mile a minute as I wait for his answer, but he's right, we can't go on like this. I'm not sure how much longer I can hold out, for one. I might just resort to throwing myself at him without being sure that's really what he wants.

'I'm beginning to get cold.'

'So get out.'

'Are you going to turn your back?' This sounds more like a demand than a request.

'Well, I could. Or you could get out while I watch.'

'And why would I do that?'

'Because you want me to. Because I want to. And because I'm sick and tired of being in a bad mood.'

'I don't see what that has to do with me,' I reply softly. 'I haven't done anything.'

'That's the point,' he says, those brilliant blue eyes burning down at me. 'You say nothing, and you think you're keeping your secrets, but you're not.' As his words echo the whispers of my dreams, those both awake and asleep, my heart begins to pound. 'There's no shame in feeling desire. No shame in acting on it.'

'Are those words for you or for me?'

'Maybe us both.'

'I don't know who you are or what you've done with bad mood Byron, but I'm getting out of the pool now, so I think you'd best turn around.' He smirks, but then he does so, and I use my arms to push myself up and out of the water, landing on my butt with a *slap*.

'I brought you a towel.'

Tilting my head over my shoulder, I watch him pull it from the glass fence, appreciating the sight of his kindness. Heck, I appreciate the hell out of him. The gold of his hair. The broad expanse of his back. The flash of colour from under his sleeve. The taut muscles of his ass. And every single part of him turns my body into a traitor. My nipples resemble small rocks and my cotton panties are damp, and neither are solely the result of the water.

And in what could be a moment of sheer insanity, I decide tonight's sex dream isn't going to be in the realms of fantasy.

'Here,' he says, handing me the fluffy towel without turning.

My feet are almost silent as I close the distance between us, placing my hand on his shoulder. His brows are pinched in a small frown as he turns, at least for a moment. For the moment it takes him to realise I'm standing before him, wet skinned, my pale underwear completely transparent, my hair likely resembling a bird's nest as my whole body aches for him.

His gaze travels over me blatantly, gliding over the wet triangle of my panties and linger on my breasts, like that's going to help the whole *poke-out-your-eye* situation.

'You smell like beer,' I whisper. His gaze clouds. Maybe he thinks I'm going to push him away? Instead, I tip up on my toes and place my lips against his. It's not exactly a chaste kiss but a stealthy one. As I lower to my heels again, I murmur, 'I like it.'

'If I'd known that was a possibility earlier, I'd have showered in the stuff.'

I bite my lip against laughing, though I really want to laugh—laugh from fear and from relief because, my God, I think this is happening.

'Are you sure you're not drunk?'

'I'm far from drunk. Unless you mean drunk on you.'

In less time than it takes to say *make mine a Pabst Blue,* Byron's hands are on me, under me, gripping my butt as he picks me from my feet. He groans as my wet centre meets his waist, and just like the first time we were in this position, his fingers are hard and questing against my skin. This wave of lust, this transfer of energy between us, it's all groping hands, clashing teeth, and sucking tongue. There's a desperation to the moment as though we're waiting for reality to come.

'*Amber* . . .' He groans my name as his fingers slip under the wet cotton. Feverish with lust, I desperately try to work my hand between us, frantic to feel where he's hard for this. *Hard for me.*

'I want you every minute of my waking hour. You're torturing me.' His voice is harsh, the stubble on his cheeks abrading my skin. 'I wake from dreams convinced I'll find you in my bed.'

'Me . . . too,' I pant in answer, not able to touch him enough, feel enough of him. Without an ounce of finesse, I work my hand under his waistband. As I grasp his cock, he utters a guttural *fuck*. His lips are at my cheek, my ear, my neck, my lips.

'What about after?' I can't quite believe I'm saying this, but the sensible part of my brain is screaming that I'm making a mistake.

'I'll probably want to fuck you again.' This is definitely a non-answer, but I take it anyway. Again and again. To hell with tomorrow and to consequences, tonight I just want to be under him. 'But for now, I want to fuck you out here under the stars.'

We stumble towards the childproof glass gate, my breasts in his face as I try to lift the high latch with shaking, damp hands. It creaks as it swings open, the unexpected momentum causing Byron to stumble, but we don't fall. We also don't stop kissing and touching as he carries us to wherever we're going. Past the darkened outdoor kitchen and fireplace, around a potted palm before he sets me down, though he doesn't let go. His roughened hands draw across my chest, slipping around behind me. One quick click, and he's drawing my bra down my arms. I gasp as he drops it to the ground, stepping into me and pressing me against a stone wall. My arms catch me on two sides of an outdoor cubicle, the walls rough and dark grey, the floor beneath my feet smooth slats of wood. Grabbing my face in his hands, Byron kisses me so deeply, it feels like he's trying to steal my air. *And I'd give it to him gladly.*

One minute, we're kissing, and the next, Byron is on his knees between my legs. My fingers are in his hair and the dips of his shoulders as I seek to prepare. I know just how good this is going to be.

'You liked that, did you?' His rasping voice sounds amused. 'In the hotel.'

'Stop talking. Just touch me.' My voice sounds husky and wanton, confirmed as he hooks his fingers into the sides of my panties and tears them down my legs. But I feel like I've be waiting for this to happen for years, not weeks.

'Jesus Christ, just look at you.' His tone holds a reverence, his gaze glued to the open place between my legs, his thumbs parting me like a ripe piece of fruit. I gasp, my head tipping skywards to where a gleaming, square showerhead hangs, the dark walls and secluded corner making sense to my sex-addled brain now. Deep green palms hang overhead, the silvery stars the only witness to our coupling.

The cool night breeze tantalises my wet flesh where he holds me open, the full flat swipe of his tongue the perfect antidote. The intrusion is so overwhelming, so sublime, I cry out.

'*Ohmygod!*' One hand still in his hair, the other scrambles for purchase somewhere—anywhere, desperate to hold on and catching on a shelf inlaid into the wall. 'I don't . . . I don't . . .' *think my legs will hold me.* And this little ledge of stone isn't going to be much help. '*Oh. Oh!*'

'I've been dying to do that for weeks. That noise you just made? It was worth the fucking wait. Cry all you like, Red. No one can hear you out here.'

With one wickedly dark smile, Byron slides his hand around the back of my knee, draping it over his shoulder, his mouth already shining in the moonlight with my wetness. The sight is obscene yet so right. I tilt my head once more, the cool air spreads through the space and a drop of cold water falls from the showerhead onto my face.

'No, you don't,' Byron's deep voice rumbles as his teeth test my thigh, the pulsing, smarting sensation throbbing in time with the rest of my being. As I look down, my breath leaves my chest in a tiny, tight sound. 'That's better. I want to watch your face when you come.' I roll my lips together to suppress a moan, his gaze dragging liquid fire across my skin. 'You'd like that? Me watching you.' I nod—how can I not?—as he runs his tongue across the indentations of his bite. 'Of course, you would, you filthy girl. And it beats listening to you touch yourself.'

'We're not talking about that now.' My voice is a bare whisper, my hips jolting electric like at the tease of his tongue.

'No, but I'm gonna see that at some point.'

'See what?' I don't have time for more questions or confused looks, not as he slides two thick fingers deep inside me. My arms flatten against the wall, and my moan is loud, carnal.

'See you touch yourself. Tell me yes, Red,' he taunts, flicking the point of his tongue against my clit. 'Tell me you'll let me watch you play with this pussy.'

'Byron, stop teasing.' His eyes are as dark as coal, his soft demands as tempting as sin.

'What? Like your dreams haven't been teasing me for weeks.' Thoughts, protests, and everything else fall away as he engulfs my clit, taking it into his hot, wet mouth.

I cry. I plead. I wrap my hands in that blond hair of his, desperate to ride his face, but as his eyes slide up my body, dark triumph shines there.

'Yes. Yes, anything. Just, please . . . don't stop.'

'You're so fucking delicious,' he growls. 'I couldn't even if I wanted to.'

His mouth meets my pussy again, the vibration of his enjoyment vibrating through my whole being because these are no tentative licks or deft flicks— no, the man feasts on me. Kisses me. Kisses my pussy like he would my mouth, his tongue and his mouth work me harder and deeper until I'm writhing and desperate. Deeply, thorough, he takes ownership of my mind and body until I'm crying out and begging for more, needing more. I frantically chase my peak, digging my heel into his back and using it as leverage to work my hips. To fuck his face.

And my actions are a red flag to a bull as Byron loses it—loses himself in me. With a grunt, he spreads me wide with his big hands as he begins fucking me with his fingers and his tongue. The brush of stubble, and his teeth threatening my clit. His whispered words of how he can't wait to be inside me—my insides are a tight spiral of pleasure drawing me higher and higher until I'm fit to burst.

And I wasn't wrong about my legs, not as Byron's hands grasp my hips to hold me. Not as he growls his praise into the very centre of me.

How delicious I am. *So fucking delicious.*

How he can't wait to be inside me. *So desperate.*

To own me. *So completely.*

Higher and higher the sensations spiral, robbing me of sense and breath, leaving me a throbbing, twitching mess.

Chapter Twenty-One

BYRON

Plastered against the wall, my hands are on Amber's pale hips, her eyes tilted skywards, her hair spread around her shoulders like Botticelli's *Birth of Venus*. If I said I didn't like how her skin retains the mark of my hand, I'd be lying.

'You really are dangerous,' I murmur, lowering her leg from my shoulder before lifting my hand to the freckles dusting her clavicle. Amber for warning. A red-coloured flag. Amber for me.

'And you really are good at that.' Her chest moves once with some semblance of a laugh, languid and sensuous.

'Enjoyed yourself, did you?'

'Whatever gave you that idea?'

'Red, anyone in a five-mile radius knows you love having your pussy eaten.' Whether the thought of being heard turns her on or the words themselves, her body bows under my hands as though reacting to some kind of sensory remembrance. It makes me wish I'd had my dick inside already. 'And to think, we could've been at this for weeks if it wasn't for stubbornness.'

'You're forgiven,' she murmurs, bringing one languid hand to my head.

This time, it's my turn to laugh. 'Takes two not to fuck, sweetheart.' Her body reacts again. Interesting . . .

'So we're both the idiots?'

'Agreed?' I place my lips low on her belly, causing her to purr like a cat.

'The question is,' she continues, 'were we idiots before or are we idiots now for complicating things?'

'Shush,' I murmur, standing and taking her pliant body into my arms to kiss her. Kiss her to silence her mind. Kiss her to compliance. Kiss her until her breaths are rapid and her hands are grasping for more.

'Take it off,' she rasps, her hands yanking on the hem of my T-shirt as I assist her with pulling it up and over my head. 'Stop looking at me like that,' she then insists.

'Like what?'

'All confident and annoying. Like you know what I want, like you can see into my head.'

'Darl, you've got your hand on my cock, that's why I'm smilin'. As for what you want, I'm hoping you've got a grip on the right thing.' I reckon but for the light, her cheeks have turned pink as she brings both hands to her mouth to hide a girlish giggle. And while I love the sound, I'm not so keen on the direction those hands are heading. 'Looks like I'm gonna have to do the job myself.' I slide my wallet from my back pocket, slapping it on the recess built into the wall, the place that houses shower gel and shampoo bottles, though not before taking a condom from the inner pocket. Then I loosen my jeans.

'Tell me you want this.' I run my hands under the open waistband of my jeans, the muscles in my abs tensing with raw need. 'Tell me you want me.'

Without answering, Amber reaches for the shelf, taking the condom from the top of my wallet before tearing it open.

My heart begins to beat like hooves, my balls tightening as she slips her fingers into the side of my jeans, flicking them farther open still.

'I like how you came prepared,' she says, her eyes flicking up shyly to mine. 'Or maybe someone forgot to do their laundry.'

'You couldn't resist that, could you, funny girl?' Pushing my jeans down my legs, I flick them out of the stone cubicle.

'Hey, you're the one with the laundry fetish.'

I begin to laugh, the sound halting as she suddenly slips the rubber over the head of my cock. My thighs tremble and my pulse pounds so hard it has to be fucking heard. I'm no longer aware of the sounds of the evening, the birds and the bugs, the feel of the breeze. All I can think is how much I need her as slender fingers slide down my length.

She gasps as I wrap her fingers in mine tight around the base, whimpers a little as I spread my hands under her thighs to lift her body *Up. On.* Her arms around my neck, her gasp a soft vowel sound as my cockhead pushes inside.

'Oh, fuck.' I guess absence does make me hard because I feel impossibly so. Hard and aching and raring to fuck as her body engulfs more than just my tip. Does absence also make it hurt, I wonder? Hurt in the best kinds of ways? Because this is borderline torturous the way I'm sliding into her inch by slow fucking inch. Hands under her fuckable arse, my thighs are trembling and every single one of my muscles vibrate with need. Need for our bodies to meet. But still I torture myself.

'Am I heavy?' she whispers.

I tighten my hands on her arse and shake my head, and as though brought to my senses, I push the rest of the way inside her with an eager grunt.

'Jesus fuckin' Christ.' My breath is laboured, my words delivered through gritted teeth, the grip of her hot walls driving me crazy, making me want to own every inch of her skin.

'Who knew blasphemy could have so many syllables?' This time, her carnal whisper vibrates through my chest. 'You're just full of surprises.'

'I'm about to deliver the best one yet.' Tightening my hands under her, I flex my hips and she groans, rolling her hips to meet mine on the next thrust. 'I'm about to fuck you so hard, you won't know where I end, and you begin.' And right then, with her body pressed between my cock and a hard place, I begin to make good on my words, delivering thrust after thrust.

Pleasure crawls along my spine and tightens my balls, causing me to grunt. And she cries out. I thrust a little harder in response, unravelling us both a little more.

'You feel so hard,' she whispers, her lips by my ear, her hands in my hair. 'So hard inside me.'

'Keep suckin' on my ear, darl, and I won't be hard for much longer.'

'I want to suck on more than your ear,' she whispers, her wicked smile ringing loud and clear and filling my head with such perfect images. Amber on her knees, my hand in her hair as I fill her, use her, feel myself in her tightening throat. The thoughts, the images, the sensation of her clenching around my cock cause my knees to almost give way. I utter a long, raspy groan, and as she tightens her teeth on my ear, my whole body ripples in response.

I can't think, I can only hold her, fuck her, as everything becomes frantic, and the tiny space fills with the noises of rutting animals. My heart feels like it could burst. Our lips smash, and I thrust my tongue into her throat, desperate to fill her, desperate for her to accept me everywhere.

My pulse pounds as I alternate between deep, punishing thrusts of my hips, small punches, and long glides of her along my length, the kind of motion that rubs her clit.

'I'm . . . I'm coming.'

But she doesn't need to tell me, not as she rocks her centre against me, not as she begins to chant my name.

'I can feel you,' I rasp into the soft skin of her neck. 'I can feel you coming around me.'

One hand still under her, I grab her by the back of her hair, exposing her throat to my mouth as I bring myself once more between her legs like a blow.

This pussy is mine—her mind and her body. And tonight, I'm not letting go.

Chapter Twenty-Two

AMBER

Back in the house, I round the counter from my quick trip to the bathroom, tucking the towel tighter to my chest when my feet come to an abrupt halt. Byron leans back against the island. Dressed in only his jeans, his hair gleams under the fancy chandeliers. Well, that and because his hair is also damp because the man decided the best thing to follow a post-coital cuddle was a cold outdoor shower. I'd squealed, like a *help, I'm being murdered kind of squeal,* and Byron had quickly apologised. It's just a shame that apology didn't extend to his gaze, not when it was glued to the hard pebbling of my nipples. The same nipples that go hard again at the *sensory memory of him warming them.*

'What have you got there?'

Byron looks up from the thing he holds in his hand with a guilty expression.

My notebook.

It's just a notebook, I intone as a vulnerable feeling washes through me. But the truth is, it's the closest thing to a journal I have because not only does it hold my best and most loved recipes, but it also alludes to my hopes and dreams. Along with the recipes, there are also a few mementos; checks from my favourite Parisian café, a couple of insta-camera pics of Emma and me outside the Louvre and one at Montmartre. A tiny flat shell from Kuta Beach in Bali, and a leaflet depicting a good luck dessert that kind of looks like a boob complete with a fleshy nipple.

And then there's more. More from the heart. Various stylised sketches of my future storefront and tiny rows of figures from my frightening attempts at number crunching.

Oh, God. Don't let him have seen those.

Maybe what it should really hold is a bunch of lottery tickets.

'Should I not be looking at this?'

'Erm . . .'

I strain to see what he's looking at. No, how embarrassing. He's looking at my sketch of the bottle of Perrier Jouët he'd ordered to my hotel room. *That night.*

'It was open on the bench, and I picked it up without really thinking about it.'

If he turns the page, he'll find a golden wrapper from the turn-down service. The chocolate he'd teased me with, running it over my lips, feeding me it in tiny increments before tasting it from my tongue.

God, I'll look like some kind of bunny-boiling nutjob.

'Amber?'

'Huh?' My eyes snap to his as I force a smile. 'Oh, no. It's fine. It's just some doodling and stuff. Just . . . just don't turn the page or you'll find how I've scored you for your performance that night.' A look of challenge rises in his eyes before I add quickly. 'And also a lock of your pubic hair.'

Challenge turns to amusement, and though he doesn't put the book down, at least he's no longer looking at it.

'I didn't see mention of any other encounters with your fellow travellers.'

'Those were written in cypher.' Taking the book from his hand, I narrow my gaze. 'Are you . . . fishing?'

Folding his arms, he snorts, sliding his hands behind him, though his expression isn't quite so derisory.

'Well, are you?' Be still my little pitter-patter heart.

'That would make me an arsehole.' He pauses, glances at his feet, then looks up again. 'Apparently, it would make me an arsehole who still wants to know.'

I bring my hand to my mouth as though this could hide my giggle. Shouldn't I be horrified? Shouldn't my inner feminist be up in arms?

Hmm . . . nope. Seems my inner feminist only wants to be in *his* arms.

'I know, I know. It makes no sense at all, yet I still want to know if you've rooted anyone since you moved in.'

'Rooted is such a ridiculous word,' I counter.

'All right, fucked. How's that word work for you?'

'That word works just fine. And you say it with such flair and panache.'

'Stalling,' Byron grumbles.

'No, sir. Not me.'

His sigh is heavy with faux-exasperation, though there's a certain light in his eye. *Sir? Really? Is that like a fantasy thing?*

'I did not,' I begin in my best fake *Arkansas-former-POTUS* accent, 'have sexual relations with . . .' Belatedly, I realise how boring this is about to make me sound. What kind of person gives up their life to adventure, and experiences said adventure celibate? Well, celibate apart from that one time. And that one time earlier in the shower.

'With?'

With a roll of my eyes and a little flounce, I announce, 'With anyone in almost a year.'

'I guess that makes me the lucky one. I certainly feel it.' His gaze holds mine, and I swear I can feel the sincerity in those three words. 'Do you miss it?' he asks, glancing at the notebook I still hold in my hand.

'Sex?'

'No, travelling.'

I'm not sure of the answer, and I'm not sure what I think as, back still against the countertop, he opens his arms, gesturing me into their circle. No girl could refuse that kind of invitation. His chest is firm and warm against my cheek as he props his chin on the top of my head. Like we haven't been avoiding this evening for weeks, and he's already held me in his arms a thousand times.

'You pleadin' the fifth?' I drop the notebook on the bench, hooking my arms around his waist as the sound of his deep voice vibrates under my ear.

'Do I miss travelling?' I muse aloud. 'At the moment? No. I've had a blast travelling, but I'm pretty happy here. I feel like I'm getting a better understanding of Australia being in one place. And I love, love, love this kitchen. I haven't had the space to bake since Paris.'

'So you only want me for my oven?'

'Yep. That and the big package you give me.'

'That sounds more like it,' Byron replies.

'I meant my employment package.'

'You keep telling yourself that, babe.' I swat his chest playfully before he catches my hand, placing it against his firm chest and covering it with his own. 'Tell me about baking. Why do you love it?'

'Baking is . . . is like therapy. Sure, there's a science to it, but the process is almost meditative to me. I can lock out everything else—thoughts, worries, even the time of the day. Baking takes my focus, quieting those voices in my head. There's something that makes me feel inherently good about baking, maybe because it takes me back to when I was small, to weekends spent with my grandmother. The nicest food always came out of her oven. At Christmas, we'd bake holiday treats for her friends and neighbours. It seemed to take a week to get it all done. I suppose when I moved to

Paris, I remembered how good it felt to bake. To feed others.' His chest moves under my ear with a chuckle. 'Don't be so perverted!'

'Takes one to know one,' he retorts happily. With a squeeze of his arms at my back, his low voice rumbles, 'Go on.'

'I didn't have a lot to do as an au pair there. The school run and a little homework supervision after school. One rainy afternoon, I pulled out the ingredients for chocolate muffins and got the kids involved. I suppose it just spiralled from there. Before long, I was looking up recipes for madeleines and canelé. Then the parents suggested—and paid for—patisserie classes. *Croissant, palmier, religieuse . . .*' My words trail off, my mind filled anew with delicious ideas, smells, and colours.

'I don't even know what any of those are.'

'No? Well, if you ever want to try, I'm your girl.'

'I like the sound of that. In fact, I could go for something to eat now.'

My eyes slide to the clock on the oven. 'It's a little late to start baking. You really want cake?'

'I'm easy,' his low voice rumbles, 'but don't go telling anyone.'

'I can keep your secret,' I reply with a small laugh, patting that firm gorgeous chest of his.

'How about pancakes? I'm pretty sure I can rustle those up.'

'You're going to feed me?' Why does this make me giddy with excitement? Am I such a pathetic girly girl? 'Let me help at least.'

'Sure. You can be my sous chef.'

As I attempt to pull from his arms this time, there's still a touch of resistance, though he eventually loosens his arms enough to let me go and untie the towel from around my chest.

'Byron!' I squeak, trying to hang onto it and my modesty in the face of his delighted smile. 'Let go!'

'Nah, I don't think I will.' With one deft tug, he leaves me standing in the middle of the kitchen, totally nude. 'My kitchen, my rules.'

'Your rules suck.' I pull a striped kitchen towel from the hook at the side of the island. 'Not to mention one-sided,' I add, holding the tiny rectangle over my torso, hiding either my boobs or my lady bits. 'What happens if the kids come down?'

'Good try, love,' he replies, his words dripping with satisfaction, his gaze moving to whichever bit I'm currently hiding with the towel. *Boobs, cookie, boobs, cookie . . .*

'Dammit!' I throw the tiny towel at his face. He catches it laughing as I swing on my toes and make my way to the pantry. 'Just for that, you can cook the damn pancakes yourself.'

'Don't be like that, love.' Why do his Aussie terms of endearment turn my insides to mush? Especially when they're delivered with such a sinful grin.

'It's your own fault if your children walk in or gasp, horror, your mom.'

'Not happening, Red,' he growls, hot on my heels. That name in that accent turns my insides to goo. *Hot, sexual goo.* As I reach the pantry door, hands on my hips, he pulls me into him again. 'You're gorgeous, and you're all mine tonight.'

'Pancakes first,' I insist. Sliding the door open, I grab the things I need, passing them into his arms, ignoring the way he looks at me. 'You said you were going to feed me.'

'I'll feed you all right.'

'Byron!' I wriggle out of his arms, opening the pantry door wide.

'Here, flour, sugar, oil, and baking powder.' I start piling the items into hands, ignoring the unamused looks he's dishing out. 'And stop looking at my cookie.' His brow furrows, and I immediate understand the terminology is a little confusing to him. 'My cookie?' I repeat, pointing at the place in question.

'Far out.' I almost giggle as the big, tattooed man rolls his eyes. 'That word was bad enough already. You know, now I'm never gonna allow the kids to use it.'

'Don't be a pussy,' I say, gesturing him over to the stove.

'Your pussy is perfect,' he says. 'Except when you call your pussy a cookie.

'Cookies are good eating,' I retort, making my way around him, bending to pull a mixing bowl from the appropriate drawer.

'Fuck me.' The expletive is more groan than anything else, the ingredients in his hands scattering across the countertop. '*You're* good eatin'.' As I stand, large hands loop around me, pulling my back to his chest. 'And if you keep bending over like that, I'll be the only one eatin' tonight.'

He bites my ear, and I almost convulse, his next words causing me to convulse with a different reason as big hands suddenly cup my breasts. 'Here, hold these for me a minute, would you? I'm making pancakes, and I'm a little bit busy.' I giggle a little at his silly suggestion, squeaking as he swats my ass. A beat later, he slides a corny apron over my head.

'This is pretty bad,' I say, pointing at the corn cock on front.

'Blame Flynn.' He begins pulling together utensils and ingredients. 'It was last year's Christmas gift.'

'You guys seem like you have a lot of love.'

'There's a lot of shit throwin' going on. A lot of dick measuring, but they're pretty great when they're not getting on my last nerve.'

'None of them were interested in the wine business?'

'Nah,' he answers with a sad smile as he adds the dry ingredients to a mixing bowl. 'Only me. Bunch of lazy bastards.'

'I'm sure that's not true.'

'It's what happens when you don't have to work.'

'Oh, wow. All of you? Actually, forget I said that.' I don't mean to be nosy except when I really do.

'Family money,' he says with a shrug. 'But there's only so much lying around on a beach a body can stand. I think they're all finding that out now.'

'So what do they all do?' I ask, leaning my forearms on the countertop as he works.

'Flynn is in property development in London. He's married now, thank Christ. Got a kid. Rafferty is fucking about the world doing Christ knows what, and Roman has decided he's gonna be a model in New York.'

'A model? Wow. Is he cute?' With an unimpressed look, Byron flicks a little flour from the bowl in my direction. 'Just keeping my options open, babe.' This time, with an expression full of warning, he lays down the egg he holds in his hand.

'The only thing you need to concentrate on is keeping open for me.'

'I should, should I?'

'Yeah, you should.' He leans over, his big hand stroking the length of my spine, making me react like a contented cat—*purrs, stretches, all the feline things*—before he unties the apron from my back, pulling the strap from around my neck up and over my head.

'I have to get *naked again*?'

Chapter Twenty-Three

AMBER

'I have to get *naked again*?'

My artificial complaint makes him chuckle as he moves behind me this time, his hands dragging liquid fire up my legs.

'You make it sound like a bad thing.'

'No, don't stop. That's so *good*.' And then I realise why. I'm wet—like, oily wet—slick and slippery by way of his hands. 'What have you got back there?' Massage oil? I can't imagine that's the kind of thing kept in a kitchen.

'You'll see.'

'Whatever it is, if you're trying to baste me up for a little butt sex, think again.'

'Wouldn't that be tryin' to butter you up, cupcake?'

'Cupcake? I've never heard it called *that* before,' I answer with a giggle. 'Butter or baste my cupcake, let me tell you, it's all in vain.'

'Sure,' he answers reasonably, leaning across me and grabbing the sieve by the flour cannister. I begin to giggle as the white dust rains down on me. 'The thought never crossed my mind.'

'Liar, liar. But what on earth?'

'Shush, you're spoiling my concentration. And stop wiggling. I bet Gervex never had this problem.'

'Who the heck is Gervex?' I twist my head over my shoulder as Byron begins drawing something on my ass with his fingertip.

'*Henri Gervex* was an eighteenth-century artist. You're not the only one with a little culture.' *A little cul-cha.*

'Oh, I'm sure.' My words waver with amusement as I strain to see what he's doing, other than making some kind of glue against my skin.

'Well, you may laugh, but the subject of *Rolla*, arguably his most famous painting, reminds me of you. All that titian hair,' he murmurs, his voice low and seductive. 'And pale, pale skin.' I shiver as his fingertips trace my spine, and I arch into his touch. 'So shockingly beautiful, she reminds me of you.'

I duck my head, hiding my resulting smile. I could get used to this talkative, complimenting Byron.

'I hadn't thought about the painting for years.'

'Where did you see it?'

'Ah, my dirty old grandad had a print of it hanging in his bedroom.' Still staring at my ass, he makes small, precise strokes of his fingers. Strokes that ignite a fire deep inside me.

'A dirty painting, huh?'

'I'm not an art connoisseur, but what I do know is the subject of the painting looks freshly fucked.' I begin to chuckle as Byron pulls back and begins admiring his handiwork. 'There.'

'Your masterpiece is complete?' I twist, trying to see what exactly his masterpiece is, but before I know it, he's grabbed his phone from where it's charging on the counter behind him, and he's snapped a pic.

'Hey!'

'How else will you see?' he asks innocently, passing the phone to me.

Yep, he tries innocent, at least. Almost pulls it off, too.

I straighten as I push the home button, the screen already dark.

'You're so beautiful,' Byron whispers, toying with a lock of my hair, not that I answer him as his phone springs back to life. And I begin to laugh—delightedly so. Covered in flour, my ass still looks pretty great, even if I do say so myself, but the thing that strikes me is that my ass isn't covered in art. Not unless you count the words 'Byron's Arse' as such.

It is a little graphic, I suppose.

'Just a reminder,' he says, laughing huskily as he swats his artwork.

'Hey!'

'You've only got yourself to blame.'

'So I deserve it?' I reply, pushing my ass back against him.

He meets my taunt with his hands. 'Only if you think you can take it again.'

'Bring it,' I whisper, resting my head against my arms on the countertop as his hands glide over my stomach and between my legs.

'*Oh, God.*' Still sensitive from earlier, my response is immediately.

'You're fucking delectable.' His fingers sweep past my entrance, causing me to whimper. 'I don't care what it's called. I could eat it all night long.'

I drop my head, my gaze following the branch of his strong, inked arms and the tanned hand that disappears between my legs. The sight is so erotic, it makes my knees weak.

'*Oh, oh, God,*' I repeat, unable to watch anymore, stretching my arms out in front of me, my breasts now flat against the cool marble.

'Just like that. I love those little noises you make,' he rasps, one hand now holding me open in a *V* as the fingers of his other hand make quick work of my orgasm, petting and teasing my clit.

'It's too much.'

'You want me to stop?' His breath is hot in my ear, his touch intense.

'No . . . *Yes! Yes! Yes! Yes!*' With each of my cries, my body jolts as though lashed by an electric line. It seems that's all that it takes to make me a panting, squirm mess.

'That was quick.' Hear that? The cocky smile in his words?

'I want you,' I say, turning in his arms. 'I want you in my mouth.'

'Fuck, yeah. You want to suck me off?' His eyes burn intensely, his hands pushing the hair from my face.

'Why is your accent so hot?'

'Fuck if it is,' he retorts, hissing as my teeth find the tiny nub of his nipple, my hands draped around his waist.

'Oh, you know you so are.'

This time, the smile isn't only in his words. It's also painted across his face. 'I think we should come back to my question first.'

'What was the question?'

'Do you wanna suck my cock?'

'Was that even a serious question?'

'I never joke about cock sucking, Red.'

'Then yes.' I bring my fingers to his chest, pushing him. 'Hell yes, I want to suck your'—I push him again— 'hard'—*push*— 'glorious'—*push*—'cock.'

His back against the double door refrigerator, I run my hands down his smooth chest and the flat plains of his stomach before making quick work of his zipper, trailing my hand down that delicious trail of downy hair, making him shiver. He's so hot and hard in my hand, satin over steel, as I free him from the confines of the seams. His groan is a low rumble that soon turns to a harsh whispered curse as I bend and inhale his fat crown. *And just his crown because I'm all about the tease.*

'Jesus, that's it,' he rasps, 'take it, beautiful. Suck me.'

The need in his voice hits my veins like a drug, his musky scent and taste only adding to the high. The man had given me three orgasms in quick succession tonight, and I'm going to repay him in kind. Because I want to and because I want to be his drug of choice, too.

'You're so fucking good at this.'

The words bloom between my legs, his praise a turn-on in itself. As I slide my lips down his length, I glance up at his face. His expression is the best—the mixture of agony and suspense, of raw pleasure and pain. It's so heady to have him like this, and as I take him even deeper, he exhales a rasping gasp.

Hand at the root of him, I work him with my mouth as his broken whispers and gasped curses paint his need in the air for me as he tells me how he's touched himself, thinking of me. The images rushing through my head make my movements sloppy, not that he complains with his hands tight in my hair, my moans driving him to the edge of his control.

'Take it,' he pleads, his eyes all intense stare. 'Take it all.'

The sounds of my own pleasure hum in the back of my throat as I do just that. Moments later, Byron's fingers are in my hair, moving the strands away from my face. For a moment, I think he'll hold me there, as he, you know . . . But instead, his eyes fall to my mouth—fall to the slide of him from my mouth. His own jaw slack, he tries to form words.

'Red . . . ' *I love how he calls me that. Love to make him groan like that.* 'I'm gonna—'

As I moan my approval, he cradles my head and, with a guttural groan, comes in my mouth.

I am a mess. The kitchen is a mess. And Byron appears to be asleep while standing up. I realise that's not true as he reaches for me, his blue eyes suddenly open, his hands cradling my face.

'Hi,' I whisper. Our faces are so close I see two of him. And two of Byron is more than any girl can handle.

'Come to bed with me.'

My heart jolts because yes, hell yes, that would be amazing.

'But what about the twins?' His expression turns pained. I wrap my hands around his forearms, pull back to better see him. 'We don't have to.'

'I want you there in my bed. But I've . . . they've . . . '

'You've never had a sleepover?'

'Red.' His sinfully, cocky smile is back. 'The things I want to do to you there aren't so innocent.'

'Again?'

He chuckles and kisses me then, his lips light and sweet. 'Yeah again. And again. And again, and again.' But then he sighs, taking my hands in his. 'We have to make hay while the sun shines, I reckon.'

Because I'm not going to be here for more than a few weeks.

The reminder is unwelcome, dark and bitter. Talk about mood altering.

'Then, I say again, we don't have to. We shouldn't let the kids see.'

'I want you in my bed.' I can feel the need in his fingers—in his words. 'We'll work something out.'

Following Byron up the stairs, my heart is in my throat. I have imagined this so many times; my hand in his, being led straight into his privacy. *Even if I've already snooped.* We don't even make it all the way up the stairs before he leans against the wall, pulls me against him, and kisses me hard. The stubble on his face abrades my cheeks, pressing a soft *hush* against my mouth.

But then he's on the move again, drifting out of my arms and up the stairs. The closing of his door behind us makes a guilty pulse between my legs.

'We'd best get you showered first.'

'Oh, right.' How is it I'd forgotten that not only am I naked but also greased and floured like a Bundt tin?

Steam swirls around the small space of the bathroom, and while it shouldn't, in theory, take long to wash, our shower is at a much more leisurely pace. A shower filled with soapy slides of hands and wandering lips. As Byron's hands dance their magic over my back, I realise I have never felt something so extraordinary in its simplicity. And I suddenly want to tell him so, but I don't. This isn't even a holiday romance.

I wrap myself in a fluffy towel, one which Byron almost immediately relieves me of, leaving it in a discarded heap on the floor as he draws back the sheets. I slide between the smooth, crisp sheets, relishing in my nakedness. And his.

I feel giddy as we lie there, staring at each other in the moonlight, and try to moderate my grin into something a little less telling.

'Oh.' I push up onto my elbow, looking over his shoulder at the nightstand.

'What are you looking for?'

'Your phone.' God only knows where mine is.

'Don't tell me.' His tone is equal parts husky and amused. 'You want to play Candy Crush.'

'No, silly.' I flop back, realising it isn't there. 'I was going to set an alarm. I don't need to be here when the kids wake up.'

'It's fine.' Reaching for my hands, he brings them to his lips. 'I wake without an alarm early, way before anyone in this house.'

'Really?' Sceptical much? But I can't understand why anyone would be eager to get out of bed every day.

'Yeah. You've probably never heard me tiptoeing around your room.'

'That's okay. I kind of tiptoed around yours today.'

At my sudden and horrified expression, a laughter burst from his chest.

'Find anything interesting?'

Only that you'll need to visit your sock drawer if we're going to have sex again, I don't say. I also don't say that I'm not sure my little cookie is ready for another round quite yet.

'I wasn't snooping,' I answer a little primly, hoping my nose isn't growing like the little wooden boy. But I might've been bringing in his clean laundry, or chasing one of the twins, or something. Right? *Right?*

'I can't imagine there'd be much to snoop.'

I don't answer, though I really want to ask about the condoms. Why do you keep them in the sock drawer? And then the answer hits me; so he doesn't forget to put them in his overnight bag when he packs. Man, that blows. Not that he's sensible about sex, just that he has sex. Probably often. Probably with women much more sophisticated and less snoopy, and I don't mean the beagle, but less insecure. More wordly. More . . . not me

Gah! Brain, shut up!

'Hey, you're not still worried about the kids walking in, are you?'

'What if they wake during the night?' True story, sort of.

'I'm a really light sleeper when it comes to the pair. The house might explode around me, but I swear, some sort of single parent early warning system tells me if they so much as sniffle in their sleep. You don't believe me,' he adds in the face of my silence or maybe my moonlit expression.

'I just don't want them to be confused.'

'Oh, they wouldn't be confused. And you can bet Mum would know in less than thirty seconds following.'

'You must've had this happen before?' Don't judge. If the man holds a shovel out to me, I'm going to dig.

'No.' The delivery of that one little word leaves me no doubt that I've been busted. 'Amber,' he adds gravely. 'I don't know if you realise this but, having you here in my bed? It's pretty much a one-off. Let me put it this way, the last woman I had in my bed was—'

His words halt, and even in the semi-darkness, I can see he's hurting.

'It's okay. I know you were married,' I say quietly. 'Sally told me.' When he doesn't reply, I continue. 'It must've been a terrible time for you.'

'Yeah. I wouldn't wish it on anyone.'

Tears prick my eyes, but I'm not going to cry. He lived through it, so what comfort would by tears bring him now?

'I want to tell you something.' He licks his lips then swallows, his fingers tightening on mine. 'I haven't told anyone this.'

'You don't have to say anything,' I add hurriedly. Yeah, so I'm a bit nosy, but I don't want him to feel like he has to say or explain anything to me.

'I want to. Katya, my wife. She'd left me. She was having an affair right before she died.'

'Oh . . . '

Oh, fuck. What's the appropriate answer to this? My mind is literally blank. I can't think of a single thing to say—I can't even muster up a platitude, not that I think I would use one even if I could think of it.

That's like a double dose of hurt.

And enough to make a person never want to get involved again.

Chapter Twenty-Four

BYRON

I swore I'd never get involved with another woman the day that Katya left me. Not the day she died. The day she *left* me. The day she walked out of the door, taking my children and ripping out my heart.

'She said she didn't love me anymore. I'm not sure she ever did. Maybe it was the lifestyle she fell in love with. We lived in Sydney for the first few years, though we partied around the world. But having kids should make you want to settle down, shouldn't it?'

Amber doesn't answer, her slim fingers tightening on mine. She might not yet be a mother, but I can't imagine a scenario where she wouldn't put any child first.

'Two years into our marriage, and with the twins barely a year old, she fed me the oldest line in the book. She was leaving— it wasn't me, it was her. Lies to cover the fact that she'd found someone else. '

'I'm so sorry,' she whispers as though her condolences have the power to hurt. And they kind of do.

'I dunno what's worse, that she was leaving or the way she told me, because she chose to do so while we were in London for my brother, Flynn's, wedding. Like I needed an anniversary reminder for evermore—like I needed to sit through a transatlantic flight with her, keeping it civil for our fellow passengers and the kids. I kept it quiet the whole time we were there, put on a brave face, drank champagne and gave a speech. And all the time, my mind was working. Where did I go wrong? What would happen with the kids? I didn't want to see them grow up only at weekends.'

'How awful.' Along with her quiet murmur, she bows her head, kissing my knuckle, tightening her hands around mine as though they were cold. Who knows. Maybe they're cold to the touch. Recalling this certainly makes my blood run cold enough.

'I haven't told another soul.'

'I'm listening, Byron. Whatever you say is safe with me.'

'Course, I started to put two and two together then. The trips she'd taken with girlfriends. The long baby showers and nights out that ran into the early hours.' The opportunities that afforded cover for her infidelity. 'Her obsession with the gym—the fucking plastic surgeon. She came clean when I confronted her. Moved out of our home within days of getting back to Aus. And she took the kids.'

'And you didn't confide in anyone?'

I shake my head. 'I could barely take it all in myself. I almost told Flynn once. I called him late at night, full of wine and fucking anger. But I just couldn't. I'm the eldest brother—I'm supposed to be the one they turn to.'

'Everyone needs someone, honey.'

'Yeah, I know.' The endearment makes me smile. When was the last time anyone called me something sweet? Taking a deep breath, I prepare myself to tell the rest of the horror story. 'There were worse things to come. Kat's cancer diagnosis. Dad's heart attack—they both happened within weeks of each other. I moved back to the vineyard because my mother needed me, even if my wife didn't. Early days, see?' I attempt a smile that this time just doesn't sit. 'Katya's relationship didn't last, of course. He was in it for the fun, not to nurse her through her last days. So she moved back with me, spending her last days here as my wife. At least, on the surface.' At least, to those watching on.

'That's very noble of you. Kind.'

'Was it?' I ask, the words sounding gruff. It didn't feel like. It felt necessary. 'I didn't see as how I had much choice.'

'Everyone has a choice. You could've told people what she'd done, vilified and blackened her name, but you didn't. Instead, you protected her. You didn't taint her memory for your daughter and your son.' She's right, of course. This woman is so full of insightful surprises. 'And that's why there's been no one in your life since?'

'Did you think I was moping around like some Heathcliff figure? Because that's not why I'm still single.'

'Why are you single, then?'

'The official answer is that I'm not prepared to feel vulnerable again. That I'm still repairing the damage that Katya caused me by leaving me twice. That I'm essentially afraid of experiencing any kind of happiness because I know deep down that I can't experience joy without also opening myself up to some degree of pain.'

'Wow, that's very insightful.'

'And a bargain at the price of seven hundred and eighty dollars.' Unwilling to allow her to watch me any longer, I pull her closer, my chin resting just about her head.

'Therapy, huh?'

I sniff as I consider my answer. I've come this far. I may as well spew the rest of my guts.

'Last year, the kids started to act out. To fight. It came out of the blue—biting and scratching, yelling and screaming. I thought it was my fault, that somehow I'd caused this change in them. So I booked us into a therapist, and she charged me a couple of hundred bucks to tell me my children were just experiencing the terrible twos at the age of three, and nearly eight-hundred bucks to tell me what was wrong with me.'

'Are you cured?'

'Nah. I didn't go back after the first couple of sessions. Those things I just said? She left them on my voicemail.'

'You've just been grieving. That's natural.'

Yeah, I'm not so sure.

I yawn quite suddenly, my mouth so wide I hear my jaw crack.

'I think we should get a little sleep.' As I nod, Amber pulls back her head, cupping my cheek in one of her delicate hands. 'But before we do, tell me about the girl called Candy?'

Man, I try not to laugh. Try and fail.

'Amber, love,' I begin, 'how am I supposed to go from telling you my deepest, darkest secrets, to telling you about the afternoon I'd needed brain bleach to forget?'

With a little pat of my cheek and a measure of steel in her tone she responds, 'I don't know, honey. But I'm sure you'll manage.'

~*~

I don't notice the lift in my mood until Mum makes a comment about it. But I can admit this past week has been good. I survived the first night of a woman in my bed, and I've survived a few since. Because when she's with me, I feel like a randy teenager again.

But there's been no hiding it from Mum. Not since we left the kitchen a mess that first night. I'd tried to play it off as a case of the munchies, explaining how I was suddenly desperate for pancakes, but that Roman had called and that I'd abandoned the effort in favour of a good yarn with my little bro.

Nah, I didn't think it'd wash, either.

She'd just sent me a funny look, her gaze deliberately grazing my phone, still lying on the kitchen bench. It was about then that I realised she must've opened it and seen the photograph of Amber's arse on my phone.

There're no flies on her, I'll tell you.

Thankfully, at least for my balls, Amber is yet unaware of that exchange. She still thinks we're keeping our very grown-up activities a secret from her. Fat chance. Though she has wondered what she's done to deserve the extra-large helping of bacon Mum heaps on her plate.

Mum thinks she's in need of protein. Apparently, feeding her my sausage every night isn't enough. I can't imagine it'll be long before Amber twigs. If Mum was any more solicitous, it'd be creepy.

'Coffee, Amber, darl?'

'No thanks, Sally,' she replies, her hands wrapped around her cup as we sit in the kitchen watching the kids play outside. 'One cup of this stuff is enough.'

'You're sure? You look like you might need a bit of a helping hand this morning. Something to put a bit of pep in your step.'

'Oh, no, I'm not tired,' Amber protests, adorably wide-eyed.

'A bit of lead in your pencil, By?' Mum holds the coffeepot aloft, her expression as blank as any mask.

'My pencil's just fine, thanks, Mum.' A bit sore, but I reckon it'll be as fit as a Malle Bull come this evening. *And just as randy.* 'Are you trying to say I look tired, too?'

'Just a bit. Now, what's the phrase I heard on the TV the other day?' She taps a finger against her chin as though searching her memory. 'That's it—you look like you've both been rode wet!'

Beside me, Amber almost chokes on her coffee.

'Easy, darl.' I rub my hand in wide circles against her back, circles that get progressively lower, mind you. Meanwhile, Amber seems to have developed a tic. 'You okay?'

'You're rubbing my back,' she says through gritted teeth.

'And?'

'And if you get any lower, your hand will be in my panties,' she sort of whisper-hisses

'Okay.' I lean back but not before hooking my thumb into the back of her jeans.

'I said that right, didn't I, love?' Mum's question is directed at Amber. 'You both look like you've been rode wet.'

'I think the end of that saying goes something like *and put away dry.*'

'I wouldn't be a bit surprised to hear you're both a bit dry this morning,' she answers easily.

'I'm sorry?' Amber squeaks.

'Nothing, love. Don't mind me.'

Edie, who seems to have a sixth sense about anyone getting any attention, comes bustling into the room, brandishing her brush.

'I've gots kookaburra poop in my hair!'

'I think that's Play-Doh, sweets.' Amber takes the brush from her hand as she lifts her up to sit on her knees. 'Yep, it's Play-Doh. Let me see if I can get it out.'

'Got much on the schedule today?' Mum asks as Edie begins to complain.

'Oh, I'm sure we've got lots on our schedules, haven't we, Edie?'

'I want to go swimming.'

'Chores first,' I reply, hiding my smile in my cup.

'And speaking of schedules,' Ma continues, pointing a finger at me. 'Don't forget Friday evening.' Placing my cup down, I groan. 'Ah-ah, you promised. Besides, it's been too long since I've seen you in a tux.' She turns to Amber and winks. 'Wait till you see him in a tux. He'd give James Bond a run for his money, wouldn't you, love?'

'If you say so, Ma.'

'Oh, I do, love.'

'I've got too much on this w—' This is as far as I get.

'No. You told Mary three months ago that she could count on you. I won't allow you to wriggle out of this. End of story.' Her pursed lipped expression brightens as she turns to Amber. 'Byron's going to be auctioned off at the country club this Friday,' she says this with an air of someone who's already won. 'For charity, of course.'

'Oh, cool,' she says . . . coolly. Almost dignified.

'It's just for a dinner,' I clarify. 'The club is auctioning a dinner, and it happens to be with me.'

'Like one of those Most Eligible Bachelor things?' Amber's gaze moves between Mum and me, seeking confirmation. 'But you're not technically a bachelor.' I'm pleased she doesn't say the word. *Widower.*

'Yeah,' agrees Mum. 'He'll probably go cheap, won't you, love? Can't even give him away!' She chuckles at her own witticisms, Amber's expression sobering as she explains. 'Mary is one of my very best friends. She lost her husband to cancer a few years ago. This is, I suppose, her way of fighting back. She does all kinds of charity work, and the auction is a bi-annual thing where the money raised goes into research.'

'Well, that's very . . . noble of you.'

That's the second time she's said that, and it still doesn't feel true.

'That's my Byron. He always does what's right. Speaking of which,' she says, putting her cup in the dishwasher before grabbing her purse. 'Don't forget to pay Amber before you step back out today.' She blows Edie a kiss before she turns to leave, thankfully missing Amber's gaping jaw.

'Was she implying . . . '

'I pay you for services rendered? Yeah,' I answer completely straight-faced.

Her face is a picture as she covers Edie's ears with her hands.

'She knows we're having *s-e-x,* and she wants you to pay me for it?'

'She wants me to pay you for services rendered like . . . looking after the kids.'

'Oh, well. That's okay, then.' Her hands fall away from Edie's ears, quickly to be replaced by my own.

'And she knows we're having *s-e-x*.'

'Hey,' my daughter complains. 'This isn't fun, you know.' She slips down from Amber's knee, running off to join her brother in the yard.

'How? We've been so careful! And you said—'

'I know what I said, but I forgot she used to spy for government.'

'She did what?'

'Not really. She's just really good at knowing things. I thought that was a mum thing?'

She shrugs, her hand distractedly pulling at the ends of her braid. 'My mom was pretty clueless.'

'Were you a naughty girl?' My hand on the back of her stool, I turn it until she's facing me and my legs are bracketing hers. 'Did you sneak out at night to meet boys to kiss and stuff?'

'Stuff? No! But she might've believed me all the times I said Dad finished off the cookies.'

My expression turns purposely sour. 'Hearing *dad* and *cookie* the same sentence does nothing for me.'

'Oh, you're a little squeamish, are you, Daddy?'

'I'm not a little anything,' I reply, taking her hand and placing it over my tightening crotch.

'Too bad we don't have time,' she answers saucily, extricating her hand as she hops down from her stool. 'Some of us have a swim lesson to attend.'

'How about I give you a swim lesson later tonight? We can dine al fresco, if you know what I mean.'

'Strangely enough, I do know what you mean. That smile you're wearing? Yeah, that's the one,' she says as I point a finger to my delighted face. 'It belongs on a well-fed cat.'

'A little pussy never hurt anyone, darl.'

'Hmm.' With a measure of side-eye, she makes her way around the island, dropping her cup into the sink on the other side of the kitchen.

Standing, I open a drawer, pulling out the cheque book. Amber falls quiet as I begin writing out her week's pay. *Like I've done every week.*

'Do we have to do it now?' Her words are part discomforted groan, the tea towel twisted between her fingertips.

'I'd love to do it now, but I have to get back to work.' I make sure to hand over the check while she's still chuckling. 'That's pay for the job you do here, right?' I duck, making our gazes level. 'The rest is all gravy.'

'You mean, like a bonus?' I nod. 'So does that mean I shouldn't expect a raise?'

'I'm pretty sure you get a raise every time I see you.' I move closer, curling my hands around her narrow shoulders.

'The children,' she whispers. But I still kiss her, though not for as long as I'd like to.

'I gotta go.'

'Me too,' she says, straightening. 'Tide and swim lessons wait for no child.' I nod even though I'm more interested in the tiny touch of colour in her cheeks. It makes me wonder if she'll always go pink at my touch.

Except there's not an *always* in this situation.

'Byron?'

'You're so fucking beautiful,' I whisper. 'You don't even know it, do you?'

The pink deepens, the flush travelling down her neck. 'I think you're the beautiful one.' She ducks her head, her fingers following the trail of ink under the sleeve of my shirt.

'Come with me Friday,' I say suddenly because suddenly, I can't think of a more perfect way to spend that evening.

Her fingers halt, her eyes rising to mine a little shell-shocked and glassy.

'To the auction?'

'Yep.'

'To watch a bunch of women fight over you?' There is a tinge of disbelief in her tone, or maybe it's jealousy. Maybe both. Whatever, it makes me smile.

'It's not like that. They're mostly just raising money for the charity.' And, by all accounts, drinking champagne and playing grab arse, according to Tom. In my defence, I didn't know that when I said I'd participate.

'Oh, I'm sure. That's why they're doing it and not just donating outright. All through the goodness of their hearts.'

'Maybe they think they're doing the male ego a good turn?'

'Your ego?' she scoffs. 'Redundant.'

'Honestly, they're usually all old women.'

'This isn't your first time?'

'Darl, I don't think this is the sort of thing you sign up to twice. Say you'll come—come protect my virtue.'

'I'm not the gambling type.'

She's really gonna make me work for it. And I would. On my knees, her perched on that tall stool. Between her pale, silky thighs, I'd luxuriate deep in the scent of her. Her fingers scraping my scalp, her hands tight in my hair while she contemplates. While she vacillates. While she makes me wait. 'Besides, you're a bit rich for my taste.' She lifts her nose and turns away from me slightly, smiling.

'You haven't seemed to mind my taste at all this week.' Fingers on her chin, I bring her face back to mine. 'In fact, I seem to recall you begging for it.'

Give it to me. I want you in my mouth. I want to suck you.

I know she can hear her own pleas. I can tell by the heat and fire in her eyes. And if she looks at me like that for much longer, I'll have her down on her knees, loosening my fly. *Because I've got a hard on like a steel fucking pipe.*

'Bottom line?' I almost whisper. 'I don't want to have dinner with anyone but you.'

'People will talk,' she murmurs.

'Fuck them.' I lower my mouth, the heat of her breath just an exhale away as the needle scratches across the vinyl of my life.

'What are you doing?' Matty sounds genuinely concerned, and though we spring apart, I find I'm not really worried. *Because it might've been worse. She might've been on her knees.*

In my dreams, maybe.

'Miss Amber has something in her eye, bud.'

'Quick thinking,' she mouths silently. I slide her a sly wink.

Of course, that's the moment Mum would choose to reappear. *Spy for the government? More like she's bloody psychic.* She pauses as she enters the room, like she senses Amber and I were on the verge of a moment—like she's seen something she shouldn't, even though there's a respectable distance between us. *Bloody psychic, see?*

'Forgot my keys,' she says a little suspiciously.

'We weren't—we weren't doing anything,' Amber splutters. 'I mean, I haven't seen them.'

'Course you haven't, darl.' Making her way to the stove, she picks them up. 'Got 'em! Now, don't do anything I wouldn't do,' she trills.

'Amber's coming to Mary's charity night with me.'

'Really?' It's not hard to see she's tickled by the idea. 'Is she gonna be your bodyguard? I can loan you some big rings in case you have to throw down.' As though the idea wasn't bad enough, she mimes a one-two punch.

'No, I mean we're going to rig the whole thing. She's gonna buy me to save me from an undesirable date.'

'I thought you said it was just dinner?' Amber chimes in.

'I did.' I glance quickly her way. 'A dinner date.'

'I'm sure you can put up with his ugly mug for one evening,' Mum supplies happily. 'Make sure he gives you his credit card because, the way I hear it, Byron has one or two fans aiming to spend big.'

Chapter Twenty-Five

AMBER

Running my hands over my thighs, I eye my reflection critically in the mirror wondering what could've possessed me to say yes to putting myself through this evening. *An evening where I get to put on makeup and wear heels and converse with other adult humans? And on the arm of a devastatingly handsome man?*

I must be crazy. Crazy lucky, maybe?

'No, he's lucky that I'm doing this,' I grumble, blowing one of the artistically styled curls out of my face. I've spent the last ninety minutes getting ready for the coming evening though I now realise ninety days wouldn't be long enough to prepare myself. There'll be looks. People will ask questions—maybe even *banging the help* type jokes may be made. And, at some point, Sally will realise I've been doing the dance with no pants with her boy. Her big boy. Her very big boy, if you know what I mean. I mean, that is if she hasn't already realised after Byron practically sat with his hands in my pants yesterday.

Then the icing on the cake that is my noisy brain is the fact that Byron has only just come home from work! We have twenty minutes until we need to leave, yet when I popped my head out of the bedroom door five minutes ago, it sounded like he was just stepping into the shower.

'Next time I'm coming back as a man.' None of the shaving, lathering, primping, blow-drying, teasing, and all that other stuff. Just five minutes in the shower and another three stepping into clothing that's already been laid out in his room, because guess who picked up his tux from the cleaners? That's right, this girl here.

I hope this dress is appropriate, I think, worrying a little more as I dust off my one pair of heels. I know an LBD is supposed to be able to carry a girl from cocktail hour to gala but I can't help stressing that it's a little tired looking. Or maybe I'm worrying because he's already seen me in it. *Ridiculous. Why would that even matter?* Because I want to impress him—I want him to feel elated to have me on his arm. I want to be responsible for the appearance of that sexy smirk, the look that says *I'm thinking of all the dirty things I want to do to you.* The same look that makes my lungs go tight and my panties turn wet.

I sigh as I look at myself in the mirror once more. *Oh, to Hell with it.* This is as good as it's going to get because there was no point in wasting my hard-earned cash on some evening gown that won't even fit in my backpack. I need to remember that in a few short weeks I'll be moving on. Something I choose not to think about, even though I should. Grabbing my purse from the dresser, I pull the door open a little ways and make my way downstairs and into the kitchen. I consider eating a muffin from the two batches the twins and I had baked this afternoon, flavours I'd called *choc-chip and what-the-fuck* along with *blueberry and what-the-hell-was-I-thinking.*

I might be a little stressed about this evening.

I decide against eating my stress-related feelings because worrying about my possibly chocolate smeared teeth—who'd choose blueberry over chocolate?—might just be one extra worry too much. Instead, I find myself pacing the room like a nervous prom date. Maybe I should be holding a corsage or something?

Finally, I hear Byron's brisk step on the stairs, so I make my way back to the kitchen to assume a kind of *1930s film star* stance. A stance of poise and elegance and absolutely not *I've been waiting here an age.*

My heart is pumping hard in my chest, and I can already feel the colour flooding my face. What if he thinks this dress isn't appropriate? What if he looks disappointed? Or even worse, doesn't look at me at all?

But then Byron walks into the room, completely unaware of my mini freak-out or even my presence in the room, preoccupied by the act of fastening his cufflinks. He drops his jacket onto a kitchen stool and I notice his hair is still damp though slicked back from his face.

I'll settle for a smile, I tell myself, though it'd be nice to be on the receiving end of a compliment. *Gee, you scrub up well.*

My breath halts as he comes to a stop, looking up with a start. His eyes travel from my face, to my hair, and down the length of the dress and all the way to my toes, lingering in all the places I like to feel his mouth the most. When his gaze finally rises to mine, I realise *this* was the reaction I craved because he's looking at me as he does when I'm naked and in his bed.

'Far out. You look . . . like a million bucks.'

'I'll take that as a compliment,' I demure as a flock of birds take flight under my ribcage. Not bad for a dress that cost me under fifty of those million dollars.

'That dress . . . turn around. Please.'

Delighted he'd even remember, I attempt a graceful twirl, coming to an abrupt stop as his hands grab my hips.

'This arse,' his low voice grumbles, his fingers roaming over my flesh. 'Absolutely stunning,' he says.

'But her face?' I say with an edge of taunt. And a desperate neediness.

'Beautiful.' His warm breath against my skin makes me shiver, his next words holding a reverence that makes my heart ache. 'From your head to your toes, and everywhere in between.'

'You don't look too bad yourself.' Turning in his arms, I slide my hands around his neck.

'What, this old thing? I thought it might help throw off your competition.'

'Gee, don't get all glammed up for me or anything.'

His mouth suddenly covers mine in a kiss that's sweet and brief but pretty darned potent. 'Who else do you think I'm dressed up for, eh?'

'The rabid mob?' I question saucily.

'Getting dressed up for that lot would be like casting pearls before swine, darl.'

His amused words rumble against my ear and though I laugh outwardly, inside I rejoice. The man wanted to look good for me—and here I was having a ridiculous freak-out! He couldn't have looked more pleased to see me. And he certainly *feels pleased* to see me.

'I'm sure they're not interested if your suit is Brooks Brothers or from Goodwill,' I say breathily. 'But what's *underneath*.' Feeling emboldened, I rotate my hips a little, rubbing my body against his very obvious erection. 'That's a very different question. According to your mother, the female masses of this town would prefer to see you in nothing but a loincloth tonight.'

'They couldn't take all this,' he says, rocking into me, his big hands gripping my butt.

'But I can?'

'You can take it, darlin'. And you take is so beautifully.' A hot pulse begins to flicker between my legs. 'And I watch you taking it on a loop in my head. Feel the hot grip of you. See your pink tongue, your mouth open, taking me deep.'

'You shouldn't say things like that,' I answer breathily.

'Why? Because it's not gentlemanly?'

'No, because I like it too much.'

Beneath my ear, his laughter is deep and rich and redolent of bedroom secrets whispered in the dark.

'Step into the laundry with me,' he whispers. His smile is heavy in his words and I realise this rubbing and brushing our bodies seem to be enjoying, that I'm definitely enjoying, has ruched the fabric of my dress up my thighs. *It currently resembles little more than a long belt.*

'The laundry? Do you need a hand looking for clean socks or something?'

'I definitely need a hand with something.'

I don't have time to answer as the door behind him swings open. My heart jumps into my throat, my hands now against Byron's chest as I push him away. I begin tugging at my dress as Matty dashes into the kitchen, followed shortly by Edie. They're both wearing their pyjamas, damp hair curling around their delighted faces as they throw their arms around their father's legs.

'Monsters! My house is full of monsters!' he roars, lifting them both up, a child in each arm.

'I'm not a monster,' Matty giggles. 'I'm a dinosaur!'

'Are you a *diplodic-u-think-he-saw-us*?' I ask as Edie holds out her arms. Well, one arm. And one thumb in her mouth.

He shoots me a wink that allays my concerns as Edie continues to lean forward. 'Do you want

Amber to put you to bed?' Edie nods then topples into my arms. 'As pretty as a picture.' There's a certain something to his words that makes my heart lift. 'What do you think, Matty? Are these two just the prettiest girls?'

Matty squints doubtfully his sister's way, I hope, but is prevented from answering by his grandmother's voice.

'And I suppose I fell out of the ugly tree, did I? I'll cry myself to sleep tonight.'

'They're the three prettiest girls!' Matty cries with a big smile on his face.

'This one's destined to be a polly,' I'm sure,' Sally says, taking Edie from my arms. 'What do you think, Edie? Will Matty make a good politician?'

'No such fing,' she answers, causing us all to laugh.

'Now, I wonder where you heard such a thing?' Sally admonishes.

'Dave-o said it,' she replies, sticking her thumb back in her mouth.

'Reckon I'll need to have a word with that man,' she says. 'And this might be just the time for your mouth to be otherwise occupied because there's no telling what that man said next.'

'You look lovely, Ma. Have you got a date?'

Sally wears her hair in a stylish chignon and is wearing a knee-length glittery black dress. I'm relieved it's not an evening gown, given my own dress.

'Hmph,' Sally answers, struggling to contain her smile. 'It's no good sucking up now, my boy. It'd serve you right if I did have a date. And a girl has to pull out all the stops when she's hanging out with women, isn't that right, Amber?'

'For sure,' I answer, though mostly out of politeness. When I'm hanging out with Emma, I don't dress for her. But I get where she's coming from and it makes me slightly apprehensive for the evening ahead.

'Come on then. Let's get you to bed and Martha can read you a story.'

'Marfa! Edie cries, throwing out her arms for the teenage girl hovering nervously at the kitchen door.

'Come in, love,' Sally directs. 'Don't worry about him,' she adds, her head darting to Byron. 'I'll sort him out if he gives you any trouble. And he's paying you and your sister double the regular rate tonight, isn't that right, son?'

'Her sister?' For the first time this evening, the old, growling Byron is back.

'Yeah, her older, so don't get your undies in a bunch. She's just parking the car. She's on her holidays from uni.'

He nods at this, seemingly now content with the arrangement and happy to hand his son over to Sally.

We say our goodbyes to the twins and the babysitting sisters and leave through the side of the house when Sally's friend arrives in her car. It seems she wanted to drive separately, in case *we young 'uns want to stay out late*.

'She means in case she does,' Byron says, holding the door open to his car. *A sleek-looking Audi.*

Looks like we're not taking the truck. The interior smells like new as I slide myself inside as gracefully as my dress and heels will allow. And I can't help but notice Byron's hot gaze fixed to my exposed thigh.

Worried? Me? As if!

Chapter Twenty-Six

AMBER

The journey to the country club feels intimate, especially as Byron reaches for my hand in an almost unconscious moment as he gives me a run-down of the evening's events. He prepares me for some mingling, and for some speculation about us showing up together. I ask him whether I'm supposed to take his arm as we enter, or if we're there as "just friends". Byron's reply is that he'll be offering me his arm, and that I'd bloody well better take it. Whether because he doesn't want to be manhandled immediately or whether he truly wants people to see me as his date, I'm not so sure.

As we pull into the parking lot, my stomach is twisted with nerves as I watch women in designer dresses glide from expensive cars, making their way into the foyer. Women of all ages and all shapes and sizes but with one thing in common; they're all obviously moneyed.

It takes me a little while to notice the car engine isn't running and that Byron is staring at me.

'You okay over there?' I swallow and nod. 'What is it? You don't have to go in, not if you're not feeling up to it. I can take you back home.'

Home. But it's not really home, is it? *It is beginning to feel like it.* I quell the ridiculous thought.

'I didn't know Australia had country clubs,' I find myself saying. I roll my lips inwards, rubbing them together to stop myself from adding *yes—let's go home*. The truth is, I'm kind of terrified. I'm totally out of my element and I don't recall ever feeling like this before.

'They're mostly golf clubs.'

'Expensive golf clubs with a side of snooty?'

'Something like that.' I take heart from the note of cynicism in his soft chuckle.

'But you're a member here?' In my seat, I turn to face him, my elbow resting on the chair, my hand cupping my cheek.

'Yeah. The Phillips family are founding members. It's mostly business for me. I'm with Mark Twain when it comes to golf.'

'I'm sure your tattoos add some colour to the green.' This time, I find myself running my lips together for a whole other reason because I'm sure he looks like a rare and exotic bird out there.

'If you're a good girl, I'll let you examine them again later.' His eyes shine with a mixture of mischief and sexiness.

'Who says I want to?'

'You did. And without words. It was quite a thing to watch, let me tell you. I've never been undressed by someone's gaze quite so . . . thoroughly.'

'Stop teasing.' I swat him ineffectually when he catches it my hand. He brings it to his lips and kisses the backs of my fingers. I can't swallow back a sigh full of longing.

'Amber,' he begins, his thick lashes peering over the top of my hand. 'You are breathtakingly beautiful and I would be honoured to escort you into the den of female wickedness over there. We'll go in, order a drink, and I'll only leave you as long as it takes me to do my thing.'

I cock a taunting eyebrow at this, which he chooses to ignore.

'You have a staggering amount of money to buy yourself a good time tonight. But a quick word of advice from the wise—'

'Oh, so you're wise as well as overconfident, huh?'

'If you choose to buy me tonight, I guarantee I'll put out.'

'I have a choice, do I?'

'It is lady's choice, though I doubt there'll be many in there.' My hand still in his, he looks over his shoulder with almost a grimace.

'Just . . . let me get this straight. I can use your money to buy someone else?' He nods tersely. 'Your money . . . for another dude?'

'For a dinner date,' he qualifies. 'It is for charity.' He adds a shrug. 'I'm not some fucking meathead.' He kisses my fingers again before turning to climb from the car.

I'm oddly deflated that he seems to care so little, my earlier worries resurfacing as the door opens. Byron holds out his hand to help me from the car.

'Thank—'

I notice his cocky grin a moment before I find myself pressed up against the rear passenger door. Only, my skin isn't touching the metal, as his hand splays low on my bare back, his other resting at the back of my neck. Instinctively, I tip my head back as he leans in, my hands rising by themselves and curling around his shoulders. He slants his mouth over mine, his kiss halting the noise in my brain and stealing my reasoning. His cheeks are smooth shaven, I realise, and he smells of the heavenly cologne he'd worn in Sydney. *The same one I'd found in his bathroom.* His chest is hard under my hands, his heart beating steadily. Shouldn't it be odd that I register these split-second thoughts when all of my fears have fallen away? His mouth is soft and his kiss tender. For at least ten seconds. When tender lips become questing and tentative strokes of tongue become something else. This is an urgent kiss. Demanding. The kind of kiss that seeks ownership.

'Red, if you choose some other bastard,' he growls hotly in my ear. 'He'd better be stumping up for dinner for three.' A delighted and girly giggle breaks free from my throat, a giggle that turns to a carnal groan as his teeth press against my earlobe. 'And you'd better be ready to put on a show because I won't keep my hands to myself.'

Pulling away, he takes my hands and this time, I'm too full of those happy kissing endorphins to worry about anything else.

'Oh, my bag.' I turn to the car and Byron clicks the fob, unlocking it. I grab it and we're back on our kiss-floaty way. As we draw nearer to the entrance, Byron lifts my hand, folding it into the crook of his arm. 'I should've left my purse in the car,' I consider in a whisper as it becomes obvious he's about to introduce me to a couple that are leaving the building. Around Sally's age, the pair aren't dressed for the gala but perhaps an early dinner.

'Here.' With a small smile, Byron takes my tiny bag, sliding it into the inside pocket of his jacket. Theres something terribly endearing about this, I find. Maybe it's because it reminds me of long-married couples, and the kinds of men who don't mind walking around with their wives' purses. Maybe it's because I've given him something personal of mine, and he's keeping it safe and close to him. The trust, the openness of this simple moment strikes a chord deep in my heart. What it might mean, I tuck it away to consider some other time.

Already, people are greeting my date—my date!— waving and telling him to wait for them inside so they can catch up. I smile pleasantly as I do my best not to cling to him like a frightened child, reminding myself this man is mine tonight. A gift, I suppose you might say. Soon to be bought and paid for.

Inside the entrance is an opulent marble lobby crowded with people in sequins and lace. There's the odd pair of shiny Oxfords and lots of ridiculously high heels, the air thick with the smell of hair spray and perfume, the noise a cacophony.

Byron guides me through the throng of bodies, oblivious to the looks we're drawing as he heads to the larger, more open space of the banquet hall. We pass Sally and he places a hand on her shoulder as he kisses both her cheek and the cheek of her friend.

The banquet hall is large and opulent. Modern chandeliers hang from the ceiling, a wall of windows overlooking gardens and a lake, equally as luxurious. Already the sky is turning a dark lavender colour, the sun beginning its lazy summertime descent as my focus is drawn back to the other dinner guests. It seems it's time to make the first of many rounds of introductions. The evening is dominated by women, which I'd come to expect, though there are one or two men who've accompanied their wives to the event. These couples are charming and gracious, the menfolk invariably making comments about swapping the dinner date auction component for a date with their lawns and so on, before the talk turns to business. Meanwhile, I'm looked up and down in both obvious and subtle ways by their wives. Unfortunately, the single women attendees aren't quite as circumspect in their assessment.

'Byron, I thought you were an eligible bachelor, what's with the date?' one woman asks. She only nods in my direction, without making eye contact.

'Cara, this is Amber.' I appreciate the way he introduces me before answering her. 'Amber, Cara.' His smile dips to where I'm holding his arm and I realise I'm holding so tight I might be leaving nail marks. I blow out a breath I hadn't realised I'd held as his gaze touches hers once more, briefly. 'Still eligible for a dining experience, if you've got the cash.'

'What's the point if we can't fool around after?' she cat-calls after him.

'The national reserve doesn't hold enough cash for that.'

I'm not sure if his answer, made through gritted teeth, was made for my ears. I laugh anyway as he guides me away from the women sending venomous stares my way.

'I can see why you needed me to come, these women want to devour you,' I whisper-hiss as he leans into me, chuckling softly.

'Come on,' he says, covering my hand with his. 'Let's get the protector of my virtue a drink.'

'I've got your back, fair Byron.'

But what I didn't expect was for him to lead me to a table before leaving to get said drink. I begin to protest, but he's gone before I can register my complaint. I fuss with the silverware, straightening it rather than looking out at the crowd, wishing I'd kept my purse, and therefore my phone, with me. Eventually, I look up to find a woman sitting at another table very obviously staring at me. I jump a little when I feel a hand on my shoulder. I turn and breathe out with relief when I see Sally. She gives me a hug.

'It's only me, darl. Where's By?' I gesture toward the bar, realising I can't see his broad shoulders there. Where's he gone?

'He was getting us drinks, I'm not sure where he is now.'

'Getting waylaid is the name of the game here. You doing okay?'

'Yes, thank you.' I nod, fighting the temptation of telling her how nervous I feel and how awkward it is being stared at by richer and older women. The woman at the other table didn't fall into the latter category, and as though drawn there by some force, my gaze moves to her table again, but she's no longer there.

Quickly, Sally is swept up in conversation with other guests again, though she stays close by. *And I love her for it.* A few minutes pass before I feel a warmth behind me, an arm wrapping around my right shoulder, a large hand holding a champagne glass. Byron leans close enough to my left ear to graze his lips against it.

'Sorry I took so long,' he whispers.

We clink glasses and drink and I empty mine in fewer swallows than is decorous, I'm sure. But I get what I was aiming for; the mellow of booze. It turns out our tablemates are very pleasant, and mostly couples, and also mostly old friends of the family. The atmosphere is relaxed and, although I'm a stranger, I'm very much made to feel at ease. I absolutely delight on the fare served for dinner, opting for an oyster appetiser and swordfish to follow, which luxuriates in a delicate buttermilk foam. Byron watches me with a mixture of amusement and something I can't place as a trio of desserts are placed in front of me.

'What have you got there?' He leans into me, ostensibly to see what I'm eating, his hand placed low on my back.

'This is a tiny choux bun,' I reply, pointing at the first confection.

'It is tiny, isn't it?' he answers, swiping it from my plate and popping it into his mouth.

'Hey! Get your own dessert.'

'You must have a sweet tooth,' one of the men at the table—Harry, I think—says to Byron. 'And I can see why.'

'If he has a sweet tooth, he should order his own dessert,' I complain, moving my plate away from him.

'I would but I'm saving myself.'

'For more wine, I shouldn't wonder,' laughs a rotund man from the other side of the table.

'This is my last, Ted,' Byron answers, holding his glass up a touch. 'I'm saving myself for cookie.' His answer may be for Ted but his gaze and his meaning are solely for me. A red hot pulse skitters through me as I lower my gaze to my remaining desserts. Byron may be speaking in code but I'm pretty sure my expression would give his meaning away.

The noise in the room dies away as an older woman steps up to a dais at the front of the room, clinking a fork against her glass in order to gain attention, a microphone clipped onto the front of her dress.

'Welcome, everyone! Thank you all for coming out tonight. I'm going to keep my speech short, as I know many of you are eager for our auction to commence.' Someone whistles, followed by a few hoots and hollers, and the odd comment. Sally leans over to me and tells me that the speaker is her friend, Mary. Next, Mary lists about two thousand people who made this event possible (yawn) followed by the next ten years' worth of events the country club will be hosting. Or at least, that's how it seems. She reminds us all that tonight's auction is benefitting cancer research, and to please only place serious bids, no matter how handsome the prize is. Cue more wolf-whistles here, along with the odd man's name shouted out.

'Rich women are pretty horny,' I say, leaning into Byron, my words for only his ears.

'I can't see anyone else in this room.' His answer makes me shiver, his finger drawing down my spine. 'All I can think about is how delicious my dessert is tonight.' He draws a little closer, his lips just a whisper away from my ear. 'Hot and wet and creaming.'

His words drag heat over the surface of my skin, making it hard for me to breathe. As he pulls away, I find Sally watching us with an unconcealed delight.

We're asked to stay in our seats to make everything go more smoothly, though I wonder if it's to stop the auction meat—I mean, men—from being mauled. I watched with strange sense of detachment as man after man is cat-called and viewed. I find it offends me deeply, which then makes me wonder if my offended nature is more because I don't want anyone ogling my man.

My man for now, I amend silently. My man for tonight, definitely.

Finally, Byron is called up to the dais. He gives my hand a quick squeeze under the table and walks to his seat through a sea of applause and whoops and whistles, very much the loudest yet.

Mary introduces him, noting his selling points like a corrupt real-estate agent with a house that needs talking up.

At six-foot-three, he's a captain of industry, but not too lofty to get down and dirty in the vines . . . getyourmindsoutofthegutters, ladies!

She has him turn around, giving the crowd "a look at the goods" while I feel mortification on his behalf. I take my eyes off the spectacle and the man I'm far too fond of, glancing around the room. Some of these so-called ladies are standing, others are craning their heads to get a good look. Some appear to be stealing the bidding paddles of other women while they're not looking, who then search around their seats frantically.

He'll make you feel sexy and strong, Mary continues with her spiel, *and a night with him and you'll feel ready to take on the world, I reckon, because he'll give you one of life's greatest pleasures . . .*

At this point, my eyes meet Sally's and I think my mouth must be open in shock. She shakes her head almost infinitesimally as though this is okay, that what her so called friend is saying isn't totally mortifying. When I look back to the dais, Byron seems to be completely unphased, the intensity of his gaze honed in on only one person. And then I get it. He's coming home with me tonight. I'm the one he'll make feel sexy and strong. I'm the one who'll be receiving one of life's greatest pleasures.

Because he'll undoubtably bring a bottle of wine to your date from his own estate.

Ohhhh.

Ladies, we'll start the bidding at five-hundred dollars.

Though my heart is beating frantically, I play it cool, refusing to immediately raise my paddle. I watch the other women going at it—women from eighteen to eighty—as I listen to the hecklers in the crowd.

'You *have* a boyfriend, Frances!'

'Like you need more dinner, Heather! Your fat ass would probably bankrupt him!'

'You had a crack at him in high school, Dianne, let someone else have a turn!'

'Grandma, *seriously*?'

The rest of the audience chuckles and banters as this goes on. Eventually the price gets too steep for the loudest mouths. One grandma is still in it, and I wonder if Byron would really mind treating her to dinner, walking stick and all. Maybe I should be the bigger woman and bow out. But as she yells, 'Come to mama,' I decide not.

I raise my paddle at a thousand dollars. At eleven hundred, the woman in the red dress raises hers. Then twelve hundred to one of the dirty look-givers

I made eye contact with before dinner. I glance back at the front of the room in time to see Byron relaxing his face from what appeared to be an involuntary cringe. A few more women drop out of the running. Grandma's ceiling appears to be three thousand dollars, and I'm left competing against the bitch in the red dress. Mary and the crowd act as though they're watching a tennis match, their heads swinging from me to her and back again. Byron looks at me when I bid, but only moves his head in the general direction of red dress when her paddle goes up. She's young and attractive, and I'd be a fool not to think that there has to be some history behind this. Maybe it's something simple like they attended the same high school and she got under his skin, or maybe it's more complicated. At thirty-five hundred, her bids become reluctant, and at thirty-seven hundred, she relents.

I've won, and I realise I'd have paid a damned sight more to protect him. My follow-up thought is that I'm being ridiculous. Everyone cheers, though maybe not as loudly as they would have if they'd all known me like they know the other bidders. Then Byron is allowed to return to his seat, while Mary placates the female audience.

'There's always next year!' she assures them, as Byron leans over to whisper in my ear, '*In her dreams*'. She then announces the dinner officially over. She thanks us all, reminds us that a band will begin shortly and that she'll be back later in the evening with a running total of the monies raised.

The crowd reverts back to pre-dinner antics, wandering and mingling, though many people start

to leave, and come to shake Byron's hand, and
mine, on the way out. I feel like the winning team
after a ball game, made to show good
sportsmanship. Sally leaves the table, saying she
sees Clarence Herrera sitting on his own.

'What a shame. Maybe he needs some company.'

Her son warns her not to get into any trouble, and
we say goodnight to her.

Byron and I stick around for a cocktail, chatting
with the director of the board of education and his
wife. They're pleasant people who have spent time
in Europe and I feel like I finally have some space to
talk. Eventually, Byron asks if I'm ready to go. My
eyes are dry and my feet feel fiery from being
cramped up in these damn shoes all night.

I am definitely ready to go.

The evening has cooled and stars fill the sky like
fairy lights. I want to ask what the deal is with the
red dress bitch but figure if he's not talking, it's for
a reason. And I can wait because tonight, he's my
prize.

'So, how did I do?' I ask, almost dancing in front
of him. 'Was I a good maid in shining armour,
swooping in to rescue you from the torment and
suffering of dining with the ferocious opposite sex?'
I make ridiculous slashing and stabbing motions in
the air.

'You're my hero,' he retorts, pulling me into his
arms.

'Heroine,' I correct, my breath suddenly taut.

'You're truly the bravest maid in all the town,
charging in to rescue a little ol' thing like me.' He

brings his hands to the sides of my face, brushing the wisps of hair away, before his fingers seem to follow the shape of me from forehead to chin.

'I am the baddest bitch.'

'You are pretty bad. I thought for a minute you'd let the granny win.' I begin to laugh as he continues. 'You took your time lifting that paddle. I'd started to worry you'd put it down somewhere and lost it.'

'Some women had theirs stolen.' Then it's his turn to laugh. 'Not by me!'

He clicks the fob but I pull him back from the passenger door by the hand he's still holding.

'Where's my reward?'

'Your what?'

'For rescuing you. The heroine always wins a *hefty reward* for rescuing the gentleman in distress.'

'Does she?'

'Read a book, Byron. Sheesh!' As I tease and cajole, I tuck my fingers into his pants, beginning to walk backwards towards a clump of trees at the edge of the parking lot.

I *am* the baddest bitch. And the bravest.

'I . . . suppose I'll have to owe you?'

'I don't take rewards on account,' I purr, pushing him up against the largest date palm in the clump. We're out of view of the club and I'm feeling like a total boss, and the way his eyes darken with want doesn't exactly hurt. 'Payment up front.' I rub my hand against the growing bulge in his pants. He pulses into my hand, his head tipped back, his face shadowed by the fronds as he offers a harsh *fuck* to the stars.

'That's a tempting offer, but maybe not here,' I murmur. Unzipping his fly, I curl my hand around him. 'But I'll take a little part payment right now.'

Chapter Twenty-Seven

BYRON

'Fuck.'

The back of my head hits the trunk of the palm as Amber slides her hand into my zipper, curling her fist around my rock-hard length.

'That's a tempting offer, but maybe not here.' Her wicked gaze flicks up my shirt to meet mine. 'But I'll take a little part payment right now.'

'Oh, Christ.' She's going to blow me in the bushes. Am I dreaming? I curl my hands around her bare shoulders to stop myself from wrapping them in her hair, my abs tight and my thighs beginning to tremble as she lifts me free from the confines of my pants.

'A very hefty reward,' she purrs, almost weighing it in her hand.

'Wet it.' The rasp of my command is in the air before I even realise it. The dark pools of her eyes find mine once more, a little shocked, and a lot turned on. 'Go on, little girl. Use your tongue.'

The nearby lamp makes a fiery halo of her head as I watch as she lowers it before her wet, pink tongue licks my length. I groan at the sensation, one of my hands threading now unconsciously into the hair at the nape of her neck. The cool night air, the vibration of her moan as she licks my slit and lap my cock like it's the tastiest of treats, blows my fucking mind.

'How was that . . . ' She pulls back, her gaze almost guileless. It's a look that would be more believable if my cock wasn't inches from her beautiful mouth. And then she seals the deal. 'Sir?' From guileless to bold and taunting. 'You like it when I call you Sir, don't you?'

'Fuck, yeah.' And that's the truth. I know it's just her way—a politeness—but I can't help the images it conjures for me. The dark things I dream of doing to her. Things I've never done with anyone else. But it's more than that. This woman makes me happy. Sure, I'm happy because I'm getting laid regularly these days, which makes me float around the property like a dog with two dicks most of the time, but it's more than that. It's like she gets me. Like she sees beyond the outer me. Sees what's beneath the surface. The soft along with the dark. And what's more frightening is the fact that she seems to like it all.

'Tell me,' she whispers, drawing her teasing tongue along my length.

'You're just so sweet, darlin'. It makes me want to sully you. Dirty you up.'

'I think I like the sound of that, sir.'

Between us, my cock jumps in response to her breathy words, an electric pulse skittering down my spine. I'd forgotten how a little role playing could feel. How all-consuming it is to step into the moment. How freeing.

'Then suck my cock, little girl.'

I bite the inside of my mouth to stop from crying out as she suddenly inhales me to the back of her throat with the best of sounds. True to my fantasy, I give her a helping hand, pressing it to the back of her head.

'Yes, that's it. Take me.' Her lips are almost at the root of my dick, the channel of her throat tight around me. 'You've been holding out on me,' I groan out, losing my mind as I lose myself in her.

With a rush of air, she pulls back, her eyes wet and glistening as she wipes saliva from her mouth with the back of her hand. But she's smiling. *Oh, fuck how she's smiling.* And her nipples are hard pebbles beneath the fabric of her dress.

'That gets you off, darlin'.' It's not a question. 'I want you to show me how much.'

Her eyes shine dark in the moonlight, her brows furrowed for a beat as she considers how. There are a few ways to meet my request, I consider, as I take my cock into my hand, rubbing the remains of her saliva into my skin. Her eyes follow the movement and it takes me everything not to beg her to get on her knees for me. But I want all of this. My cock in her mouth, her exposing the dark side of herself. I want it all and I want her to do it for me. And she does, her fingertips skimming the fabric of her dress up her thighs.

'Fuck, yeah.'

I don't know what it is about this dress that drives me fucking mental. Maybe it's how it exposes her creamy skin to my touch. Or maybe it's how the fabric moves with her like a second skin. More likely it's because I know what she's wearing underneath.

Not. A. Fucking. Lot.

Amber exhales a long tremulous breath as the hem breaches her hips, the dark triangle of her underwear exposed, gossamer thin and transparent, the neat strip of her red curls on display beneath the wet fabric.

'You're shivering.' She nods, her dark eyes full of need. 'Is it the cool evening breeze on your pussy? The thrill of being caught?'

'It's the way that you're watching me.' She arches her back. Does she realise how tempting she looks with her tits thrust out?

'Give me your underwear,' I demand, giving my cock a swift tug. 'Give me your underwear and get on your knees.'

Her breath is tremulous as she hooks her thumbs into the thin band at her hips, sliding the scrap of fabric down her legs. Then, like a good little girl, she does as she's bid, but not before I slide off my jacket, placing it on the ground in front of me.

'You're so good to me, sir.' Her taunting expression changes as I take her undies from her hand, bringing them to my face.

'I can smell your sweet cunt. And I'm gonna eat it all night long.' I slide her underwear into my pocket then, leaning into her, I press my hand against the back of her head. Maybe it's the boldness of my words or that her pussy is exposed to the air that has her inhaling me sloppily to the tip with a carnal groan. 'Shush, Red. Unless you want an audience.' She moans again, this time in a high pitch, making me chuckle. At least, until she begins to use her tongue in the wickedest of ways.

'You're so fucking good at this.' In response to my hoarse words, she sends a lust-filled, hazy glance my way.

'And you're so big,' she whispers against my wet flesh.

Jesus Christ, she's gonna kill me. But I'll go with a smile on my face.

The night is filled with the sounds of our coupling and though the air is cool, my skin burns, the feeling expanding and growing as I edge closer to coming. Then, coming I am, and the part of me that would tell her—hat tiny vestige of gentlemanly honour—is long gone as everything blurs, good, bad, should and ought no longer have meaning as a white heat barrels through my body. My hand cradles her head, pulling her closer, my knees threatening to give out as I explode into the back of her throat.

My chest heaves as I stare up unseeingly at the stars peeking through the fronds of the palm. The last time I felt this boneless was after an Ironman Triathlon. I feel like I've run a marathon, rode a bike around the world, and swam an ocean, leaving behind a husk of a man. But a happy husk. A vacant, smiling, ready for the nut house husk. My eyes drop to the woman still on her knees in front of me, her hair now wild and her complexion flushed. She smiles up at me and my heart aches with the beauty of the moment. The simplicity. And though my heart recognises it already, my brain is playing catch up.

This woman means so much to me.

Yep, I'm well and truly fucked.

Chapter Twenty-Eight

AMBER

The house is quiet when we get home, and Sally's car is missing from the drive. Byron drops his crumpled jacket to a kitchen stool before making his way into the family room to pay the sisters for babysitting. As I begin to load glasses and the odd cup into the dishwasher, I wonder what this says about the schizophrenia of my position while Byron ushers the pair to the door. Maybe I'm seeking to reinforce the fact that I'm the hired help, even though I'd entered the house on Byron's arm, dressed like the lady of the house. As I catch a glimpse of my reflection in the darkened kitchen window, I give up. There's no fooling anyone over the age of seventeen into thinking I look anything other than truly fucked.

The sisters leave and Byron moves around the downstairs turning off the lights. There's something in the quietness of his movements. Something he isn't saying. He won't look at me and he barely spoke to me in the car. *Though he did hold my hand.* Maybe the enormity of what's happening between us is hitting him, too. Or maybe it's more that he's dragged me into the dark and he doesn't like what he sees when I'm there.

You're in charge of his beloved children, Amber. Maybe you shouldn't have been so noisily into blowing him.

But I couldn't help it because I was into it. I couldn't help myself.

He comes to stand behind me, his reflected expression warm, wanting, making the noise in my head recede. He wraps me in his arms, then takes my hand, pulling me from the room.

We move up the staircase, pausing at the children's room to peek inside. Matty lies snuggled under his covers like a cherub in a classical painting, but for his pirate bed linen, while Edie lies sprawled across the top of the covers, her thumb still jammed into her mouth. I find that we're both smiling as Byron pulls the door mostly closed. He turns off the hall light before turning and taking my head in his hands.

Our lips meet, and if moments can be measured in kisses, this kiss is destined for our history book. Soft lips and teasing tongue, our lips seems to say what our mouths cannot.

I want. I need. You mean something to me . . .

'Tell me I'm not the only one feeling this.' Byron's husky whisper blows across my skin, his lips teasing my neck as I tilt back my head back giving him better access to my heated skin.

'I feel it.' Lord, do I feel it. I feel it so much that I flatten my palms against the wall, fearful of him realising exactly how deeply I need him as he kisses a trail of fire over my bare shoulder, pressing his teeth in the place where it curves to my neck. I whimper, my knees almost giving out, my insides suddenly pulsing a frantic beat.

'Thank you. Thank you . . . for outside earlier. For being you.' I tip my smile to the ceiling, my eyes suddenly glassy from sensory and emotional overload. 'Don't hide from me,' he rasps, tilting my head back, our lips meeting again. 'Never hide from me.'

Tongues dance and lips brush as I pull his tie, then work a few buttons of his shirt loose as his fingers tease the fastening of my dress. But he doesn't loosen it. Instead, he lets his fingers trace a line down my bare back, my flesh breaking out in goosebumps at his touch.

'Turn around,' he whispers, so I do, my palms and elbows resting against the wall. I shiver as his lips touch my neck where it curves into my shoulder, and draw in a sharp breath as he loosens the clasp on my dress. The soft fabric falls away with a sigh. Or maybe that's me. It puddles around my heels as Byron's hands cup my breasts.

'I'm so hard for you.' A soft kiss to my neck. A swipe of his tongue. 'I want you all the time.' His hands fall away as his mouth trails a line of kisses down my spine.

'Please,' I whisper as he pulls on my hips, widening my stance. My eyes flick to the window above the grand front door, the glass at mezzanine height. *Would anyone be able to see us like this?*

'Would you like them to?' His voice is laced with taunt and husk.

The only response I can summon is a whimper because I would and I wouldn't and that right there scares me.

'Would they see your silhouette or your skin? Would they see me spreading your legs for my view?' With his dark words, he does just that, wrapping his fingers around my ankle as he lifts it. 'But this view,' he says, his tone now a little awe-filled. 'I'd keep to myself.'

'Oh, God, please.' My cheeks burn with my position, my nipples taunted by the cold wall. But most maddening is how my insides pulse emptily, desperate for him.

'Please what?' With an edge of taunt and touch that's all tease, he slides his fingers, parting my wetness, his breath hot against my flesh.

'Please, Byron, touch me.' Touch me before I burst.

With a noise that makes me feel like I'm the best thing he's ever tasted, he presses his mouth against me, his tongue tearing a cry from my mouth.

'Shush, sweetheart.' I nod and press my mouth against my arm, rocking back against him in a silent promise to be good. 'I heard you in your bedroom that night. I wanted it to be me making you cry out. I want to make you beg for me every night.'

They're just words, I remind myself. *Words whispered in the darkness don't necessarily carry the same meaning into the daylight.*

Then he kisses me—kisses me as he would my mouth. Soft lips and probing tongue as he whispers those midnight sentiments I wish I could bottle for evermore. Between his promises, his tongue, and his deft finger work, I struggle to stay upright, crying into the crook of my arm, biting the flesh to keep myself both quiet and sane. As my orgasm crawls though me, as I push back, grinding into his face feeling every inch his goddess and his whore. I'm so desperate for more—for more tongue, for more fingers, for this ache to be fulfilled.

'You're so beautiful when you come,' he rasps. 'Come for me, Amber. Come on my face.'

And I do. Oh, I do, my orgasm crashing over me, the shock of it so powerful it's like nothing I've ever experienced. I'm crying, tears streaming down my face, my whole body shaking. The feeling is intense—immense—as I give in, give up, give over to the power this man has over me as I rock against him wild and unrestrained, chasing my climax to it's very ends.

It takes me a moment to realise Byron is standing, then turning me to face him, his mouth and chin shining wickedly with my wetness.

'I knew you were dangerous from the moment I saw you in my kitchen. Amber,' he breathes, pressing his mouth against mine. *Me wicked? He's the one with the Devil's smile.* 'Taste yourself, Red. You're like liquid fire.' He presses his mouth to mine as I wonder if I'm fire, will it stop me from being burned?

My hand in his, we make our way to his bedroom, my weak legs hitting the mattress as he pulls the bed linen back, sliding off my heels and tucking me in. I feel cossetted. Good. And lucky to be watching him finish the job I'd started out in the hallway as he sheds the rest of his clothes, his ink just shadows in the darkness. I will never forget what it feels like to experience his weight over me, how it presses me down into the mattress, his hands framing my face. The sound he makes as his cock touches me, brushes my wetness, will stay with me until I'm old and grey.

The muscles of his back ripple beneath my fingertips, the flex of his hips welcomed against the cradle of my own. We kiss and we kiss until my body begs for his, my fingers tight on his hips as I work myself against him, as though to draw him in.

'Red, I don't have a condom.'

'They're in your sock drawer,' I whisper, slightly delirious. Though his dark chuckle puts a stop to that.

'Thanks, darl, but I know where they are.' He rubs the underside of his hard cock against me and I'm pretty sure my eyes roll to the back of my head. 'What I'm trying to say is that I want to feel you.'

'Oh.'

'I want to come on you. Come inside you.'

Ohhhh.

'But you're not on the pill, are you?' I am and I have been the whole time I've been travelling. No girl wants to experience their period while at the beach or on a long haul flight. 'Amber,' he groans, flexing again. 'Hang on.' He makes as though to pull away but I wrap my legs around him. The change in position brings his crown right *there*.

'Jesus,' he rasps, holding himself over me on his hands. Another remembrance for my old lady scrap book.

'I want you like this, do it.'

Before I have the chance to tell him I'm on the pill, he takes the invitation, pushing inside me with a carnal groan.

'Jesus fucking Christ. You're so tight. And so *wet*.' His deep exhale blows across my neck. 'You feel amazing. I promise I'll pull out . . .

Who needs words of romance when you have Byron Phillips pressing his promises to your lips, his words becoming nothing more than a carnal groan that echoes through your bones.

He pauses, his weight towering over me, acclimating to the feel of my body around him. His eyes screwed tight, his arms tremble as he withdraws as though the slow slide drives him almost delirious. A small stab of his hips pushes me physically up the bed and I cry out, everything drawing taut and tight and on the precipice of shattering.

The sounds of his uneven breaths. The sight of his hair falling across his face. The slow, deep feel of him. I don't think it had ever felt so good. So perfect.

'Fuck . . . just look at you.'

'Oh . . .' I wrap my legs around him as his words cause an explosion of sensation inside.

'Jesus. Not gonna last. Need you. To come.'

I don't have any words but I don't need them anyway, not as he drags my leg from his hip, spreading me wider across the bed. The change of angle is instant, the friction against my clit the best kind of torture as he begins fucking me in deep but eager thrusts.

'I love . . . love the way you feel. The way you hold me,' he rasps with a roll of his hips. And I'm done for, my muscles flexing around him as the entirety of my being becomes nothing but waves of pleasure and joy. 'That's it . . . that's it. You're so lovely when you come.' And with a shudder and a hot gasp, he pushes up to his knees, holding himself in his palm. I've little time to consider who's the lovely one as he paints my stomach and between my legs with white-hot lashings of his cum.

Chapter Twenty-Nine

BYRON

'You're in a good mood,' Mum says as I come into the kitchen the morning after the night before. The night before that has the muscles of my abs and thighs the best kind of sore.

'Ma, how can you say I'm in a good mood when I've only just walked into the room?'

'A mother just knows,' she answers in the tone of someone who should be selling time on a TV commercial for a psychic hotline. I consider throwing the paisley tea-towel her way with a suggestion that she could wrap it around her head. You know, if she's going to be seeing into the future and shit, when she adds, 'And I heard you whistling as you came downstairs.'

I find myself chuckling as she slides me a look. *You know the one.*

'I know what you're thinking,' I tell her. 'And it's not that.'

'You couldn't guess at my thoughts, not if I gave you a million years to guess.'

'You're thinking I'm happy because I've had sex.'

'No, *yesterday* you were happy because you had sex. And I wager that was the reason the day before that and the day before that. This morning you're happy because you've realised you have a connection beyond the bits of the pair of you that fit together. You know, your dangly bits?'

'Thanks, Mum. I'm pretty sure I know how it works.' Jesus Christ on a fucking bike, I do not need this conversation with my mother this time of the morning. Or at any time in the next century, preferably.

'You've realised you have a chance of something real.'

Way to wipe the smile off my face, Mum.

'Yeah, well, don't get too excited. She's leaving in a few weeks. Any connection we have won't extend beyond that.' No matter what my mother thinks.

'It won't if that's your attitude,' she answers pointedly, bringing her coffee cup to her lips.

'It's not up for discussion, okay?'

'That was pure fact, not a debate, son.'

Refusing to be drawn into this discussion, I make my way over to the coffee machine, disappointed not to be greeted by Amber's dark and heavenly brew.

'She must have had other things to do,' Mum adds.

As she opens her mouth to speak again, I point a finger her way with a censorious, 'Don't.'

'I wouldn't dream of it,' she answers with a measure of sass, walking out of the room.

But there was a moment last night where I realised everything had changed. I'm not talking about what happened in the garden or upstairs. There was a moment before the auction where I could see my present become my future. And that moment was all her. *All Amber. All authentic. All the way.*

I can't say why, though I can pinpoint the moment. I'd watched her from across the room as she'd thrown back her head and laughed in response to something Mum had said. I just knew it right then and there, knew it in the pit of my gut and in my fucking veins that she was no longer a casual fuck. *If she ever could be such a thing.* We'd crossed that line without even realising. I have feelings for her. Big feelings. The scary kind. And sure, she'd induced all kinds of feelings in me since I'd walked into the kitchen and found her drinking coffee with my parent, as casually as you like. Feelings of surprise and delight, of suspicion and anger, quickly followed by more delight and all kinds of physical reactions. Sore muscles from fucking, a semi-permanent stiff cock. But these kinds of feelings aren't easily chased away or replaced. And while I don't want to put a name to something that I know I'm not meant to have, it definitely begins with *l* and ends in *ove*.

Yeah, that other four letter word.

So that's me fucked.

~*~

It seems the days following the country club auction are accompanied by my whistling soundtrack. And why wouldn't it? I woke in the morning listening to the birds getting their breakfast and looking at the red hair cascading across my pillows. Some mornings I stayed until the sun crested her head setting her auburn locks aglow and turning her creamy skin into gold. Other mornings, I woke with her head burrowed under my chin, those same auburn locks tickling my nose. And God, I love it. Every morning it kills me to get out of bed because I just want to stay in that moment, Amber's warm skin against mine.

I might be prolonging the agony, making it worse for myself, but I've decided to take this bit of joy while I can get it. She's supposed to be leaving, but who knows what another few weeks might bring? Maybe she'll come around to my way of feeling all on her own.

And until then, I'll enjoy my time with her to the fullest. Take this morning, for instance. I'd delayed my exit from bed until the very last moment, giving myself only a few minutes to shower. But a few minutes wasn't nearly long enough, especially not as Amber had followed me stealthily in, sleepily taking the soap from my hands. We'd gotten good and soapy until I turned her in my arms, pressing her back into the cold tiles as I'd hooked her leg around my hips.

'What if the kids come in?' she'd panted, the hot air in the room swirling between us.

'Didn't you lock the door?' I'd rasped into her neck.

'What, you mean like you did?'

'We'd better make this a quick fuck, then.'

Despite my assurances, she still stresses, but at least she's stopped trying to creep back into her bed before I wake. Still, it's only a matter of time before the kids bust us in some graphic grope-fest or semi-state of dress because I can't keep my hands off her. I survived my parental grope-fests, I'm sure my two will, too.

I reckon we'll have to cross that bridge when we come to it.

Same as persuading her to stay.

There, I said it. Or thought it. Whatever.

If you don't ask, you never get.

Maybe she'll even say yes.

And maybe I'm forcing us to take increasing risks in the subliminal hope that we'll be caught. That this thing between us will be forced into the open. That then it'll be real.

I consider this for a moment.

Nah. I reckon I'm just hard for her all of the time.

My whistling continues as I unlock the door to my office and leave it open to the cool of the morning. Making my way to my desk, and as always, power up my computer ready to answer my emails.

'What the fuck is that noise?'

I look up to find Tom leaning against my open door. 'You look as rough as guts,' I tell him with a smile and probably a little too much pleasure. Half of his shirt is untucked from his pants and all of it looks like it's been slept in. 'Are you auditioning for a part in the theatre production of that vampire thing?' I ask, gesturing to his sunglasses. 'What was it called again? Nightfall or some shit?'

'It's *Twilight*, you drongo.'

'You'd know, you being the teenage expert.' As a teacher, I mean.

'It's a bright day out,' he protests. 'Plus, I've got this.' He pulls off his sunnies revealing an impressive looking black eye. 'It's not fucking funny.'

'Isn't it?' I answer, still chuckling. 'Who's missus have you been rooting lately?'

'It's worse,' he says, stepping into the room and pulling the door closed behind him. Under the artificial lighting now, his skin has a nasty grey pallor. 'I got this from a woman.'

'Fuck off.'

'It's true. I think I'm in love, and it's your fault.'

'Me? What the fuck have I done?' I fold my arms across my chest, delighted to be the apparent cause of his woes. 'Tom the Tomcat met a bitch with bigger claws, eh?'

'Don't call her that,' he says with a glare my way.

'Fair enough.' I shrug. 'When you tell me who the fuck she is I'll call her by her name. Actually, I'll shake her hand—fuck, I reckon I'll buy her a beer! It's about time you got a taste of your own medicine.'

'Her name is Rose. She's a backpacker.'

'Someone working on my place?' I ask with a frown. The last thing I need is his sorry arse turning up and mooning all over some kid who has no interest in him, beyond a quick ride of his dick.

'Nah, but her mate is. The redhead the whole town is talking about?'

'Never mind the whole town. Who are *you* talking about?'

'I've got better things to do with my time than talk about you, mate. It's the town that's asking who she is. Sweet looking girl by all accounts. And you haven't growled at anyone in weeks. And I just heard you fuckin' whistling!'

'So?'

'So, what's the deal? Is it the redhead or are you on drugs? What is it? Coke? Meth?'

'Yeah, you got me,' I deadpan. 'I've been smoking ice in my downtime.'

'Reckon it could be Fentanyl. One of the teachers at school was saying you can get it in a patch now. Come on, whip your daks off and let me see your thighs.'

'Settle down, pervert.'

'Must be her magic pussy, then.' I refrain from answering, instead sending a scowl his way. 'Or love.' But I'm still not biting, even if it might be that. He'd be the last person I'd confide in. 'Word on the street is that you were auctioned off at some kinky night club last weekend, too. You've been a busy boy, by the sounds of things. They're sayin' you went home with some hot escort.'

'Word on the street, eh?'

'Yeah, well, the staffroom. You gonna make me a cuppa, or what?'

'Or what. If there are kink clubs around here, you're more likely to be a member than I am.'

'Yeah, that's true,' he concedes. 'Wonder what they're talking about, then?'

'It was the bi-annual auction last weekend. Remember the one you're no longer invited to since you confused what construed a dinner date entails?'

'I can't be held responsible for the mayor's wife taking out my dick before the fish course. I felt obligated, you know! So who bought you?' he asks after a moment.

'Apparently, a hot hooker.'

'You've got far too much money, mate. You hired a hooker to buy you, doubling your spend? I've heard of people having tickets on themselves, but that takes the biscuit, mate.'

'Did you fall when this backpacker punched you? Maybe bump your head?' Before he can retort, my mobile phone rings. 'Hold that answer.'

'Hi, Byron.' At the sound of the feminine voice, my heart sinks, my expression falling just as quickly.

'What's wrong?' In response to Tom's whisper-hiss, I hold up my hand.

'Yep, Byron speaking,' I answer, feigning ignorance as I wish to God I didn't recognise the high-pitched voice. *Fucking Rebecca Keogh.* No one else's voice grates like hers.

'Byron, it's me, Becci.' Her voice is sweet and a little silky, and does nothing for me but turn my blood lukewarm.

'Hi, Becci.' My gaze flicks to Tom's as he mimes stringing himself up from the neck by a rope. 'What can I do for you?' Or not, as the case will definitely be. Unless she needs help moving out of town, that is.

'At the country club at the weekend . . .' She leaves her statement hanging, though it should be an apology she's making after she threw herself at me and then had the ridiculous notion to actually *bid* on me.

'Some things are best left alone, Becci.' Like you, I don't say, even though I know it to be true.

'I tried to bid on you—I thought if I could get you to sit down to dinner, you might give me the chance to explain.'

'There's nothing to explain.' And no table big enough, either.

'You're always just out of my reach.'

And you're always a few sandwiches short of a full picnic, I don't say, creating a silence on the line that causes her to huff out an annoyed little sigh.

'Was that all you wanted?' I ask with a flat tone.

'Yes, just dinner. I just want to see you again. You know, without you turning in the opposite direction.'

'Good luck at next year's auction, then.'

'Byron, how can you be like that?' she cries, more with frustration than distress. 'I don't like how things ended for us. There was so much more I was looking forward to with you.' Yeah, I'm sure. Let me check them off in my head: my cheque-book, my wallet, my bank account. 'I just want a chance to explain.'

These calls still happen occasionally even though I've blocked her number. *Three of them, in fact, so far.* I've always been firm but polite in deference to her family's links to mine. And also because I've come to think she's definitely a bit of a nut job. But what I've never done is say this:

'Becci, I'm seeing someone. You're wasting your time calling again.'

'Oh, are you? I didn't know. Was it . . . the redhead at the auction?' she asks, her now steely tone covered by sickly sweet.

And now I know where the rumours have come from.

'It doesn't matter because if it wasn't her, it'd be someone else. Anyone else.' My gaze drifts to Tom again who appears to be offering to bend me over my desk. Covering the mouthpiece with my hand, I mouth to Tom. 'Mate, I'd rather root you than her, but be serious, you'd be my bitch, not the other way around.' Tom sets off cackling almost silently. 'It's time for you to move on,' I say into my phone this time, along with, 'See you around.'

Her protests are cut off with a satisfying *click*. I place my phone down and take a few deep breaths, my hands reaching for a file on my desk. I flip through it though see nothing all, my mind flitting between these two very different women. *Becci and Amber.* When I think of the former, it's like my balls want to crawl up into my body, while thoughts of Amber have the opposite effect. Just thinking about her makes me feel sublimely relaxed. If I close my eyes and think of her at home now, taking care of the twins, laughing and cooking, I find that I smile. And when I think of her in my arms or my bed, or bent over every other surface imaginable, the muscles in my body tighten in the best kind of way.

So that's what I choose to think about, pushing Becci aside without another thought. *Until next time she calls. Or catches me in the street somewhere. Who knows, maybe I'll have convinced Amber to stay by then.*

'That's the go,' I say quite suddenly to myself.

That's what the answer to this is. Not to get rid of Becci, but for all the other things.

I need to convince Amber to stay. I need to tell her how much having her around means to me—how much *she* means to me. I need to tell her I love her, that the kids love her, too, because it's fucking obvious they do, one mimicking her accent and the other insisting she wear her hair the same way day after day. And how they've both recently decided they're going to *cook people food* when they grow up. *I kinda hope that means they'll become chefs rather than cannibals.*

I'm gonna go home and get down on my knees and tell her I want us to be a family. That I want to give her family—give her children. I'll promise to take her on a thousand holidays to wherever she wants in the world.

If only she'll love me back.

If only she'll stay.

'What's the go?' Tom asks. 'By the way, I knew it was the nanny. I was just busting your balls, man.'

'Sure you did,' I mutter, glancing down at the file in my hand.

'So, when can I speak to her about Rose?'

'How about the twelfth of never.'

Chapter Thirty

AMBER

This morning I take the twins to a playgroup, not because they want to but because I think it might be good for them to have a little socialising outside of their own bubble. *They've been squabbling quite a bit this week.* But . . . I might've made a mistake because the place looks more like a miniature demolition derby than a calm place to play. *I'm not sure Byron would appreciate his children making friends here.* Tambourines and maracas fly through the air as tiny tots careen around the place in peddle cars like they're bumper cars at a fair.

'Is it a full moon?' a young mum asks, her face wearing a worried frown. Dressed in tie-dye from head to foot, I guess if anyone was to ask this sort of question, it'd be her.

Maybe your head is in Uranus because these kids are hellish miscreants, I don't reply. Even though I might be thinking it.

'Maybe they just served the wrong type of orange juice?' Like the kind with a half-litre of vodka in.

'I don't like it here,' Matt says, tugging on the leg of my shorts.

'Jeez, it's going off in here!' Edie's voice is full of exuberance. 'Man, these kids are feral!'

'You could be right,' I answer, wondering where she's picked up this very Aussie turn of phrase. Maybe from this playgroup. Or more probably from her own father.

'Come on, let's get out of here.'

We leave while our sanity is still somewhat intact, though I'll admit I'm a little bummed. I'd expected it be the kind of place the kids would play while I daydreamed a little about their dad. I know, I should be fired. But banging the boss does have its benefits!

Outside the building there's a small pond surrounded by a paved trail. I decide to walk Matty and Edie around it to expend some energy and we take a few minutes to look at the minnows swimming in the shallows. Matty asks for the snack pack that I carry around in my bag, and he throws a few pieces of cereal in to lure some of the bigger fish over.

'I'm going to catch one!' he proclaims.

'Oh, no you're not!' I respond, making to grab the back of his shorts as he ignores me, leaning over the water, his pudgy hands on his knees. I know what's coming and it all happens in slow motion before I can get my fingers into the back of his waistband. A bigger fish, or a turtle in this case, pokes its head above the surface of the water to snatch the treat. In turn, Matty lunges for it.

'Dammit,' I grumble as the fabric of his shorts slips through my fingertips. Matty falls to his hands and knees in the shallow water, crying out from the shock of the experience. Thankfully, he quickly scrambles up, looking down at his soaked shirt and pants indignantly.

'You look like you peed,' Edie says, laughing and pointing a finger.

I sigh, but then find myself chuckling, which as Sally would say, goes down like a one-legged man in a butt kicking contest. That is to say, Matty doesn't appreciate the humour in the situation.

'I told you not to,' I say as he scowls in my direction, his hands balled into little fists.

'Ha-ha! You'll have to go home wif no clothes on,' his sister crows.

'That's not nice, Edie,' I caution, then watch on as Matty bursts into tears. 'Don't worry, little buddy. In this weather, you'll be dry in no time!' He'll also be mightily smelly from the pond water, but whatever.

I wring out his clothes and we sit in the shade for a little while, devouring the remaining snacks and talking about pets versus wild animals. Edie says she'd like to own a polar bear while Matty and I agree that some animals are fun to watch from a distance and should be left in their natural habitat. Matty also states that fish are too slimy to handle, and I agree.

Before long, my little charges are looking sleepy, Matty especially, his little eyelids drooping. Picking him up, I take Edie's hand and walk back to the car, strangely contented by my morning and my company—my chatty silver-haired princess and the weight of her brother in my arms. As I fasten them into their car seats, I try not to think about leaving them, about moving on with my travels, because it only brings a lump to my throat. And not just because I'll be leaving them.

Oh, Byron. What have we started?

This past week, Byron's whole attitude seems to have changed. He's still as sexy as the devil himself, but he's warmer. We touch more. Cuddle more. Talk more. Steal moments in the laundry where we can't seem to touch enough flesh, unable to get close enough, or touch hard enough, as though we're desperate to leave our mark on the other. Then there are the sweeter moments where we pass on the stairs, exchanging a hot glance or quick kiss, sometimes a naughty compliment. It's like we can't be trusted to be alone. Take this morning, for instance. The twins followed Sally to her small place out back and, no sooner had the door closed behind the trio, Byron slid his hands under my short dress.

'You're as good as a warm sugar bun,' he'd said, grinning as he'd palmed my ass, giving it a healthy squeeze as he'd pulled me into him, his mouth sliding over mine. 'You know how much I love your sugar,' his deep voice had rasped. 'And you know how much I love your buns.'

'Hey! Sexual harassment in the workplace,' I'd trilled, pulling away more than a little flustered.

'I agree. You shouldn't be wearing those floaty little summer dresses to tempt me.'

'I could wear overalls and your hands would still gravitate to my buns.'

'You got me there,' he'd answered. 'I could write a book about the things I love about your arse.' As though to prove a point, he'd dropped to his knees covering my ass cheeks with raspy, stubbled kisses, pulling my panties between my butt cheeks. 'An ode to Amber's buns,' he'd declared solemnly.

Who knew the man could be such a goofball?

Once the kids are loaded into the car, I drive along the last road out of town, the road that eventually turns into the Phillips driveway, and decide I'll whip up a batch of buns as the pair take a nap. I just hope I'm around this evening when Byron comes home to a plate of warm sugar buns on the counter.

I might even display them in pairs.

At home—I know, I'm not helping myself—and with the twins sleeping, I head downstairs to the kitchen, flipping through my trusty notebook for a suitable recipe. I'm examining the pages having, as usual, meandered into my bakery fantasy, when the rather grand doorbell chimes. It's unusual in the way that it rarely sounds. Usually, company will buzz from the gate at the end of the drive, or they might walk up and knock a couple of times at the kitchen door at the side of the house. I think I've only heard the front doorbell ring once this whole time.

I open the front door to a woman dressed in a tight, white dress. She carries a blue Chanel purse and wears matching high pumps and a pair of sunglasses that would look at home on Jackie O. Sunglasses I can see my messy reflection in. The whole ensemble is the kind of outfit you might expect to see a rich woman wearing on the French Riviera.

'Hi, how can I help you?'

'Who are you?' Her tone is curt, and I resist a similar response, the words poised at the end of my tongue.

'I'm Amber,' I answer evenly instead.

'The nanny,' she sneers.

If you knew, why'd you ask?

'Yep,' I answer brightly before I ask again, 'Can I help you?' Maybe like, help you out of here? Kick your ass down the driveway?

'Yes,' she responds taking a step closer. 'You may excuse me.'

And you may kiss my ass.

'I'm afraid I can't,' I reply instead, closing the door until it's open only to hip-width. I also place my sneaker behind it. You know, just in case. 'I can only let people in who are on the list of expected company. If you want to leave your name, I'd be happy to let the family know you called.'

Because, lady, if you think you're getting through this door, you are in for one helluva shock.

The woman scoffs and looks to the sky for a moment before she slides off her glasses, her eyes narrowed on me.

'Listen, *babysitter*, I'm a special friend of Byron. Possibly not the kind of friend who'll drop to her knees at the click of his fingers, but some of us are a little more circumspect.'

I can literally feel the colour draining from my face. Does she mean . . . she saw us? At the auction? Saw me . . . you know? With a sudden horror, I realise where I've seen her before. She *was* at the auction—she threw eye daggers at me!

'Classy.' Her expression is pure disgust. 'Your mother must be so proud. Now, get out of my way. He's expecting me.'

'Oh, really,' I reply, the colour rushing back into my face, this time from anger. 'You must be the kind that enjoys watching. And as I'm on this side of the door, watching must be all you're good for.'

Burn . . .

'I have never—'

'Well, that's probably where you're going wrong,' I answer evenly as I plant my feet a little firmer. There's no way in hell this woman is getting past me. Not today, sister of Satan.

'Listen . . . you! I *am* going to come inside and I'm going to leave my own message for Byron, and if you give me any more trouble about it, I am going to let him know.' Ohhhh. Scared. Not. 'You won't be the first babysitter he's had on their knees, and I dare say you won't be the last.' Her gaze flares as though with malicious thought. 'The last one got fired, you know. Ask him about Candy.'

'Nanny.'

'Excuse me?'

'Nanny, not babysitter. I'm not a teenager called in on a whim. I'm an educator and I'm currently part of this family as the full-time caretaker of Edana and Matthew. I'll be sure to tell their father you asked after their welfare today.' I smile smugly though imagine it looks more like a grimace. 'And while I'm expected on the property, you are not. Have a good day, *love*.'

She blocks the door with her arm as I attempt to close it.

'It's easy to see what you're trying to do here,' she sneers.

'Get you to leave, you mean?'

'But let me tell you,' she continues, ignoring my comment. 'Men like Byron don't go for women like you. You're the help—you're nothing to him. Just a hole he can use. He won't settle down with you— he'll choose someone like me. He will see me!'

I wish *I* wasn't seeing her right now. I am beginning to feel like I'll either punch her in the nose or throw up on her shoes.

'Ask yourself how many women have taken this job hoping to get close enough to fuck him, to make him theirs.'

'Oh, so you're here for an interview!'

'Do yourself a favour and quit.' Again, she attempts to push past me, and for a split second we might be about to throw down. Maybe wrestle on the lawn?

'Lady, and I use that term loosely, I suggest you come back later because my patience is wearing very, very thin.'

'Oh, no, is the poor little babysitter getting upset?' She uses the same kind of baby-voiced mocking tone you'd expect to hear in grade school. I want to laugh. No, I want to punch her in the nose, and then laugh.

I draw in breath, with the intention of letting it out in a slew of unladylike suggestions, when I feel a soft hand on my shoulder. Sally has appeared by my side in the doorway and I suddenly feel a little embarrassed. *The things she might have overheard.* I step aside, ducking my head as she opens the door a little wider.

'Rebecca,' Sally greets her cheerily. 'It *has* been a long time hasn't it?' She reaches out to grab a hand that Rebecca hasn't offered, shaking it vigorously. 'How's your dad? I hear he's been laid up?'

'He's beginning to feel better, thank you,' she replies, her venom and volume receding rapidly. She's also quite pink. Maybe I'm not the only one embarrassed by her behaviour.

'That's good. It must be terrible to conduct business and go about life as normal when you can't even get off the toilet for ten minutes. Runs in the family, though, doesn't it? No pun intended, of course. Why, I remember just a couple years ago when—'

'Thank you, Sally,' the woman mutters, cutting her off as she slides a mutinous look in my direction. 'I was just here to see Byron.'

'Yes, but you know he's never home this time of day. I'm sure you're on important business, an errand for your father, is it?'

'Well, erm, not exactly. It's more of a personal matter.'

'Oh, I see,' Sally says, feigning concern. 'Of course, you don't need us taking down a message about a personal matter, do you?'

'Exactly,' she says, relief evident in her voice as, this time, she shoots me a piercing glance. Sally nods knowingly and my stomach turns at the thought of now having to admit this bitch into the house.

'We understand. He'll be home around seven o'clock, love.' Sally begins to close the door, a stuttering Rebecca leaning her head to the side to retain eye contact as the space diminishes. 'See you!'

Click.

The door finally shuts and I peer out the sidelight window next to it. It takes Rebeca a few moments to get the message—maybe she's stunned?—before she walks briskly down the driveway, her heels sinking into the gravel. *I hope they're ruined.* I watch her throw her purse down into the passenger seat, climb in, and slam her door shut.

'That self-absorbed, spoiled bi—' I stop the waterfall of muttered insults spilling so naturally from my mouth when I remember I'm standing right next to Sally.

'Oh, you got that right. But only by half. The woman is a nightmare.' She begins walking back towards the kitchen so I follow her, but not before locking the front door.

'I guess you've dealt with her before?'

'Well, you know, she's always been around. Her father has been in and out of business with our family for decades. He's not a bad man, but he's never been a real success at anything. I reckon he encourages his only daughter's pursuit of rich men. Byron's not the only one,' she adds with a shrug. 'Don't go thinking he's special.'

'She still lives with her dad?'

'Oh, yes, though I'm sure he'd be pleased to get her off his hands for more than one reason! She's got to be thirty-five and she's never been married or in a long-term relationship, though she's been around the block, if you know what I mean? Even before Byron was married, she seemed to imagine herself in this house. In fact, any of my boys would've done at one time. They stayed well clear. Well, other than Byron. But don't go blaming him.

'Really, Sally, it's none of my business.' She smiles knowingly and I find words tumbling free from my lips. 'Could Byron not see what an awful woman she is?'

Sally's eyes linger on me for a moment before answering.

'Not really my place to say, but for a while, it seemed . . . Well, it never went anywhere. Byron's usually pretty astute when it comes to reading people, but her? I suppose he needed something to take his mind off his wife after she passed. And, well, I suppose she's a tough woman to miss in that situation.'

'You mean she's an opportunist.'

'Don't let her get under your skin,' Sally says with a vague wave. She'd like that way too much. You don't need to stoop to her level, darl.'

It might be a bit late for that advice. I'm sure Sally heard some of what I had to say.

'I saw her at the auction Friday night,' I murmur, moving the conversation away from the altercation at the door. 'She was stealing other women's paddles from the tables.'

Sally laughs. 'Yep, sounds like her! She's a devious bitch, 'scuse my French.'

'*Putain*,' I spit. 'And I won't ask you to excuse *my* French, Sally.'

'Was that as nasty as it sounded?' she asks with a smile.

'Pretty much,' I admit. I just called her a whore. 'I noticed Byron looked very uncomfortable when she started bidding.' If I dig anymore, I might end up in China.

'Yeah,' she says with a sigh. 'He's been trying to outrun that woman for a while now. Some people just don't take no for an answer. I can't say I'm happy to see her around again.' She places a hand on my arm, her eyes kind. 'Don't you worry yourself about what she means to him.'

I smile weakly. I want to say that it doesn't bother me, that I have no interest or investment in her son's personal life, let alone his dating life, but I can't bring myself to lie. Besides, if I open my mouth now, I'll only make myself sound more like a fool.

Sally wanders over to the kitchen counter where my notebook still lies open. She peeks in, asking what I'm planning to bake. I can't trust myself to say *warm sugar buns* because I no longer feel like making them.

Chapter Thirty-One

AMBER

The rest of the afternoon passes in a blur. The kids wake, we play, we make gingerbread men, no sugar buns here, then it's time for an early dinner, showers, then bed.

'Will Daddy be home soon?' Edie asks, untangling her arms from my neck and dropping onto her mermaid bed.

'I'm sure he will.' He'd called earlier to say he has a telephone conference with a buyer from Europe and would be late. I didn't mention our afternoon visitor though I wonder if Sally has. 'Even if you're asleep, the first thing he does is come upstairs to kiss his two favourites.'

After he's kissed this favourite thoroughly . . .

Seemingly satisfied—not hard when you consider the two drinks of water, one trip to the bathroom, and three stories the pair have coaxed from me—they snuggle deeper into their pillows, their almost translucent lids fluttering closed.

'Night, monsters.' I pull the door partially closed as two little voices whisper back.

'Love you.'

I'm not crying happy tears, you are, I tell my reflection in the bathroom as I clean away the detritus the pair have trailed through the upstairs. A more cynical person would say this is the reason they love me.

Good job I'm not cynical, then.

I run my hand through my hair in an attempt to tidy it, realising I don't have any make up on, and that I haven't all day. I look down at my clothes, my stained T-shirt and old denim cut-offs. This isn't a look that would be at home on the French Riviera. Except maybe as a member of a yacht crew.

Byron likes the way I look, I tell myself. *And I like to be comfortable.*

My flip-flops slap as I move down the stairs, making my way into the kitchen to grab a bottle of wine from the magic cabinet. After a generous pour, I make my way into the family room, plumping cushions and straightening drapes. Anything to distract myself from the events of the afternoon.

Why do I feel so antsy? Is it her? Is it me? Something is making me jumpy.

I make my way back into the kitchen to top up my glass and pick up my phone, noticing there's a missed call and a text from Rose.

Hey, babe, I know you're pretty settled where you are but we're moving on tonight. Long story short, the foreman of this place is a total homophobe and he gave Sven

some shit last night when he found out he's bi (turns out he is, so there's hope for me yet :P) Methinks it's a case of the asshole do protest too much. Or in other words, the foreman has latent homosexual tendencies and dammit, I saw Sven first!

Her stream-of-consciousness text is quickly followed by another. *Also, I slept with some guy at the weekend who keeps hassling me. He's a total douche canoe and he's boring me with his desperate pleas. The D was good but come on! Move on already.*

And one more. *No worries if you're staying but don't lose my number. You never know where we might meet, girl!*

I text her back immediately. *That's too bad. I hope Sven is okay but given he's built like a building. I feel certain he is. I'm bummed we're not getting to say goodbye, cause you're right, I am settled here.* For now at least. *The pay is great and the conditions even better. Safe travels, my friend. I hope we meet soon. Maybe at the top end?*

We'd both planned to visit Kakadu National Park at the top of Australia, working our way from Sydney up. Who knows, maybe we'll both be there at the same time, because if this experience has taught me anything it's that you just can't tell what's waiting for you around the corner.

Like the man of your dreams who asks you to stay . . .

Maybe. Like I say, you just can't tell.

When it becomes apparent Rose isn't about to respond immediately, I put my phone down and take a mouthful of my wine when I hear what sounds like a woman crying outside. My heart skips a beat—maybe something has happened to Sally? Or maybe it's one of those noisy Australian birds— but I soon realise the noise is too high-pitched to be Sally's and too human sounding to be anything else. Plus, it doesn't sound like someone in physical distress but maybe emotional?

I move to the window but there's no one in the yard or the pool area, as far as I can tell, so I open the side door and peek out. It's dark and I can't see anyone, but whoever was crying has stopped now. Then over the sounds of cicada song I hear a soft female murmur, a melancholy sound. No, it's a whiny sound. One that's almost familiar.

My heart sinks but . . . surely it couldn't be. Could it? Has she been hiding in the kids cubby all afternoon?

Merde . . . The putain is back.

I step out into the evening, skirting the wall until I reach the corner of the building where I pause. And I listen—listen so hard—though I'm not exactly proud, especially as my grandmother's words suddenly echo in my ear.

People who listen at keyholes rarely hear good of themselves, Amber.

Yeah but sometimes, Grams, they hear the truth.

'. . . but Byron, an itinerant worker, really?' Rebecca's laugher fills the night air. It's a dainty, tinkling sound that turns my blood cold as I strain my eyes though the darkness, noticing her white dress so close to Byron's larger form. Her hand drifts up to touch his face, her words ringing crystal clear in the night. 'I can understand the attraction. She's very pretty in that fresh faced kind of way.'

It's hard to make out Byron's answer, his low tone sounding little more than a deep rumble. But more than that. He doesn't pull away.

'It'll never last. Yes, a clean break, I think. That way neither will be hurt.'

Is she talking about me? About us? I guess I'm the itinerant worker—didn't he call me that himself on my first day? But a clean break. What's that about? Eight weeks he said. Despite how things seem to have changed between us, he's intimated nothing else.

With this realisation that we might not be on the same page, I suddenly feel very small. Small in both age and size as I find myself shrinking against the wall. Rebecca may not be that much older than I am, but she has a clear advantage. She's obviously been playing this game a lot longer than I have. If I was worried before, now I feel ill. Sick to my stomach that he would even let her touch him. I look down at my palms and the half-moons of deep red my gripping nails have caused. And yet, here I still stand, though the only thing that's keeping me here in this place, in this house, is the fact that I can't hear what he's saying. Unfortunately, I can hear her earlier words still as they swirl through my head.

I'm a particular friend of Byron. Possibly not the kind of friend who'll drop to her knees at the click of his fingers, but some of us are a little more circumspect.

Putain!

I watch as Byron turns his head back to the house. He doesn't appear to notice me, but a sudden breeze carries his words in my direction. I hear them as clear as a bell rings.

'I don't want to get involved.'

My heart plummets to my stomach, dissolving in bile and acid. My fingers scrabble against the brickwork in my hurry to get back to the comfort of the house.

But it's not comforting.

And it never will be again.

I hear footsteps along the side of the house and I can't help myself—I have to look. And I have to bite my lip to stop the sound of my sob.

Byron walks down the driveway, Rebecca's hand in the crook of his elbow, her face turned up to his, looking like a couple out for an evening stroll.

How stupid I am, I think as I slide down the wall, my butt hitting the floor with a *thump*. But I won't cry, I decide, because I have just a small window to save myself.

I finally find my legs again, making my way into the kitchen to grab my phone. As fate or luck would have it, the little blue dots are dancing, indicating that a lengthy text message is in progress from Rose. I don't wait for an answer that's no longer appropriate, instead I text back:

Change of plans/mind. When can you pick me up?

Her answer is immediate. ***Half hour.***

I sweep through the rooms downstairs, gathering my belongings, then make my way upstairs, pushing my LBD to the bottom of my backpack with more feeling than I can deal with right now. I begin then to punch the rest of my clothing inside, along with any dirty laundry I find. I don't have time to be neat or thorough though it helps that my methods of packing are making my arms ache.

Something else to concentrate on.

In the bathroom, I ignore the children's toys, things that make my eyes leak, swiping my toiletries into the waterproof bag they arrived in. I pause at the twins bedroom door and though my heart aches to see them one last time, I refuse to go inside. I kiss my fingers and press that kiss into the door instead with a whispered, 'Goodbye, my little monster friends.'

Back downstairs, I open the front door and throw my pack into a dark corner when I notice Byron's silhouette walking up the long driveway. His hands are thrust into his pockets, his eyes on the gravel beneath his feet. It's a strange thing to feel your blood run from hot to cold and back again. Fresh eyes, I tell myself.

Better I find out now rather than later; be it eight weeks or a year, I can't stay here.

Pour rien au monde. Not for love nor money.

I close the front door quietly, making my way into the kitchen where I hope I can be a good enough actress for the next ten minutes. I'm not strong enough for a scene and I'm not built for the histrionics I can feel building inside of my chest. Friends had commented in the past how my relationship breakups seemed to leave me unfazed, wondering how it could be possible that I remained friends with most of my exes. I thought it was just me—the way I was built. Easy, breezy Amber. Too nice to hurt or be hurt.

I now see this wasn't true. I'd just never cared enough. I'd just never been in love.

Wine glass in one hand, my phone in the other, I look up at the sound of Byron entering.

'You are a sight for sore and sorry eyes,' he says, making his way over to me, pulling me into his chest.

I'm thankful for the stool. Thankful for the cloak of numbness I've willed as I deeply inhale the scent of him one last time. As he pulls back, he ducks, bringing our eyes level. And he does look tired but maybe lies are tiring. Will he mention her? Will he say? What does he see in my gaze?

'You okay, sweetheart?'

Of all his silly terms of endearment, sweetheart has become my favourite. Maybe because it's the most recent he'd bestowed on me. Not that it matters. Not anymore.

I sit a little straighter and nod. 'Just a big day. And I have to go out in a bit to see Rose. I hope that's okay?' His expression works through a range of emotions—confusion to irritation, irritation to acceptance.

'Ah, yeah. Rose.' He tugs on his ear. 'I heard about that.' I'm not sure what he means and I can't bring myself to ask. 'Tom, my mate, called into the office this morning. He can be a bit of a tit at times, no doubt your friend will confirm that.'

'Oh, really?' I ask, almost by rote. Then I ask him the million dollar question. Despite packing and asking Rose to come get me, whether I stay or go might just depend on the answer to this. 'Any other interesting visitors today?'

His eyes narrow but they don't leave mine as he says, 'No one of note.'

I suppose I have my answer then.

My phone lights with a text. ***Your carriage awaits. Front gates are locked. We're on the road.***

I hop down from the chair, throw back the rest of my wine, then wind my arms around his waist. 'Take care of yourself,' I whisper into his chest.

'What was that?'

'I said I'll see myself out.' With a smile that makes my cheeks numb, I move away one step at a time.

The kitchen door closes quietly behind as I take a deep breath to steady myself, then make my way to the front of the house to grab my bag from the shadows of the front porch. I hurry down the driveway hoping Byron doesn't come out to see why he can't hear the car start. Rose is standing by the open door of the van and she takes the bag from my hand, passing it to one of the other travellers inside. I've no idea what she sees on my face but whatever it is, it causes her to pull me into her embrace. As the van trundles down the long drive, I take one last look at the Phillips house before letting go of my choking tears.

Chapter Thirty-Two

BYRON

She didn't come back last night. In fact, it's pretty clear she's left for good.

I mean, what the fuck? Didn't I deserve an explanation?

After her quick goodbye hug, which in hindsight was a bit strained, I made and inhaled a quick sandwich before carrying the half bottle of wine she'd left into the family room, kicking my boots off and my feet up on to the coffee table. I didn't want to go to bed without her—I reckoned I couldn't. Next thing I'd known, I'd woken in the same position, an empty bottle curled by my side.

I'd panicked, of course I had. The knot in my gut as big as the root of a tree. I called her phone—fucking frantically, the thing going straight to her message bank—as I'd yanked open the kitchen door to find her little car was there. Somewhat relieved, I headed upstairs.

My bedroom was empty. Hers was bare.

I'd wanted to vomit last night's wine and sanger up right there.

I felt ill. Bereft. Fucking betrayed.

She'd left me without a word—left us. *Was she really that big of a bitch? Was I played?*

Pulling off my work gloves, I make my way into the kitchen. Ma and the kids are playing cards at the island, the atmosphere morose. Sensing I'm not in the mood for another round of *where's Amber*, Edie hops down and treats my knees to a hug.

'Don't worry,' she whispers, as though if she says it quietly enough it won't really hurt. 'You know who will be back as soon as she's finished her holiday.'

Fuck me sideways. Have I somehow made the speaking of her name forbidden, or are my children so intuitive to my pain?

Without answering, I pick up my daughter and pop her back on her stool as I watch the trio play another round of half-hearted Snap. I can't help but notice that Ma seems just as out of sorts as I do. For me, I'd think a foul mood is considered as they say par for the course. For Mum, it's a rare day when she's not as bright as a ray of sunshine.

'Well, I think I'll make some lunch,' she announces, dropping her cards. 'Why don't you two go and sit at your little desks and colour?'

Now what? I ask myself. Is she gonna bend my ear? Interrogate me? Ask me what the hell I did to run Amber off? If she does, I hope she's ready for my answers.

I don't fucking know. And I wish I did.

'Son, you should know that Rebecca came by yesterday while you were gone.'

Fuck, I'd forgotten about her. So she was here twice in one day? Last night she'd turned up at the office saying her car had blown a tyre nearby. She's said she'd called to have it fixed but that she needed a lift home quite urgently. Fuck, she nattered on about her new boyfriend, then asked me a few questions about Amber, or the new nanny, as she'd called her.

Colour me suspicious, but I can't think what she could have done to cause this.

'What happened? Did Amber say anything?'

'She handled herself very well. I wasn't there when Becci arrived but I ended up stepping in and chasing her off. I thought Amber seemed okay when it was all over, but I think I might've been wrong.'

Was my mother wrong? Or was I wrong for not mentioning Becci's appearance to Amber? *Even though she'd asked*. I didn't mention it because she doesn't mean anything to me. I didn't mention it because I didn't want to rehash the past and run the risk of spoiling our evening. And I didn't say because I still can't quite believe I was stupid enough to get involved with the woman in the first place.

With an expression I can't make out, Mum hands me a note which looks to have been torn from Amber's ever-present notebook. I open it up to her narrow, half-cursive handwriting. Is it odd that I'd recognise it anywhere?

'This was in the post-box this morning,' Mum says quietly. 'It was under the newspaper.'

My heart pinches as my eyes begin to run across the words.

Byron,

Thank you for the opportunity to work within your home and experience the joys of your beautiful family. I will always be grateful for the opportunity. Also, thank you for allowing me access to your beautiful kitchen, even if I sometimes took advantage of the privilege. I'm sure you already know this but I wanted to say that you're raising two wonderful human beings. The world will undoubtably be a better place for having them in it, and I wouldn't be at all surprised to find Edie in charge of the planet at some point, ruling with her sweet brother by her side.

Please tell them I'm sorry I couldn't be there to say goodbye in person.

There's a mark here. Is it a splash of wine, or is it a tear? And if it is a tear, is she crying because she'll miss the kids?

It's probably wine, my inner cynic mutters as I carry on.

I truly admire your work ethic and recognise that your life revolves around maintaining a successful business. In that way, you have inspired me to continue pursuing my own business goals, once I've finished seeing the wonders of your beautiful country.

On a more personal note, I want you to know that I've enjoyed every minute with you, from the bottom of my heart. I'll miss you, I think it says next, though the words are heavily scored through.

I have to move on before

Before what? I prepare myself for more platitudes.

I've decided to focus my energy on other things—

What other things? What the fuck does that mean?

—I will therefore no longer be available to you as a nanny. I know that you will find someone who is loving and kind to step in.

Thank you,
Amber.

As I fold the paper in half, my thoughts are in a jumble, though I try to keep my expression blank. Mum then hands me another folded square of paper.

'She left me a note, too.'

Sally,

    I apologise for whatever inconvenience this may cause you. I know you won't hesitate to step in and watch the children for as long as need be, but please don't let it get in the way of your travel plans. You are going to have such a marvellous time on your journeys, and I hope that you'll send me a photo or two.

This is my Facebook profile: facebook.com/AmberHardy321

I will miss you all.
Love,
Amber.

I hand her the note back and swallow hard. I swallow anger, and frustration, and even pain. I swallow the resolve I'd decided as a course of action this morning—a fuck her kind of thing. Suddenly, it no longer seems to matter. Whatever the reasons behind her leaving, she's doing what's best for her. Keeping her here would've been wrong. She needs to travel. To see the world. Experience all the things that I can't give her. To keep her here would be like clipping the wings of a bird.

'I'm sorry I didn't do more to soothe her yesterday,' Mum says, staring down at her note, her brows wrinkled with concern. Maybe even misplaced guilt.

'I don't think that was it. Becci was here last night again. There had to be something behind that. '

'You mean she hassled her again,' Mum asks, her head coming up sharp.

'I dunno.' My answer is strained. I feel too foolish to recount the whole scenario. The car that had obviously had its tire slashed on purpose, right outside of my house. Her strangely worded questions and the way she'd been friendly and tactile, without throwing herself at me, her usual MO.

I push my stool back, my hand reaching for the note I feel I can't leave.

I walk around the house aimlessly, then stalk out to the fields, heedless of the strong afternoon sun. I fold the note between my fingers, creasing the lines hard as I try to imagine how Amber must've felt as she'd written those lines.

Was she hurt. Did she feel betrayed. Foolish?

Well, I'll bet she didn't feel nearly as foolish as I do right now because I didn't tell her how I feel, and maybe if I had, she'd have had a little faith in me.

Shoving the note into the back pocket of my jeans, I roll my hands into fists, lashing out at a nearby fence post, once, twice, three times, and a fourth, until my knuckles bleed. And then I do what I always do when things go tits up. I move along. When my dad died, I moved home. When my cheating wife became ill, I took her back in. When Becci fucked me over, I brushed it under the carpet.

Business, family, and seasons call, and I move the fuck along with them all.

Because if I stand still I might realise what I've missed.

I spend the next few days in the office but I'm not beyond a bit of hard yakka—a bit of hard work. It's what I get lost in today. *Work of the backbreaking kind.* I dig up huge, dead vines, trim nearby tree branches, and help wherever I can just to numb my brain. But it doesn't work, though.

Same as any other day since she left, I go home as the sun sets, my mood unchanged.

I eat dinner with the kids, courtesy of Mum's mediocre cooking. And as she puts them to bed, which I'm grateful for today, I cast a resentful glance at the empty kitchen before moving in the opposite direction. I usually head to the yard, but I can't cope today with the recollection of her swimming in her underwear because it just leads to other imaginings. Like seeing myself holding her up against the wall, my fingers seeking her wetness. Her lips at my ear and the delicious sharp sting of her teeth against the lobe.

Not today, wank-inducing Satan.

I head for my study, a place I barely use. Cracking open a window, I throw myself forcefully into the old oxblood leather desk chair causing it to creak. I pull open the top drawer of the desk, thinking I probably have a packet of cigarettes stashed there.

And I do.

I take one, leaning back in the creaking chair, bringing my dirty work boots up onto the desk. Then I decide on another vice as I lean down and pull out the bottom drawers to grab the bottle of whisky there. I fill the empty glass sitting on my desk and I drain the contents in one swallow, relishing the peaty burn. Refill and repeat and then repeat again before I drag myself up to an empty bed.

The French doors are open, the windows wide to the night-time sounds as I strip and slip under the sheet. For a while, staring at the ceiling holds some appeal but whisky aided sleep eventually weighs my eyelids down. My final thought before succumbing to slumber?

I wish Amber was here.

The morning arrives and with it, torrential rain. I'm slower to rise than usual, reluctant to leave my dreams. Also, I feel as rough as guts as I drag open my eyes. My mouth feels fucking feral, courtesy of the half bottle of whisky. Slowly, I work my way out of bed and into the shower, then into clean clothes. As I head downstairs, I mourn the fact that there's no scent of coffee to greet me. I make my own, but it tastes like shit. I'm not in the mood for breakfast, so I take myself over to the office as soon as Mum appears in the kitchen.

'Morning, darl.' She pats her damp hair. 'Sleep well?'

'Well enough,' I respond shortly, grabbing my jacket from the back of the chair.

'Byron.' As she full names me, my feet come to a halt and I turn.

'You've got to be kidding me.' I rake my hand through my hair as she makes as though to hand me a manila folder—a folder I know holds the old nanny applications. A folder I don't take.

'I'm not asking you to replace Amber,' she says, dropping it on the island standing between us. 'I'm just saying we need to find a new nanny. It doesn't have to be today, but it has to be done. And the sooner you do it, the better for everyone.'

'And if she comes back?'

'She's not psychic, By.' Ignoring her expression, I make my way out into the rain, more words following me. 'And why would she come back just to work?'

Chapter Thirty-Three

BYRON

'Go the fuck away.'

It's still dark as my phone begins to ring, my hand shooting out from under my chest to silence the thing as I glare at the screen. I consider turning it off or maybe throwing it at the wall but I've decided to make a concerted effort not to be so childish this week.

'What do you want, Flynn?' My voice is raspy with sleep, the light from the screen on my phone ghostly in the dark room.

'Mornin' to you, too, you fucker.'

'It's not morning.' I scrub the heel of my hand against my eye. 'It's the middle of the night.'

'Eh,' he answers, 'what do I care. By the way, I'm pleased Chastity isn't here. She doesn't need to see your junk plastered across the screen.'

'What?' His words pull me fully from sleep.

'Look where you're holding the camera, arsehole.'

Straightening my phone, I groan at the sight of him all bright-eyed and dark haired. It's a reflex reaction to cover how my heart pinches tight at how much my brother looks like our father in his younger years.

'That's better. The sight of your hairy ball sack was putting me off my granola bar.'

'I'm sorry for you.' I yawn, pulling myself higher up the pillows. 'Sorry you got the short end of the family pricks, that is.'

'Ha, you reckon. Wanna have a look? Maybe refresh your memory?'

'For fuck's sake,' a Scottish voice growls from somewhere . . . wherever Flynn's office is in London these days. 'Can you no' talk about anything else other than your genitalia?' Keir says.

'Oh, that's a big word,' Flynn responds, his gaze no longer on the screen but rather over it. 'Usually you like a bit of cock talk.'

'Fuck you.'

'Nah. I don't do gay for pay.'

'You would if Chastity told you to,' comes Keir's response.

My brother's wife is a purveyor of ethical, female porn.

'As lovely as it is to hear you squabble with Keir, could we get to whatever the fuck it is you want?' My next yawn almost unhinges my jaw.

'Right, I'll get to the point. Mum called. She's worried about you and, to be honest, you do kinda look like a bag of shit.'

I sigh. 'Because it's the middle of the night. Excuse me for not taking your call in my top hat and tails.'

I tamp back the frustration that I must be the current hot topic of my family's conversations. 'And the fact that she called you means I'd better get her tested for dementia.'

'She called me because I'm a happily married man. A *very* happily married man,' he adds nauseatingly.

I try and fail to stifle my second, much more annoyed sigh. As the eldest brother, it's my role to dish out advice, not this fuckwit.

'I know, I was there at your wedding. Did you know, I used to be married, too? And while you were still married to your hand.'

'Hey, were you a fly on my bedroom wall last night? Chastity's in Poland on a shoot,' he says by way of explanation and with a mile wide fucking grin.

'Left you with the baby in one hand and your dick in the other, did she?'

In the background, Keir groans again.

'You're just jealous because you're not married now. What happened there, eh?'

'Well, I didn't kill her, if that's what you're insinuating.'

'She's still gone.'

'Flynn,' I growl, 'I'm going to fucking sleep now.'

'Hang on, hang on! But seriously, Mum says there was a girl.' The rest of his words fall in a rush. He's been issued with a directive from the mum-ship and fuck if he isn't going to deliver it. 'You fucked up, didn't you?'

'So. She left. End of, Flynn.'

'Get over yourself. Reach out to her.'

'It's not that simple,' I find myself saying. 'She's backpacking around the country. Why would she want to be stuck with a widower and his four-year-old twins?'

'I dunno, maybe because she was happy with you? Maybe because she wants to be with you?'

I think sleep deprivation is the reason behind this conversation. With any luck, I won't remember any of this when I wake.

'How could you possibly know?'

'Because Sally the oracle said so. And her mate saw her crying when the campervan pulled up at the servo that night.'

'Servo?' Keir repeats.

'Yeah, the service station. You know, where you refuel your wheels? Anyway,' Flynn says, his attention moving back to me. 'What you need is a grand gesture.'

'What I need is a frontal lobotomy, listening to you.'

'I'm serious. Chicks dig that sort of shit. How'd you think I won Chastity over? Come on, out of all the men in London, how'd she end up with me?'

'She was unlucky?'

'Not even a little.'

'Then I guess a chloroformed hanky and a basement somewhere must've done it.'

'No, mate. The grand gesture was what won me the fair Chas.'

'Go on, then. What do you suggest I plan?'

'I don't fucking know, do I? It depends on the woman. It's no good sending her a flash mob if she hates crowds. What does she like? What are her interests?'

'Baking and fucking me.'

Flynn's brows pull together so I guess he might be thinking.

'A cookery course?' he suggests.

'Lame. What's grand about that?'

'A trip to France?'

'She's already lived there, and I don't know whether you know but I have a business to run.'

'I got nothin' then.'

'Nicholas Sparks movies,' Keir offers from somewhere beyond.

'Don't they all die?' Flynn says, his eyes moving away once more.

'What was your grand gesture?' The minute the words are out of my mouth, I'm regretting them. Not because I don't want to hear his suggestions but because of the evident delight on his face. This is going to be bad. So bad.

'Right, so this was twofold, okay?'

'If you say so . . . '

'First, I let her film me, you know, to gain her trust—'

'Hang on, you let the lady pornographer film you?'

'I let my *future wife* film me,' he corrects.

'Like, *film you*? Far out. Am I in danger of seeing this anywhere?' Talk about spoiling your viewing pleasure.

'I set her a dare,' he says, carrying on. 'If she won, she could do what she liked with the tape.' That's fucking ballsy. 'And second, I told her I'd give her a kid.'

'Yeah, well, you've got one,' I answer, confused.

'I'm aware,' he deadpans. 'The little fucker barely sleeps. But this was before, before she knew she needed me.'

'So you offered to impregnate her? What kind of fuckery is that?'

'The fuckery that works. Impregnating porn is a thing, you know—a kink. Not that it's her kink. Chastity wanted a baby, not some fantasy forced pregnancy. And what I'm telling you is in the strictest of confidence, right?'

'This is not the kind of stuff I'd repeat,' I reply, wondering if I'm having a nightmare.

'Awesome. Good chat. Let me know how it goes.'

'So that's it? No ideas or advice. Just . . . knock her up?'

With a wink and a cocky grin, he replies, 'It worked for me, didn't it?'

~*~

Amber left, and my mood seems to be getting worse, not better. While I hate that she left without giving me the opportunity to explain, I think I get why. I'm hurting, of course. It smarts that she left. That she could think so little of me. But those thoughts should spark sadness, shouldn't they? When all I feel is anger. And I think I know why.

It's my fault things have gone tits up. I should've been up front with her. Told her how I felt but I was too much of a pussy to be straight with her. It's me I'm angry with, not her.

Sure, it takes two to open up, two to build a relationship, but I should've taken the first step, because I was the one in the position of power and she was the one with everything to lose.

I spend the rest of the night contemplating this. Contemplating Flynn's mad phone call. And when morning comes along, I think I might have a plan.

I'm pleased to report, it doesn't involve chloroform, basements, or forced pregnancy.

Chapter Thirty-Four

AMBER

If Sydney is hot, the heat in Cairns is closer to that of hell. Let me tell you, it's a whole other level. What that basically means for me is that I'm hot, red, and frazzled on a near constant basis, and not even *factor whale-lard* sunscreen has helped in my ever constant battle with freckles.

'I'm going to be one giant freckle before long,' I complain to the mirror, my fingers fanned across my face.

'I think that's called a tan,' Rose says from her position on the top bunk in our dorm room. Just four bunk beds in this one—positively swish! Not really. 'Urgh, look,' she huffs, pointing behind me. 'There are ants in here again.'

I glance over my shoulder to where a line of tiny black bugs march.

'They look like a line in wallpaper.' If the room had wallpaper, that is. It doesn't. Just white-washed bricks.

'Lines in wallpaper don't move,' Rose gripes. 'Unless you've had a few too many beers. Plus, wallpaper doesn't make my skin crawl. Or bite.'

'They're only ants,' I answer with a forced brightness. I hate the constant presence of ants, too. But I try not to think about them.

'Tell that to the kid who got anaphylaxis after a bite from one of those green fuckers.'

'Well, sure. That was scary. But it was a good job he had an epi-pen.' And that I, the only adult in this place, had the gumption to pop the kid. 'But it's not so bad here. I mean, it's not a room with my own en suite. But at least there's a decent sized kitchen. It's just a shame it's too hot to cook.'

'Girl, you're crazy. What you should be saying is it's a shame there's no strong, tanned, inked Aussie arms to lull you to sleep here.'

'I'm regretting telling you about him,' I say with a frown.

'Yeah, well, I can't believe you left like that. You should've asked the guy what the deal was with that other chick.' She slaps down the travel magazine, pushing herself up on her elbow. I won't be drawn into this conversation because it still hurts. What's done is done. And sure, I might do things different if I had that evening over again but that changes nothing. Besides, 'As I've told you, there wasn't any point. I was just a bit of fun to him.'

And I was too involved.

'You don't even know that,' she says, flopping back against the mattress. 'Why oh why hasn't this place got air conditioning?'

'Because it's a cheap hostel and not a five-star hotel. Oh, shoot! I'm going to be late to the café.' At least I'm not working outdoors, although the place I work opens out onto the outdoor view of the Cairns Esplanade. No doors, no windows, no air conditioning. Just the very occasional sea breeze and some overhead fans. But at least the view is pretty.

Azure skies. Tropical sea. Palm trees swaying in the scant breeze.

'Bring me back a frappe?' she asks, batting her long lashes prettily. 'I'm gonna get my head down before work tonight.'

Rose is working in a riotous backpacker bar. It's loud and it's brash and she loves the place as much as I loathe it.

'Sure.'

'Hey, Amber!' As usual, Brianna greets me with her perky, Aussie enthusiasm. The nice thing about Cairns is it's too hot for people to be grumpy. Seriously, it's just not worth the extra layer of sweat you work up. 'You're early today,' she says, almost vibrating with enthusiasm.

'Hey, Bri.' I send her a small wave as I stow my bag under the counter, wrapping the regulation black café apron around my waist. 'You know what they say, five minutes early is ten minutes late.'

'Not in Cairns it isn't,' she replies with a chuckle. 'Watermelon, pistachio, and two cookie-dough, all cups.'

I look over to the glass gelato counter to where a young couple with two small children stand, the kids with their hands splayed out on the cool glass.

'Hmm. I say . . . two vanilla cones and two choc-chip cones.'

It's a silly game we play when we're having a slow day. *Guess-what-the-customer-is-about-to-order.*

'You should've been here earlier today. There was this guy?' I love how Bri's accent gets thicker the more excited she gets, the tail-end of her words rising and rendering statements as questions. 'He was such a spunk!'

I almost choke on my bottle of water. She gets me at least once a shift with her favourite (seminal, to my mind) description of a hot guy.

'Did he order an espresso?' Bri seems to think there is some correlation between rich guys and their choice of coffees.

'No, a ristretto!' she answers, all wide eyed as though these are the most salacious words she's ever uttered. 'A rich guy with *tattoos.*'

'Ya' don't say.'

I bet he drank his coffee and rode his skateboard, not his Maserati, home. But I won't burst her bubble. Life will do that to her all on its own. Gah! I brush the miserable thought away.

As the family indicate they're ready to order, Bri turns to the glass counter with a wide smile on her face. *Maybe that's why she gets better tips.* And before long, the four leave with gelato choices neither of us had guessed.

'Those boys were so stinkin' cute, weren't they?'

'Very,' I agree.

'You reckon they were twins?'

'Maybe.'

'Twins must be so hard, don't you think? Double the cost. Double the work. Making sure everything is equal and stuff.'

'Oh, I don't know. I suppose it depends on the twins.'

As is often the case lately when cute kids turn up at the café, I find myself wondering what Edie and Matty are up to. I hope that in the time that has passed they've found someone kind to look after them. Maybe someone who doesn't mind collecting the eggs from the angry chooks to save Matty's tiny toes. Maybe someone who likes to bake. Someone who can braid Edie's silvery hair. With a sigh, I pick up a cloth and begin wiping down the countertops, hoping to stop my mind from wandering elsewhere.

To the outdoor shower.

His bedroom.

The memory of being held in his arms.

'Oh, I forgot to tell you, the ristretto guy? He was looking for you.'

My stomach suddenly twists itself into a pleasurable kind of knot.

'Me?' Bri nods enthusiastically. 'Did he say who he was? Leave a message?'

'He did not. I kinda think it was 'cause Claus was giving him the whole *battering lashes* thing.' Claus is a Swiss backpacker who does the early morning shift. 'Maybe the spunk thought he'd keep the number for himself?'

My heart skips a beat, my mouth suddenly dry. 'You're sure he didn't leave a name?'

'Nope. All I can tell you is that he was a tall, blond drink of inked Aussie water. Someone you met at a bar, maybe?'

'Nope. I haven't met anyone new lately.' Other than the pair of German girls who only stayed in our room for one night before moving on. 'You said he had tattoos?'

'Totally hot.' She mimes fanning her face.

'Kids with him?'

'His only baggage was a backpack,' she answers with a shrug. 'Same as the rest of us.'

At this, my heart rate drops. Byron wouldn't be schlepping through Cairns with a backpack. *Monogrammed luggage, maybe*. Also, silly brain, but Byron wouldn't be schlepping through Cairns looking for me.

Besides, he has my number if he wants to talk.

The rest of my shift passes without note, though I find myself watching the crowds that pass, my stomach lurching occasionally and unnecessarily at the sight of tall blonds. I grab a takeaway salad and a frappe from a nearby place before starting my hot walk home. It's early evening and the bats in the city are making themselves known, which I always find a bit creepy. Cairns is a small city, the gateway to the Great Barrier Reef, not that I've made it out there yet. But I have high hopes.

I pass all manner of buildings on my walk back to the hostel. Wooden Queenslanders built on stilts, traditional pubs with wide verandas, and towering apartment buildings and hotels. When I get to our place, a not quite so salubrious building of mud-coloured brick veneer, I find Rose isn't in our room, or the communal rooms. And I know without looking that she won't be in the pool as she reckons that's just an invitation to an infection.

I flop on my bed and pick half-heartedly at my salad as I contemplate shower number three for the day. Then I begin flicking through my notebook, still bummed I'd lost my old one between Riposo Estates and here.

My recipes and my mementos, my little sketches and rows of scrawled figures, all gone.

Maybe I'll call and ask Sally if I left it there one of these days. Or maybe I'll be too embarrassed to ever speak to her again.

With a sigh, I lie back against the mattress and decide I'll close my eyes for a short while.

'*Eww*, wake up, Amber, you're covered in ants!'

'What?' I jump from the bed, bumping my head on the metal frame of the upper bunk. 'Oww! *Eww!*'

My skin suddenly feels pricked by a million pins. 'Get them off me! Get them off me!' I begin to dance around the room, whipping my clothes off as I travel, brushing my arms and legs, twisting to swipe at my back.

'It was the salad—you went to sleep with the container open.'

'Put it in the garbage outside!' I sort of squeal.

'No way. I'm gonna go grab a can of *Raid*.'

'I've got to shower,' I whimper, my hands in my hair, the rest of my body wriggling and writhing like I've been possessed. 'They're in my hair, Rose. Help me, they'll burrow in my ears! Why are you laughing at me?'

'I'm sorry, you just look crazy.' I must be crazy for backpacking, I think, heading for the door. 'No, come back, Amber. It's the guy's allotted time for the showers.'

'I don't care,' I shriek, dashing out into the hall in just my underwear.

The hostel we're staying in is small and pretty basic and, as of last week, there's been an issue with the male shower room. This has meant a reduction in our nightly rate (yay!) but a sharing of the only shower left (boo!) Males and females have alternate afternoons and mornings, but as my butt hits the door, I don't care that there might be guys in there. Hell, there could be a sasquatch having a party in here and I wouldn't give a damn as the entirety of my being screams for relief.

'Coming in,' I squeal. 'Your modesty is safe with me, I promise, but I can't speak for these ants!'

The door bangs against the wall and I keep my eyes lowered to the white tiled floor, noting the sound of a nearby shower. Whipping back the shower curtain, I step into the first stall, flicking on the switch as I begin to rub my scalp vigorously before proceeding to do the same to every inch of my skin. And I do all this trying not to squirm and squeal.

My eyes are stinging from my running mascara as I finally turn off the shower. I twist my hair, wringing out the water, grabbing the fluffy downiness of a towel that's fed into my hands.

'Thank you so much,' I whisper, reluctant to turn fully to face this stranger in my underwear. 'I'll wash it for you later.' I rub it under my eyes, hoping it's not a white towel while knowing my recent luck means it is.

'No worries,' the amused voice answers. 'That was pretty entertaining.'

'I'm pleased you're amused.' My chin comes up, my tone dripping now with asperity. 'Maybe you'd like to—'

I halt in my answer, playing back his words, or rather his voice, as I turn my head Through my limited stinging vision, I notice an inked forearm. I look up, and up again.

'Byron?' I can't believe what I'm seeing—who I'm seeing. 'What are you doing here?'

Because, yes, the man himself stands before me, his blond hair darkened by water, the front flopping over his face, every other wet inch of him on display, including a pretty impressive semi—

'You—you've got no clothes on!'

'Most people shower naked, darl.'

His eyes make a slow perusal of my body, so much so that I duck my head to be sure I am actually wearing my underwear.

For what it's worth, I am.

It's not worth very much as far as modesty goes, the fabric wet and very much see-through.

I bite my lip against further ridiculousness, not sure if I should return his towel or cover myself with it.

'You're a sight for sore eyes.' Byron shakes his head as though he can't quite believe I'm standing in front of him. 'Do you know how many backpacker hostels there are in Cairns?' I shake my head dumbly. Dumb because I don't have any words, let alone thoughts. 'Me neither but there are fucking heaps of them.'

'Have you been looking for me?' My voice is small, almost as though I fear the answer.

'What do you think?' he asks a little more sardonically as he reaches out hesitantly, his fingers brushing my cheek. I'm not sure whether it's the brush of his calloused fingers or the look in his eyes that causes my stomach to flip.

'I think I've probably been bitten by ants and I'm having some kind of hallucinogenic reaction.'

'Does this feel like you're hallucinating?' he growls, pulling me into him. He's hard where I'm soft and my whole body yields to him. My heart is wild in my chest, the fire of anticipation rushing through my veins as his eyes darken, flicking to my mouth before he covers my lips with his own.

He asked me a question, didn't he?

Am I hallucinating? If my mouth wasn't already engaged I'd answer yes, because his kisses make me feel as though I'm floating on air. His flesh is warm under my fingers, his eyes burning with their shrewd intensity now as he pulls away, creating a distance between. One appropriate only for lovers.

And then I remember we aren't.

Because I left to protect myself.

'What are you doing here, Byron?'

'Well, it's like this. Some fuckwit suggested I try winning you back with a grand gesture.'

I look down at the towel in my hands. 'Is . . . this it?'

'It is and it isn't.'

'It either is or it isn't. Which is it? And while we're battling the difficult questions, why don't you tell me how Rebecca is.'

'That's not difficult to answer. The woman is off her rocker. I'm sorry you had to deal with her and I'm sorry I didn't explain the whole fucked up business to you—and I will. But not right now. Not in the middle of my grand gesture.' I look down at the towel again though this time he grabs it out of my hands. 'You've been sunbathing.' His eyes travel over my shoulders and down my arms.

'No, if I had all this would be freckly, too,' I retort, indicating the pale flesh of my torso.

'Be still my aching—'

'Stop that,' I say, guessing where he's going with that.

'I want to kiss each and every one of your freckles, Red.'

'I don't think that's happening any time soon.' At least, not in this bathroom.

'Have you got a bunk bed?'

'Yes.' Hasn't everyone in this place? 'And also, a roommate.'

'Fuck, that complicates things.'

'How? Why? God dammit—what are you doing here, Byron!'

'Isn't it obvious? I'm coming travelling with you.'

Chapter Thirty-Five

BYRON

So that might not have gone as well as I'd planned, even though, in my opinion, my offer was better than any homemade porn. But as Amber had suddenly found another ant crawling between her breasts, she'd squealed and begun to slap at herself.

I did what any man would do in that instance. I switched the shower on again, stepping under the spray with her this time.

I'd rinsed her hair. Pulled her folded arms from across her chest, slipping her bra down her arms. Then I'd hooked my thumbs into the hips of her underwear, pulling them down her legs.

It was a hand job—I mean a hard job. But one I'd volunteer to do every day as I'd set about the task of ridding her of her little ant friends. It wasn't very sensual or even sexual. Just functional. I'd wrapped her in a towel then, stepping into my shorts without towelling off, I'd taken her to my room.

My private room.

With a bunk bed, for fuck's sakes.

'I miss you,' I say, getting down on my knees on the unfortunate looking industrial carpet. 'The kids miss you, too.' I take her hands in mine and kiss her fingers, bringing them under my chin.

'I miss all of you,' she answers quietly. 'But—'

'No buts. Cards on the table, sweetheart. I was going to ask you to stay the night you left.'

'The night I saw you with her, you mean.'

'The night she played you,' I counter.

'She told you to make a clean break of it, and you agreed.' Her voice is a little harder and I'm pleased we're getting somewhere. 'By leaving, that's what I was giving you. I was giving you that clean break.'

I cast my mind back, my recollection not meeting hers. 'I don't remember any of that. I told her she was off her gourd—that she was nuts if she thought she'd ever be anything to me. And you leaving as you did was anything but easy. It nearly broke me.'

'I had to leave,' she whispers hoarsely. 'I thought you were done with me. She's like an orchid and I'm . . . I'm more like a daisy.'

I chuckle at her analogy, but she's not wrong. And not for the reasons she thinks. She's pure and uncomplicated. Show her a little love and she just blooms. And Becci? She's more like one of those carrion flowers. Striking to look at, hard to maintain, and fucking rancid under the first leaf.

'Well, you're the loveliest daisy I've ever seen. I've never felt like this about anyone. Ever. And I reckon I never will again. And I'm going to make it up to you—and she's going to tell you the truth.' After a little parental intervention, a word from Sally's lips to Becci's father's ear. 'But you have to *want* to come back first.'

'Come back for what?' she asks softly.

'For all of it. For me, for the twins, for Mum, the whole deal. For good. And for this.'

It's time to pull out my trump card. I lean over to grab her notebook from my pack, holding it in the palm of my hand as the pages fall open to where I'd placed the architects plans.

'What are these?' she asks, unfolding the scaled down A4 plans.

'A commercial kitchen and a shop front. For when you're ready to go into business.'

'What?'

'You said you were inspired by me. Well, you got that wrong. You're the one with the big ideas. So this is me, giving you a start on the path to your dreams. One of them, anyway. I hope me and the kids feature in those dreams, too.'

'I don't understand,' she murmurs, running her fingers over the computerised elevations and floorplans.

'I have a few provisos, of course,' I blunder on, not giving Amber time to ask questions or say no. 'I want you to open your bakery at Riposo. If you look at the plans, there's even the option for a bit of a café down by the creek.'

'The creek? But that's such a perfect spot.' The instant the words are out of her mouth, she rolls her lips inwards, her cheeks turning pink.

'Yeah, I know. I saw how you'd sketched it in your notebook. I also wondered if you'd like to make stuff to serve at the wine-tastings. Maybe even expand into events.' Over her lipless mouth, my Amber's eyes go wide. 'But I'm getting ahead of myself. First things first. The provisos. Our conditions.'

'Who's conditions?'

'Ours. We'll need to meet your parents—your swinging parents. And you'll need to meet my brothers, too. You'll also need to undertake to add to our numbers.'

'What numbers? What are you talking about?'

'The way I see it, we'll need at least three more Phillips's under our roof.'

'You mean . . . babies?'

'That condition came from Edie and Matt. But I'm not averse. In fact, I can't think of anything I'd like more than to see you round with our child.'

Fuck, does that sound kinky? It does, doesn't it?

'I . . . I think you've gone mad. You want me to open my bakery on the estate, and you want me to give you three kids?'

'No, you misunderstand. The twins want two more brothers or sisters. The third new member of family Phillips?' The notebook still balanced in my palm, I flip to the back page. There, taped to the back cover is something sparkly that I hope she'll love.

'You . . . you're . . . '

'Amber Hardy, will you become Amber Phillips and make an honest man out of me?'

'You want me to marry you?'

'Please.' I nod. 'I really do. Plus, I really *don't* want to be single for next year's man-meat auction.'

'That's why you want me to marry you?' She sounds a little incredulous but her dark eyes are merry and glistening.

'Well, yeah. That and because I'm madly in love with you.'

Like some kind of magic or alchemy, our lips begin to gravitate closer when Amber places a hand on my chest.

'Wait—which was the grand gesture? The bakery or your strange proposal?'

'The bakery, sweetheart. Would it help if I said I'd chuck in a week's stay in the Shangri-la hotel?'

'That five-star beauty? Hell, yeah, it would. Let's go pack my bags. I'd marry Dave-o the foreman to get away from these ants.'

'I could've saved a few grand and just brought a can of *Raid*. Wait.' I peel the clear tape from her engagement ring, slipping I onto the fourth finger of her left hand.

'No backsies. I mean it. For life.'

'It's so perfect,' she says, staring down at it.

'And so are you.'

'Who knew you were such a romantic?' she murmurs, feeding her arms around my neck.

'Only for you,' I whisper, pulling her closer. 'Tell me you love me, Red.'

'I love you Byron Phillips. Now, get me to this hotel and take me to bed.'

'Only an idiot needs to be asked twice.'

'Really? You want me to repeat myself?'

The End

Acknowledgements

Thanks to my gorgeous family, as always. And to Michelle for stepping into the breech and also for looking after the flock.

My thanks also to Lisa. Luff your face, lady! And also to Elizabeth. I appreciate your input and your wry comments make me smile. Wishing you a blessed year ahead, lovely.

And to the Mo-Fo's. The secret society. Or the society with secrets, it's hard to tell. You're a whole lot of awesomeness and positivity.

Thanks also to the usual suspects in the Lambs. You're all super fab and so helpful!

And to you, the reader.

About the Author

Donna writes dirty stories, according to her family. She hopes you find them funny, too. When not bashing away at a keyboard, she can usually be found hiding from her family and responsibilities with a good book in her hand and a dog that looks like a mop by her feet. She likes her humour and wine dry, her mojitos sweet, and her language salty.

Printed in Great Britain
by Amazon